The Canadian Connection

To: Jim,

A true patriot and friend of old warriors and veterans of 'yesteryear.'

Darden

The Canadian Connection

A Novel

Darden Newman

iUniverse, Inc.
New York Lincoln Shanghai

The Canadian Connection

Copyright © 2007 by Darden Newman

All rights reserved. No part of this book may be used or reproduced by any means, graphic, electronic, or mechanical, including photocopying, recording, taping or by any information storage retrieval system without the written permission of the publisher except in the case of brief quotations embodied in critical articles and reviews.

iUniverse books may be ordered through booksellers or by contacting:

iUniverse
2021 Pine Lake Road, Suite 100
Lincoln, NE 68512
www.iuniverse.com
1-800-Authors (1-800-288-4677)

This is a work of fiction. All of the characters, names, incidents, organizations, and dialogue in this novel are either the products of the author's imagination or are used fictitiously.

ISBN: 978-0-595-43674-3 (pbk)
ISBN: 978-0-595-88003-4 (ebk)

Printed in the United States of America

Chapter 1

Change of Pace

Shortly after six that morning Dan had put on his robe over his sleeping shorts, put on his house shoes, went to the kitchen of the condo and started a pot of coffee. After that he went outside to get the morning newspaper, *The Knoxville Journal*. The first thing he always checked was the classified ads under 'Business Opportunities.' He had looked at several small business prospects in the past five years but had never found one that seemed to be within his field of endeavor. As usual there were no prospects in today's paper.

Dan poured himself a cup of coffee and turned to the headline story on the first page of the paper with the dateline of August 25, 1988.

US Warship Downs Iranian Airliner

A U.S. warship fighting gunboats in the Persian Gulf yesterday mistook an Iranian civilian jetliner for an attacking Iranian F14 fighter plane and blew it out of the hazy sky with a heat-seeking missile, the Pentagon announced. Iran said 290 persons were aboard the European-made A300 Airbus and that all had perished.

"*The U.S. government deeply regrets this incident,*" Adm. William J. Crowe Jr., chairman of the Joint Chiefs of Staff, told a Pentagon news conference.

The disaster occurred at mid-morning over the Strait of Hormuz, when the airliner, Iran Air Flight 655, on what Iran described as a routine 140-mile flight from its coastal city of Bandar Abbas southwest to Dubai in the United Arab

Emirates, apparently strayed too close to two U.S. Navy warships that were engaged in a battle with Iranian gunboats.

The article continued to reveal additional details about the accident. After reading the story, Dan was convinced even more than ever that eventually the United States' military presence in the middle east would precipitate an incident that would probably involve America in another land war with one of the Islamic nations in the region.

Dan had popped some packaged pancakes into the microwave and after they had heated, he covered them with butter and maple syrup. He had just about finished them along with his second cup of coffee when the phone rang.

Who would be calling this early? Dan thought.

"Hello."

"Hey, you old dog-robber, where you been … I called you yesterday afternoon."

"Hey, Stump. I just got back from St. Petersburg yesterday and got your message off the machine but I thought it was too late to call you."

"Well I hope you were using one of our planes … I need the business," Stump laughed. "Now that you're back you can get back to your routine, playing golf every day and flirting with all the gals sitting around the pool,"

"Yeah, Stump. It's pretty hard to take," and Dan laughed in reply. "But, to tell you the truth I could stand a change of pace."

"Well, I just might have something here that will do just that for you. How about instrument time … have you had any lately?"

"Yep, as a matter of fact I took a trip over to Charlotte last week to visit my old friend Ed Mynatt, and Knoxville was socked in when I got back so I had to come in on the gauges. Also got in a night landing on that trip." Dan paused and then continued. "I know you well enough to know that you are trying to suck me in on some deal, Stump. What's up?

"Yeah … well, I think I've got something here that you will be interested in doing. You can combine a little fun with a little business."

"O.K., why don't you let me in on your little scheme and I'll see if I'm interested," Dan chuckled.

"Here's the deal. I have had a 1987 King Air out on lease to a company and they recently decided they wanted to buy a new jet from us. Now I've got a prospect on the King Air with a mining supply company in Anchorage and they want to take a look at our plane as soon as possible. My problem is that all my sales people are involved in other projects and are going to be tied up for the next four to five days and I need to get that plane up there … pronto! I need the type of guy who can sell refrigerators to Eskimos so I immediately thought of you. Also, I know I can trust you to get my plane up there in one piece."

"Wheeew," Dan whistled. "Anchorage, huh? That *does* sound interesting. Alaska is one place I've never been to and always wanted to visit, so how much is it worth for me to ferry it up there and close the sale?" Dan asked.

"Tell you what ... the prospect has put up five G's to bind the contract and if you close it for the price I quoted, you can have the deposit. How does that grab you?"

"Hmmm, sounds pretty good to me." Another pause. "O.K., what about expenses?"

"Geez! You haven't changed a bit, have you?" Stump chuckled. "O.K. I'll get you one of our company American Express cards and you can charge all legitimate expenses. Now remember, I said *legitimate!*"

Dan had to laugh again. "O.K., I guess I can struggle along with that. When do you want me to leave?"

"You can leave when you want but I need the plane up there within two days, Dan. And here's some more good news, the plane is sitting right in your back yard ... over at our old stomping grounds ... Island Home airport." Stump replied.

"O.K., you've talked me into it. Deal."

"Man ... what a bloodsucker you are!" Stump laughed. "Why don't you drop by our office at the airport this afternoon if you can. You know our manager, Bob Fields, don't you?"

"Sure do. He gave me my bi-annual check ride a few months ago."

"Good. I'm calling him right now to tell him to cut you a check for an advance of fifteen hundred and to let you have one of our American Express cards. Now, don't you go and put a 'ding' in my airplane, you hear?" Stump chuckled.

"I'll try not to, Stump. Good to hear from you again, ol' buddy."

"Oh! Say, Dan, how's Mary Beth and Tom getting along?"

"They're just fine, Stump. Both are doing well ... working hard but I still don't have any grandchildren yet. How's Frances and the boys?"

"Frances is fine and Bill's wife Elizabeth has one 'in the hangar' and I just know it's going to be a boy."

"Hey, congratulations! You're getting way ahead of me ... I'll be looking for a cigar from you."

"You got it! Good luck and have some fun up there in Alaska, Dan." Stump said.

"Thanks, Stump. See ya.'"

After hanging up, Dan thought about the long relationship he had with his old friend James "Stump" Reynolds. It went back to his college days at the University of Tennessee where he had met Stump in their freshman year. They both had dreams of being pilots and had worked part time during school to pay for flying lessons. Dan's ambition at that time was to be an airline pilot but developing astigmatism had put an end to that. After graduation Stump took a sales job with Southeastern Beechcraft, where they both had learned to fly, and now he was Vice-President of sales in Greenville, South Carolina.

* * * *

After lunch, Dan went out to Island Home Airport where he and Stump had gone to flight school. Dan entered the office and found Bob talking to one of the employees. Bob saw Dan and walked over to greet him.

"Hello, Bob," and Dan extended his hand.

"Good to see you again, Dan," and they shook hands. "Are you all packed and ready to go?"

"Just about but I thought I would come out this afternoon and get all the details taken care of so I can get an early start in the morning."

"Good idea. Stump called and I've got a check here for you," Bob walked over to the desk, picked up a sealed envelope and handed it to Dan. "Your check is in there along with an American Express card.

He then continued, "How long since you have been in a King Air, Dan?"

"Oh ... let's see ... it's probably been at least a year, Bob."

"Would you like to take a turn around the pattern?"

Dan knew that Bob was really saying, 'how about demonstrating to me that you still know how to fly the thing.'

The two of them walked out to the King Air sitting on the line and both of them made a 'pre flight' check together before getting in the aircraft which also included checking to make sure the wing tanks had been 'topped off' with fuel.

They both got in, Dan in the left seat and Bob in the right. They proceeded to go through the pre start-up check list and then Dan fired up both engines, taxied to the end of the runway, performed the final check list and Dan took the aircraft off into the wind.

After two 'touch and go' landings, Bob seemed satisfied enough and had Dan taxi back to the hangar.

"Well, I would say you haven't lost your touch. You got all the charts you need, Dan?"

"They're in my flight case in the car. By the way, Bob, can I leave my car here while I'm gone?"

"Sure thing, Dan. In fact, I'll put it in the spot where the King Air usually sits so it will be inside the hangar while you're gone." Bob smiled and said, "I sure wouldn't want anything to happen to that Mercedes 380-SL while it's under *my* care!"

"Thanks, Bob, I appreciate it."

"Have a nice flight, Dan." They shook hands and Dan headed back to the condo.

Chapter 2

▼

The Kids

As soon as he arrived back at the condo, Dan called his old golfing buddy, Don George, at his office and told him he was flying up to Alaska early in the morning so he would not be around for their regular golf game on Saturday. Don told him that he thought he was "nuts" but go ahead and prang himself on some mountain peak up there in Alaska. Dan laughed and told Don that was not allowed ... it wasn't his airplane.

Then he called Tom.

"Tom Nichols, speaking."

"Hey sport, how's the 'lawyering' going?"

"Oh ... hi Dad! When did you get back?"

"Last night around six. I had dinner out and didn't get to the condo until around eight o'clock ... I was pretty well beat so I didn't bother to call."

"Did you have a nice trip?"

"No, not really, Tom ... in fact I kind of wish I hadn't gone."

"Just not the same, huh?"

This kid was pretty savvy to be just 25 years old. "That's right, son. Sometimes it's difficult to realize that you just can't go back in time." Dan took a deep breath to control his voice then continued, "Are they keeping you busy?"

"They sure are, Dad. A client of the firm has run into a little trouble with the IRS and the senior partner has assigned me to accompany him on his meeting with the auditor."

"Well, that should be interesting. Look, Tom, what I'm calling about is that your 'Uncle Stump' called and asked if I would ferry a King Air up to Alaska to see if I could close a deal they have going with a mining supply firm up there. I shouldn't be there too long but I will call you when I arrive and let you know where I am and about how long I will be there."

"O.K., Dad. Why don't you spend a few days looking around up there. I understand it is really beautiful country."

"I plan on doing that, Tom. By the way, how is Jane getting along with her third graders?"

Tom laughed. "Oh she's doing as well as can be expected with about twenty-six nine year old kids in her class."

"Well, you tell her I was asking about her and I will see both of you when I get back."

"O.K., Dad, you take care of yourself, you hear?"

"I will, Tom. Love you, son."

"Love you too, Dad."

After he had hung up, Dan had a fleeting thought: *I wonder if Alaska just might provide the opportunity I have been seeking for the last five years.*

* * * *

The next call Dan had to make was to his daughter, Mary Beth.

"Hello."

"Mary Beth?"

"No, this is Cathy. Who is this?"

"This is her Dad, Cathy."

"Oh! Hi, Mr. Nichols. I'm sorry but the hospital called Mary Beth in early today and she won't be home until around midnight."

"Well, look, Cathy. Would you be sure and tell her that I am delivering an airplane up to Anchorage, Alaska for a friend of mine and I will call her when I get up there."

"Alaska! Are you *really* going to Alaska, Mr. Nichols? Boy, that is one place I am going to see if I ever get enough money to make the trip!"

"Yep ... I'm really going, Cathy, and you be sure and give her the message, all right?"

"I sure will, Mr. Nichols, and you be careful, hear?"

Dan laughed, "O.K., Cathy I will be careful."

Mary Beth was in her first year of nursing at St. Mary's hospital in Knoxville and she and her friend, Cathy, were sharing an apartment not too far from the hospital. Ever since Mary Ann had died Mary Beth had assumed the position of surrogate wife ... or even worse at times ... a surrogate mother. Dan would put up with this to a point but eventually he would have to firmly remind her that she really was just a daughter.

CHAPTER 3

North to Alaska

The night before, Dan had laid his charts out on the kitchen table and plotted his route from Knoxville to Anchorage, Alaska. The flight plan would take him to Nashville, St. Louis, Sioux Falls, Great Falls, Spokane, Bellingham and then direct to Anchorage. He came up with a total of 3,134 nautical miles. If he could average 290 knots ground speed, the trip would take ten hours and forty-eight minutes flying time. He would, of course have to make a fuel stop and he would allow at least an hour and a half for refueling and a little break.

*   *   *   *

The next morning, the wheels of the King Air were retracted into their wells at exactly 7:05 a.m. Eastern Daylight Time and Dan had an uneventful flight all the way to St. Louis. Air traffic was light and he only talked with ARTCC (Air Route Traffic Control Centers) four times thus far. These contacts had pertained only to aircraft in the vicinity that the Centers were making him aware of.

At St. Louis, Dan switched one of his communication radios to a Flight Service Station for a weather up-date. Talking with a weather specialist, Dan received a confirmation of the forecast that he had received upon leaving Knoxville. There was a cold front moving through the west producing a line of severe thunderstorms, with hail in certain areas, on a line extending from northeast to southwest. At the present time the line was from Cranbrook, Alberta to Walla

Walla, Washington, and moving eastward at approximately 30 miles per hour. Dan thanked the controller and returned to the ARTCC frequency. This was foreboding news for this storm was directly in his line of flight.

Chapter 4

Rough Ride

Approximately 200 miles from Great Falls, Montana, Dan began to encounter turbulence and he was in and out of cloud formations. Fifteen minutes later he began to encounter moderate rain and the turbulence increased somewhat. He was just beginning to think of calling Salt Lake City Center to alter his flight plan when there was a flash of lightning that practically blinded him, the King Air shuddered and Dan had self recriminations concerning his stubbornness to deviate from his route before now. The King Air was bucking like a wild horse and it became difficult for Dan to maintain his assigned heading. Rain was now pelting against the aluminum sides of the ship and it sounded as if someone was taking pails of nails and throwing them against the aircraft.

Just when he thought things could not get worse there was a great flash of lightning and a resulting clap of thunder which shook the King Air like a paper kite in a windstorm. The bottom fell out of everything and the Jeppesen charts in their binders, which had been in the right seat, were now momentarily floating in midair. Dan was straining upward on the straps and then suddenly there was a huge jolt as his butt made contact with the seat and he realized his teeth were aching from the pressure he was putting on them. The smell of ozone permeated the cockpit.

Dan called Salt Lake City and asked the controller if he was painting a thunderstorm cell in their vicinity.

He answered, "Ah, sir, there is one about three miles off your right wing but you should be out of it in just a few minutes."

"Comforting thought," Dan said to himself. *"I should ask him where the hell he has been for the last ten minutes but better just forget it. Those guys have their problems in weather like this just the same as us nuts up here in it."*

Dan called Salt Lake again, "Center we are really getting kicked around down here. Do you have a PIREP[1] that indicates smoother air at a higher altitude?

"Negative, four five Kilo. United flight in your vicinity reporting turbulence up to flight level three four zero.[2]"

"Ahhh, thanks anyway, Salt Lake, four five Kilo."

Dan managed to steady the aircraft enough to look at his chart. He called Salt Lake Center once again.

"Salt Lake Center, King Air November zero four five Kilo."

"Go ahead zero four five Kilo."

"Sir, are you painting any cells southwest of my line of flight?"

"The weather appears to be moderating approximately sixty to seventy miles southwest of your location, four five Kilo."

"Ah … Roger, Center. Request change of flight plan from present location direct Billings VOR, direct Salmon VOR, J-52 to Spokane, landing Spokane International, four five Kilo."

"Roger King Air four five Kilo. Stand by one."

Fifteen seconds later Salt Lake City Center approved Dan's change in his flight plan and just as the controller said, the turbulence and rain diminished appreciably the further southwest they traveled and the King Air continued on to Spokane, Washington, in much improved weather conditions.

---

1. Pilot Report
2. 34,000 feet

Chapter 5

▼

Next Stop—Anchorage

Sitting in the snack bar in the main terminal of Felts Field in Spokane, Washington, Dan took a big bite out of a ham and cheese sandwich which he washed down with a swig of cold milk. The taste caused Dan to wonder how long that ham had been curing between those two pieces of whole wheat bread. A week maybe? Dan was pouring over his charts as he ate and decided to file his flight plan from Spokane to Bellingham and then direct to the Sandspit VOR with final destination, Anchorage. This route would take him over water but still close enough to land so that if he should lose both engines simultaneously he would still be able to glide to an onshore landing. Anyway, the odds of losing both engines simultaneously were very, very remote. According to the charts It looked as if he still had about 1,436 miles to go and if he averaged the same 285 knots as on the last leg, it would be a flight of just about five hours. It was now 12:10 p.m. Pacific Daylight Time and if he could get off by no later than 1:00 p.m., he would be in Anchorage by around 5:00 p.m. as he gained an hour going up. *"Sounds like a winner to me."* Dan thought as he washed down two Oreo cookies with the rest of the carton of milk and stuffed the remaining Oreos in the pocket of his flight jacket. They would come in handy in a couple of hours. Dan took his thermos over to the counter and filled it with coffee, grabbed his chart bag, paid his bill, and started looking for the pay phones.

He found a couple in the lobby and using his credit card, dialed the Anchorage number that Stump had given him. A pleasant sound of a female voice answered, "Intermont Mining Supply." Dan asked if Mr. Albert Switzer was there and learned that he was not. Dan then told the lady who he was and that he planned on having Mr. Swtizer's King Air at the Anchorage airport around five-thirty p.m. this evening. *Making it five-thirty should allow for any unexpected delays,* Dan decided.

"Oh, I know that Mr. Switzer will be pleased to hear that. He is out of town but I expect him back before noon tomorrow. Will you be needing a room for this evening?"

Well, now, this sounds like some right neighborly people. "Yes, I will ... thank you very much."

"There is a nice Courtyard by Marriott just a mile or two from the airport. Would that be satisfactory?"

"Yes, maam,' a single room with a queen or king size bed will be just fine."

"I'll certainly take care of it, Mr. Nichols, and, incidentally, I am sure I can arrange for a representative from our firm to meet you at the airport."

"Well, that will be just great. Tell your man that I will park the King Air at the Stevens Air Service hangar and will be waiting in the flight office."

"I'll certainly do that, Mr. Nichols and you have a nice flight up to Anchorage. Goodbye."

"Thank *you*, maam,' and I hope to see you tomorrow. Bye."

*   *   *   *

Dan paid the local FBO for refueling the King Air, boarded the aircraft, fired up the engines, ran his check list and received clearance from the tower for take-off. Spokane Departure Control cleared the King Air according to Dan's IFR flight plan and by 1:20 p.m. they were already climbing out of five thousand five hundred for twenty thousand.

The weather was about as good as the forecaster had given him over the 'phone in Spokane but the visibility was more like ten miles than the twenty that he had predicted, but he could live with that. Also the clouds were scattered now and the wind had moderated to something like ten to twelve knots out of the northwest so it looked as if they would have a very pleasant flight. The DME indicated they were making 295 knots across the surface so perhaps they would get into Anchorage by Dan's estimated time of arrival, 5:00 p.m. local time.

They were following the J-501 Airway out of Vancouver and at the Sandspit VOR, Vancouver Center bade them "G-day" and turned them over to Anchorage Center. Another 803 miles up the road and Anchorage Center turned them over to Anchorage Approach at the NOWEL intersection where they were cleared down to 6000 feet for vectors to the final approach course to Runway 6 Right at Stevens Anchorage International. A light rain had begun to fall.

At 1,600 feet Anchorage Approach vectored them onto the ILS[1] for the approach and they were given a "cleared to land" by Anchorage Tower. A little too much speed 'over the fence' resulted in a slight jolt on landing but not too bad, and Dan was able to make a turn off at the second intersection where he had no trouble finding the Stevens Air Service facility. With both engines stopped and all switches off, Dan made the perfunctory entry into the logbook with a notation in the total time column of five hours and five minutes. Good trip.

In the FBO office Dan informed the attendant on duty that the aircraft that he had just brought in had been purchased by Intermont Mining Supply and one of their representatives would be arriving shortly to make the decision as to whether they would want the aircraft either tied down or hangared. Dan then went to find the men's room to wash up a bit in an effort to be a little more presentable when the Intermont rep arrived. After that he picked out one of the naugahyde overstuffed chairs, dropped his frame into it and tried to relax. The Breitling read 6:25. He had just picked up a copy of a month old *Air Transport Pilot* when the door to the FBO office door opened.

In walked a stunning young lady in a black raincoat over a tailored black pant suit that matched her shoulder length black hair. She also was wearing silver earrings, a belt with a silver buckle and black leather ankle high boots. The silver and black contrast accentuated her beautifully sculptured facial features. She appeared to be about 5 feet 9 inches or so and at first glance Dan would have thought it was Rita Hayworth, the movie actress. Well, she looked enough like her to be her sister. Even from the distance of about five feet, Dan could see a pair of flashing dark brown eyes that signaled there just had to be a brain behind them with a high degree of intelligence. She first glanced towards the counter and then towards Dan. Since he was the only male waiting in the office she confidently walked over and said, "Mr. Nichols?"

Dan fumbled and dropped the magazine in an effort to rise. "Uh, yes … that's right."

Her full, red lips curled ever so slightly at the corners creating two very small dimples. She extended her hand and said,

---

1. Instrument Landing System

"I'm Jessica Lane, Mr. Switzer's assistant." Dan took her hand. It was very warm and Dan had a fleeting thought about the old saying, 'warm hand, cold heart.'

"Uh, I'm glad to meet you, Miss Lane." Dan reluctantly released her hand as he felt hers relax. *Why does my face feel so damn hot? Surely I'm not blushing!*

"Shall we sit for a few minutes while we go over a few details?"

"Uh, sure." Dan waited until she had sat down in a chair that was facing the one that he had been sitting in.

"What do you suggest that we do with the plane?" she asked.

"Do with it?"

"Yes ... you know ... until we take possession of it, that is."

"Oh ... yeah. Well, it may cost a few extra bucks but I would recommend that it be put in a hangar tonight. I'm sure that you will want an A&E[2] mechanic to check it out and it would be more convenient for him if it was in a hangar."

"Certainly. Would you mind seeing to it, please?" she requested.

Damn, Dan, what the hell is wrong with you? You've been around beautiful women all your life. You should have the 'upper hand' here. After all, you must be at least six or seven years her senior!

"Sure, Miss Lane, I'll take care of it just before I leave."

"My friends call me, Jess, Mr. Nichols," she said with a disarming smile.

"And mine call me, Dan, Miss ... uh ... Jess."

"Fine, now we have that out of the way. Do you have the papers on the aircraft?"

"Uh, sure." *Why are you starting every sentence with an 'Uh,' you dolt?*

"They are right here in this brief. The logbook is in there too." With that Dan reached into his flight case and pulled out a small zippered briefcase that Bob Fields had given him with all the records on the King Air. She reached out, took the briefcase and placed it in her lap as she sat on the edge of the chair with her back as straight as a ramrod.

"I'll take this and have it in the office for Mr. Switzer when he arrives in the morning. Why don't you come to the office about 11:30 a.m. He has been out of the city so that will give him time to clear his desk and look over the papers on the plane. I am sure that he will want you to go to lunch with him so that he can ask any questions he may have about the aircraft. Later we can settle the financial arrangements."

"That sounds fine with me."

---

2. Aircraft & Engine

"Good. Shall we go?"

"Go?"

"Why, yes," *another one of those ice melting smiles again.* "You don't think I am going to be rude enough to abandon you to this God forsaken hole for the night, do you?"

"Uh, well" *dammit ... did it again!* "the lady I talked with in your office earlier said something about a room at the Courtyard by Marriott so I thought I would just grab a cab ..."

"Nonsense!" I am going right by there, so you come along."

With that she rose with the fluidity of a ballet dancer and headed towards the door.

"Oh, Miss ... er, Jess."

"Yes?"

"The plane ... you know ... hangar arrangements?"

"Of course. How forgetful of me"

Dan went to the counter and informed the clerk that the King Air needed to be hangared overnight in the name of Intermont Mining Supply. He also informed the clerk that an A&E mechanic would probably be along in the morning to check it over.

Dan walked back to the door where Jess was standing. "O.K., that's taken care of so we are off." and Dan attempted one of his best imitations of a Clark Gable grin.

They walked out in a misting rain. She pulled a set of keys from her purse and headed for a metallic blue Corvette. Dan moved a step ahead and opened the driver's door for her.

"Why, thank you, Dan," and smiling, she slipped behind the wheel in one fluid motion.

As soon as Dan shut the door on the passenger's side the atmosphere was permeated by a very subtle, yet very provocative odor of expensive perfume. Dan glanced to his left and saw that the lights from the instrument panel were illuminating the exquisite features of Jessica Lane's face. Possibly sensing Dan's stare, Jess turned her face towards him for an instant, curling her red lips in a smile. Dan smiled back, took a deep breath and felt an unusual feeling in his stomach. He thought, "*it must be the result of my not having eaten anything substantial today. Or was it ...? Damn, Dan. Pull yourself together, man; you are acting like a high school kid!*"

Jessica Lane drove the Corvette out of the parking lot and onto the road leading from the airport in a manner that clearly demonstrated that she drove just as she obviously did everything else … well. In less than ten minutes the Corvette pulled up to the front entrance of the Marriott Courtyard. Dan exited the car with his bags, leaned inside before shutting the door and said, "Thanks, Jess. I appreciate the hospitality very much."

"The pleasure was all mine, Dan. There will be a key to a rental car at the desk for you in the morning with instructions on how to get to the office. See you at eleven thirty." And she flashed another final alluring smile.

Dan closed the door, stood and watched as the tail lights of the Corvette trailed off into the evening mist, leaving him standing in the aura of the lingering smell of her perfume. That old familiar feeling that he got when he was around a woman he was attracted to was still in the pit of his stomach. *What the hell have I gotten myself into?*

Chapter 6

Taejang Chong Hi Lee

Taejang[1] Chong Hi Lee had departed from Pyongyang just fifteen minutes ago after attending a meeting of the Secretariat of the Central Committee where President Kim Il Sung had been present. Admiral Chong was sitting in the first row of seats aboard a Russian built Lisunov Li-2 aircraft which the Russians had been licensed to build during World War II by the Douglas Aircraft Company. It was a replica of the American DC-3 which had been obtained from the Russians by the North Korean government to be used as a military aircraft. Admiral Chong did not enjoy flying in the least but it was the most expeditious means of returning to his headquarters in Toejo Dong. As a result of the meeting, the Admiral was now charged with accomplishing a mission about which he had grave misgivings.

As the ancient aircraft lumbered through an overcast leaden sky, the Admiral began to ruminate about history which had led him to this point in his varied career. His native country of Korea had been at odds with Japan since the late 1890's and after several military encounters they succumbed to Japan. However, when the Russo-Japanese war started, Korean leaders decided their best interests would be served by allying themselves with Japan in this conflict. Unfortunately they made a tragic assessment and their decision led to the complete control of Korea by Japan which became official in August of 1910.

---

1. Four star Admiral

Rebellious Korean factions would not be quelled however, and in 1919 the March First Movement demonstrated the first act towards Korean independence. They asked for assistance from other countries so they would not have to fight against Japan alone. Many countries wanted Korean independence but none came forward to aid Korea in their movement. Japan looked upon this movement as an act of rebellion and they were not about to allow Korean independence to take place. The result was an outbreak of violence by the Koreans who destroyed police stations, courthouses, and schools, all of which were under Japanese control. Hundreds were killed on both sides and thousands of Koreans were thrown in prisons. The end result was *complete* domination of Korea by Japan. There was a consolidation of schools and the Japanese language, culture, and traditions, were taught to Korean children. Even when Japan was at war with other countries, Koreans had to fight for Japan and were usually on the front lines. This was where Chong Hi Lee found himself in 1941, in the Japanese Navy at the age of seventeen.

The Japanese heavy cruisers *Myoko* and *Haguro* were escorting the light aircraft carrier *Shoho* in the Coral Sea on May 7, 1942 when all three ships came under bombardment by the United States Air Corps. All three ships were hit but the *Haguro* escaped serious damage while the ship that seaman Chong was on, the *Myoko*. received a direct hit and had to be abandoned. The *Shoho* was also fatally damaged and began to sink. After the bombardment was over, the *Haguro* began to pick up survivors. Seaman Chong miraculously had been blown clear of the *Myoko* and found an empty life raft. He noticed an area of burning oil had surrounded a group of his shipmates and he paddled furiously to the area and began to beat the flames with the oars in the life raft, clearing a path for his shipmates so they could board the raft. Shortly thereafter the sailors in the raft were picked up by the *Haguro*. Chong's heroic act was later recorded by an officer who was in the rescued group and seaman Chong received The Order of the Rising Sun 7th Class medal for his act of bravery.

After World War II, Chong received a discharge from the Japanese Navy with the condition that he would return to his native Korea, which he did. He immediately enrolled in the Kim Jung-sook Naval Academy. He was an industrious student and with his previous naval experience he graduated at the head of his class in 1949 with the rank of *Chungwi*.[2] The outbreak of the war with South Korea in 1950 provided Chong with leadership roles and rapid promotions. Admiral Chong's thoughts then turned to the incident that would bring him to the attention of the President of North Korea, Kim Il Sung.

---

2. Lieutenant Junior Grade

Kim Il Sung was born to a peasant family in Mangyondae, Korea in 1912. His parents fled the oppressive Japanese and went to Manchuria. Kim attended schools there and in 1932 he led a group of Korean partisans in a number of raids against Japanese outposts in Korea. In 1941, Kim fled to the Soviet Far East, received military training under the Soviets and eventually became a major in the Soviet Army. In 1945, Kim returned to his homeland and the Soviets put him in charge of a provincial government in Soviet occupied Korea. In 1948, he became the first premier of the Democratic People's Republic of Korea. In 1950, Kim received Stalin's permission to launch an invasion of the South which took place on June 25th of that year. But it was only thanks to a massive Chinese intervention that Kim's regime survived the United States led counteroffensive in the fall of 1950. In 1953, Kim and his Soviet guardians chose to settle for half of the country. However, Kim never accepted the division of his country and continued to fight for consolidation.

During the early days of the Korean conflict, the North Korean Navy operated 45 small vessels which were charged with transporting supplies and replacements to forces advancing along both coasts. Also the navy was involved in a bold strategic attempt to seize Pusan by landing 600 troops near the port city. Pusan was one of South Korea's largest ports and its location in Southeastern Korea, across from the logistic support bases in Japan, also made it vital to the South Korean and American cause. Unfortunately for the North, the landing craft came under heavy fire from the US Navy and the attack failed. Although the attack was not a success, the boldness of the plan attracted the attention of Kim Il Sung and he issued an order for the naval officer who had planned this mission to report to him at headquarters in Pyongyang.

Chong Hi Lee remembered well the meeting with the President. He recalled how he, a young *Chungjwa*[3] of 27 years of age, had trepidations about being called into the presence of the ruler of the country. Because of the defeat the vessels under his command had suffered, thoughts of a court martial were not too far removed from his mind. To his great surprise he was complimented on his bravado in planning a raid that would have dealt a devastating blow to the enemy had it succeeded. The result of the interview was that President Kim assigned him to the Office of Naval Warfare and soon after Chong was promoted to *Sangjwa*.[4] The war with the South stalemated which resulted in a truce but both sides continued to maintain a military state of preparedness. As the North contin-

---

3. Commander
4. Captain

ued to expand its military forces, Chong Hi Lee continued to play an important role in the development of the Naval Forces which ultimately resulted in his becoming the *Taejang,* four star Admiral of the Fleet.

The Admiral's reverie was interrupted by a sudden change in the rhythm of the engine sounds coming from the Lusinov Li-2. It automatically caused Chong to grip the armrests until he realized they were apparently making their approach into the military airfield at Toejo Dong. The "Fasten Seatbelts" sign was now flashing on the overhead above the door to the pilots' compartment. Soon the engine noise abated as they descended and he heard the 'chirp' of the wheels as the aircraft touched down on the asphalt runway. Disembarking down the airstair door the Admiral received a salute from the naval military policeman at the foot of the stairs which he returned. His automobile, bearing the four stars of his rank, was waiting with the driver holding the door for him.

"Welcome back, Admiral," the driver said and saluted smartly. "Headquarters?"

"Thank you, Uen, it's good to be back ... yes, to my office." The military sedan departed.

When Admiral Chong arrived at his office he sat at his desk, picked up the phone and called in his aide, *Chungjwa*[5] Kim Mi-young. Commander Kim entered the office, bowed from the waist and said,

"Welcome back, Admiral."

Admiral Chong replied, "Thank you Mi-young. I have a task for you. Please get Admiral Kwan on the military line in Wonsan and direct him to report to my office here at his earliest convenience."

Commander Kim bowed again, clicked his heels and said, "Immediately, Admiral," turned on his heel and left the room.

After Commander King had exited the room, Admiral Chong placed both of his forearms on top of his desk, intertwined the fingers of both hands and stared straight ahead. *It will be good to see my old friend Kwan again but I have some serious trepidations concerning our carrying out the assignment the Central Committee has given the two of us.*

---

5. Commander

Chapter 7

Anchorage Marriott Courtyard

True to her word, Jess had arranged for Dan to pick up the keys to a Hertz Honda Accord at the desk of the Marriott Courtyard the next morning. There was an envelope addressed to Dan and upon opening it, it read, "Directions to Intermont offices. Leave the Marriott and turn right on Spenard Road. When you run into McRae road, turn right to Minnesota Drive and then turn left on Minnesota. Continue until you come to 5th Avenue, turn right and the office is at the intersection of West 5th and E Street. Parking lot is at the rear of the Seward Building and we are in Suite 505, fifth floor."

Dan showed the instructions to the desk clerk and asked him how long it would take him to drive to that address. "Oh, at this time of the morning I would say it might take you no more than 20 or 25 minutes." It was then only 9:05 a.m. Dan still had two hours to kill so he picked up a copy of the *USA Today* and went into the coffee shop. A very attractive brunette waitress arrived at his table with a menu. She smiled brightly, and as she poured a glass of water she said, "Would you like a cup of coffee?"

"Yes, please … black." Dan noticed that her name tag said 'Judy.' She departed and was right back with the coffee and a menu.

"Do you have poached eggs?"

"Yes, sir, we sure do."

"O.K., I'll have two poached medium, crisp bacon and wheat toast."

"How about some hash browns?" she queried.

"No, thanks, but I will have some grits," and Dan looked her in the eye to catch her expression.

She didn't bat one of her textured eyelashes and said, "Where in the south are you from?"

"Knoxville, Tennessee."

"Well, sir, I think you are going to have a long trip in order to get your grits," and she flashed a set of perfect white teeth as she smiled her answer.

Dan couldn't help but watch her as she turned to leave the table. *Male genes, I suppose.* He became engrossed in the paper, reading the headlines:

Ramstein Air Base, Germany:

On August 28, 1988, more than 300,000 people gathered at Ramstein US Air Force Base near Frankfurt, West Germany. They had come to watch performances by aerobatic teams, the annual Flug Tag Air Show. The day turned to tragedy when three jets of Italy's Frecce Tricolor (Tricolor Arrows) collided above the crowd. Approximately 500 people were injured (most of them burned) and 69 people were killed at the base or died later from their injuries.

The story went on detailing the horrible events which took place after the aircraft had crashed in a huge ball of fire, spreading flaming jet fuel into the spectators.

Judy returned, with Dan's order, refilled his coffee cup, smiled and moved to another table close by where some guy who looked close to Dan's age was having breakfast with an attractive female that looked quite a bit younger. In studying the contrast between the two, Dan immediately thought of Jess and himself. They were laughing and seemingly were enjoying one another's company immensely. Judy moved to a nearby serving table and returned to the couple with a coffee pot. He watched her refill their cups and then he forced himself to return to the newspaper and tried to concentrate on the financial page.

About twenty minutes later Judy returned once again. "Anything else, sir?"

"What? Oh, no thanks. Just the check please."

"Here you go. You have a nice day, now."

"Yeah ... thanks. You too."

Dan reached for his billfold, pulled out two bucks and left them on the table. As he got up to leave he passed by the table where the couple were sitting and heard her say, "Well, Jim, when two people enjoy each other's company as much as we do then what else really matters?" He smiled, and replied, "You've got an excellent point there." Dan had to agree, that *was* an excellent point. Dan paid the cashier for the breakfast, looked at the Breitling and noticed that it was only 9:55. He still had about an hour to kill.

Back in the room, Dan made sure that all of the aircraft papers were in order and neatly placed in his small briefcase. He wondered if he should check out and then decided not to since he really didn't know what lay ahead for the afternoon and also didn't have a clue yet as to how he was going to get back home. So Dan walked to the 'phone, dialed in his credit card number and then the number which went directly to his son's office 'phone.

"Tom Nichols"

"Hi, son, how's it going?"

"Oh, hi, Dad, where in heck are you?"

"I'm at the Marriott Courtyard in Anchorage and I thought I had better call and let you know that I will be here for at least another day or two. Here's the number if you need me." Dan looked at the number on the 'phone and gave it to Tom.

"O.K., Dad. Everything is going great here. I picked up that Wallace account so that should bring in some pretty big bucks for the firm and maybe even a bonus for me."

"That's fine son. I'm really pleased to see that you are liking your job. There isn't anything much worse than having to work in a job that you don't enjoy and isn't rewarding."

"You planning on being up there much longer?" Tom asked.

"I really don't know just yet. Since it is my first trip to Alaska I thought I might take a week or so and just do some sightseeing."

"I don't blame you for that. I hope that maybe some day Jane and I will be able to take a vacation up there. I would imagine that it is really a beautiful place."

"You remember how your mother and I used to take you and Mary Beth up to the Smoky Mountains and how we all enjoyed being in the mountains so much? Well, they have mountains up here that put the Smokies in the shade so I am going to be sure and see a lot of them and some of the other scenery while I'm here.

"Well, just keep in touch and let us know how you are getting along. And one other thing, Dad, take care of yourself."

"I will son and tell Jane I said 'hello.'

"O.K., I will, Dad. Love you, g'bye."

"Good bye, son."

At the front desk Dan told the clerk that he had decided to stay over at least one more day. The clerk clicked some keys on the computer keyboard and acknowledged Dan's request. Dan left the desk and stepped out into a clear late August morning with a forecast high of 65 degrees according to the *USA Today*. The desk clerk told him that the car should be parked in the area just in front of the portico. Dan looked and saw two Honda Accords there; the tag that his key was on indicated that his would be the four door sandalwood brown. Dan slipped into the driver's seat, turned the key in the ignition and the smooth running six cylinder engine responded immediately. He found the exit onto Spenard Road and had no trouble following the directions down to West 5th Avenue where he made a right turn. Five blocks later, Dan saw the Seward building on the right, turned in beside the building and parked in the lot to the rear. Inside the building were two banks of elevators and he entered one just as two gentlemen were getting off. Dan punched in the 5th floor button and the Otis machinery moved the car smoothly upward. It was 11:25 a.m.

Chapter 8

Intermont Mining & Supply Co.

The door opened at the fifth floor and immediately across from the elevator Dan saw a solid door with the lettering, 'Intermont Mining Supply Company.' A turn of the knob and he was inside the waiting room. He walked across the carpeted floor towards a beautiful solid oak desk with a lady seated behind it who appeared to be close to retirement age. She was dressed in a tailored dark blue jacket with a white blouse and a gold pendant attached to a gold chain which showed beneath the white collar. She was a rather attractive lady, wearing glasses, and as soon as Dan approached the desk she smiled pleasantly and asked, "May I help you?" Dan recognized the voice as the one he heard on the 'phone when he had called yesterday.

"Yes, my name is Dan Nichols. I believe Mr. Switzer is expecting me."

"Oh, yes, Mr. Nichols. You're the gentleman who delivered the new aircraft, aren't you? I am Virginia Stewart;," and she extended her hand to Dan who took it in his and replied,

"Yes I am and I want to thank you for making the reservation for me. The Mariott was very nice."

"I'm so glad. Would you have a seat please?" She picked up the telephone and pressed two buttons as Dan sat down in a leather upholstered chair with arms, next to an end table that held a table lamp and assorted magazines. He placed his brief on the floor beside the chair and picked up a copy of a magazine from the end table entitled *Mining Engineer's Monthly*.

In about ten minutes Virginia Stewart's phone buzzed, she answered it and said to Dan, "You may go in now. It's the second door on the right." Dan got up and walked to the door that had 'Albert Switzer, President' inscribed on it. As he opened the door he was greeted with the distinct smell of cigar smoke. It was a rather large corner office with two large windows with draperies on the left wall and two on the wall straight ahead. The windows offered a view of Cook Inlet in the background. Rich beige carpeting blending perfectly with the walnut upholstered chairs, tables and desk in the spacious office. Albert Switzer arose from behind the executive size desk as Dan entered the room.

"Ah, Mr. Nichols it's good to see you." He smiled and moved around the desk to meet Dan. Al was a rather large man, about five feet eleven and appeared to weigh somewhere around two hundred thirty pounds or so. Round face with ruddy complexion, a furrowed brow below which were two piercing blue eyes. His hair, a light brown, was thinning and grey was becoming the predominant color of his temples. Age should be somewhere in the early to mid-sixties. His suit coat was open and a rather portly stomach was evident. He held out his hand and Dan was not surprised when he shook it to find his handshake was very firm. The skin of his hand was rough giving the impression that he possibly had performed manual labor at some time or another in his lifetime.

"It's nice to meet you, sir," Dan said as they relaxed their handshake.

"Yes, yes. Please have a seat. Would you care for a cigar?"

As Dan dropped into a comfortable leather chair opposite the desk, he said, "No thank you. I don't smoke."

"Ah, a wise man. A dirty habit at the best."

Dan noticed that Mr. Switzer breathed a little heavily and the redness of his face indicated that perhaps he was a man who might have high blood pressure.

Dan replied, "Well, I did smoke at one time but I managed to break the habit about twenty-five years ago."

Al Switzer sat down at his desk and said, "Tell me. What do you think of our fair city?"

"I really haven't had an opportunity to see very much of it but what I have seen so far looks very nice. At least it appears that you have clean air here."

"Yes, that's quite true. Fortunately we don't have any industrial plants nearby that pollute our air. Did you have a nice trip coming up?"

"Not too bad. I ran into a cold front coming across the plains states that had some pretty rough weather in it but the King Air handled it very nicely."

"Ah, yes … the King Air. Tell me a little about this airplane that I have just purchased."

Switzer opened up a hand carved wooden box on his desk and took out a Cuban cigar and lit it from what appeared to be a sterling silver desk style cigar lighter. Dan spent about the next fifteen or twenty minutes telling Al Switzer of the attributes of the King Air, elaborating on the passenger comforts and the history of reliability and safety of the aircraft.

"So you think I made a good buy, eh?" Switzer queried.

"I think you made an excellent buy, Mr. Switzer."

"Oh, you don't have to call me 'Mr. Switzer,' Dan. Al will do very nicely. We don't tread on formality at Intermont."

"Well, thank you, sir. That is very kind of you."

"Good! Shall we get down to business then? You have the bill of sale and other necessary papers, of course?"

"Yes, sir, I do." Dan picked the brief from the floor, set it in his lap and proceeded to open it. He took out the papers and handed them across the desk to Al.

'Hmmmm, well I see the price is exactly as we agreed upon. Good!"

Switzer pressed a button on an intercom box on his desk.

"Miss Lane. Mr. Nichols is here. Would you come in, please?"

The door to the office opened and Dan arose to see Jessica Lane coming in dressed in a traffic stopping red business style suit. Her brunette hair was immaculately done with not a hair out of place. Dan's eyes were drawn to two simple gold earrings with a gold pin holding her crisp white collar together. This time she was wearing a skirt and Dan had to pull his eyes away from two very shapely legs. She was so lithe it appeared as if she drifted across the room.

"You know Mr. Nichols, of course, Jess?"

"Of course, sir. How are you this morning, Mr. Nichols?" she asked as those red lips curled again at each end.

"Uh, I'm doing just fine, Miss Lane." Dan responded as he got a whiff of that perfume again. *Alright, Dan, keep cool, man.*

"Fine. You two have a seat and let's see if we can wrap this thing up. Do you have the check for Mr. Nichols, Jess?"

"Yes, sir, I do … right here." She had a leather covered legal pad which she opened and produced a check which she handed to Dan.

"Is the amount satisfactory, Dan?" Al asked.

Dan checked it against the copy of the bill of sale that he had retained and saw that the amounts agreed. It was also a cashier's check so that took care of that detail as well.

"Yes, sir. It is exactly as it should be."

"Good. Now I took the liberty of having Stevens Air's aircraft and engine mechanic perform a primary check on the aircraft this morning and it looks as if everything is as it should be. Of course, we still have to go over all the engine and airframe logs and make sure that all the AD's, if any, have been performed. You understand, of course?"

Ah, ha! The old boy knows more about aircraft than he has indicated.

"Oh, yes, sir. Southeastern Beechcraft warrants the aircraft to be everything that they represented or they will bring it up to standards. I think you will find that in the sales agreement."

"All right then, we've got a deal." With that Switzer stood up, smiled, and extended his hand across the desk and Dan shook it.

"Now let's all go get a bite of lunch. What do you say?"

"That sounds just fine to me, sir" Dan replied

All three of them proceeded to the parking lot at the rear of the Seward building and as they approached the cars in the lot, Switzer took out a set of keys, handed them to Jess and said, "How about you driving, Jess. Dan, you sit up front with her and I will get in the back." Switzer and Jess led the way to a silver Jaguar Vanden Plas. Jess clicked the door button and all three took their assigned places. Switzer sat directly behind Jess.

As they pulled out of the lot, Jess asked, "Where to, sir?"

"Well, why don't we go to the Petroleum Club. I think they usually have steak and lobster on the menu on Fridays."

I wonder if this club is affiliated with the one in Evansville where Mary Ann and I had dinner?. They do have affiliates in different cities, Dan thought.

Jess whisked them down West 5th and turned right on "C" Street. From the way she drove, Dan could tell it certainly wasn't the first time that she had been behind the wheel of the Vanden Plas.

In about ten minutes they turned in between two brick pillars which had marble insets that read, 'Petroleum Club of Anchorage.' They all went in and were greeted by the maitre d' who immediately picked up three menus and said, "Good afternoon, Mr. Switzer. Your usual table?"

"That will do just fine, John. Thank you."

They were ushered to a table for four in a far corner of the dining room and they had no sooner been seated when a waiter appeared with a water carafe and asked,

"Your usual, Mr. Switzer?"

"Yes, thank you, Alfred. What will you have, Jess?"

"I'll have a glass of Chenin Blanc."

"And what about you, Dan?"

"I'll have a vodka on the rocks with an olive."

A smile spread across Switzer's face. "Ah, a two fisted drinker."

With that, Alfred, bowed slightly and departed.

"Well I don't usually have a vodka for lunch but since I am not driving or flying I thought I would seize the opportunity."

"Now that is what I like to hear ... a man who will seize an opportunity." Switzer replied. "Incidentally, Dan, what are your plans when you leave Anchorage?"

Upon hearing that question from Switzer, Jessica turned her face slightly toward Dan and raised a beautiful arched eyebrow in an inquisitive look.

"Oh, I imagine I will just go back to Knoxville and do what I have been doing."

"Which is?" Switzer pursued.

"Just being a part time pilot and a part time golfer."

Alfred returned with the drinks and after all three of them had been served, Switzer raised his glass and so did Jess and Dan. As Switzer said, "Here's to us," the three glasses were clicked together and Dan offered, "Hear, hear."

"So, what you apparently are telling me is that you don't have to work in order to support yourself or your family?" Switzer remarked.

"My wife died a few years ago, Mr. Switzer ..."

"I'm very sorry to hear that, Dan." Al replied with a sincere tone in his voice.

"Yes, well, Al, I don't have the responsibility of a family; my daughter is a registered nurse, single, and employed in a hospital in Knoxville. My son is a new attorney and married to a young lady who graduated two years after he did and she is presently teaching in a private school so I am unencumbered as far as a family is concerned."

"You don't look old enough to have children that age, Dan." Switzer seemed honestly surprised.

Dan laughed quickly, "I may be older than you think I am."

Jess cut her dark brown eyes towards Dan as she took a sip of her wine.

"You haven't even reached the prime of your life yet," Switzer chuckled. "I'm sure you haven't been a pilot all your life. Tell me a little about your background."

"Well, sir, I graduated with a BS in Business Administration, major in accounting, minor in marketing, and went to work for a local bank after graduating. Six months after employment they put me in the investment banking department. One of our clients was a real entrepreneur who had started his own manufacturers' representative business and he and I hit it off well. After we had known each other about a year he prevailed upon me to join him in his business."

Dan stopped and took a sip of his vodka before continuing.

"To make a long story short, I became a rather valuable asset to my benefactor by not only becoming his most successful salesman but also by having the ability to fly an aircraft. We leased a Beech Bonanza and expanded our coverage into five states. After the business began to expand rapidly, my benefactor who was ten years my senior, offered a proposition that would allow me to purchase up to forty percent of the business based on increase in sales, growth, and profitability. In twenty years our business quadrupled and my partner lived up to his offer. Just prior to my wife's death our biggest competitor offered to buy us out and my partner, who was then sixty, was ready to accept."

Dan paused again and took another sip of his drink. "So was I since I wanted to devote more time to my wife, who, at that time, had been diagnosed with terminal cancer. So we accepted the offer and my wife and I traveled for several more months before she died. I'm now in a position where I don't particularly have to worry about financial security and can devote a considerable amount of time to doing what I like best and that is flying and golfing."

At that moment, Alfred returned with three menus. "Are you ready to order, Mr. Switzer?"

"Yes, Alfred, I'll have the filet mignon and the lobster tails."

"What kind of salad, sir?"

"The Caesar salad will be fine."

Jess ordered the broiled chicken breast and a salad. Dan never was one to eat a large lunch so he ordered a fried chicken salad with the house dressing. At that point the conversation turned to topics of local interest and both Al and Jess mentioned some of the features of Anchorage and its' environs that Dan might want to take a look at while he was in the area. They even brought up the possibility of his visiting Talkeetna where he could take a day trip to view Mount McKinley and some of the more interesting scenic areas.

Alfred arrived with the meal and they all began to partake of their dishes. The food was delicious, well prepared and the service was, of course, superb. After finishing their meal, Al looked at his watch and said that he needed to get back to the office.

The three of them got back into the Vanden Plas in the same positions that they were in previously. When they had reached the parking lot at the Seward Building they all entered the elevator and exited on the fifth floor. As they entered the main office, Jess 'officially' introduced Dan to the receptionist, Virginia Stewart. All three of them were standing in the lobby when Al turned to Jess,

"Jess why don't you take Dan into your office. I have a 'phone call to make and I will join the two of you there in a few minutes." Jess and Dan walked across the lobby together to the door of her office. The plaque on the door read, 'Jessica Lane, Vice President'. They entered a large room that had a plush carpet in a warm light brown color which blended perfectly with the swag drapes with window treatments. She had a beautiful mahogany desk with matching credenza and in front of the desk was a glass topped oval shaped coffee table with four leather chairs in a half circle around the table. Jess invited Dan to have a seat.

"Nice office," Dan complimented. "Business like but still very lady-like."

"Thanks. Glad you like it." She sat down in one of the chairs at the coffee table and Dan sat in the one facing her.

"So what else do you do besides fly and golf?" she asked.

"Not a heck of a lot, really. I like to read good books and exercise. I have a knock-off on a Nautilus machine in my condo and I try to work out on that just about every day."

"Do you like to dance?" she asked.

"Well, yes, but it's difficult to do unless you have a partner."

That remark seemed to amuse her and she laughed, "I wouldn't think that you would have too much difficulty in getting young ladies to dance with you," and she looked at Dan with those brown eyes rather coyly.

"I'm not one for 'quantity' as much as I am 'quality,' Jess." Dan replied.

"Oh?" She raised her eyebrows and crossed her legs, "so you are particular, huh?"

"I'm just an old fashioned guy I guess. If I can't find someone that I really enjoy being with I would just as soon not be with anyone," Dan answered.

"Well, I don't see anything wrong with that."

Just then there was a slight knock on a paneled door in her office that apparently was a connecting door. Jess said, "Come in." The door opened and it was Al. Obviously the door connected with his office. He directed a question to Dan.

"Dan, are you planning on being around here over the week-end?" he asked.

"I suppose so. I really haven't made any plans, Al."

"I would appreciate it if you would stay over and drop back in to see me on Monday, say around eleven o'clock. The company will pick up your motel bill for those extra days."

"There's no need for that, Al. I'll be glad to stay over if you want me to."

"Fine. Jess, would you have someone call the Marriott where Dan is staying and tell them to send his entire bill to our office?"

"Certainly, Al ... I'll take care of it," Jess replied.

"Good." Al walked toward Dan and he got up out of the chair. He extended his hand which Dan shook. "I look forward to seeing you on Monday morning then, Dan."

"Thank you, sir, I'll be here. Al went back into his office. Dan turned to Jess and said, "I suppose I will see you Monday, as well?"

"No doubt," she smiled and went to the door of her office and opened it for him.

Just as Dan was about to exit, he turned and asked, "I, uh ... well, Jess, I thought perhaps that you and I ..."

She interrupted, placed her hand on the one that he had just put on the doorknob smiled and said, "Thanks but I have other plans tonight, Dan. Perhaps another time."

Dan felt his face flush. *Damn dummy! You should know that a beautiful woman like Jess would have an engagement for Friday evening!*

"Oh, well ... sure, Jess. Thanks for everything today and I will see you Monday for sure."

Dan felt just like he did the night he was refused a dance by a girl at his first high school prom.

As he went by Virginia Stewart's desk, he spoke to her. "Hope you have a nice week-end, Virginia." She wished him one in reply. Dan exited the main office, boarded the elevator and went to the parking lot where he unlocked the Honda, fired it up and headed for the Marriott Courtyard.

Chapter 9

Lonely Friday

Friday evening and Dan didn't have a damned thing to do. Well, he sure wasn't going to mope around the motel all evening, watching TV and feeling sorry for himself. He went to the room, freshened up and opened the Yellow Pages to 'Restaurants.' Dan found where Anchorage had an Outback Steakhouse. At the front desk he asked if they happened to have a map of the Anchorage business district. The clerk reached under the counter and produced a folder which, when opened, provided a diagram of the downtown streets and gave the location of several restaurants, motels and hotels. Dan located the Outback at 101 W. 34th street, oriented himself and went out to the Honda and headed downtown.

Even though there were a number of people waiting, the fact that he was a 'single' worked in his favor. He was seated at a small table within fifteen minutes. His waiter arrived soon after and he ordered a Grey Goose vodka on the rocks with an olive. The waiter left while Dan perused the menu. He suddenly realized that he was rather hungry. The baked chicken that Dan had for lunch had been well digested several hours ago so he settled on a 10 ounce rib-eye steak with a baked potato, small 'bloomin' onion and tossed salad. The Grey Goose arrived, Dan gave the waiter his order and sat back to sip on the drink and look around. At his one o'clock position there was a couple sipping on two glasses of wine.

A candle flickered on the table and the girl sat her glass down, reached across the table and the young man took her hand and rubbed the back of it with his right thumb. She looked at him rather dreamily, smiled, and they became engaged in conversation. Over to Dan's immediate right there were two young couples and they too were having some drinks and were in animated conversation. Once when one of the young men finished speaking they all erupted in laughter. Obviously a joke had been presented which they all no doubt enjoyed. Then one of the young men raised his glass and evidently proffered a toast to which they all hoisted their glasses, clicked them and sipped their drinks. Once again they all became involved in lively conversation. Dan suddenly felt very much alone. His loneliness recalled to mind the evening of the last vacation that he and Mary Ann had at their favorite condominium on Indian Rocks Beach in St. Petersburg.

They both knew that the cancer Mary Ann had would be taking her away very soon. They had been sitting on the veranda overlooking the beach where the setting sun had painted the sky with exotic hues of aquamarine, reddish gold and silver just as the sun slipped beneath the blue water of the Gulf of Mexico.

Dan remembered he was sitting in one of the deck chairs with his after dinner drink when Mary Ann had gotten out of her chair, came over and sat down in his lap, put her arms around his neck and looked directly into his blue eyes. She had told him, "Dan, I know why you insisted that we come here. I know that I am going to be leaving you very soon now and I want you to promise me something."

Dan remembered putting his drink down on the table beside his chair, as he took both hands and placed them around Mary Ann's waist. Then he had told her "I'll promise you anything you want, honey, just name it."

"I want you to promise me that you won't live alone for the rest ..."

It was then that he had quickly taken his right hand and put two fingers on Mary Ann's lips. "Anything but that ... you know that I'll *never* forget you."

Then she had replied, "I don't want you to *forget* me, Dan. I know you won't do that, but you are still a young man and you will probably live at least another forty or forty-five years and you are the type of person who needs the love and support of a woman."

Dan had recalled this incident hundreds of times in the past five years and try as he might, he had not been able to erase it from his mind.

The waiter had returned with his meal and as he placed it before Dan he said, "Will there be anything else now, Sir? ... Sir?"

"Huh? ... Oh, I'm sorry," Dan replied as the waiter broke into his reverie.

"Uh, no ... that's all for right now, thank you."

Dan picked up his knife and fork and began cutting into a rib-eye steak that had a pink center cooked to perfection. Had the chef been close by he probably would have uttered an expletive as Dan took ketchup and A-1 sauce, mixed them and dipped bites of the tender steak into the mixture.

Within minutes after finishing the meal, the young man returned with the check, Dan glanced at it and handed him his American Express card. When he returned, Dan added a five dollar tip. Stump could afford it especially after that 'beating' he had taken on his way up here. Dan picked up the receipt and his AMEX card and departed.

*   *   *   *

Back in his room, Dan sat down at the small desk and began to think about things that he had to take care of immediately. First thing he needed to do was call Mary Beth. He picked up the 'phone, punched in his credit card number then hers and the 'phone began to ring.

"Hello."

"Is that you, Mary Beth?"

"No, it's Cathy."

I've got her roommate again!

"Oh, hi, Cathy. This is Mary Beth's Dad."

"Hi, Mr. Nichols. You just missed her … she had to report in a little early tonight. One of the regular day nurses is sick and they are having to split shifts to fill in for her."

"Oh. Well, will you be sure and tell her I called, Cathy, and I'll keep trying until I get her."

"I sure will, Mr. Nichols. Are you still in Alaska?"

"Yes I am, … in Anchorage."

"Is it snowing up there?"

Dan laughed, "No, Cathy, it isn't snowing. They probably won't have snow up here for a couple more months."

"Oh, heck. Well, I sure would like to be somewhere where it snows at Christmas."

"This is the place to be, Cathy. It's almost guaranteed. Maybe you can come up here sometime."

"I hope so. Well, I'll be sure and tell her you called, Mr. Nichols. 'Bye."

"Thanks. Cathy. Talk with you later." Dan replaced the receiver in the cradle.

Dan decided that if he was going to hang around here awhile he definitely was going to need more clothes than what he had brought along and they needed to be something more fitting with the environment around here. He picked up the

Marriott pen and notepad lying by the telephone and began to make some notes of items that he possibly might need. Definitely a pair of blue jeans, probably a wool shirt and maybe even a denim jacket to go with the blue jeans. He had brought along his University of Tennessee ball cap but he might also look for some kind of hat or cap that would provide more rain protection plus a little more warmth. The only other shoes he had brought was a pair of Nike's so maybe he should also get a pair of leather mid-calf boots, waterproof of course. Well, that was all he could think of at the moment but once he got to looking around he probably would think of something else. Now ... where to find these items? Where else but the Wal-Mart. Dan would tackle that in the morning.

He looked at the chronograph ... it was nearly nine o'clock already. He undressed, took a shower and slipped on his boxer sleep shorts plus a 'T' shirt and turned on the TV to see if he could catch any news. Dan flipped through the channels and saw Clint Eastwood. It took him just a minute to recognize this was a re-run of *Magnum Force* so he started watching it but couldn't keep his eyes open. When he woke up, Clint was long gone and some movie he had never heard of was on. Dan took off his watch to put it on the nightstand and noticed that it was ten after eleven. Dan turned out the lights. *I wonder who Jess was out with tonight. Probably some guy about her age who looks like Sean Connery. I hope he spills coffee all over her dress.*

Chapter 10

▼

Anchorage Weekend

As had been his habit for years, Dan woke up early. The room was still dark and rain was hitting his window. Dan looked at the luminous dial on the Breitling lying on the nightstand and it said 6:55 a.m. Geez! he didn't want to wake up this early, especially on a Saturday morning. Dan lay there for awhile, hoping to go back to sleep but it was no use. He finally got up, shaved, brushed his teeth, showered, got dressed and headed downstairs to the lobby. Dan picked up a copy of the *Anchorage Daily News* at the front desk and walked toward the restaurant.

There was only one couple in the dining room and they were sitting at a table next to the window. Dan selected one that was quite removed from them. It was just getting daylight and the rain was still coming down. In just a few minutes he saw his favorite waitress approaching.

"How are you this morning, sir?" And she gave Dan her customary smile. It was nice to have someone with a good personality waiting on you on a morning like this.

"I'm fine, Judy. Look, I'm going to be around here for at least a couple of more days so why don't we just get on a first name basis. My name is Dan."

"Well, I'm glad to *officially* meet you, Dan. Do you have a clue as to what you want this morning?"

"No, I really don't so why don't you just leave the menu while you bring me a cup of coffee."

"Let's see ... you take it black, is that right?"

"That's right. You have a good memory."

She put down the menu and turned to go for the coffee pot. When she came back with the coffee she asked,

"Now. Have you made up your mind?" She poured the coffee and then sat the cup down.

Still looking at the menu Dan said, "Yep. I'll have some French toast and two strips of crisp bacon."

"Any grits?"

Dan looked up to see a very nice smile move across her face.

Dan chuckled, "O.K., Judy, you got me. Guess I will just have to wait on the grits until I get I get back to Tennessee."

Having finished his breakfast and signed a ticket for the meal, Dan started back to his room through the lobby and noticed a guy walking through in athletic shorts, tee shirt, cross-trainers and a towel slung over his shoulder. Dan walked over to the counter in the lobby and spoke to the clerk.

"You guys got a workout room here?"

"Sure thing. I've been told it's the best of any of the motels in Anchorage. We've got a really big indoor pool too … almost Olympic size."

"You're kiddin' … where is it?

"Just turn to your left and then at the first corridor turn left again. Keep straight ahead and eventually you will see a sign that says 'Exercise Room.' Go in the room and then you will see the entrance to the pool."

"Thanks." Dan followed his directions and found the exercise room which was filled with just about every type of exercise machine imaginable. He then walked through the door to the indoor pool and the guy was right, it was one of the best looking, and largest, indoor pools Dan had ever seen in a motel. He was going to check this out this afternoon.

Dan headed for the main entrance and was glad to see that the rain had turned to a mist. He cranked up the Honda and headed for the Wal-Mart. As usual the parking lot was almost full and the crowd inside was already getting quite large. He found all the items on his list plus he picked up two pair of wool socks and a couple of extra pair of Hanes jockeys and tee shirts. Having found out about the pool at the Marriott, Dan picked up a pair of swim trunks. He also found a cap that looked like a ball cap with earflaps and it had a wool liner in it. It looked like it would really keep his head and ears warm.

After exiting the Wal-Mart, Dan noticed a Barnes & Noble bookstore close by so Dan dropped in there and browsed around for awhile to see if there were any new books on aviation; either fiction or based on fact, it didn't make any difference to him. He saw a paperback copy of *Fate is the Hunter* by Ernest Gann and he bought it. Dan would read it again for the third time.

Not having much else to do, he headed for the Anchorage/Lake Hood Seaplane Base to see what was out there. Dan had found out that Intermont had an Otter and his curiosity was getting the best of him since he had never gotten a seaplane rating. Dan found the place which was really impressive and there was just about every kind of seaplane imaginable there but Dan did not see the Intermont Otter. After knocking around for an hour or so he headed back to the Marriott. Dan took his packages up to the room, put on his athletic shorts, Nike's, tee shirt and wrapped his swim trunks in a motel towel and headed for the exercise room. He worked out there for an hour and just as he was about to leave, he found out they had saunas; one for men and one for women. Dan went in the men's sauna and cooked himself for about 20 minutes, took a cold shower in the men's shower room … well almost cold, put on his swim trunks and did about a dozen laps in the pool. By that time he felt like a limp noodle. Back to the room and showered off again, dressed and about six o'clock he headed for Applebee's to get some of their baby back ribs.

The place was crowded … naturally, being Saturday night, so Dan sat at the bar and had a vodka on the rocks with an olive. A guy sitting next to him started up a conversation and it turned out he was a truck driver who drove the Alcan highway delivering mining supplies and equipment up to Deadhorse for the Alyeska people. The waitress came back so Dan decided to just eat at the counter. He ordered baby beef ribs and talked to the driver for over an hour. He was a real interesting guy and seemingly well educated. The driver said he could make more in Alaska in six months driving a rig than he could in twelve months back in the states. Finally Dan finished his dinner, shook hands with the driver and left him still sitting there eating a little and drinking much. When Dan got back to the Marriott, he got ready for bed and sat down in the easy chair to read *Fate is the Hunter* by Ernie Gann. What a guy and what a life *he* led. Dan was pretty well shot from the exercise and swim so he turned back the covers, got in the bed and turned out the light at ten o'clock. He had managed to kill Saturday.

Chapter 11

The Picnic

Sunday morning was one those awakenings when you wondered just where you were. The sight of the familiar furniture in the room of the Marriott finally brought Dan to reality. He looked at the Breitling on the nightstand and it informed him that it was twenty minutes after six o'clock. *Dang! I wish I could learn to sleep later.*

There was no sound of rain and as Dan pulled the drape back slightly he could see from the parking lot lights that there was dry pavement outside. That should be a sign that possibly a good day lay ahead. It then dawned on him it was Sunday and he wondered what the heck he would do all day. After performing his morning ablutions, Dan flipped on the TV and tuned in FOX news to see what was going on in the world as he dressed. He shouldn't have bothered … wasn't there any *good* news anymore?

He purposely killed a lot of time before going downstairs to the dining room but it was still only seven thirty when He sat down at a table. Only one other guy was in the room besides him and Dan nodded to him as he looked up when Dan entered. He acknowledged the nod and went back to his newspaper.

The waitress arrived and it wasn't Judy. Dan supposed Sunday was her day off. Although he had a lot of food at Appleby's last night, Dan was surprisingly hungry this morning so he ordered a cheese omelet with sausage and biscuits. Evidently all that exercise he had yesterday had worked off a lot of calories. The waitress came back with his black coffee and as he sipped on it he watched as the dawn began to fill in the shadows outside. It had all the earmarks of a nice fall day. Soon his meal arrived and Dan attacked it with the vengeance of a man who had been deprived of food for days. As he was starting on his second cup of coffee, the desk clerk came into the dining room, looked around and then approached his table.

"Mr. Nichols, there is a 'phone call for you."

Dan followed him back to the lobby desk where there was a 'phone sitting on a stand to one side of the desk. Dan picked up the handset.

"Hello?"

"Hi. I'm glad I caught you."

It was Jess! "Hey, well I'm glad you caught me too. What's up?"

"Do you like to go on picnics?"

Dan laughed slightly, "Well, it's been a long time … but, yes, I *do* like picnics."

"Great! I'll pick you up at ten o'clock in the lobby. And you had better wear something warm 'cause where we're going it's going to get cool before we get back."

"Where are we going?"

She laughed that lyrical laugh of hers. "It's a surprise. You just be ready, O.K.?"

"Right. I'll be in the lobby at ten."

And with that she was gone.

Wear something warm. Well, my trip to the Wal-Mart was very timely. Dan put on all the heavy stuff he had bought and crammed the cap with ear flaps in the pocket of his blue denim jacket. Hopefully he wouldn't need it but it would be there if he did.

By nine forty-five Dan was standing in the lobby and at three minutes to ten he heard the unmistakable rumble of a Harley Davidson engine. Jess pulled up under the portico on a Dyna Super Glide Harley, cut the engine and slipped out the kick-stand with her booted foot. She dismounted, removed her helmet and shook out her jet black hair. She was wearing leather boots with a high heel, cuffed blue jean pants and a leather jacket and leather gloves. She was absolutely gorgeous and Dan felt his heart skip a beat. She walked towards the lobby grinning and showing those perfect white teeth. Dan opened the door and she stepped inside.

"Hi. You ready to go?"

"Where in the world did you get *that!*"

"Oh, it belongs to a friend of mine and he lets me use it once in awhile."

Sean Connery I'll bet.. Crud!

"It's nice to have friends like that."

She ignored the comment. "Do you like to ride?"

"I used to have a '74 OHV way back in the dark ages."

"No kiddin'? Well, that's great! Do you think you can hang onto the buddy seat?"

"Well, now, I just might be able to do that," and Dan returned her smile.

They walked out to the Harley and Dan noticed she had an extra helmet strapped to the bike. He put it on and made the necessary adjustments.

"I'm glad you took my advice and wore something warm," she said and swung her right leg over the bike. After she settled on the seat Dan got on behind and noticed there were no hand-holds on the buddy seat.

"O.K., hold on," she instructed.

Dan placed his hands on her hips.

"Oh, for crying out loud!" she laughed. "*Hold on!* I won't break."

With that Dan put his arms around her waist and locked his hands. Dan felt the adrenalin kick in as he pressed his body against hers. She had a firm solid feel.

She flicked the electric starter and the Harley came to life. She shifted her weight to balance the bike, retracted the stand, revved the engine, slipped the clutch and they were off. She deftly leaned to the left as they exited the driveway and then made a right turn down Spenard Road.

They motored on down Spenard and soon were on Glenn Highway heading east out of town. Conversing with one another was impossible due to the helmets and the roar of the engine, so Dan just held on and moved with her body as she leaned the bike into turns. After about ten minutes Dan felt very much at ease as he realized that she obviously was an experienced rider. Soon they were on the outskirts of Anchorage and Jess increased the speed up to sixty miles per hour. The road was smooth and the traffic was light so they were making good speed to wherever it was that they were headed.

After a while Dan saw a sign ahead that said, "Chugach National Forest." They motored on until another sign appeared: "Eklutna Lake. Exit mile 26." When the Eklutna Lake sign came up Jess slowed the bike, down-shifted and made a left turn onto Lakeside Trail. She shifted up to a higher speed and they continued on the road as it began to curve following the contour of the mountain on their left. They were also gaining altitude as they went along and occasionally Dan could catch a glimpse of mountain peaks as they weaved back and forth on the winding road. Finally, she slowed once more, then braked and made a left turn onto Cob Ridge Trail and Dan realized it was well named; it was little more than just a trail. They followed that road as the incline increased markedly and after a couple of miles Jess practically stopped and made a right turn onto a dirt trail. They dodged overhanging tree branches and crept along until suddenly they were in a clearing where she stopped.

"Dan, you hop off and get that flat rock over there for me," and she pointed to the rock with her right forefinger. Dan went for the rock and brought it back.

"Now put it under the kick-stand when I release it." He followed her instructions. She put the end of the stand on the rock and then dismounted. *Smart girl ... she recognized the ground would be too soft and the kick-stand would dig into the ground and the bike would fall.*

Dan removed his helmet and she did the same, shaking her long black hair and then smoothing it with her hand. *Dan got a whiff of that perfume again. Damn!*

They placed their helmets on the bike and she said, "Follow me."

Dan fell in a couple of steps behind her and they walked about twenty yards down a slope and then Dan realized they were on a bluff and far below he could see Eklutna Lake and to the right and left he could see snowcapped mountains in the distance. It was absolutely one of the most outstanding vistas he had ever seen in his life! Dan had thought the Smoky Mountains back home were great but they were nothing compared to this.

"How did you find this place?"

"Oh, I came up here once or twice with some bikers and I think it is one of the more outstanding places in the park so I come back here whenever I want to show it off to a friend." She turned her head to face Dan and smiled.

"Well, I am greatly honored, Maam," and Dan did a mock bow and returned her smile. That amused her quite a bit and she laughed at his little act.

"O.K. You ready for the picnic?"

"Hey, I'm starved. Where's the food?"

"Where do you think it is, silly? Don't you remember what saddle bags are for?"

Dan followed her back to the bike and they opened both of the bags and began to unload a number of items. There was a very large Eskimo blanket which apparently was hand woven in beautiful colors of red, black, blue and yellow. Also there were some Rubbermaid containers which obviously held food and a thermos which must contain coffee. Also, a collapsible zippered ice chest which Dan was sure contained some condiments. Evidently Jess had packed quite a meal for them. Dan was right on all counts. She had prepared potato salad, fried chicken, some cuts of baked ham, lettuce, a tomato, mayonnaise, potato chips, and whole wheat bread, Also, there was a large bag of Oreo cookies. The thermos did hold coffee and there was also a plastic container of cold water. They spread it all out on the blanket which had been placed close to the overlook so they could enjoy that magnificent view as they ate. They also made sure that the paper towels she had brought were placed so that they wouldn't soil the blanket with the food. Jess insisted on preparing the sandwiches while Dan just sat there, had a cup of hot coffee and watched as she arranged the food for serving.

"Aren't you afraid of wild animals around here.? Dan questioned.

"No, not really. Mostly small animals like coyotes, lynx, some red foxes, wolverines, and otters. Once in a while a black bear will come wandering along ... especially if it smells food." She was on her knees and she looked up at Dan with a big grin.

Then Dan told her, "I'll tell you what. If a bear shows up, you try running him off while I go for help."

She laughed loudly and said, "Don't worry. If worst comes to worst I think we can handle him with this." She unsnapped a pocket on her leather jacket and pulled out a Colt 38 Detective Special. Dan noticed that all the cylinders held bullets.

"Ah, it looks as if we have a former Girl Scout here ... be prepared."

"Normally if a bear comes around he can be persuaded to leave by yelling at him and beating on a pan or something. But, whatever you do, don't panic and run. I'll take care of you." and she gave Dan that sly smile again.

They sat on the ground and ate their lunch and made small talk about flying, biking, and a little about the business. Dan was stretched out on the blanket, propped up on his left elbow and holding a cup of coffee in his right hand. Finally he got around to asking some questions that he had on his mind.

"What's a girl like you doing in a place like this anyway?"

"I wondered how long it was going to take you to get around to my jaded past," she smiled. "Well, to start way back, I have always been a spoiled kid in spite of the fact that my older brother and my Mom tried to prevent it. But my Dad would have no part of it; I was always the apple of his eye." She picked up an Oreo cookie and munched on it for a minute before continuing.

"I was born and raised in Fairfax, Virginia, and my Dad was a lawyer so we always had just about everything that we needed. I went to public school there ... my Mother and Dad both insisted on that. Then when I graduated I went to Columbia University and then on to George Washington Law School, determined I guess, to follow in my Dad's footsteps. After graduating from there I went to Wharton where I got a MBA and majored in Environmental and Risk

Management. I thought that I wanted to work for the EPA in Washington but I got sidetracked. I got married."

Jess paused for a moment, sat on her behind, pulled her legs up and hugged them with both arms as she rested her chin on her knees. Her face took on a somber look and in a few moments she continued as she stared straight ahead beyond the overlook.

"I was twenty-six years old and Ben was twenty-seven. He was going to Wharton also and was majoring in Finance and Investment Banking. It wasn't like it was one of those spur of the moment romances. We had dated for a year and a half and we both were too dumb to realize that we were headed for trouble. He had a stubborn streak in him and so did I and we found ourselves arguing over just about everything from politics to what our economic goals were to how to make love. But we ignored those signals and plunged ahead with a wedding.

"It was one of those high society weddings ... you know the kind. We had it back home and my Mom and Dad spared no expense. It was held at the country club and it had all the trappings of a three ring circus. I think that my poor Dad must have dropped about thirty grand on that affair. Then to top it off, they paid for our honeymoon in Aruba. When we came back from the honeymoon we moved to Minneapolis."

"Minneapolis?" Dan asked.

She relaxed her position, stretched out like Dan was, propped herself on her right elbow and stared at him. She had plucked a small mountain flower and was twisting it nervously with her fingers.

"Yeah ... Minneapolis. I hated the damn place. Ben had been solicited for a position with an investment firm there so that was where we went. No consideration for whether that was what *I* wanted and no consideration for what I might want to do with *my* life. So there I was with nothing to do except freeze to death in the winter and burn up in the summer. Oh, we did the country club bit and I played tennis with the other socialites, if that was what you could call us. We had our little luncheons and all that crap but then it happened. After eleven months I got pregnant." She paused again, and sat up and poured herself a glass of water. After taking a few swallows she went on.

"I lost the baby during childbirth. A little girl." Her voice quivered when she said 'little girl' and Dan saw a tear trickle out of her right eye.

"Neither one of us could handle it. I started drinking too much, the arguments got more heated and all I wanted to do was sit around the house and feel sorry for myself. Whenever we went out to dinner or had friends over I went through the motions but I felt like I was married to a stranger and he felt the same about me. After about six months of that, I packed up and went back to Fairfax. My Mother and Dad tried to smooth things over by telling me that it would take time and I would change but I never did ... I didn't want to. Ben and I were finished. So, we got a divorce and I went to work for a law firm in Washington that specialized in environmental and ecological lawsuits. After a year of writing briefs and doing research I was beginning to get bored and my social life was as dull as a butter knife."

Jess stopped, poured herself another cup of coffee, sipped on it for a minute and then continued.

"One of the partners in the business was a good friend of my Dad's and he took a special interest in my situation. He came in my office one afternoon and asked if I was really happy there. Of course I told him I was but he was a shrewd old guy and he knew better. He sat down in a chair across the desk from me and said, 'You know, a change of scenery just might be the ticket for you.' It was then that he told me about this friend of his who was operating a mining supply business in Anchorage and needed a good attorney on his staff and someone who was informed on environmental matters. So, Al sent me an airline ticket. I came up here and never went back. Oh, I've been back to see my Mom and Dad but I love this place. It is one of the most unique places that I have ever been in and I'm at ease here and love what I am doing."

Jess paused again, sat up, crossed her legs and had another sip of coffee. Then she said,

"You know, I don't know why I am telling you all of this. You are the only person other than my Mom and Dad who knows this much about me now."

"Well, Jess, sometimes it does a young woman good to confide in an older man," Dan smiled.

She looked at Dan and furrowed her brow, "Hey, you're not an *old* man."

"Well, let's look at it this way, I think that when you were born I was in the fourth grade so you go figure."

"I remember your telling Al that you were older than you look but you don't look that much older than me ... or act it, either."

Dan smiled and in his best southern drawl he replied "Well, thank you, Maa'm. It's mighty nice of you to say that."

Suddenly she crawled the five feet between them on her hands and knees and gave Dan a light kiss on his left cheek, grinned and said, "You're welcome, and besides ... I think you're kinda cute, Dan Nichols!"

Dan was so surprised that all he could think of to say was, "Thanks," and he felt the blood rush to his face. *Damn. I hope it didn't show.*

They cleaned up all the utensils on the blanket, put the leftovers in a plastic bag that Jess had brought along specifically for that purpose and loaded everything back in the saddle bags.

Jess asked, "You want to drive back?"

"Are you kidding? Not today, but I may take over the controls a little later when we are on level ground."

They donned their helmets, took their positions on the bike, Jess fired up the Harley and they retraced their way back down the mountain to the highway and headed back to Anchorage. It was getting cool as the sun had disappeared behind the mountains and by the time they got back to the Marriott the temperature must have dropped into the high forties. Fall was definitely in the air. They pulled up under the portico and Dan got off.

"Jess, I had one of the best times I have had in about five years but there's one thing I just have to say. You don't *have* to be nice to me."

She looked straight into his eyes and without a sign of a smile she said, "Dan Nichols, I don't *have* to be nice to anyone and you just remember this. I think you are one of the nicest guys I have met in a long while."

Dan hesitated a minute then said, "Do you like to swim?"

"I *love* to swim. I was on our high school swim team and I was the anchor on the relay team."

"Well, would you like to go for a swim?"

"Are you nuts? Where and when?"

"Right here. They've got one of the best indoor pools I have ever seen."

Jess hesitated a minute, then said. "I'll have to go to my apartment and get my swim suit. It will probably take about thirty minutes."

"That's fine with me. I'll be here in the lobby."

* * * *

About thirty-five minutes later she came driving up in her blue Corvette, parked it out front and walked towards the lobby. She had changed into a black pant suit and had on a leather jacket with a large navy blue canvas bag slung over her shoulder. Dan opened the door for her as she came into the lobby.

She smiled, looked at Dan and said, "Hi again."

"Hi yourself," Dan replied.

"Where do we change?"

"Would you believe in my room?"

Her smile disappeared and she looked at him rather suspiciously then said, "O.K."

Dan led the way to the elevators and as they got on another couple got on also and they went up to the second floor. When Dan and Jess exited the elevator, the couple went in the opposite direction.

As they walked towards Dan's room, Jess said,

"Now I know how a kept woman feels. Did you see the way they looked at us?"

He just gave a little laugh and said,

"Jess, your imagination is running away with you."

Dan put the key in the lock and opened the door. She stepped into the room almost as if she was looking to fall into some kind of trap.

"You go first," Dan said and pointed to the bathroom. She walked in and shut the door. He went over and turned on the TV to the Weather Channel. The local forecast came on and for tomorrow they were predicting another fairly nice day with highs in the low 40's and partly cloudy skies.

The door opened and Jess stepped out in a black one piece swimsuit. She was holding a robe over her left arm and also had on a pair of clogs. She looked like a New York swimsuit model. Dan would have guessed she was about 38–24–36 with a pair of legs as shapely as he had ever seen on any female.

"Wow!" was all Dan could think of to say and Jess smiled appreciatively.

"Your turn," she said.

Dan picked up his trunks, robe and Nike's. He had failed to remember to buy any clogs. In five minutes he was ready and within ten minutes they were standing at the edge of the pool taking off their robes. There was only one couple in the pool with a young boy who looked to be ten or twelve.

Jess said, "I'll race you down to the other end and back!"

"You're on," Dan answered and they both plunged into the water. It was no contest. She had made the turn at the other end when Dan was about three yards back. By the time he turned, she was a good five yards ahead and when he was within twenty feet of the end of the pool she was sitting up on the side laughing at him. When Dan got close enough he reached up, grabbed her by the ankles and she screamed out as he pulled her into the water.

Before Dan realized what was happening, she had her legs wrapped around his waist and she had taken the palms of her hands, put them on top of his head and used his head to leverage her body straight up. She was forcing Dan under the water with her weight and he was thrashing around like a whale. Suddenly she loosened her grip and was swimming away towards the opposite end of the pool.

When she got out of the pool this time she was sitting on her crossed legs and laughing at the top of her voice as he swam towards her.

"O.K.," Dan said. "I give up"

She was still grinning when she said, "You sure?"

"Yep, I know when I'm licked."

She slipped gracefully into the water and stroked towards him where he was treading water. She put her two arms on his shoulders and locked her hands behind his neck as they both kept their bodies moving to keep afloat.

"You're an o.k. guy, Dan Nichols." She was smiling as she loosened her hands and then back stroked away and went the length of the pool and back again as Dan did his slow Australian crawl towards the same end of the pool that she was headed to.

They both continued to swim for about another thirty minutes and then decided to get out. Dan had brought a couple of the towels from the room and they patted themselves to a semi-dry state, put on their robes and shoes and went back to the room. When they had gotten inside she asked,

"Do you mind if I take a shower? I always like to shower after a swim."

"Sure ... you go ahead, Jess. You will notice there is a wall mounted hand dryer near the second lavatory."

Dan could hear the water running and she was humming some song but he couldn't make it out over the sound of the shower. The water sound stopped and a couple of minutes later he could hear the hand dryer blowing. She had left her clothes lying on the bed and in a few minutes the door opened and she stepped out in her robe, holding it closed with one hand and fluffing her long black hair with the other. Dan stood there with his heart beating like a trip hammer.

She stood there looking at him and said, "Well?"

"I think I had better go in there and take a cold shower."

She tossed her head back and let out a loud laugh. Dan went into the bathroom and he did take as cold a shower as he could stand.

She was dressed when he came out in his robe. He started to pick up his clothes and go back into the bathroom when she said,

"Do you have your shorts on?"

"Yeah, I've got them on."

"Well, I've already seen you in your swim shorts so why not dress out here if you want to ... I won't bite," and she smiled at him again.

Dan thought to himself, *she's either testing me concerning my morals or else she has to be the most naïve girl I have ever seen and I don't think she is at all naïve.* He took off the robe, picked his pants up off the bed, put them on and continued to dress. She didn't stand and stare, she just went back into the bathroom and continued to fix her hair and make-up. *Just like an old married couple*, Dan thought.

When they started down the hall to the elevator Jess slipped her arm through Dan's and it remained there until they went into the dining room. The dining room was about three fourths full when they walked in and Dan was somewhat surprised when about two thirds of the people in there turned and stared at them. After the waiter seated them and took their drink order, Jess looked at Dan and turned up the corners of her lips as she said,

"We must make a rather handsome looking couple, don't you think?"

"*I* think they were looking at *you* and all the men were jealous of *me* and the women were jealous of the way *you* look."

Jess propped her elbows on the table, linked the fingers of her hands and rested her chin on them. She leaned forward, smiled even more and said,

"And *I* think you've got the greatest line of B-S of anyone I have met in a long, long time ... but you know what?"

"What?"

"I *love* it!" And she laughed loud enough that several of the couples turned and looked their way.

They each had a drink, ordered their dinner and just thoroughly enjoyed talking to each other as the evening wore on. Finally, Jess looked at her watch.

"Oh, my gosh! You know what time it is ... it's after ten. Where did all the time go?"

Dan signed the check and he told Jess to wait in the lobby while he ran up and got her jacket and navy shoulder bag. She looked at him coyly and said,

"Well, I could go up there with you, you know."

"Dammit, Jess," he grinned, "you've caused me enough pain in one evening to last at least a week. You stay right here until I get back."

She laughed again and sat down in one of the lobby chairs. He was up and back in ten minutes, slipped the jacket around her shoulders and walked out to the Corvette, unlocked the door for her and after she had gotten in he handed her the keys.

While the door was still open she said, "Come here." Dan leaned over and she kissed him lightly on the lips.

"I've had the best day today that I probably have had since being in Alaska, Dan. I just feel real comfortable being around you."

"I feel the same way, Jess. It really has been a most wonderful day."

The Corvette moved away into the night and Dan was left standing there smelling the lingering aroma of her perfume. *I feel exactly like an addict ... the more I am around her the more I **want** to be around her. Damn! What **am** I going to do?*

Chapter 12

Chung-Jang Kwan Il Soong

The chauffeur driven 'North Korean made' 1987 Mount Paikdu, which was a poor copy of the Mercedes-Benz, was wending its way northward on the coastal highway from Wonsan to Toejo Dong. Admiral Kwan Il Soong sitting in the back seat was attempting to reconcile in his own mind whether or not the forthcoming meeting with his superior, Admiral Chong Hi Lee, would be a pleasant one or if it would reveal additional demands being put upon their already overtaxed and under funded Navy. Requests for acquisition of more modern equipment for their submarine fleet had been shelved in favor of additional spending on the nuclear program. No doubt the addition of nuclear weapons would enhance the nations' posture for bargaining with China, Japan and the United States but continuing to ignore the basic needs of the military could possibly result in their being unprepared for a strike by an aggressor nation on their homeland.

This hardly could be the reason for a summons to the Toejo Dong headquarters, however, as this information could easily have been communicated to him by a telephone call from Admiral Chong. What was even more puzzling was the time set for the meeting. He had been requested to arrive at Admiral Chong's office at three o'clock in the afternoon. This would assuredly mean that he would have to stay overnight whereas a morning meeting would have allowed him to drive back to Wonsan the same day. It was now two o'clock and judging from their present location, it appeared they would easily arrive at the appointed time.

At ten minutes until three o'clock, Admiral Kwan was escorted into Admiral Chong's office by his aide. Kwan Il Soong walked into the room, bowed from the waist and said, "Your servant, Kwan Il Soong reporting as ordered, honored sir," then returned to an upright position. Admiral Chong had already started moving towards Kwan and as Chong neared Kwan, he extended his hand which Kwan took. Chong then placed his other hand on top of Kwan's and spoke.

"It is good to see you again, old friend," he smiled.

"And it is equally good to see you, my Admiral," Kwan replied.

"Come. Please be seated," Chong offered and Kwan took one of the plush upholstered leather chairs opposite Chong's desk.

The two had met years ago when they were both students in the Kim Jung-sook Naval Academy. Chong was senior to Kwan by two years but they both joined the Communist Party and became better acquainted once they had graduated from the naval academy and participated in Communist party activities. Their career paths had followed more or less parallel paths and they had become even more closely related during the military engagement with South Korea. They had opportunities during their long friendship to discuss their political theories and beliefs as well as their analysis of military science and tactics. The two of them were often amazed at how closely they were aligned on such topics. Their mindset only increased the bond between the two.

Most of the remainder of the afternoon was spent in an assessment of not only the activities of the Eastern Fleet but also part of the discussion concerned the performance of the entire North Korean Fleet under the command of Admiral Chong. It was only fitting that Admiral Kwan be apprised of such matters as he apparently was the heir apparent to Admiral Chong's position once he retired.

As the afternoon wore on, finally Admiral Chong said,

"My friend, I would be honored if you would allow me to extend an invitation to you to have dinner at home with me this evening. I suggest you dismiss your driver and have him drive to the enlisted men's quarters where he will be taken care of for the evening. After dinner I will have my driver take you to the visiting Admiral's quarters at the Toejo Dong Naval Base."

"I would be honored to have dinner with you, sir." Kwan replied.

*   *   *   *

The Chinese Red Flag limousine bearing a flag with four stars on the front of the vehicle was making its way to the outskirts of Toejo. Inside the vehicle was the driver and Admirals Kwan and Chong in the rear seat. Soon the automobile arrived at a walled compound with two Korean Navy military policemen standing at the gate. As soon as the car turned into the entrance, the two military policemen brought their rifles to the position of a salute and the iron gate was opened. The automobile proceeded into the compound and came to a halt at a low one-story structure typical of a wealthy Korean landowner.

The home, although not ostentatious, was of typical Korean architecture. The blue tile roof was curved up at the eaves to provide covered space for outdoor activities as well as protecting the interior of the building. The walls of the home were made of native stone and dark wood and the grounds were a combination of small gardens and natural landscaping.

The driver exited the vehicle and opened the rear door for the two Admirals. They walked up two steps onto the elevated main floor and were ushered into the foyer by a Korean houseboy who bowed as the two officers entered. He then took their great coats and presented two pairs of sandals for the officers. They removed their shoes and put the sandals on. The houseboy opened two sliding translucent rice paper paneled doors and escorted the two men into the main sitting room. The room had a number of cushions and mats plus a large teakwood table which sat on legs that appeared to be about eight or nine inches in height. There was also a floor lamp in the room which projected light toward the ceiling. Also standing at the entrance to the room was a woman dressed in a brilliant green long full skirt with a short matching jacket. Admiral Chong introduced her to Admiral Kwan as his wife. She bowed, greeted the visitor and immediately retired down a hallway to another section of the home. Admiral Chong turned to his houseboy, "Jon-wi, escort Admiral Kwan to the guest room so that he may prepare for dinner."

Jon-wi bowed and motioned for Admiral Kwan to follow him down the long *ondol* hallway.

Admiral Kwan realized as he walked that the entire house must have the *ondol* heating system. This system was a series of pipes running underneath the wooden floor which carried circulating hot water. This provided an even warm heat for all of the rooms in the house which was perfect for comfortable sleeping as the occupants slept on mats instead of on beds. Jon-wi opened another sliding door which revealed a small room with a table holding a wash basin plus a towel. There were also two sleeping mats and several large cushions in the room. On one of the mats was a medium blue cotton jacket and a pair of pantaloons as well as a beautiful black silk robe decorated with gold fillagree. Jon-we explained, "The garments are for you, sir, as the dinner will be quite informal. I shall return when dinner is ready to be served." Jon-wi departed.

In approximately thirty minutes, Jon-wi returned and knocked on Admiral Kwan's door. The door opened and Jon-wi said, "Dinner is ready, sir. Please follow me." The two walked back down the hallway until they came to two sliding doors which opened into the *sarangbang*, or the front quarters. This was the room which was used exclusively by Admiral Chong. In this room there was a desk, a table lamp, and a chair. Other than these two pieces of furniture there was a low table with several large cushions around it and one floor lamp in one corner of the room. Admiral Chong was dressed in a charcoal colored jacket, pantaloons and a dark blue silk robe trimmed in gold cord. He was standing near the table which had several steaming dishes on it. He motioned to Admiral Kwan, "Come in my friend. We are ready for dinner," and he smiled at Kwan.

They both seated themselves on cushions at the table which held two bowls of *maeuntang* for each of the two men. This was a hot, spicy seafood soup that contained white fish, vegetables, boybean curd and red pepper powder. The main dish, sitting in the middle of the table, was *pulgoki*, one of the most popular Korean dishes. This literally meant 'fire beef' or Korean barbecued tender slices of beef marinated in a sauce. In addition there were two vegetable dishes and a bowl of white rice for each man. To top it off there was also a dish of *kimchi* which was necessary for every Korean meal. This was a relish made with pungent pickled vegetables such as cabbage and turnips with chopped garlic, onions, and salted fish.

Admiral Chong picked up a bottle of *soju* wine and poured a goblet for Admiral Kwan. He then sat the bottle down and Admiral Kwan picked it up and poured a goblet for Admiral Chong. It was a bad breech of etiquette for a Korean to pour his own drink. Admiral Chong lifted his glass and said, "To a long life and much happiness, my friend." Admiral Kwan lifted his glass and touched it to Admiral Chong's. Admiral Kwan sipped his wine and sat the glass down. He then picked up his chopsticks which was a signal to his guest they could begin eating.

Chong spoke to his friend, "It is time for us to end formalities, Soong. We should remember our early friendship when we were both students at the Naval Academy and refer to one another by the names we knew each other by at that time."

Kwan replied, "It will be difficult for me, my friend, as I have always looked upon you as my superior as I have the utmost respect for you and your ability as a leader."

Chong smiled and said, "I understand but please try. I wanted you to visit with me this evening in my home for two reasons. First, to convey to you my appreciation for your long lasting friendship and to thank you for your confidence in me. I trust after this conversation is over this evening that you will still think of me in the same light."

Kwan was surprised by the frank statement but replied, "I assure you that whatever is said that I will continue to have the utmost respect for you and anything that is said will be kept in strictest confidence."

Chong continued, "You are aware, of course, that I just returned from a meeting of the Secretariat of the Central Committee and the President was in attendance at that meeting."

"Yes, Lee. I am aware of that." Replied Kwan. He then took the final spoonful of *maeuntang* ... it was an absolutely delicious soup.

"I have real concerns for the course that our leadership is taking, Soong."

Soong now knew why he was invited to Chong Hi Lee's home. The State Political Security Agency had no listening devices here.

Kwan respectfully waited until Chong had finished his soup. To proceed on to the next course without waiting for his host to pick up his chopsticks would have been an insult.

Chong continued, "When we were young members of the Party, we were hopeful that the proletariat would at last have an opportunity for economic improvement under the leadership of President Kim Il Sung. And, for a while, it appeared that would be the case."

Lee had now picked up his chopsticks and began to eat the *pulgoki*. Soong followed his lead.

"I do not have to tell you the effect that the war with the South has had on our comrades, Soong." Lee continued. "They have regressed economically to the state they were in prior to 1950 and it appears their situation will worsen. The economy of our country is being drained by the expenditures made by the party in order to become a nuclear power, and to what end?" Lee paused and took a sip of the rice wine. "Because of this program I am afraid that our hope for a peaceful reuniting with the South, and an economic welfare program for our people, is being dashed by a small group of anarchists."

He continued. "We are both acutely aware of what happened to Japan when they awoke the sleeping tiger. And, instead of using our nuclear power to enrich the lives of our comrades we are seeking ways to tantalize the tiger by building nuclear weapons. That idiot child of the President, Kim Jong-Il frightens me, Soong. I do believe that if he becomes the President, upon the death of his father, that he will unleash a nuclear weapon upon the Yankees if he thought there was any possibility that it could be done."

"Oh, surely you really don't believe that, Lee?" Soong questioned.

Lee paused while he spooned some of the white rice on his plate. When finished, Lee looked Soong directly in the eye.

"There is no question in my mind but what he would do it if he thought it would succeed." Lee said in all sincerity.

Soong felt a slight chill run up his spine. He took a large sip of the wine.

"I tell you this," Lee continued, "because my time is coming to a close and there is little doubt but what you will be my successor. I doubt there is little you or I can do to change the course of events but I thought it only fair to make you aware of what is going to befall you when you become the Admiral of the Fleet."

Suddenly, Soong had a feeling of despair. *What could one or two officers do in such a situation?* Soong finished the last of the wine and as he sat the goblet down, Lee immediately refilled it.

"Now, my friend," Lee said, "I have to tell you the rest of the story. You know of course, that we do not have a missile submarine, correct?"

"Yes, Lee, to my knowledge we do not."

"Then, would it make sense to you that there is a movement under way to develop a missile similar to the Yankee 'Trident' missile?"

"What in the name of Buddha, for?" Soong replied.

"It is my understanding that to build such a missile is a tricky process. There is an accelerator needed in addition to the nuclear components. Normally, it is possible to obtain this isotope in the process of producing nuclear energy but our scientists have been unable to do so. Our President, or his son … I don't know for sure which … have even threatened our scientists with their lives but they still have not been successful. China, India and even Germany have small quantities of this isotope but they refuse to sell it to us and that has infuriated our leaders even more. So, it appears that a plan has been devised for us to steal it from the Canadians."

"*Steal it?*" Soong exclaimed.

"Yes … and, my friend *you* are going to be instrumental in carrying out the plan for the theft."

Soong felt a few beads of perspiration begin to form on his brow. Perhaps it was just the wine, he conjectured. After a moment he composed himself enough to ask. "Suppose we are successful in obtaining the isotope, what happens next?"

"I assume that it will take time to build the weapon and test it successfully. If that program is successful then stage two of the plan will be put into motion," Lee answered.

"And that would be …?" asked Soong.

"Build the vehicle." Lee replied.

"Build the vehicle …" Soong had a perplexed look on his face for a moment … then, "You mean a *nuclear submarine?*"

"Exactly." Lee said in finality.

"Then it would be possible to *definitely* hit the United States' western coast with a nuclear missile." Soong felt that chill run up his spine for the second time this evening. "But that would take several years,"

"The idiot child can be a patient man as long as all parties involved are making progress," Lee added. "But he has little patience with failures."

The two friends had finished their satisfying meal and they were on their third glass of wine. At least some of the more fearsome thoughts running through their minds were being numbed to a degree by the rather strong alcohol content.

"When you leave here tonight, my friend," Lee continued, "I will give you an envelope containing sealed orders. You are not to open them until you return to Wonsan. When you are alone in your office, open the orders and put the wheels in motion for undertaking the mission. Once that is done, put the orders in your safe. No one but you is to ever see these orders. Do you understand?"

"Yes, my Admiral. I understand perfectly."

Chapter 13

The Interview

The last thing Dan thought about before closing his eyes Sunday night was that he *had* to get in touch with Mary Beth on Monday for sure. He woke up at 6:30 with that thought on his mind. It took him just about a full minute to realize that it was 10:30 back in Knoxville and Mary Beth probably got home around 7:30 or 8:00 a.m. her time. Dan decided he would give her about two more hours to get some sleep then he was going to call. Arising from the bed, he showered, shaved, dressed and went down to the dining room for breakfast. Judy took care of Dan in her usual fashion and at 8:05 a.m. Alaska time, he picked up the phone in his room and dialed Mary Beth's number.

"Hello." A voiced filled with sleep answered.

"Hi, hon ... it's me."

"Oh, hello stranger, where are you now?" She still sounded a little groggy.

"I'm still in Anchorage. I apologize for not having called sooner but I just haven't been able to catch you."

"That's o.k., ... I know. Cathy's told me you have called a couple of times. How do you like it up there?"

"I really like it, Mary Beth. It's a beautiful place and I intend to spend some time visiting some of the points of interest and seeing all this beautiful scenery.

"Aren't you going to get awful lonesome up there not knowing anyone?" Mary Beth asked.

What is she ... clairvoyant? I never was good at keeping secrets from this kid!

Well, I have met a few nice people and I spent a great day yesterday with one of the young ladies who is an officer of the company that bought the King Air.

"I see. (silence) Who is she?"

Dan sensed that Mary Beth was suddenly wide awake.

"She's the vice-president of the company that bought the King Air, honey. She's a very nice person as well."

"Did you say, '*young*' lady?"

"Well, she's probably about seven or eight years younger than me."

"*Daaad!*" Dan could just visualize Mary Beth now sitting straight up in the bed.

"Oh, come on, Mary Beth," Dan said rather irritated. "There may be eight years difference age wise but she is mature beyond her years. She's a very smart person; has a law degree and a masters in environmental engineering."

"And, I suppose she is beautiful as well." she said somewhat sarcastically.

"You wouldn't want me to become involved with someone that looked like an old hag, would you?"

"*Involved!* Just how *involved* are you with her, Dad?"

"Aww, that was a poor choice of words, Cookie. Actually we just met … really. She and I have a lot in common. She's got a great personality, witty, and I know you would like her if you met her."

"I see. And what other traits does she have that mother didn't have?" she said somewhat bitterly.

"Now, that's a low blow, Mary Beth!" Dan replied, somewhat indignantly.

"You're right … I shouldn't have said that and I apologize."

"That's o.k. Are you getting along o.k.?"

"I'm doing fine, Dad. They told me at the hospital that my work ethic was so good that the next floor supervisor's job that comes open will be mine."

"Hey, that sounds great! Any boy friends yet?"

"I'm dating one guy that's real nice but it's nothing serious."

"Well, I'm glad to see that you have a social life. You need some outside interests; you know the old saying about all work and no play."

"I know, Dad. Working the night shift makes it tough but I hope that I will be on the day shift before too long."

"Well you take care of yourself, Cookie, and I will try to do better about calling."

"That's o.k." Mary Beth paused … "And, Dad, …"

"What honey?"

"Oh, nothing. I love you Dad."

"I love you too, Cookie. You're the greatest in my book. Bye."

"Bye, Dad."

*I'm glad to get that over with. I guess I could have just not mentioned Jess but I would have had the same feeling as when I used to try and keep secrets from my Mother. Damn! At times that girl is **worse** than my mother. But, it was nothing more than I expected. I knew that once I met someone that it would be tough for Mary Beth. She was so close to her mother and no one could ever take her place. Well, that is as it should be. No one could take Mary Ann's place in my life either but I have to get on with my life too.*

Dan picked up his brief case and went back down to the lobby desk and got a free copy of the USA today and went back into the dining room. Judy saw Dan come back in and came over to the table with the coffee pot.

"I'll bet you are back for a refill aren't you?"

"Yeah, I just had to leave awhile and call my daughter back home and now I still have some time to kill."

"I'll bet she was glad to hear from you," Judy said.

"Well yes and no. With my daughter it's pretty much like reporting in to my mother when I was a teen-ager."

"Oh? And have you been a bad boy?" Judy smiled.

"No, not really. It's just that since my wife died my daughter feels like it is her responsibility to see that I don't fall into bad company."

Judy laughed aloud. "Well, you just have to keep in mind that you are the only Dad she has and that she loves you very much."

"Yeah, I know. She really is a great gal and I need to have patience with her."

"Well, you just make yourself at home and I'll keep the pot hot for you."

"Thanks, Judy, you're a pal."

Judy walked away and Dan picked up the *USA Today* and looked at the financial page. It being Monday there wouldn't be any stock market reports so he just looked it over to see if he could find where some corporate leech had screwed some of the stockholders again. He continued to keep a check on the time and when 10:30 finally rolled around, he picked up his brief case and headed for the Honda.

∗   ∗   ∗   ∗

Dan walked into the Intermont reception room at ten minutes 'til eleven. Virginia was on the 'phone so he just dropped into a chair and picked up a copy of *Newsweek* and started reading all the bad news. Virginia hung up.

"Good morning, Mr. Nichols. How are you this morning?

"Just fine, Virginia, just fine, and by the way, why don't you just call me Dan? Al himself told me that Intermont is a very informal organization so you and I probably should follow his example, don't you agree?

"I'll try, Mr. Nichols. I'll see if Mr. Switzer is ready for you." She dialed an extension number and then placed the handset in the cradle.

"He said to give him about five minutes," and she smiled at Dan over the top of her bifocals.

In just about that length of time the door to Al's office opened and he gestured to Dan.

"Come on in, Dan. It's good to see you this morning" Al stuck out his hand which Dan shook as he entered his office. Dan then noticed another man was sitting in one of the chairs opposite Al's desk.

"Dan, this is Fred Robinson, our Vice President of Finance."

Fred Robinson reminded Dan of Jimmy Stewart when he was about 50 years old. Tall, slender with an angular face on which wire framed glasses sat. He had light brown hair which was beginning to grey at the temples. Fred stood and extended his hand.

"Hello, Dan. I'm glad to meet you. I have been hearing some good things about you from Al."

How could that be? I haven't been with Al more than three hours so far. Perhaps Al has been making some 'phone calls back to the States.

"Well, thanks, Fred. I'm glad to meet you also."

Al had walked around his desk, sat down in his large upholstered chair and took a Cifuentes y Cia cigar out of the carved wood box on top of his desk. He extended the box across to Dan.

"Cigar, Dan?" Dan extended his arm with the palm at a ninety degree angle to his wrist.

"Oh, that's right. You don't smoke. I admire your will power. One of these days I am going to try to do the same."

Al pushed back in his chair. "We might as well get right down to business, Dan. I wanted Fred to sit in on this conversation since he is concerned with keeping a lid on the 'money keg.'" Al chuckled at his little witticism.

"Dan, when we had finished our lunch the other day my suspicions of you were confirmed. I had a hunch after the first few minutes of our initial conversation that you were more than just a pilot; that you probably had either been in business for yourself or you had been in upper management for some organization. As our conversation at lunch continued and I learned more about your business background, you must have experienced many of the problems involved in building a business and making a success of it."

Al inhaled from his cigar and then blew out a cloud of smoke as he continued.

"Our business has grown markedly in the past five years and we have been flying by the seat of our pants in just trying to serve our customers and keep them loyal to us. We do that by cutting some good deals for them and giving them faster delivery than our competitors. This means that we are working on less margin than our competitors so we need to keep very close control of our operating costs." Al paused, took a deep puff on his Cifuentes y Cia again, exhaled and continued.

"Frankly, we have very little factual information related to the cost of operation of our aircraft and we badly need a system of nailing down our cost of delivery by our planes. Now, I am going to let Fred give you an idea of what we need."

Fred turned in his chair and faced Dan. "Dan, have you ever heard of Crossair?"

"Yes, I have. They are a very large contract air freight outfit I believe."

"That's correct. I happen to be very well acquainted with their comptroller and not long ago I had an opportunity to meet with him for dinner one evening. I was telling him about our problem of attempting to arrive at an absolute cost figure for operating our aircraft and he told me about a software program they had purchased which has provided their company with excellent operational cost data for each of their aircraft. He furnished me with the name of the software company so I contacted them and they sent a promotional video tape on their program. Al and I were both so impressed that we purchased the program."

Fred paused for moment then continued. "Have you had any experience with a computer?"

"Well, yes, Fred. I had to become somewhat computer literate so that I could satisfy the same basic needs in my company that you are now facing. I use Windows and can move around in Word, Excel and other basic programs."

"Good! I was hoping that you would have at least the basics of computer literacy."

Fred turned back towards Al. "Al, you want to wrap this up by telling Dan what we are looking for?"

Al got up, walked over to the window of his fifth floor office and gazed out over Cook Inlet. He took another puff of the cigar and then turned to face the two of them.

"Dan, we need a man with your knowledge of aircraft and how they can be used as an effective tool to serve our customers efficiently and at the same time be a factor in making a profit for the company. For the past several years we have operated our aircraft in a very inefficient manner. Just to be very truthful about the matter, we don't have a reasonable guess as to whether the air fleet is making money for us or not. Both Fred and I believe that you are the man that can give us what we need to make our air operation run efficiently and profitably. And, we are willing to pay a reasonable amount for your efforts. We may as well cross that bridge before we go any further. So, let me toss this out on the table. How would $60,000 dollars a year sound to you with a provision that if you get the operation shaped up within six months and it is making money for the company we will add an additional $10,000 per year to your base salary. Other benefits such as health and life insurance will be part of the package as well. What do you say?

Suddenly Dan began to feel flushed and the walls of the room seemed to be closing in somewhat. Nervous anxiety?

"Well, this is quite a surprise, Al." Dan replied. "I really didn't expect to come in this morning and be offered a job, however I must admit that it is attractive because of the fact that it is something I really love to do. Why don't you go ahead and spell out exactly what you have in mind before I give you a definite 'yes' or 'no?'"

"Fair enough," Al replied. "O.K., Fred, the ball is in your court again."

"Let's start with people, Dan. At present we have two pilots, Harry Abelson and Tim Morrison, and both of them will be reporting to you. Harry has been used to running things his way and consequently Tim, being our junior pilot, has had very little guidance insofar as being responsible for his performance as a pilot, maintaining records and turning in a detailed expense account. From now on not one of our three aircraft are to leave the ground without your approval. You will have total responsibility for scheduling the aircraft and assigning the pilot for the trips. Also, Harry and Tim are not to spend one dime of the company's money without your approval and when they do, they are to present a receipt to you for the expenditure." As Fred proceeded with his presentation, Al sat back down in his chair and put the stub of his cigar in the silver ashtray on his desk.

"Also, you are to develop a system of maintenance for the aircraft and see that all FAA requirements are met for each aircraft. In developing cost figures for each aircraft you will also provide estimates for periodic inspections, engine overhauls and general maintenance. We lease a section of one hangar from Stevens so you will need to incorporate that cost in your expense program as well. We have worked well with Stevens in the past and have had a good relationship with them but this is not to say we are married to them. If you find that you can significantly reduce our maintenance and service costs by going elsewhere then Al and I are open to your recommendations." Fred paused for a moment.

Al looked towards Fred. Anything else, Fred?"

"Yes. We have some office space available in our section, Dan, and I think it would be wise for you to keep all of your records in that office. There is also a computer there and the software that I mentioned has been installed and is functional. I would like for you to take a look at it at your earliest convenience. Any questions, Dan?"

Dan could feel a dampness on his forehead and his heartbeat was definitely elevated.

"No ... no questions, it's just that this is all so sudden. There are so many things for me to take into consideration." Dan replied.

"Well, if there is something that we haven't explained adequately or if there is some more information that you need we certainly will be pleased to allay any fears that you may have." Al added.

"It isn't that, Al," Dan said, "it's just ... well, this would call for an entire change in my life. Geographically it's a long way from home and I would be making a very drastic change which, frankly, gives me some pause to consider all aspects of your proposition."

"I see," Al mused. He exhaled a puff of cigar smoke and exchanged glances with Fred. "Then are we to assume that you are just not interested in our offer?"

"Oh, I wouldn't say that, Al. But I would be more comfortable if I had a little time to consider all the ramifications of making such a move."

"And how much time would you need, Dan?"

Dan quickly thought ... two days to get home and five days to give it some real thought.

"Suppose I give you a call a week from today, would that be satisfactory?"

"That sounds logical to me. What do you say, Fred?" Al asked.

"Well, Al, we have been sitting on this thing for about six months so I don't see where another week will make that much difference." Fred answered.

Al stood and Dan and Fred followed. "So be it then," and he moved from behind his desk. Dan turned and shook hands with Fred then Al moved towards Dan, shook his hand and ushered him to his office door. He put one arm around Dan's shoulders as they walked.

"You give this some very serious consideration, my boy, and we will be looking forward to hearing from you."

Dan looked Al square in the eye. "I really will, Al."

When Dan walked into the reception room he asked Virgina if Miss Jess was in her office.

"No, she isn't, Mr. Dan. She had to run an errand downtown but said she would be back soon."

"Well, when she returns would you tell her I had to leave town unexpectedly but I will giver her a call."

"I certainly will, Mr. Dan. Will you be gone long?"

"I don't know, Virginia ... I really don't know. But you take care."

✳   ✳   ✳   ✳

Dan was standing at the elevator waiting for it to reach his floor when he heard the elevator bell 'ding' and the doors opened. Jess was exiting the elevator.

"Well, so we meet again," Dan said.

"Oh ... hi! Did you accept?"

Both paused just outside the elevator door while the doors closed and the elevator started down.

"You mean the job ... so you knew?"

"Of course I knew. After all I am an officer of the company," she smiled.

"That's right. And did you cast a vote for me?" Dan smiled back at her.

"Why, certainly I did. Don't you remember what I said last night as I left you?"

She is teasing me again.

"That you felt comfortable when you were with me." Dan replied

"That's right."

"Well, you may change your mind."

"Why is that? Jess asked.

"I didn't take the job, Jess"

"You *what?* Why not?" She went from a smile to a look of incredulity.

"I hope that you can appreciate this. Really the least thing I expected from Al this morning was a job offer and I was just totally unprepared for it. Here I am about two thousand miles from home, my family is back there and the environment here is rather different to say the least. To say nothing of the fact that I go from a life of leisure into one of a significant amount of responsibility. Can you understand where I am coming from?"

"Well ... yes I can." And there was just the hint of a smile at the corners of her lips.

"Good. Now I can also tell you this. I did not shut the door ... I told Al I would go home and seriously think about the deal and give him an answer in a week."

"Great! I feel better already." and the smile reappeared. "I know that you will do the right thing." She paused for a moment and then, "I guess this is good-bye then."

Jess reached down and took his right hand in her left, pulled him towards her gently and gave him a kiss on the lips. Not a lingering kiss but one of tenderness.

"I can see right now that you are bribing me." Dan said.

There was that lilting laugh of hers and she replied, "Well, you might say that. Good-bye, Dan and you be careful."

"I will. Good-bye, Jess, and I will give you a call."

"I'm counting on it."

The doors to the elevator opened, Dan stepped inside, turned around and faced Jess. The doors closed.

Chapter 14

Back to Knoxville

Dan checked his bags at Stevens International and then went to a pay phone and used his credit card to make a phone call.

"Tom Nichols speaking."

"Hi, Tom, it's Dad."

"Hey, Dad, how's it going?

"Well it's going all right. I'm about to get on a Delta flight to Atlanta. I will connect with Delta Flight 343 for Knoxville which is scheduled to arrive at McGhee Tyson at 3:10 p.m. your time. I'm wondering if you might be able to get off and pick me up."

"No problem, Dad. What happened, why the sudden decision to come home?"

"I'll give you all the details when I see you, son … O.K.?"

"Sure, Dad. Have a good flight."

Out of habit, Dan checked his watch as the Delta 757 lifted off the runway and he noted they were twelve minutes late. That should present no problem once they reached cruising altitude. The prevailing westerlies should boost the ground speed of the 757 to the point where they would more than make up for the lost time.

Probably for the first time ever in an aircraft, Dan went to sleep reading a magazine and slept for more than two hours. He realized that he was just mentally fatigued.

* * * *

Dan was right. The Anchorage flight pulled into Atlanta Hartsfield twenty-one minutes ahead of their scheduled time. Flight 343 left Atlanta for Knoxville five minutes late and they arrived in Knoxville just about on time. Tom was waiting for his Dad in the concourse.

"Hey, Dad, you look a little tired."

The two of them embraced. Many fathers and sons shake hands but Tom and Dan had given each other a hug on meeting for many, many years. It was a true expression of the closeness that the two of them shared.

"Well, I must admit, son, that things have been moving a bit fast for your old Dad."

Tom gave his Dad a playful punch on the shoulder, "Where do you come off with the 'old' stuff. I'll bet there are few men your age who are in the physical condition you are."

"Well, we won't argue that point but right now I look forward to a few days of doing practically nothing."

"So what's been going on up north?"

Dan proceeded to fill Tom in on all the details which took place at Intermont but he failed to mention his relationship with Jess.

"So you came home to shake out the cobwebs and make a decision, right?"

"That's about the size of it."

They loaded Dan's bags in Tom's car and as they were driving back towards Knoxville, Dan spoke up. "How about you and Jane joining me for dinner tonight?

Sure you are up to it."

"You bet."

"O.K., I'll drop you off and give her a call from your condo and see what she says."

"Great."

Chapter 15

▼

Man of Leisure

Dan awoke the next morning to find that he had slept almost an hour later than his normal time. As he went through his normal exercise routine before taking his shower he realized just how stressful the past week had been but now he was completely refreshed.

Dan slipped on his robe and house shoes and quickly dropped into his old routine; making a pot of coffee, reading the morning paper and having a light breakfast of toast and cereal. He wondered why he continued to read the paper and be discouraged by the political situation in the country and also the mess that the world in general was in.

Reaching for the phone on the kitchen counter, he dialed a familiar number.

"Hello."

"Hi, Don, it's me."

"Oh ... so you are finally home. Did you have a good trip?"

"Yep ... very interesting trip. I'll tell you and the guys about it when we play golf. You think you can set up a game with Frank and Bill for tomorrow?"

"I'll see what I can do and call you back."

"Oh, and one other thing, Don ... I'm going to play with either Frank or Bill."

There was a pause and when he replied there was a change of inflection in Don's voice.

"Well, O.K.! If *that's* the way you want it!

"That's the way I want it. Bye."

After getting dressed Dan began to sort out the extra clothes he had brought back from Alaska, deciding which ones needed to be washed and the ones that needed to be dry cleaned. Bundling the clothes in two groups he left the condo and drove to the cleaners and then to the post office to pick up the mail that he had held while he was gone. From there he dropped by the bank and then back to the condo.

Looking at the Breitling he noticed that it was after noon and this would be a good time to give Mary Beth a call as she should be waking up about now.

"Hello." There was a sound of drowsiness in her voice.

"Hi, Cookie ... it's Dad. I hope I didn't wake you early."

"Oh, no. I was lying here awake just trying to get up enough energy to get out of bed."

"Oh? Have a hard time last night?"

"You wouldn't believe it, Dad. They brought in some drunk that had tried to kill himself with a knife plus there was a horrible car wreck on Broadway. Five people in two cars were mangled up pretty bad and one kid eighteen years old didn't make it."

"My gosh, baby. You really see some bad stuff, don't you?"

"Somebody has to do it, Dad. At least I feel like I am doing something worthwhile. Did you have a great trip?"

"Yes, I really did. It's a beautiful country up there and I enjoyed the flight up. I got to see some of the country in the U.S. that I had never seen before, too."

"Well, at least you got that out of your system."

"Well, I'm not so sure about that, Mary Beth."

"What do you mean by that, Dad?" Her voice had increased by at least five decibels.

"Intermont offered me a nice position, Cookie, and I came back to think things over."

"It's that damn woman again, isn't it?" Her voice was pitched even higher.

"Now, don't you start on that again, Mary Beth!" Dan said indignantly. "We've been through that before and I'm trying to make a decision based on logic and what will be best for me and also for our family."

"Well, as a member of *our family*, I can tell you right now that I'm opposed to it."

"O.K ... O.K, I can see that trying to resolve this issue with you over the telephone is hopeless." Dan paused a moment ... "I think the best thing to do is for you, Tom, Jane and me to have dinner together and hash this thing out. Are you agreeable to that?"

"Yes!"

"Fine! I'll arrange a time with Tom and Jane and get back to you."

For a few minutes after the call, Dan tried to figure out which side of the family that Mary Beth's antagonism had come from. *Is it just me that she is antagonistic towards me or is she that way with other people as well?*

That afternoon Dan took an 8-1/2 x 11 tablet and, like the accountant that he had been, made what is known in the accounting trade as a "T" Table. One horizontal line across the top and one vertical line down the middle of the page. On one side of the vertical line he wrote the word "Benefits" and on the other side he wrote "Liabilities." One the left side of the vertical line, he began to list as many things as he could think of that would be a benefit by his going back to Intermont and on the other side the reasons why he should stay at home. When he finished there were quite a few more items on the left side than on the right.

Chapter 16

Friendly Opinions?

It couldn't have been a better day for golf. The temperature was in the mid eighties, no clouds and the humidity level was low. Dan flipped a coin to decide his partner and he paired up with Frank while Don went off with Bill. Don was in something of a "funk" for the first four holes but on the par three fifth hole he made a birdie. He grinned, and looked at Dan as if to say, "Take that, you moron." When they finished up on the eighteenth, the score was dead even. For a minute they discussed a playoff hole but Dan said, "I think it would be better if we left it this way." The other three concurred and they migrated to the nineteenth hole for a beer.

Sitting around the table in the card room having their beer, the three friends pressed Dan for details about his Alaska 'escapade.' Dan gave them an almost detailed line for line description of the entire trip and ended with the employment agreement that Internet had offered. He just omitted one small detail … there was no mention of Jessica Lane.

Approximately twenty minutes of discussion bantered back and forth between the three friends and the long and short of it was they unanimously agreed that Dan belonged in a squirrel cage if he considered going back. Dan had no further comment.

They all parted by shaking hands along with some back-slapping and Dan went back to the condo to find there was a message for him on his answering machine from Stump Reynolds.

Dan dialed his friend's number.

"Stump Reynolds, here."

"Hey, Stump, it's me."

"Where in the freakin' hell have you *been*?" Stump's voice had the level of a tornado. "I send a guy off with a million dollar airplane and all I get back from him is a letter with a signed contract and a check. I called up there Monday and they told me you had caught a plane and left. For all the hell I knew you could have gone to China! You never have gone off on one of my trips before without calling me afterwards!"

"Yeah, I know ... I've had a lot on my mind lately."

"Well, that's mighty damn hard to believe seeing as how the cavity between your ears is about ninety percent air!"

"Hey! If you don't calm down, I'm going to come down there and punch you in that bulbous nose of yours!" Now Dan was agitated.

"Well, shall I remind you of the last time that you tried that? You ended up in a swimming pool with your clothes on!"

They both broke out laughing and Dan finally stopped laughing long enough to say, "Yeah, I remember ... it took three days for the stuff in my billfold to dry out, you bastard."

"O.K., Dan. I apologize for teeing off on you like that but I was actually worried about you."

"I know you were and I should have called you. But let me give you a run-down on why I am in such a snit." And Dan proceeded to give Stump the compete story ... including Jessica Lane.

"Oh ... I should have known. So there is a woman involved. Well, I hope you got laid ... that's something you have needed for five years."

"Come on, now, Stump ... she's not that kind of lady." Dan said indignantly

"All right. So you want me to tell you what you should do, right?"

"Well, your opinion would be important to me, Stump."

"Hey, ol' buddy. We have been through thick and thin for how long ... thirty years? I love you like a brother but I can't make this decision for you but I sure can sympathize with you. I have Frances and Bill and Elizabeth and I've got grandkids too. I can certainly appreciate the void you have in your life. Sure, you've got Mary Beth and Tom but they aren't there when you come home at night and I can't visualize what my life would be like without having Frances waiting for me. Sorry pal, but this is one you alone will have to make the call on."

"Thanks, Stump. Whether you realize it or not, you have been a big help. I hope we can get together sometime soon."

"Me too, buddy. See ya.'"

Chapter 17

▼

Peace At Last?

Being at loose ends on this Thursday, Dan decided after breakfast that he just might run over to Island Home Airport and see if by some chance some of his old buddies from his early flying days might be hanging around. He knew that Jim Bowers, one of his old flying pals, still kept his Beech Bonanza hangared there and he might catch him on the ground.

Traveling across the Henley Street bridge he came to where he would ordinarily make a left turn onto Island Home Pike which would take him to the airport. For some unexplainable reason though, he continued straight ahead on Chapman Highway which eventually would lead to Highway 441 and would wind its way up to Sevierville and on to Gatlinburg.

Passing Sevierville, Dolly Parton's home town, Dan continued on a few miles more to Gatlinburg. Although the little town was crowded, he found a parking place, got out and mingled with the vacationers who thronged to this place during the vacation months. He remembered this was one of Mary Ann's, Tom's, and Mary Beth's favorite places when they were young because of the many, many souvenir shops. Dan could never see the attraction himself, because practically every trinket in the stores was stamped "Made in Japan" on the bottom.

He stopped in the Black Hearth and had a sandwich for lunch then returned to the 380-SL, motored on to the eastern city limits and saw the sign, "Welcome to the Smoky Mountains National Park." He wound his way up the mountain and enjoyed the drop in temperature as the Mercedes climbed. Finally he parked in the Clingman's Dome overlook area, got out of the car and sat on the natural stone wall and looked down on the thousands of acres of trees which were discernable for miles through the bluish smoky haze.

He heard car doors opening and observed one family of four from Ohio who were just getting out of their car; a husband, wife and two children. The mother was a blonde and the two children looked to be about ten and eight, the boy being older than the girl. They reminded Dan of his family and their trips to the mountains. They had really loved this place.

Dan's mind began to think about various events that had transpired in their lives over the years and eventually he thought of Mary Ann's and his last trip and her last wish for him.

I don't want you to <u>forget</u> me, Dan. I know you won't do that, but you are still a young man and you will probably live at least another forty-five years and you are the type of person who needs the love and support of a woman.

Strangely enough, instead of a feeling of sorrow, there was a feeling of peacefulness that engulfed Dan. He got back in the car and drove home. He called both Tom and Mary Beth to tell them they would have dinner together tomorrow night.

CHAPTER 18

▼

CROWING SOUNDS

The chauffeur driven North Korean made 1987 Mount Paikdu, which was a poor copy of the Mercedes-Benz, was approaching the guard shack of the North Korean Naval Base at Wonsan. In the rear seat was *Chung-Jang*[1] Kwan Il Soong. The Vice Admiral considered himself fortunate to be riding in a vehicle of class even though the doors did not shut properly due to unmatched window sections. The car was manufactured at the Mount Sungri factory in Tokchon City. Although production of all automobiles manufactured in North Korea was touted to be 20,000 units annually, the Admiral had reliable information that the production numbers were more in the range of six to seven thousand units per year. Nevertheless, he at least, was afforded the automobile whereas senior party officials, public agencies and noteworthy businessmen had to resort to bribes in order to obtain a vehicle of any sort. At times, being in the military, with proper connections, did afford one some special benefits.

The driver slowed at the guard shack where two uniformed members of the Korean People's Navy challenged the driver and the Admiral for their identification cards. The two individuals in the automobile were given more than just a cursory glance. The guard on the driver's side checked the appearance of both the driver and the Admiral against the photographs which appeared on their ID cards. After the military policeman was satisfied, he rendered a salute to the

---

1. Vice Admiral

Admiral and motioned the Mount Paikdu through the gate. Admiral Kwan Il Soong was certain that a report would be rendered to the State Safety & Security Agency that he had passed through this checkpoint at such and such a time and on this specific date. Agents of the State Safety & Security agency manned agencies in each province and every city, both large and small, in the country. It was rumored that total personnel in the agency had approached 50,000 persons. These people were charged with counterintelligence responsibilities at home and abroad; they searched out anti-state criminals, economic crimes, supervised camps for political prisoners, monitored political attitudes and reported slander of the political leadership. When director Lee Jin-soo died in October 1987, he was not replaced and the agency fell under direct control of Kim Johng-il, the son of President Kim Il Sung. All reports of major consequence were forwarded directly to the president.

When the driver approached the quay where the submarines docked, the Admiral directed the driver to stop. The driver immediately exited the car and opened the rear door for the Admiral. Admiral Kwan Il Soong was not a tall man, about five feet ten with a body that would possibly indicate that he had done some wrestling at some point in his life. Slightly overweight for his size, he had a ruddy complexion that belied the hours exposed to the sun, wind and rain while on the conning tower of a submarine or the deck of a fast coastal patrol vessel. He had a neatly trimmed mustache which was just about all white now, matching his hair. His steel grey eyes were half-hidden by eyelids that had crows feet at the corners and were almost frozen into narrowed slits to protect the pupils from hours of glaring into the sun while on the decks of various naval vessels.

He strolled with a rolling gait down the quay and looked over the first ship tied to the stanchions. It was a SOJU which was the North Korean version of the Russian OSA-1 guided-missile patrol boat equipped with 4 STYX missile launchers. Although rather small in size, their high speed provided quick interception of any intruding vessels into coastal waters. Sailors aboard the patrol boat were performing routine duties while some were painting any areas that had been badly weathered. The next boat was a ROMEO Type 033 Diesel-Electric submarine. North Korea obtained their first ROMEO's in the early 1970's from China who then proceeded to assist the North Koreans in building their own versions of the ROMEO which were still in production. This particular one was one of the later models.

Sailors had formed a human chain up the gangplank for supplies which were being loaded onto the submarine, probably in preparation for another patrol in the next day or so. The officer of the deck noticed the Admiral strolling by and promptly saluted. The Admiral caught the salute out of the corner of his eye and returned it. He then paused as he reflected on what had taken place in his office earlier in the day.

The morning after returning from Wonsan he entered his office and removed the orders from his wall safe which had been given him by Admiral Chong Hi Lee. He had been tempted to open the orders during his return trip but years of discipline refused permission for him to do so. He returned to his desk chair, took an opener and slit the envelope. He sat engrossed in reading and contemplating the plan which was presented for him to execute. It was a little more than intriguing and certainly presented a challenge and a certain degree of danger for the junior officer who would execute the plan. Admiral Kwan began to consider the qualities of the various submarine captains under his command. After devoting a great deal of time to the matter he reached his decision. The man for this assignment had to be Commander Johng Ho Kim.

The commander was a graduate of the Kim Jung-sook Naval School, the very academy that he and Admiral Chong had attended. The Commander had fourteen years of service in the Navy and had served in patrol boats as well as submarines and all of his superior officers had given him excellent reviews. Admiral Kwan Il Soong took a memo pad, scribbled a message on it and called in his aide. When the aide had presented himself, the Admiral handed him the memo and instructed him to send it as a coded message to Commander Johng on the submarine UB-235 immediately.

The Admiral's recollection ended and he continued his slow walk down to the end of the quay. The hours of daylight were diminishing now as the earth tilted on its' axis away from the sun. It was getting late in the afternoon and the sun was dropping rapidly beneath the western horizon. The rays of the sun streamed from west to east and presented a display of maroon, aquamarine and purple hues against a bank of cumulus clouds which were several miles offshore over the Sea of Japan. Admiral Kwan stood at the very end of the quay with his hands clasped behind his back drinking in this indescribable display of nature. Seagulls were gracefully swooping down to the waters' surface and then climbing back towards the sky again. The smell of the salt air caused the Admiral to expand his chest and drink in this wonderful elixir which had kept his lungs so healthy over the years. The Admiral was not a very religious man but at this particular time he pondered for a few moments, wondering if the God of the Americans actually did exist. Who else but a Supreme Being could be responsible for such beauty.

These God fearing Americans had portrayed his country as the lunatics in charge of the asylum and unfortunately he had to agree that the rulers' lack of concern about the welfare of his countrymen had caused him a great deal of anguish. His entire adult life had been spent in the military and he was dedicated to protecting his country, and its' people, at all costs. However, the military doctrine had shifted drastically in December 1962, away from the doctrine of regular warfare to a doctrine that embraced people's war. At the Fourth KWP Central Committee meeting in that particular December, Kim Il Sung made the decision to arm the entire population; to fortify the entire country; to train the entire army as a 'cadre army'; and to modernize weaponry, doctrine, and tactics under the principle of self-reliance in national defense. Since that time the burden of not only the enforcement of this doctrine but also the cost, had been placed squarely upon the backs of the populace at a terrible price. Life, as his ancestors had known it, ceased to exist. The principle of self-defense had now given way to the primacy of the offense. The new doctrine stressed that decisive results could be obtained only through offensive operations. The offense had three objectives; the destruction of enemy forces, the seizure and control of territory, and the destruction of the enemy's will to fight. This new doctrine strategy would embrace four key tactics: combined-arms offensive operations, battlefield mobility, flexibility and the integration of conventional and *unconventional* warfare. The admiral had been made privy to information that in the area of unconventional warfare, chemical and nuclear weapons would be considered. He was reminded of the often cited statement attributed to former Indian Army Chief of Staff Sundarji: "*one principal lesson is that, if a state intends to fight the United States, it should avoid doing so until and unless it possesses nuclear weapons.*"

And now, Admiral Kwan thought, that pompous little wing flapping, strutting rooster, is making crowing sounds that could be the death knell of millions of his countrymen. The gods help us when Kim Il Soong dies and his son assumes his father's role. His mind snapped back to the present with the thought that somewhere out on that Sea of Japan, Captain Johng Ho Kim and the U-235 were making headway towards Wonsan to play their role in this deadly game of what the Americans referred to as "chicken."

Chapter 19

The Dinner

Around noon, Dan called Bill Regas, the owner of Regas' Restaurant, and asked if he could reserve a certain table in the restaurant that evening for a party of four to arrive at 7:30. Bill recognized the table location that Dan was speaking of and told Dan that he would hold it for him. Dan wanted this particular table as it was in an alcove and would provide some degree of privacy.

Dan made it a point to be there around 7:15 and ten minutes later Jane and Tom arrived. Jane was a slim young lady and the sleeveless dress with a scoop neck accentuated her attractiveness. Tom had on a dark pin-stripe suit and wore a black bow tie. They both looked like they were dressed for a formal affair.

"Hi, Jane, my ... you look stunning tonight!" Dan offered.

"Thanks, Dad, you cut quite a figure yourself in that suit." And she gave her father-in-law a big hug.

"Hey, Dad," Tom said as they shook hands across the table.

They had just started some small talk when Mary Beth arrived. She was dressed in a sheath with a matching elbow length jacket and wearing a faux pearl necklace with matching earrings. Her hair was perfectly coiffed and she just radiated style and beauty.

As Dan rose to embrace her he thought, *My Lord! My little girl is now a beautiful woman!* Dan held her chair as she sat down.

The waiter appeared with menus and Dan ordered a bottle of sparkling champagne which the wine server opened and poured for each one. Dan offered an appropriate toast and a few minutes later the waiter presented each one with a menu. They ordered and continued with their conversation until the meal ended and they had finished dessert. It was then that Dan spoke.

"You all know why we are here tonight …"

Before he could say anything else, Mary Beth extended her right arm and put her hand over that of her father's.

"Dad, before you say anything I want to say that I have been a perfect ass in this whole affair and I want to apologize to you right here, right now, before Jane and Tom."

Dan was startled to say the least. "Well, Cookie, I must say that you have taken me by surprise and I don't know what else to say but 'thank you.'"

Dan continued, "All of us know why we are here tonight but before I begin let me say that I love every one of you from the bottom of my heart and I want you to know that a great deal of thought and consideration of your needs, as well as mine, has gone into what I have to say.

"I think you probably have already concluded that I am going back but I also want to tell you why." Dan paused to take a drink of water.

"You all know me well enough to know that I am an energetic person and I have always felt like I had a purpose in life. For the past several years now I have felt like I have *no* real purpose in life. I feel like a flower that is withering away. When I go back to Intermont I will be accepting a task to assist them in developing an efficient air freight department which will increase their competitiveness and also increase their bottom line profits. Also, I will be doing some flying which each of you know has been an activity that has inspired me in several different ways. This will not only give me a feeling of accomplishment but also a purpose that has been lacking.

"Now, one other thing. You also know that I have met a lady in Anchorage that is around seven or eight years my junior but her maturity level reduces that age difference. To say that I do not have a romantic interest in Jess would be to tell you a lie. However, both she and I are mature adults and she has been divorced and, as you know, I am a widower. I think that works in our favor because each of us will be very sure that we are entirely compatible should we, and I emphasize *should we,* ever decide to be married. Furthermore, once you meet her I know you will approve of her. Now, I think each of you should have an opportunity to ask any questions that you may need to have answered."

"Well, Dad," Tom spoke up, "Jane and I have discussed this and 'yes' we did think you would probably go back. I don't think either of us have any questions and we just want to offer you our full support and wish the greatest of happiness for you."

Dan looked over at Mary Beth and tears were trickling down her cheeks. He removed a handkerchief from his pocket and handed it to her. She carefully began to wipe away the tears.

"Dad," she sobbed, "the greatest reason I have acted like I have is because I don't want to lose you!" and she began to convulse as she cried.

Dan moved his chair around until he could put his arm around her. "Hey, Cookie. You aren't going to lose me." He took the handkerchief and began dabbing her cheeks. "Tell you what … what if I promise to be home every Memorial Day, Labor Day and Christmas. Would that help?"

"Would you really do that, Dad?"

"You bet I will."

Mary Beth removed the handkerchief and looked her father in the eye. "Oh, I love you *so much,* Dad!"

"I know you do, honey and I love every one of you too and I promise that I will make at least those visits home each year and more if I can."

"Now, let's wrap this thing up." Dan continued. "Mary Beth, I want you and Cathy, if you want her as your roommate, to move into the condo. You can do what you like with the furniture … keep it or sell it and furnish it as you like."

"Jane, I know that you have always cast an envious eye on the 380-SL. I sure can't take it to Alaska so I want you to have it."

"Oh, Dad, I can't do that!" she squealed.

"Oh, yes you can and you *will!*" Dan replied.

Jane jumped up out of her chair and moved around to Dan, put her arms around his neck and kissed him on the cheek.

"Well, Tom, that leaves you and unfortunately I can't leave anything of a material nature to you at this time but you know that if you ever need anything I have, that it's yours."

"I know that Dad. You already have done more than enough for Jane and me and we appreciate what you have done very much."

"O.K., kids. That does it. I have some packing to do and a few other small details to take care of. I will call Intermont on Monday and will be leaving Tuesday. I will see each of you again before I leave."

They all arose, exchanged hugs and departed together.

Chapter 20

The Return

Saturday morning Dan went to a nearby restaurant for breakfast and then to the post office and gave them a change of address. He spent the rest of the day scouring the condo for items that he wanted to either take with him on the plane or pack to be shipped to Anchorage by Federal Express. After that he called the airline and made his reservations. That evening he watched a movie on TV and went to bed early.

Sunday he went to church with Mary Beth, Tom and Jane and then took all of them out for Sunday lunch. That afternoon he called Don, Frank and Bill and told them he would be leaving Tuesday and he would be sending them his new address and phone number. He also called a few other acquaintances and told them good-bye. He was burning his bridges.

Monday, Dan placed a call to Intermont.

"Good morning, Intermont Mining & Supply."

"Hello, Virginia. Is Al in?"

"Oh ... Mr. Dan! Yes ... yes he is. Hold on a moment."

"Hello, Dan! How are you, my boy?"

"I'm doing fine, Al. How about yourself?"

"Oh, I'm sitting here on pins and needles awaiting your decision."

"Well, you can get off of them, Al, I'm coming back."

"Praise the Lord! That's the best news I have had in a long, long time. When will you be arriving?"

"I'll be in Tuesday on Delta flight 4032 from Atlanta, arriving at 4:35 p.m. your time."

"Wonderful! Someone will be at the gate to meet you."

"That really isn't necessary, Al. I can grab the airport limousine over to the Marriott."

"Nothing of the sort, my boy. Someone will be there and that's that."

"O.K., Al, if that's the way you want it."

"That's the way I want it, Dan."

* * * *

Tom called Monday evening.

"Dad, Jane has taken tomorrow off and wants to know if it would be O.K. with you if she could take you to the airport tomorrow."

"I think that's wonderful, Tom. Are you coming along"

"No, this is something that she thought of all by herself and I want her to do it alone if that is O.K. with you."

"Tell her I will feel honored, Tom."

* * * *

Jane pulled up at the condo the next morning right on the agreed time. Dan could tell that the 380-SL had been freshly washed.

Dan was out of the house with his two bags before she could get out of the car.

"Hi, Dad. I hope this arrangement is O.K. with you."

Dan threw his bags in the back seat, got in, leaned over and kissed Jane on the cheek.

"It's just fine with me, Jane. I think it is wonderful that you wanted to do this."

"I just wanted you to see how carefully I drive your 'baby' and I will take good care of it."

"I know you will, honey, and I hope you enjoy it for a long, long time."

When they arrived at the airport Dan told Jane to just drop him off at the terminal and it was not necessary for her to come in. He watched her drive away as the porter came to pick up his bags.

A door had closed on a chapter of his life and a new one was about to begin.

* * * *

The flight up to Anchorage was uneventful and Dan finally finished reading, for the third time, the renowned pilot Ernie Gann's *Fate is the Hunter*. There were not many people in the world that Dan had envied but Ernie Gann was one of them. *Damned astigmatism.*

Flight 4032 pulled up to the gate just thirteen minutes late. Dan pulled down his carry-on from the overhead bin and walked up the jetway to the terminal. Someone from Intermont was, indeed, waiting for him in the concourse.

She was wearing the very same outfit that she had worn the evening that she had first picked him up on his arrival at Stevens Aviation. Dan set down his carry-on.

"Well," Jess said stone faced.

"Well what?" Dan replied rather stoically.

"Aren't you going to kiss me?" and she smiled.

They both embraced and this time it was not a short kiss.

Chapter 21

Welcome Back

Dan had checked into the Marriott on Tuesday evening after having had dinner with Jess at one of the better restaurants downtown. He arose at his usual time of 6:00 a.m. on Wednesday morning, after going through the ablutionary and dressing routines, he stopped by the desk to pick up a copy of the USA Today and carried it into the dining room with him.

Dan was so engrossed in the paper he didn't realize someone was approaching his table.

"Well, good morning, stranger."

Dan looked up to see the smiling face of his waitress friend, Judy.

"Hi, Judy. Yes, I'm back."

"How long are you going to be here this time?" She had picked up his coffee cup, sat it on her serving tray and was pouring him a cup of black coffee.

"For a long, long time I hope. I'm moving here permanently, Judy."

"Get outta' here! A boy from Tennessee trading in his coonskin cap for one of bearskin?"

"Yep, I've been offered what I hope is a permanent position with Intermont Mining & Supply Company so I will be looking for a place to live in a couple of days."

"Well, that's wonderful! I hope you really enjoy your life here. Can I fix you a couple of nice poached eggs, crisp bacon and whole wheat toast this morning?"

"You've got a fantastic memory, Judy. That will be just fine.

Once again, in her usual efficient manner, Jess had arranged for a Honda to be delivered to the motel for his use. He stopped by the desk, picked up the keys and was in the car heading downtown at 7:40

* * * *

Dan opened the door to Intermont very quietly, peeked around the door and saw Virginia typing away on the keyboard and concentrating on what was appearing on the computer monitor. Very stealthily he walked across the carpeted floor until he was just a few feet from her desk.

"Good morning Virginia."

He accomplished his goal … she was completely startled as she turned and saw Dan standing at her desk. "Oh! Mr. Dan! Oh, it's so good to see you back!" She practically jumped up from her chair, walked around the desk and took his left hand in both of hers.

"You just don't know how happy I am to see you again, Mr. Dan."

"Well, thank you, Virginia. I'm very pleased to see you too. Is Al expecting me?"

"Indeed he is." She walked back around her desk, picked up the phone and punched in Al Switzer's extension. "Mr. Switzer, Mr. Dan is here."

Putting down the phone she said, "He said for you to come right in."

Before he could open the door to Al's office, it was opened by Al Switzer who had a huge smile on his face.

"Dan! Come in, my boy! It's wonderful to see you again!"

"It's good to be back, Al," Dan replied as Al pumped his hand repeatedly.

"Have a seat. I just believed all along that you would make the right decision and be back with us again." Al said as he walked around his desk and sat down.

"It wasn't an easy decision, Al. But after I weighed all aspects of the situation I had my mind made up by Saturday of last week. My family is reconciled to my coming back and that was the thing that was uppermost in my mind."

"Of course it was. After all our family is the greatest treasure that all of us have, right?"

"Yes it is, Al. And I may as well get this up front before we go any further. I promised my son and daughter that I would be home on every Memorial Day, Labor Day and Christmas."

"I can't see that will present any problem, Dan. You can take your vacation any time you like as long as you make arrangements to have the bases covered while you are away."

"No problem there, Al. I will make sure that is taken care of."

"Fine, now are you ready to resume where we left off when you left?"

"Any time you are, Al."

"Good, now let me see if I can get Fred in here. I told him you would be here this morning and to try and keep his desk clear."

Al called Fred and he told Dan that Fred was on his way. In about five minutes Fred came into the office and he and Dan exchanged handshakes.

Chapter 22

The Agreement

When all three had settled in their chairs, Al picked up the conversation.

"I think it would be prudent for us, at this time, to review the details of our agreement. And, Fred, I think it would be wise if you would draw up a formal written document stipulating the expectations we have for Dan and his income should be incorporated in that document. Let's review the matter of income so that we all concur.

"As I recall, Dan, our offer was $60,000 per year as a base salary and if the goals are met within six months and the aircraft division is profitable at that time an additional $10,000 per year would be added. Also, benefits such as health and life insurance would be included. Is that the way you remember it?"

"That's exactly as I recall it, Al." Dan replied.

"Good. Fred, I think you made notes pertaining to the other matters we discussed prior to Dan's departure, is that correct.?

"Yes, I did. Do you want to review them now?" Fred asked.

"No ... no, I don't think that is necessary. Just draw up a draft of the agreement and Dan can review it and any necessary changes can be made later."

"Do you have anything to add at this time, Dan?"

"Well, this is outside of the agreement but what about the personnel in the aircraft department?"

Fred took up this subject. "At present we have two pilots, Harry Abelson and Tim Morrison. These two men will report to you. Harry has been used to running things his way and consequently, Tim, being our junior pilot, has had very little guidance insofar as being responsible for his performance as a pilot, maintaining records and turning in detailed expense reports. From now on not one of our three aircraft are to leave the ground without your approval, Dan. You will have total responsibility for scheduling the aircraft and assigning the pilot for the trips. Also, Harry and Tim are not to spend one dime of the company's money without your approval and when they do, they are to present a receipt to you for the expenditures."

As Fred proceeded with his presentation, Al put the stub of his cigar in the ashtray on his desk.

"Also, you are to develop a system of maintenance for the aircraft and see that all FAA requirements are met for each aircraft. In developing cost figures for each aircraft you will also provide estimates for periodic inspections, engine overhauls and general maintenance. We lease a section of one hangar from Stevens so you will need to incorporate that cost in your expense program as well. We have worked well with Stevens in the past and have had a good relationship with them but this is not to say we are married to them. If you find that you can significantly reduce our maintenance and service costs by going elsewhere then Al and I are open to your recommendations." Fred paused for a moment.

Al looked towards Fred. Anything else, Fred?"

"Yes. We have some office space available in our section, Dan, and I think it would be wise for you to keep all of your records in that office. There is also a computer there and the software that I mentioned has been installed and is functional. I would like for you to take a look at it at your earliest convenience. Any questions, Dan?"

"No, you both have laid it out quite well and I see what your objectives are. The first thing I would like to do though, is to go over to the hangar and look over the DC-3 and the DHC Otter. You both realize that I will have to be checked out in the DC-3 and get a seaplane rating for the Otter. I don't foresee any problem with the DC-3 but I'll probably have to put in six to eight hours in the Otter in order to get a seaplane endorsement on my ticket."

"You got any problem with that, Fred?" Al queried.

"Not at all, however I would like for Dan to start gathering his cost information as soon as possible."

"Well, Dan, what do you think?"

Dan sat for a moment, stroking is chin with his right thumb and forefinger. "You can assume by my returning that I am willing to give the assignment my very best shot. I like the six months arrangement ... let's call it a 'trial period.' If at the end of that period you are not satisfied with my performance or, if for some reason, I am not satisfied with my situation, we part as friends. Agreed?"

Al stood up and grinned at Fred. "What did I tell you about this young man, Fred? He's a square shooter if I ever saw one." Al got up from his chair and walked around the desk with his hand outstretched. Dan and Fred stood also and Al shook Dan's hand and Fred followed suit.

"Oh, one other thing, Fred," Dan asked, "is there by any chance a laptop available in your section? If I had one, I could install the program in the laptop and I could do quite a bit of work at night. After all, my social activities here aren't going to be all that great ... at least I don't foresee any right now."

Fred furrowed his brow in thought. "I know that we have at least two ... I'll see what I can do to free one of them up for you."

"O.K., that's it then," Al said.

Fred and Dan were practically out the door when Al said,

"Dan, could I see you just a minute. I thought of one other item you should be aware of." Dan turned and walked back into the office as Fred left.

"Come in and sit down, Dan."

Dan sat down in front of the desk while Al walked around and sat in his usual chair. Al leaned forward resting his arms on the desk and shook the ash from his cigar into the ashtray on the desk.

"Dan, I am going to be perfectly honest with you. We have a problem with Harry Abelson that you need to be aware of."

"Oh, what's that?"

"Harry is an alcoholic. He is supposed to be going to AA meetings but I know for a fact that he falls off the wagon from time to time. Al leaned back in the chair as if relieved to have this off his chest.

Oh, crap! All I need is an alcoholic pilot! Dan thought.

"Have you ever seriously considered getting rid of him, Al?" Dan asked.

"Yes, but if we can possibly keep him on I would appreciate it. There are certain extenuating circumstances that I am not at liberty to divulge right now. But I would consider it a personal favor if you can work with him, Dan."

"I'll do the best I can. But, I have to be honest. If I ever find him drinking on the job or if I determine that he has been drinking and he sets foot in one of our aircraft, I will have to ground him, Al. I am sure you recognize the liability that could be incurred by the company by his killing someone or damaging property while flying one of our aircraft under the influence."

"Yes, I have been well aware of that, Dan, and frankly it has caused me great concern on more than one occasion. You certainly have the prerogative to ground him under those circumstances."

With that, Al stood as did Dan and the two of them walked towards the door. Al opened the door for Dan and gave him a pat on the shoulder as he left the office. Virginia Stewart was on the 'phone so when she looked up, Dan just gave her an acknowledgement with a nod of his head and a smile. She returned the smile and Dan went out of the main door into the hallway. He punched the "down" button on the elevator and when the doors opened, out stepped Jess.

"Well, so we meet again," Dan said.

"Oh … hi! Did you get all the details worked out?"

Both paused just outside the elevator door while the doors closed and the elevator started down.

"Yes, I think that we covered everything very well."

"So you are to be in complete charge of all the aircraft and the personnel as well."

"Yes, that's the way I understand it."

"Good. Do you remember what I said prior to your leaving about having people working for me that I felt comfortable with?"

"That you felt comfortable when you were with me." Dan replied. "Uh, huh. What about having *capable* people working with you?"

"Dan, it's obvious that you are capable for the job. I would much prefer to have a capable person running the aircraft division that I can get along with."

"Meaning that you couldn't get along with the person who was running it?"

"Meaning I didn't like the person who *thought* he was running it. The man is a complete moron. Oh, he can fly an airplane all right, but he can't get along with anyone but himself. I just cannot for the life of me understand why Al hasn't gotten rid of him."

"Thanks for the information. I am going to try and do my best to get along with him because we need proficient and capable pilots, but if he proves to be otherwise then he won't be flying for me."

"I hope I can count on that," Jess said.

"You can make book on it. Oh, by the way. I've got a little problem that you may be able to help me with. I need to find a place to live."

"Well, I just might be the gal who can help you out with that problem. Come on in to my office."

They both went back through the lobby and into her office. She went around her desk, took a seat and motioned for Dan to sit down in one of the chairs in front of her desk. She looked in her 'phone list and dialed a number.

"Is Jean Smith there?" There was a pause of about 30 seconds.

"Hello, Jean? This is Jess Lane at Intermont. I'm fine, thanks. Say, Jean, we have a new manager by the name of Dan Nichols and he's looking for an apartment. Can you help him out? Good. Hold on a minute." Jess put her hand over the mouthpiece. "She wants to know when you can drop by her office?"

"How about four this afternoon."

"Would four o'clock be o.k., Jean? Fine … he will be there." Jess placed the handset back on the 'phone.

"That was Jean Smith with Prudential Realtors and they specialize in listing a lot of apartments. She said that she was sure she could find you something you would like. Here … let me draw you a little map of how to get there."

Jess took a piece of plain paper and drew a map showing their present location and how to get to the Prudential office.

She is the only woman I have ever seen who could give directions that were perfectly clear. Like I said, she does everything well.

"Thanks a lot, Jess. Now, just one other thing and I will leave you alone."

"Is that a *promise?*"

She's smiling again … this gal is a real tease.

"No … you know I'm not going to promise you *that!* and Dan smiled back at her. "I've got to get some wheels. You think it would be o.k. if I was a little late coming in tomorrow morning?"

"That will be perfectly satisfactory, Mr. Chief Pilot, you just get yourself settled in. We are going to need you around here."

Jess got up and walked around the desk and as Dan arose she took hold of his left arm with her hand.

"Welcome aboard, Dan." she was smiling again.

"Thanks, Jess. I think I am going to enjoy being here."

"I'll see to it," she said.

Another one of her little innuendo's. She was still holding on to his arm as they both walked to the door.

Stopping at the door Dan said, "Thanks again for help with the apartment, Jess. I've got to go out to the airport now and 'beard the lion in his den'."

"Meaning Mr. Abelson?"

"Yeah … meaning Mr. Abelson."

"Well, good luck. Others have tried it and have come up short."

"I very seldom, if ever, come up short, Jess." And he smiled at her as he left.

Chapter 23

Harry and the 'Gooney Bird'

At the airport Dan turned into the driveway that led to Stevens Aircraft but found there was one of those gates that one had to insert a card into in order to raise the bar across the entrance way. So Dan had to park the Honda in a visitor's area and walk to the FBO office. Going inside Dan saw what appeared to be two charter pilots, one slumped on the sofa and the other one in an easy chair. The one that had four stripes on his shoulder epaulets was drinking coffee and reading and the other, who had three stripes, was putting current charts in his Jeppesen manual. It was the same old story of pilot seniority; the captain was relaxing while the co-pilot did the nitty-gritty stuff. Dan walked over to the customer counter and asked the young lady on duty if the manager was in. She wanted to know who Dan was and then she dialed a number and then spoke to Dan. "Mr. Timberlake will be right out."

Norman Timberlake was a tall broad-shouldered guy who looked like he maybe had been a wide receiver on his college football team. Maybe in his late thirties, blonde hair, blue eyes and had those Roman features. Dan thought, *The guy should be making movies instead of running a fixed base operation for an aviation outfit.*

"Norm Timberlake. What can I do for you, Mr. Nichols?"

"Name is 'Dan,' Norm. I am what is supposed to be the new chief pilot for Intermont Mining."

Timberlake's broad smile revealed a set of the most even white teeth imaginable. *What else but?*

"Well, we just heard about you coming on board. Come on, let's go back to my office. How about a cup of coffee?"

"I could go for that. Black if you please."

Norm poured both of them a styrofoam cup of black and they headed down the hall to his office. Once there, Norm pointed to an upholstered chair and then went behind his desk and sat down.

"How do you like Anchorage?" Norm said as he linked his fingers behind his head and leaned back.

"Not bad, not bad at all. I am sure the weather will take a little getting used to by a good ol' boy from the south." and Dan laid his best 'suthin' accent on him.

Norm laughed, "Yeah, I would say that you will have some interesting times flying in this weather. Where you from?"

"Knoxville, Tennessee."

"Oh, is that right? Back when I was newly married the wife and I took a flying tour of several of the states and we stopped off in Knoxville for a side trip to the Smoky Mountain National Park. I don't remember the name of the airport, but it was a small strip in the middle of a river."

"That was Island Home Airport, Norm. That's where I learned to fly." Dan said.

"No kiddin'? Small world isn't it? Well, what can I do for you this morning?"

"We can begin by your telling me what you know about the Intermont aircraft."

Norm sat up straight, picked up his cup and took a sip of coffee.

"The old 'Gooney Bird' is really in petty good shape for the shape she is in. I think the papers said that she was built by Douglas back in 1943. Of course she has had some mods[1] pulled on her down through the years. Far as we can tell, and the FAA too, there is no evidence of corrosion. Seems like the old bird has been taken pretty good care of which is really unusual. Now the Otter is a dandy. Good radios, good paint and the inside is clean as a pin. I don't remember how much time is on the engine but I don't believe it has been overhauled. And, the Wipaire floats are in good condition too; neither of them have leaks as I remem-

---

1. modifications

ber. Of course you know all about the King Air. Looks like Mr. Switzer got a good buy on that one."

"He did. It's in tip top shape and a good flying aircraft too. Now, do you have a checkride pilot that can check me out in the DC-3? I have a little stick time in it but I would feel more comfortable having a qualified instructor give me some time."

"How about me?" and Norm flashed those pearly whites again.

"You? You got time in a "three?"

"Man, what are you talking about? Soon as I got my multi-engine rating I flew co-pilot on the 'Gooney' for nearly three hundred hours and then another two hundred in the left seat. Alaska Airlines was running a daily trip to Nome at the time but they finally got a Dash-8 and got rid of the 'three.'"

"Well what the heck are you doing chained to a desk?"

"Got married, plus two kids. The ol' lady said it was time for me to get out of the wild blue yonder and plant my feet on terra firma. I still run some charter flights for Stevens though. That was part of the deal. I told them in the beginning I would never completely get rid of the flying bug so they agreed to let me get in two to three runs a month. Works fine for me."

"Great. Say, one more thing before I forget it, can you fix me up with a card so I can get through the gate?" Dan asked.

"Sure thing." Norm got up and went to a vertical file cabinet, took out a small lock-box, opened it with a key from his key ring and handed Dan a card. Then he went over to his desk and took out a ledger, flipped over to a page and recorded the number on the card along with Dan's name.

"Security, you know. The Feds want to know everything about who is coming on the field. You need to go over to the main terminal and go to the security office. They will fix you up with a pass so that you can have access to the tarmac as well as certain buildings. They will tell you which ones are off limits. You have to wear the pass so it can be seen when you are roaming around. Here is mine." Norm unclipped a card from his belt and showed it to Dan. It had his picture, a serial number, who he was employed by and his title.

"Thanks, Norm. I'll take care of that before I leave today. Now I think I will go out and look at the ships if you don't mind."

"Sure thing. Let's go this way." Norm led Dan to the hallway, turned right and they went through a door that exited into the hangar. "Tim Morrison is on a trip with the Otter but you can see the 'three' is still here."

There she stood with her nose in the air and her tail on the ground. The veritable old tail-dragger. The number N9140R was painted on her vertical stabilizer and no doubt on the top of one wing and the bottom of another.

"Just help yourself, Dan, and when you get through come back in the office and we will set up a time to get you behind the wheel of the old gal."

"Thanks, Norm. I appreciate it."

Dan walked around the DC-3 inspecting the exterior, checking the ailerons and elevators for any unusual wear. The aluminum skin looked excellent considering its age; there didn't seem to be a patch anywhere on the fuselage. He looked over the tires on the landing gear to see if they still had adequate tread and also checked the three bladed props to check for nicks. As he walked around to the fuselage and touched the aluminum skin, Dan thought ...

"If you could only talk what tales you might tell. Were you in that pre-dawn darkness of June 6, 1944, on your way to drop paratroopers of the 82nd Airborne onto the soil of Normandy? Or, were you perhaps flying the "hump," the Himalayas, to deliver badly needed supplies to General 'Vinegar Joe' Stillwell and his troops as they labored over the building of the China-Burma road? Then, when you became a civilian did you perhaps fly for Allegheny Airlines over the Adirondacks during the stormy nights while St. Elmo's fire flashed and danced around your propellers? Or maybe you were even piloted by Ernest Gann as he made a night approach into what he called the 'black hole' which was the cinder runway of the Newark airport. Here you are over 40 years old and you are still on the job."

November niner one four zero Romeo had double clam shell doors on the right side of the fuselage so that large pieces of equipment and crates could be easily loaded. There was an airstair on wheels close by so Dan wheeled it over and clambered up to open one of the doors. He found that this was not an easy thing to do as when the large door was opened outward it was necessary to move the airstair backwards. It was definitely a chore for two men or more. However, Dan was persistent and finally got the door opened far enough so that he could step inside.

The inside was like a small cavern. No seats and the windows had been covered over to prevent breakage from the cargo being hauled. Everything in the interior had been stripped so that it could be maximized for hauling cargo. The floor was stressed aluminum and had tie-down 'dogs' so that the cargo could be secured. Dan made his way up to the cockpit and dropped into the left seat. He began to rummage around, looking in the seat pockets for the checklist and also for any aircraft documents he could find. Dan opened one manila envelope and found the history of the aircraft:

1942 March 11		Manufactured by Douglas Aircraft as a C-47 Construction #4898
1942 March 20		Accepted by United States Army Air Force at Randolph Field, Texas. Assigned to 8th Air Force.
1943 December 10		Service from Bury St. Edmunds, England
1944 August 15		Service from Duxford, England
1945 July 22		Service from Frankfurt am Main, Germany
1946 March 15		Stricken from Service
1946 July 12		Sold by the United States War Assets Administration to Ozark Airlines, registered as N8326.
1949 August 22		Sold to Southern Airlines, Atlanta, GA
1957 May 30		Registration changed by Southern to N50SA
1966 August 15		Sold to Midwest Aircraft Sales, Omaha, Nebraska
1967 September 10		Sold to Caufield Air Service, Wichita, Kansas
1984 February 22		Sold to Trans Texas Air Freight, San Antonio, Texas, registered as N9140R.
1986 October 15		Sold to Cal-Tech Air Service, San Diego, California
1987 March 30		Sold to Intermont Mining Supply Co., Anchorage, Alaska

The old girl had been around the block a few times. Dan gathered up this information plus the Aircraft & Engine log and the checklist, all of which he would take back to the apartment and study tonight. About that time he heard a noise at the rear of the aircraft.

"Hey, what the hell are you doing up there?" came a shout.

Dan turned in the seat and looked towards the cargo doors. A heavy set individual who looked like an NFL blocking back with a head of rusty colored hair mounted on a bull neck had just entered the aircraft and was moving towards the cockpit. Dan didn't answer him. The stocky individual lumbered up the cargo floor until he was about three feet from the cockpit door. Dan continued to stare at the ruddy face with two close set beady eyes which were shadowed by two bushy eyebrows. His ruddy face was screwed into a menacing look.

"I *said*, what the hell are you doing here?"

Dan's reply to him was, "Who the hell are *you?*"

"That's none of your damn business. Now you get the hell out of *my* aircraft!"

"You must be Harry Abelson."

"Well ... what if I am?"

"If you are, then you work for me." Harry Abelson looked as if he had just taken a punch to his solar plexus. His beady eyes opened just a little more.

"You ... uh, you Dan Nichols?" He said in a somewhat subdued voice.

"That's correct. Do you always greet strangers in such a diplomatic manner?"

"Well, I didn't know who you were. Hell, for all I knew you might be some guy tryin' to sabotage the plane."

Dan got up from the left seat and moved to the cockpit door.

"Yeah, well if you will get out of my way I have to get over to the main office. By the way, I want to see you and Tim Morrison here in the hangar at eight o'clock Thursday morning ... sharp."

And with that Dan moved by him towards the cargo door. As he neared the door Dan heard Harry say, "Sure ... I'll be here."

Opening the door from the hangar into Stevens Aircraft, Dan walked down the hall and glanced into Norman Timberlake's office. He wasn't there so he continued on until entering the lobby of the main office. Norm was standing at the counter talking to someone. He excused himself and came over to where Dan was.

"Did you run into Harry Abelson?"

"I did."

Norm grinned, "From the look on your face you must have had an interesting conversation."

"We did." Dan couldn't help himself ... he had to smile.

Norm laughed, "Not exactly the 'hail fellow well met' type is he?"

"Is he always like that?"

"About ninety percent of the time. I don't know what's wrong with that guy." Norm paused for a few seconds then continued, "Yes I do, too. Ever since he got busted out of Alaska Airways for drinking he has been walking around with a huge cinder block on his shoulder."

Without so much as a smile Dan offered, "He'd better get rid of it or he's going to get busted again."

Norm narrowed his eyes slightly, "I'll bet you're a hard ass, aren't you?"

"I can be if I need to be."

"How about another cup of coffee?" Norm offered.

"Sure. Make it black."

They stood around for a few minutes drinking their coffee and Dan made an appointment with Norm for one o'clock tomorrow afternoon for Dan's first ride in the DC-3. Dan then asked Norm for directions on how to get to the airport manager's office and made his way over there to see about getting his security pass. The airport manager's secretary pointed Dan towards the office of airport security where he had to fill out an application and be fingerprinted. After looking at the application, checking his FAA pilots' license, and asking about ten minutes of questions, the security officer issued Dan a temporary pass. He said that after the FBI checked out his background he would get a permanent pass. It suddenly dawned on Dan why all this security … Russia was not that far away. Evidently there must be a great deal of contraband being passed through Alaska.

Dan looked at the Breitling and it said that it was twenty-five minutes after three. He had been so engrossed in what he had been doing that he had forgotten all about lunch. Dan grabbed a canned Coke and a package of peanut butter crackers from one of the vending machines in the airport, walked out to the parking lot, cranked up the Honda and headed for the Prudential office.

Chapter 24

The Apartment

Jean Smith was a 40'ish lady with what appeared to be natural curly tinted blonde hair; a vivacious smile, friendly green eyes and a very trim figure. She had walked out to the lobby in a light brown two piece business suit to meet Dan and then ushered him back into her office. She asked Dan to sit down and then proceeded to ask him what he had in mind in the way of an apartment.

"Well, I don't know just what is available, of course, but if I had my 'druthers' I would prefer a one bedroom apartment with bath, sitting room with a fireplace, pullman type kitchen, dining area, and a balcony if possible. I would like for the facility to have a spa, fitness area and a swimming pool. Since I don't have any furniture I would prefer that it be furnished but if that isn't possible I suppose I can either buy or rent some furniture."

Jean smiled, "Well, you certainly know what you want, don't you? Let's see what we can dig up here."

She turned to her computer, made some entries on the keyboard and up came three possibilities on her screen. One in particular looked very interesting. It had all of the features that Dan had specified, however it had two bedrooms, two baths and a half, combination dining living area and a compact kitchen. It also had the fireplace Dan wanted plus a balcony. The complex also had a swimming pool and a spa/hot tub facility in the fitness center. It was also a gated facility with nice looking grounds according to the photograph which was on the screen. It was not furnished but Janet informed Dan that they also represented a furniture rental company so that would not present a problem. The rent on the apartment was $875 per month and the furniture would probably run somewhere in the vicinity of $150 a month. That sounded like a deal to Dan. Jean looked at the 'phone number on the screen, dialed it on her deskset and contacted the apartment manager. Jean told her that they would be there in fifteen minutes. Jean opened a file drawer, selected a file folder and extracted a plastic card which Dan assumed would be the entrance key to the gate.

Seventeen minutes later they pulled up to the gate of the Alpine Apartments on Mockingbird Drive in Jean's Mercedes. Jean Smith inserted the plastic key in the gate control and after the bar raised, they were driving along the entranceway to the apartment building which housed the manager. Entering the manager's office, Mrs. Thelma Thompson greeted them warmly and after exchanging pleasantries she just handed the unit key to Jean and she and Dan proceeded to the second building on the right and went upstairs to unit 224.

The walls of the spacious apartment were painted in a warm light beige color with white ceilings. Jean said that the floor plan indicated it had 1020 square feet. Dan opened the sliding glass door to the balcony where he found that one could see the snow capped mountain peaks of the Chugach State Park in the distance. Dan always had a fair knack of being able to visualize how furniture would fit into rooms and it looked like an ideal arrangement to him so he told Jean that they had a deal. They then went back to Thelma Thompson's office and discussed the details of a lease. Dan explained his situation concerning his employment to her and she reluctantly agreed to a six month lease if he would pay a penalty of one month's rent if he terminated the lease after six months. Dan agreed, signed the lease, and gave her his check for one month's rent in advance plus a security deposit of five hundred dollars. Jean drove Dan back to her office and as they got out of her car Dan asked her,

"You mentioned you knew a place where they rented furniture. Do you know by any chance if they happen to stay open in the evenings?"

"Well, I don't know," she replied, "but we certainly can find out."

They went into her office, she looked up a number and dialed. She talked with a Mrs. Finley who told her they stayed open in the evenings until seven o'clock. Janet gave Dan the address and directions how to get there. Dan thanked Jean, they shook hands and in five minutes Dan was on his way.

Dan decided to go ahead and take care of the furniture matter so twenty minutes later he drove into the parking lot of the rental furniture place at 101 Muldoon Road. Dan was pleased with the exterior appearance of the building as he walked to the entrance and even more pleased when he went inside and saw the quality of the furniture on display. A rather matronly lady who appeared to be in her late forties was walking towards him and introduced herself as Martha Finley. Dan introduced himself and immediately she replied,

"Oh yes, Mr. Nichols. Mrs. Smith called and told us you would be in this evening. Now if you will give me some idea of what style furniture you are interested in I will be glad to help you."

"Well, Mrs. Finley, I don't know beans about furniture styles, but can we just make a short tour of the showroom and maybe I can point out what I like as we go along?"

Mrs. Finley turned out to be a very patient and accommodating saleslady and in a little over an hour they had everything nailed down pretty well. She said that she would work on the cost figure and have it available for Dan tomorrow morning. He told her that he would look over her proposal when he received it and call her back.

One more stop before calling it an evening. Although Dan was getting rather hungry, he was on a roll and wanted to finish this thing up. He had made up a list of miscellaneous items he would need for the apartment so now it was time to head for the Wal-Mart. By the time he got there it was six-thirty. Dan went inside, grabbed a cart and headed for the sporting goods department. He had decided on his next trip here that he needed a pair of 'shoe packs' to wear in the snow instead of the boots he had bought on his previous visit. By the time he got the buggy full he had some cooking utensils, can opener, drinking glasses, a set of dishware, and other odds and ends including an alarm clock. The bill came to one hundred sixty-nine dollars and seventy two cents. Dan had the feeling that he had forgotten something but he was pretty sure the Wal-Mart would still be in business when he returned.

Dan stopped at the Pizza Hut on the way back to the Marriott, got a couple of bottles of Fosters at a convenience store and took it all back the motel. He just left all the junk from the Wal-Mart in the Honda and locked it. He thought, "*If someone steals it I will just battle it out with the rental car insurance company.*

After eating the pizza and having a Fosters, Dan clicked on the TV, flipped through the channels and couldn't find anything interesting so he watched about twenty minutes of the CNN channel. He looked at the clock and it said it was five minutes after ten so he removed his clothes, took a hot shower, brushed his teeth and went to bed. Dan clicked off the light and lay there for a few minutes in the dark. *Am I positive that I did the right thing? In the past I was always so meticulous about investigating all facets of an organization before making a move and here I am, involved in a job that I know nothing about with a company that I <u>absolutely</u>*

know nothing about. Why not be honest with yourself, Dan. You know deep inside that you were heavily influenced by just one individual ... Jess. Well, why not? You may have sat on your ass in Knoxville forever and never found a person like her.

Chapter 25

The Jeep

Judy was back on duty in the dining room and started over to Dan's table as he sat down.

"Hi, Dan. What's for breakfast this morning?"

"I'll have a couple of soft scrambled eggs, link sausage and wheat toast."

"And some grits?" she kidded with a smile.

"Yeah, and some grits." and Dan returned the smile.

She came back in about ten minutes with the breakfast which he ate as he went over the latest news in the *USA Today*. Dan finished his meal and Judy came back with a second cup of coffee.

"This is my last meal here, Judy, and I just want you to know that I appreciate your taking care of me."

"I hate to see you leave, Dan. It's been a real pleasure serving you." She gave Dan a genuine smile as she finished pouring his coffee and then left to go to an adjoining table.

Dan picked up the check as she left and put a ten spot on the table. *What the heck, it's only money.*

Dan called Mrs. Finley from the room and she told him that his rental charge would be $225.00 per month; about $75 per month more than what Janet Richards estimated but he would rather pay more and get some nice stuff than pay less and not be satisfied with it. Also, Mrs. Finley told Dan that if he decided to purchase the furniture within six months, 65% of the rental charge would apply towards the purchase price. That being the case Dan would only be paying $78.75 per month for rental. Of course they would no doubt have him locked in to paying a higher than normal purchase price but you can't have it both ways he supposed. Dan asked her if they could possibly deliver the furniture today and she assured him it would be in place in the apartment and ready for occupancy by no later than four o'clock this afternoon. Dan gave her the address and told her he would drop by sometime today and give her his check.

After that Dan had to go somewhere and find some 'wheels.' He went down to the lobby and bought a copy of the *Anchorage Daily News*, sat down in a lobby chair and turned to the classified ads, looking under 'Automobiles.'

Dan scanned several ads and then came upon one that read, "JEEP GRAND CHEROKEE LAREDO '84—4X4, very clean, loaded, white/gray cloth, 6 cyl., auto. 1 owner, garage kept 210K $7500. Affordable Used Cars—929 E. 8th Avenue. 272-1218." Dan tore the ad from the paper, went out and got in the Honda and started for Affordable Used Cars.

Dan pulled the Honda into the Affordable lot at five minutes 'til nine and saw an office that probably was about twenty feet long and maybe twelve feet wide. It had one large window in the front and he could see a balding man sitting at a desk reading a newspaper with a big, fat cigar stuck in his mouth. Dan parked the Honda and walked into the office. As he went through the door the guy behind the desk stood up. He looked to be about five feet nine with a protruding stomach which would have overlapped his pants had it not been for a pair of suspenders which held them up. He had a ruddy round face and two rather beady eyes which sized Dan up.

"Name's Ed Beasley. What can I do for you?" and he extended a hand which Dan shook. It felt like he had grabbed the Pillsbury Doughboy.

"Dan Nichols. I saw an ad you have in the morning paper." Dan reached inside his jacket and pulled out the ad that he had torn from the Anchorage Daily News. Ed looked at it.

"Oh, yeah. What do you want to know about the car?"

"Well, for starters, will it run?"

Ed didn't appreciate Dan's sense of humor.

"Sure it will. Runs like a top. Ain't nuthin' wrong with *that* car. You see where it says it's a one owner car, don'tcha?"

I imagine in his mind that was supposed to be as good as a written warranty.

"Do you mind if I take it for a test drive?"

"Not a'tall, not a'tall. Here." Ed turned and pulled a tagged key from a large peg board nailed to the wall that was filled with hooks and an assortment of keys.

"You just go down to the next to last car on the second row and take it for a spin. Dan could see right away he was in a 'self-service' used car lot.

The car was right where Ed said it would be and Dan circled it before getting in. It looked fairly good on the outside; just a few dings where car doors had hit it. There was one small dent in the left rear panel but other than that it wasn't too bad. Paint had no check marks that he could see. Not much tread left on the tires though. Dan opened the door. The floor mats didn't have any holes in them and although the upholstery was worn he couldn't see any cuts or burn marks. Evidently the previous owner had not been a smoker as there was no detectable smoke odor in the car. The odometer read 42,552 miles.

Dan turned the key to "Start" and the engine fired right up. He gingerly made his way to the exit and turned in the direction from which he had arrived. He had passed over a railroad track about a mile back so he headed for that. Traffic was light at this time of the morning and although it was after nine, it still was not completely daylight so as he exited the lot, Dan turned on the headlights. They worked so he turned on the wipers which worked as well. The railroad crossing was about a block away.

Dan increased the speed to forty miles an hour and hit the crossing. He made it across and as far as he could tell nothing had fallen off and all four wheels were still on. Also, the shocks did not bottom out going over the crossing. Dan turned and circled the block and headed back to the lot. As he neared the lot, he looked in the rear view mirror and saw no one following him so he slammed on the brakes and the Cherokee slid slightly but did not swerve to the right or left.

Turning into the lot, Dan placed the Cherokee in its' proper slot, got out and started walking towards the office. As soon as he entered, Ed remarked,

"Well, whad'ja think? Great little car, ain't it?"

"It will do for what I need it for. Tell you what ... I will write you a check for it right now for $6500."

Ed gave Dan a look as if he was trying to make off with the family jewels.

"Naw, Naw ... no way! That car is worth $7500 if it is worth a penny."

Dan put on his cap and put his hand on the doorknob to the office.

"Now hold on a minute," Ed said. "Let's be reasonable about this thing. I might come down just a little bit but not what *you* are offerin.'"

"O.K. I'm a reasonable man, Ed. Tell you what I will do. You put a new set of snow tires on the car and I will give you $6900 for it."

"Big freakin' deal, for Chrissake! You want me to put a four hundred dollar set of tires on the car and you up the offer four hundred. What kind of nutcake do you think I am?" By now, Ed's face had taken on a rosy hue and a couple of beads of sweat were appearing on his forehead.

"O.K., Ed. You give me your rock bottom price for the car with the new tires."

"Seventy-two hundred, take it or leave it!"

He's beginning to sweat a little more now.

"Seventy-one hundred'" Dan offered.

"Aw, Geez, man. You are killin' me! Awright, seventy-one hundred and not a penny less!"

Dan stuck out his hand and this time it seemed that the Pillsbury Doughboy was even more lumpy than it was the first time.

They sat down and Ed began to make out a bill of sale and application for title and license tag. Dan wrote out a check for the seventy-one hundred and handed it to him and he gave Dan the necessary papers to title the car. Dan then told him he would be back around four this afternoon and pick up the car with the new tires installed. Ed grimaced as Dan mentioned the tires but Ed said the car would be ready.

Dan looked at his watch and it was only 10:15 so he headed the Honda for the new apartment, slipped his new plastic entry card into the gate which promptly opened and he drove down to the complex where his apartment was located. Dan had just started taking stuff out of the Honda when he heard a female voice.

"Moving in?"

Dan turned, and it was a young girl who looked to be about twenty-four or twenty-five, blonde, about five feet two and dressed in a blue denim jacket, light beige cotton blouse, blue jeans and dressy black ankle top boots.

"Yeah, I'm going to be in 224. Name's Dan Nichols," and Dan stuck out his hand.

The girl took Dan's hand and shook it. "Michelle Piper. We're gonna be neighbors ... I live in 230 with my girl friend. Here, let me give you a hand."

"No, you don't have to do that," Dan said.

"Oh, yeah I do ... that's what neighbors are for."

And she proceeded to load up with a bunch of the stuff and they walked up the staircase to the second floor. Dan was about to turn right when she said,

"Going the wrong way ... it's down here." and she turned left. They walked down to 224, Dan opened the door with his key and they went in and sat the stuff down in a place where it would be out of the way of the movers. She stayed right with Dan until he had everything out of the Honda. After the last load, they stepped out onto the landing and Dan told her how much he appreciated her help.

"Sure, glad to do it. See you later, Dan." and she walked down the walkway towards her unit. *Well ... if everyone else here is like Michelle, it's going to be a nice place to live.*

Dan was determined to have a better lunch than he had dinner last night. He remembered having passed a Morrison's Cafeteria so he headed for it, put the Honda in their parking lot and went inside. Dan was one of the first in for lunch apparently as the line was very short. He selected a meat entrée, some vegetables and a piece of pie for dessert. Dan finished up his lunch with a second cup of coffee and saw that it was just a few minutes after twelve. Plenty of time to get out to the airport for his lesson in the DC-3.

Chapter 26

Captain Johng's Destiny

Sojwa Johng Ho Kim stood on the conning tower of the Undersea Boat 235 facing forward watching the knife shaped keel of the submarine slicing through the whitecaps of the running sea. Occasionally the breeze would whip the cold froth from the whitecaps and blow it back into the face of Captain Johng. Rather than turn his face from the wind he would take a deep breath and breathe in the salt spray as if it was an elixir having been mixed by the God of the Sea, Neptune. The moon laid down a silver shimmering path upon the sea which the UB-235 was chasing towards the horizon and the stars above twinkled almost as if they were encouraging the submarine to an even greater effort to win the race.

Standing in the tower, Johng Ho Kim was thinking back to the very small village of Anju some 100 kilometers north of Pyongyang. His father, mother, two brothers and sisters lived in a squalid little hut and worked in the rice paddies and little garden they had, trying to eke out a living. There was a small school in the village which Kim was determined to attend in spite of his father's occasional beatings which were rendered in an effort to keep Kim working in the rice paddies. His mother, on the other hand, saw a spark of determination in her eldest son and continued to persuade her husband to let the child attend the school Fortunately a compromise was reached and Kim was allowed to attend for which he would have the extra duty of milking the goat and making the cheese in addition to his part time work in the paddies.

Kim would never forget the day that Eun Kong visited the school, resplendent in his uniform of the Navy of the Republic of North Korea. Kong had attended this very school and as he stood and told of his adventures in one of the Navy's patrol boats and how they had harassed their enemy to the south during the war, Kim sat wide eyed and took in every word. Kong emphasized that he had been able to rise to the position that he was in at that time due to his determination to study and learn so that he could pass the entrance exam into the North Korean Naval Academy. From that day forth, Kim took a vow that he, too, would achieve the same goal as that of his former schoolmate.

At the age of seventeen, Kim told his mother, father and his siblings good-bye and traveled south to Huchon where he boarded a train to Najin. There he enlisted in the North Korean Navy and passed the exam which would allow him to enter the Kim Jung-sook Navy School. Four years later, after graduation, Kim was appointed to the rank of *Sowi* [1] and reported for duty at Toejo Dong which was the city where the headquarters of the East Coast Fleet was located.

Because of his rank in his graduating class, Kim was assigned to a guided-missile patrol boat which was a choice assignment for a newly appointed officer. The patrol boat was equipped with the SS-N-2A/STYX antiship missile which operated primarily in the coastal waters and calm seas. Though small in size, the high-speed boats could respond quickly to intruding vessels. After six months, Kim was promoted to the rank of *Chumgwi* [2] and assigned to the Soviet built OSA-1 guided missile patrol boat which was somewhat larger than his former boat. While serving on this boat, Kim applied for service in submarines and six months later he was transferred to the naval base at Wonsan.

Upon arrival at Wonsan, Kim was assigned to the Submarine UB-205 as the engineering officer. He served with distinction in that post and at the time of his next performance review his commanding officer recommended him for the rank of *Sangwi*. [3] Kim continued to perform at levels above standard and at the age of 28 he was transferred to the UB-220 to serve as the Executive Officer. This duty called for promotion to the rank of *Taewi* [4] Kim served in this capacity for four more years until an opening for captain of a submarine became available. His

---

1. Ensign
2. Lieutenant Junior Grade
3. Lieutenant 2nd Class
4. Lietuenant 1st Class

commanding officer on the UB-220 recommended Kim for the position and the review board selected him. Thus, he was promoted to the rank of *Sojwa* [5] and became the captain of the UB-235 on June 10th, 1985.

He had been captain of the UB-235 now for three years and as he stood on the conning tower that night and reflected on how he had persevered over all obstacles to achieve his goal which had given him a great feeling of satisfaction. There was one dark blot that stained his burning desire to excel in his career of being the best. The thought of this caused his brow to furrow and his eyes narrow to slits.

The capitalist Yankees used the submarines of the North Korean Navy as their prey in their eternal game of 'cat and mouse.' It was almost certain that every time the UB-235 would journey into international waters their sonar would pick up the sound of one of those Yankee submarines which would stalk them. "Boomers" they called them. Where did they find such an asinine term for a submarine? Whenever the Yankee sub would begin to ping their vessel, Kim would burn with envy knowing there was absolutely nothing that he could do to outmaneuver or outrun them and get them into a situation for a simulated torpedo attack. These "Boomers," as they were known, were ten times larger and almost three times faster than his ROMEO class submarine plus he carried only 18 conventional torpedoes compared to their OHIO class subs which carried 24 Trident long range missiles and 42 Mark 48 torpedoes. Kim had read where the Mark 48 torpedo was a heavy weight torpedo with a warhead of 290kg. If the capitalist pigs were to unleash one of those on his boat, all of his crew and boat would be an indistinguishable mass of metal lying on the floor of the ocean.

He longed for the day when all of this would change. There were rumors running through the fleet at this very time indicating the possibility of the introduction of a new submarine that would put their Navy into a position of being battle worthy against the imperialist dogs. As the cold spray from the Sea of Japan bathed his face once again, he looked at his waterproof chronograph, sighed and called the lookouts down from the conning tower. It was time to submerge into the depths that were all too familiar to the submariner.

When they had submerged, Johng Ho Kim turned the command over to his Executive Officer and retired to his cramped quarters. He removed his heavy sea coat, wool scarf and cap and called for his orderly to bring a cup of herbal tea to his quarters. After the orderly had left, Kim opened the safe in his quarters and read the orders again for the third time. The UB-235 was in for a long journey. Admiral Kwan Il Soong had called Kim to his office and had presented the orders

---

5. Commander

to him personally. The Admiral had explained the grave importance of the mission and the absolute necessity of completing his mission successfully. Kim knew that if he failed, his career in the North Korean Navy would be at an end. He replaced the orders in the safe, spun the dial, finished his tea and retired to his bunk. Kim dwelled upon the mission for what seemed an hour before he fell into a fitful sleep.

CHAPTER 27

'GOONEY BIRD' CHECKRIDE

When Dan arrived at Stevens Air he went by Norm's office. Dan rapped on the door frame and peeked around the open door to find Norm sitting at his desk alone in his office.

"Hey, I just wanted to let you know I am here. I'll have the bird brought out on the ramp and you can join me whenever you are ready if that's o.k.?"

"That'll be fine, Dan. I shouldn't be more than ten minutes or so," Norm replied.

Dan went into the hangar, found a Stevens employee and asked if he could get the DC-3 out on the ramp. The line boy hooked up the tow unit to the "three" and pulled it out of the hangar onto the ramp. Dan then did the 'walk around,' inspecting the control surfaces of the aircraft and checking the tires while the line boy checked the oil in the engines and the gas caps on the wings. The line boy and Dan pulled the props through three times on both engines and between the two of them, got the clam shell doors open. Dan then went up to the cockpit, pulled out the checklist and began to look it over while he waited for Norm. After about fifteen minutes Dan heard the cargo door slam and Norm made his way up to the cockpit.

"You got it all figured out by now? Norm grinned.

"Well, I wouldn't say that but I've got a few of the details down pretty well I think."

"O.K., let's see if you can get it cranked up."

Dan moved the prop controls full forward, cracked the throttles and moved the mixture controls to about the middle of the idle cutoff scale. Battery switch to "On," generators "On," and ignition master switch "On." Right magneto lever to "Both," Right fuel booster pump to "On," prime switch to "On Right." Then Dan flipped the start switch to "On Right" and listened for the right engine beginning to turn over. About four or five seconds after that Dan moved the right vibrator switch to "On Right" then moved the three-position switch to the "Down" position. When the engine fired off, he moved the vibrator switch to the "Off" position. Then Dan moved the start switch to the "Off" position and moved the right fuel mixture control lever to the "Auto-Rich" position. He switched the prime switch to the "Off" position and the fuel booster pump to "Off." The right engine was turning over beautifully and then he repeated this process for the left engine.

After both engines were running, Norm punched Dan on the right arm and said, "Good! O.K., now let's see if you can taxi this thing." Norm flicked the microphone switch, called ground control and got clearance to runway six left. Dan gingerly moved the throttles forward, then retarded the right throttle and stepped on the right brake. The DC-3 began a slow turn to the right and when he had it lined up with the taxiway he moved the right throttle even with the left, tapped the left brake slightly and evened the nose of the aircraft down the centerline of the taxiway. Norm looked over at Dan and said, "Think you are smart, don't you?" and gave Dan another grin.

When They got down to the end of the taxiway, Dan stopped the aircraft, set the parking brake and ran the right engine up to 1800 rpm, flicked the right magneto switch to "Left" then to "Right" and noted the drop in rpm's. The RPM's did not fall off more than 50 RPM's on either the right or left mag. Dan then retarded the right throttle and ran the same procedure on the left engine using the left magneto switch. The left engine checked out o.k. as well. Dan then pulled the manifold pressure lever back to the detent and then full forward to cycle the variable pitch control for the left propeller and then repeated the process for the right prop.

Norm called the tower and received clearance for take off. Dan eased the plane out onto the runway and turned to the left. He used a little too much power on the right engine and overshot the centerline but he jockeyed the throttles and got the DC-3 lined up pretty well. Then Dan called for Norm to put in ten degrees of flaps.

"O.K., let's go," Norm said.

Dan advanced the throttles, prop controls and mixture controls to full forward and they began to pick up speed down the runway. At 65 knots, Dan could feel the rudder control in the foot pedals as the slipstream passing around the vertical stabilizer brought that control into play. Soon thereafter, the tail began to rise. Shortly Norm called out "V1," which is the speed at which a decision must be made to continue the takeoff or stop if something wrong is detected. All the gauges were in the "green" so they continued. At 85 knots Norm called out "V-2" which is the safety rotation speed and shortly thereafter he called "rotate" and Dan pulled back on the yoke. The DC-3 lifted from the runway and they were airborne.

Dan let the airspeed build to 105 knots and noted the altimeter increasing as well as the rate of climb indicator, signaling they had a positive rate of climb established. The altimeter indicated that they were 500 feet above ground level so Dan called out, "gear up," and Norm moved the landing gear handle to the "Up" position. At 110 knots Dan called, "flaps up" and Norm moved the flap handle to the "up" position. Norm clicked on the intercom and said, "Level off at 2,000 feet, Dan, and stay in the pattern for a landing."

At 1,000 feet Dan began a slow 90 degree turn to the left and continued to climb to 2,000 feet. When the altimeter read 2,000 Dan began another 90 degree turn to the left and reduced the throttles to keep the airspeed at 120 knots and pulled back on the prop levers to 2200 rpm. Norm called the tower,

"Anchorage tower, Douglas November niner one four zero Romeo is on downwind for Runway six left, request touch n' go."

"Roger, four zero Romeo, you are number two following Air Alaska seven thirty-seven. Approved for touch and go."

"Four zero Romeo, roger. We have the seven thirty-seven in sight." Norm acknowledged.

Dan reduced the speed to 100 knots and turned on the base leg, had Norm drop one-quarter flaps and they began a descent of 300 feet per minute. With the runway in sight out of the left window, Dan turned onto a heading of 065 degrees and Norm dropped another one-quarter of flaps. At the outer marker, Norm lowered the gear and Dan made sure the mixture controls were full rich, advanced the props to full forward and maintained an airspeed of ninety knots. The Air Alaska 737 had touched down. Dan ran the GUMPS[1] check and hung the airspeed needle on the 'blue line.' Crossing the fence he began to pull back on the yoke slightly and reduced the airspeed to 85 knots. Back on the throttles a lit-

---

1. Gas-Undercarriage-Mixture-Props-Speed

tle more while raising the nose to where the aircraft was in a slight tail down position, airspeed eighty knots. The wheels went "squeak-squeak" and Dan pushed the yoke forward slightly to keep the wheels on the ground; he held what he had until the tail began to drop more then he shoved the throttles to the forward stops and they were moving down the runway for another takeoff.

"Good! For your first landing that was damn good!" Norm said. "O.K. we are going out of the pattern this time for some airwork."

They left the traffic pattern at twelve hundred feet and went out over the Gulach where they climbed on up to eight thousand feet and did some power on and power off stalls. Dan found that the DC-3 was a relatively docile lady and after four or five stalls he was getting the hang of recovery pretty well. Norm looked at his watch and noted that they had been up for about forty-five minutes so they headed back to Stevens Anchorage International airport where Dan went for another wheel landing. No doubt the first one was pure luck because this time he had a "bouncer" but recovered nicely and brought the aircraft to a full stop. Taxiing back to the hangar was an interesting exercise in throttle and differential braking control, i.e. using a combination of throttles and brakes on one or the other of the wheels. Dan's path down the taxiway was not exactly in a straight line but for a beginner, he did quite well.

Once at the ramp Dan went through the shut-down procedure and set the parking brakes. The mechanic came up and chocked the wheels as Norm and Dan exited through the cargo door. They both walked back towards the hanger.

"Not bad for your first ride, Dan. Next time out we will go through an 'engine out' procedure and an emergency landing. After you get the hang of that I believe you will be ready to take the 'Gooney' on a trip solo if you want to. Right now I would suggest you have either Harry or Tim with you."

"Thanks, Norm. I appreciate your help and just put your charge for your time on our regular bill, o.k.?"

"I'll do it, Dan, and it was my pleasure." By that time they had reached the hanger, Norm opened the door for Dan and they went into the hallway that led to the main office. Dan went into the lobby and sat down at the visiting pilot's phone. He dialed Jess' office.

"Jessica Lane." Hearing her voice actually caused Dan's heart to beat a little faster.

"Hi."

"Oh, it's you. Where have you been, stranger?"

"Well, as a matter of fact I have been working for a change."

"What a nice change of pace." Dan could tell she was smiling.

"Since you have been slaving over a 'hot desk' all day I was wondering if you would have dinner with me at the Crow's Nest tonight."

"The *Crow's Nest!* Dan, have you ever been to the Crow's Nest?"

"Something wrong with the place?" Dan could hardly keep from laughing.

"No except it is one of the most exclusive places in Anchorage."

"Is that right? Do you think they might let a lowly freight hauling pilot in there?"

"Sure. They are willing to let almost anyone in who can pay the freight."

"In that case I will drop by your apartment about seven thirty. Is that o.k.?"

"That sounds great to me. I'll be ready."

Chapter 28

The Crow's Nest

Dan had plenty of time left so he headed downtown to the Intermont office building, went up to the fifth floor, into the office lobby and asked Virginia how to find Fred Robinson's office. She told him to go down the main hall to the last door on the left, go in the General Offices and someone would direct him from there. When he opened the door to the General Offices, he received something of a surprise. The room was full of small cubicles, maybe ten or fifteen, and Dan gathered this was where the personnel and accounting people hung out. A young man was coming towards him down one of the aisles and Dan asked where he might find Fred Robinson. He pointed towards an enclosed office in the room. On the door of the office was a plaque that read 'Fred Robinson—Vice President Finance.' Dan knocked on the door and a voice said, "Come in." Fred was sitting behind a desk in a spacious carpeted room with windows that looked out over a building next door.

"Hey, Dan, what can I do for you?"

"I thought I would drop by and see if you had any luck on finding a spare laptop."

"As a matter of fact, I did." He turned around in his swivel chair, opened a sliding door on his credenza, picked up a Dell laptop and handed it to Dan. "I intended to call you and tell you it was here but I got involved. I had one of the girls delete all the files on it, Dan, and it should be clean of everything except

Microsoft Windows which will have Excel and Word.. The name of the program you are looking for is called Airspex and you will find it under 'All Programs.'"

"That's great, Fred. I appreciate this very much. I was by the hangar and picked up some information on the DC-3 so I thought I would spend some time during the evenings getting started on the program."

"Good man. I certainly will be looking forward to seeing some hard figures on our aircraft operating costs."

"I hope to have some figures for you no later than the end of next week. Thanks again, Fred and I will be in touch soon, no doubt about it."

On the way out Dan passed by Virginia's desk. "Virginia, do you know how to get in touch with Tim Morrison and Harry Abelson?"

"I sure do, Mr. Dan, they both have 'beepers.'"

She never was going to call me just plain 'Dan.'

"Oh, I almost forgot" She opened one of her desk drawers. "Here's a 'beeper' that Miss Jess gave me just this morning for you to have. You will find your number on the back."

"Thanks, Virginia. When Tim and Harry call in, would you please remind them that the three of us will have a meeting at eight o'clock sharp in the morning at the Stevens Air office?"

"I certainly will, Mr. Dan."

"Thanks, Virginia."

Dan looked at his watch and it was a little after three-thirty. Not much time left to accomplish anything else so he went out to the parking lot, jumped in the Honda and headed for The Crow's Nest which was on the top floor of the Hotel Captain Cook at 5th Avenue and "K" Streets. Stepping out of the elevator on the 5th floor of the Captain Cook Hotel, Dan went to the Crow's Nest receptionist's station and found the maitre d'. Dan had a few words with him and went back to the parking lot.

Next stop would be the "Squire's Shop" which Dan had found in the Yellow Pages. It was advertised as being a men's shop for the 'discerning gentleman.' They were located at 1252 Seward Highway which was just a few miles from the hotel.

The clerk that greeted Dan was a nice young fellow, 30 'ish, with a nice personality.

"Can I help you, sir?"

"Yes, I'm looking for a jacket and pair of slacks I can wear to a semi-formal affair. Should take a 42 long in the jacket and pants with a 38 inch waist and 31 inch inseam."

"Yes sir, right this way."

The young man slipped a midnight black suede jacket on Dan which fit him to a tee.

"You look really sharp in that jacket, sir. Fits nicely on the shoulders and the sleeve length is just right also." The young clerk smoothed the jacket along both shoulders.

The salesman then found a pair of grey slacks, 38 waist and 31 inch inseam. Dan went into a dressing room, tried them on and they fit perfectly.

Dan stepped out of the room and looked at his outfit in the mirror. *Pretty sharp.*

The salesman was approaching with a white shirt. "I believe this shirt should do the trick."

Dan looked at it and saw that it was a 16 inch neck with 33-34 sleeves. "That's my size all right. Now how about a nice pair of shoes."

In the shoe department Dan found a pair of black Johnson Murphy wing tips that were on sale. All that was left was a nice tie and a black leather belt.

"I think this silver grey tie will go really well with your jacket." the clerk said as he pulled one from a rack.

Dan agreed and he rounded out his purchase with the belt.

The two of them walked to the front of the store where the salesman packaged everything neatly and rang up the purchases on the cash register. The total was $396.85 including tax. Dan wrote the young man a check for the amount, took his package and hung the plastic bag containing the slacks and jacket on the coat hanger over a hanger above the rear seat of the Honda then headed for the Hertz Rental Agency.

At the agency, Dan signed off on the charges and asked the clerk if there was someone there that could take him to the Affordable Used Cars lot where he had purchased an automobile and needed to pick it up. Since Dan had been such a good customer the clerk agreed and had one of he attendants drive him over there. Dan took his newly purchased garments out, gave the attendant a five buck tip and went into the office where Ed Beasley was sitting behind the desk with his usual cigar in his mouth reading the newspaper.

"Afternoon, Ed. You got my jalopy ready?"

"Of course I have. Affordable Cars is always ready to serve our good customers." *He was actually smiling!* "Here's the key … I put five gallons of gas in it for ya.'

He's all heart.

"Thanks. Good doing business with you, Ed." *Might as well leave on a friendly note.*

"You, too. Be sure and come back and see me when you want to trade up."

"Yeah, I'll do that, Ed."

Dan walked down to the Jeep, put his clothes in the back and checked to find a drive-out tag on the back window. There were four new Goodyear snow tires on the Jeep. Good enough. Off to the apartment.

On the way he passed a supermarket that wasn't far from his apartment. Dan looked at his watch, it was four-thirty. He still had time so he stopped and forty-five minutes later he had a cart full of groceries including eggs, milk, coffee, a couple of ribeye steaks and other odds and ends. Arriving at the apartment, Dan climbed the steps to 242, inserted the key into the lock and stepped inside. Voila! The furniture had arrived and whoever did the arranging had done a good job. There would be very few things that Dan would need to rearrange in order for it to come up to his expectations. Dan put up the groceries and then spent the next hour putting away just essentials. The rest of it would have to wait as it was time for him to get dressed and pick up Jess for their dinner at The Crow's Nest.

Dan punched the button for the door chime on Jess' apartment at exactly 7:25 p.m. She came to the door and when she opened it, Dan just had to take a deep breath. She was standing there in a stunning sleek, styled black dress with her hair up and a few loose curls which gave her face a soft look. A pair of diamond and pearl earrings were all the jewelry she was wearing but they were so unusual … they surely were heirlooms. Her shoes were black pumps and looked like they probably had come from a high-end store like Neiman Marcus.

"Hi, you want to step in?" she smiled.

"Well, our reservations are for eight so we probably should go."

Jess turned and picked up a fitted jacket which matched her dress as well as a small evening bag. Dan stepped inside the door.

"Here, let me help you with your jacket," and he took it from her and then slipped it around her shoulders. Dan caught a scent of that perfume and that old ache hit him in the pit of his stomach again.

"Thank you, Dan," and she turned her face towards him with an alluring smile.

They walked down the sidewalk with her holding on to his arm then he opened the door to the Cherokee for her.

"What in the world is *this?!*" she asked.

"Why, it's your golden chariot, madam" and Dan made a flourish with his arm as she slipped into the right front seat.

Jess started laughing so hard Dan thought she was going to ruin her makeup.

"What's so funny?" he said.

"Oh, nothing ... I just pictured you as the Jaguar or BMW type and you drive up in *this!* It's just too much."

"Hey, you are looking at the proverbial Mr. Scrooge here. I can drive this crate for six months and just walk away from it if I have to."

Jess looked at him with something of a pained look on her face. "Dan, you aren't thinking of leaving at the end of six months are you?"

"I'm not *planning* on it but I dunno. You know the deal that Al made ... he said we would take a look at the situation at the end of six months."

She reached over with her right hand and placed it on his right arm which was holding the steering wheel. "I hope things work out where you can stay."

Dan glanced at her and saw those brown eyes looking at him rather somberly.

"I hope so too, Jess. I'll give it my best shot." and he gave her a reassuring smile.

They both were rather quiet during the drive downtown where Dan turned into the parking lot at the Hotel Captain Cook. They exited the car, walked into the building and took the elevator to the fifth floor. They stepped out into the lobby of the Crow's Nest and there was one couple waiting ahead of them. As soon as the maitre d' returned, he lifted his eyebrows in recognition.

"Ahhh, Mr. Nichols and Miss Lane. How are you this evening?"

"Just fine, Maurice ... and you?" Dan stole a glance at Jess and her mouth partially opened in complete surprise.

"This way, please. I have your table waiting for you." Jess and Dan walked towards a candlelit table next to the windows which offered the best view of Anchorage. Maurice pulled the chair back for Jess and Dan walked to the other side of the table. After she was seated, Dan sat down. Jess leaned across the table and spoke softly.

"I thought you said you had never been to the Crow's Nest before."

"That's right, I haven't"

"Then how did the maitre d' know you and *me?*"

"It was worth every penny of that twenty I gave him this afternoon when I made reservations."

"You *didn't?* she exclaimed.

"Oh, but I *did!*" and he grinned from ear to ear.

"Dan Nichols, you're *incorrigible."*

"I sure as hell hope so."

A tall slender Greek god type approached the table.

"My name is Jason and I will be taking care of you this evening. May I bring you something to drink?"

Dan spoke up and said, "I'll have a Grey Goose vodka on the rocks with an olive and the lady will have a glass of Chenin Blanc."

Jess quickly spoke, "I think I will have a Gibson instead." The waiter bowed and retreated.

"A Gibson? My, what brought that on?"

"This is a special occasion tonight," she almost whispered in reply and looked at him impishly.

"Oh, really, and what might that be." Dan asked.

"I just want this to be a memorable night for the two of us." Her eyes bored into Dan's as if she was trying to look into his innermost soul and fathom his thoughts.

Jason returned with the drinks and after they had been served, Dan raised his glass. She did the same and they touched the glasses together.

"Here's to our special occasion." Dan said and they both sipped their drinks.

Jason returned and presented them with menus. Jess chose the oven roasted king salmon with wild mushroom and white bean ragout, olive oil poached tomatoes and truffle vinagarette. Dan saw something on the menu that he always wanted to try. Pepper crusted American bison sirloin. With it came porcini-infused yellow corn palenta, ragout of wild mushrooms, braised winter greens, and oven dried black currant gastric. Jason departed with the menus and the two of them engaged in looking at the downtown lights and occasionally Jess would point out an item of interest. Of course, Dan saw the rotating beacon at the Stevens International Airport and pointed that out to Jess.

Shortly, four males in tuxedos returned and served their meal in grand style. The Crows Nest, Dan found, excelled in not only preparing food in gourmet fashion but served it in the same manner. Their food was indescribably delicious and it was the beginning of a night that would be the special occasion that Jess promised.

After dinner, Jess and Dan sat sipping their brandy, listening to the string ensemble that had been playing throughout dinner when Dan noticed a couple dancing on the small dance floor in front of the dais that the band was on.

Dan asked Jess, "Would you like to dance?"

She replied, "Yes I would, thank you."

They both rose and walked to the dance area. Dan took her right hand with his left and slipped his right hand around her slim, firm waist. She immediately put her head on his right shoulder and began to follow Dan around the dance area. There was that perfume again.

"I have been meaning to ask you, Jess. What is the name of that perfume you are wearing?"

She pulled back slightly, raised her face and smiled, "It's called Hypnotic Poison by Dior." Dan looked into her brown eyes and chuckled, "No wonder it is killing me."

The ensemble moved right into an old Glenn Miller favorite of Dan's, 'Serenade in Blue' and Dan thought, *God, I can't take much more of this.*

Without moving her head from his shoulder, Jess said, "Do you like Glenn Miller?"

"My very favorite of the old Big Band orchestras. He had a sound like no other."

"Yes, I know," Jess replied, "I have all of his recordings." There was a slight pause and then she continued, "He isn't dead you know ... that is just a rumor."

"C'mon, Jess. He went down in the English Channel in a Norseman in '44."

She lifted her head, smiled at Dan and said, "Prove it."

"O.K., you win," Dan chuckled. "I guess he will live on forever in the hearts and minds of some of us."

They continued to glide around the floor. Jess was very light on her feet and followed Dan perfectly as if they were just one entity in motion with the music. Finally the ensemble paused for a break and the two of them returned to the table.

Dan looked at his watch and it was 10:35. "I suppose we had better think about leaving as much as I hate to."

"Yes, I know. Unfortunately I have a big day ahead of me tomorrow."

"Me too." Dan rejoined. "I have a meeting with Tim and Harry in the morning and maybe another training flight as well."

Dan signaled Jason for the check and he brought it over immediately. Dan produced his American Express card and Jason moved away to the front desk.

"What's your big day tomorrow?" Dan asked.

"Oh, one of the mines has sent in some environmental reports they want me to look over before they send them out to the EPA."

"Does the company charge for those services?"

"It depends. If it is a company that we really do a lot of business with, we usually do it gratis. If it is a small account we do make a charge but it usually is less than what they would be charged by a consultant. This is one means we have of encouraging them to do more business with us."

"Hmmm, pretty slick. I'll bet you're the one that thought up that deal," Dan said.

"You're a real perceptive guy, you know that?"

"Well, you have to remember that I'm a guy who tries to figure all the angles, too."

"Yes, I know," she smiled coyly, "I have noticed you have tried to figure out some of *my* angles."

"Get outta here! Dammit, Jess, you are always trying to make me out the lothario ... actually I am the perfect gentleman." Dan was grinning all the way.

"Uh, huh. I noticed that when I took the shower in your bathroom that night." she was still smiling.

"Oh, I give up! Let's get out of here." Dan laughed.

Jason returned with the check, Dan looked it over, added a generous tip and signed the tab. The waiter removed the customer copy, bade both a good evening and departed. Dan got out of his chair, moved behind Jess's chair and helped her on with her jacket.

They left the Crow's Nest and went the five stories down on the elevator to the parking lot and stepped out into the evening air. The sky was clear and the stars were shining brightly in the heavens. There was a cold chill in the air and Dan put his arm around Jess as they walked to the Cherokee. Dan helped her in and then hurried around, got in behind the wheel and started the engine. They both shivered a little waiting for the heater to come on as he moved the Cherokee out of the lot. Jess moved close to Dan with her left arm underneath his right arm and placed her head on his shoulder. Soon the warm air began to fill the car and they made very little conversation as Dan drove back to her apartment. Dan parked the car, went around to the passenger side and opened the door for her. Once again he tried to give her a little protection from the cold air as they walked to the front door.

Jess took the key from her purse, opened the door, reached inside and flipped on a light. She turned, "I would ask you in, Dan, but it is getting quite late."

"I know, Jess. Maybe some other time, huh?"

She simply said, "Yes," and Dan could tell from her movements that she was going to kiss him on his cheek. Dan quickly moved both of his hands and cupped her lovely face in them. Dan leaned forward and kissed her full on her lips. She put both palms of her hands on Dan's chest and at first he sensed a slight resistance and thought she was going to push away but instead she slid them up around his neck and pressed her body fully against his. The kiss became more passionate as if both of them were attempting to excoriate any remnants of hurt or pain from previous experiences. They both clung together for what seemed to be several minutes.

Finally Jess pulled away slightly, placed her head on Dan's shoulder and he felt her body convulse in a sob.

Dan pulled back so that he could see her face and said, "Oh, hell, Jess. I didn't mean to *offend* you!"

"Oh, you didn't offend me, Dan, it's just that …" her voice trailed off and he saw two tears trickle down her cheeks. Dan reached in his pocket, removed his handkerchief and dabbed her tears.

"It's just that what, Jess?" Dan asked.

"It's just that …" and she sobbed again. She took his handkerchief and blotted her eyes. "It's just that I moved up here to *un*complicate my life and now it's getting complicated again."

Dan pulled her back close to him and she put her head back on his shoulder. Dan spoke to her,

"Jess, we both have had tragedy in our lives but we just can't afford to go on living in the past. We have a lot of good years ahead and we both need someone to share them with. It's possible for us to feel close to one another and share our feelings with one another without screwing up our lives."

She looked up into his face, "Oh, I hope you are right Dan." She then put both of her hands around his neck, pulled his face forward and kissed him softly on the lips. Then she looked into Dan's eyes and said,

"Good night and you be careful, hear?"

"Don't you worry. I will." And, with that she stepped inside the door and gave him one last smile before it closed.

Dan retreated to the Cherokee, started it up and drove back to the apartment thinking, *What a night. Jess was right … it* would *be a memorable one.*

Chapter 29

Al Switzer

Al Switzer turned around in his office swivel chair and looked out on the Knik Arm of Cook Inlet, watching a small coastal freighter making its' way south. From his viewpoint he could also see the 'O Dock' Road which ran parallel to the Knik Arm and just make out the roof of the Intermont Mining warehouse. There was probably close to two hundred thousand dollars of various items in that warehouse for the mining industry. A couple of rebuilt diesel generators, cable, pumps, casing, piping, blasting supplies, exhaust fans and much more. Al took a few more puffs from his cigar and let his mind wander into the past, thinking about the early beginnings of his family and his life. He began to think back to the story that his Dad had told him about his grandfather.

His grandfather was Nicklaus Stoanovich and was born in Kolubara, Yugoslavia. Nicklaus grew up in a poor family and as a young man he worked in the largest coal mine in Yugoslavia. His grandfather had made friends with a young man in his neighborhood by the name of Anthony Lucas. After going to the mines he lost track of Anthony but later he made an effort to find his old friend. Inquiries revealed that Anthony had joined the Austro-Hungarian navy. Lucas encountered so much discrimination in the navy that on a trip to the United States he jumped ship and remained in Louisiana illegally. He obtained a job there and in 1899 he noticed an ad in a local paper advertising for workers in the oil fields of Texas. It had been placed in the paper by a Pattillo Higgins who had brought in the famous Spindletop oil gusher in Texas. Anthony answered the ad and received a reply from Higgins who suggested he come to Beaumont, Texas for an interview. He made the trip and after being interviewed, he was hired by Higgins.

Anthony prospered in his relationship with Higgins and, in need of an experienced man he could trust, Anthony remembered his old friend back in Kolubara who had experience in drilling and use of explosives. He wrote his friend Stoanovich and said that he would sponsor him if he wished to come to America. Of course Nicklaus accepted the offer and eventually was working for Lucas in Beaumont, Texas. Lucas left Higgins to go out on his own with his friend Stoanovich in tow. With financial backing from two Pennsylvania oil men, Lucas brought in the 'Lucas Gusher" on January 10, 1901. Lucas was so appreciative of Nicklaus' efforts in their endeavor that he rewarded NIcklaus handsomely and, in time, Nicklaus became moderately wealthy.

Soon thereafter, Nicklaus Stoanovich applied for American citizenship and had his name legally changed to Nicklaus Switzer. In 1902 he met a young Texas lady by the name of Madelyn Armstrong and he married Madelyn in August 1902. Twelve months later they had a son named Theodore and two years after that, they had a daughter and named her Evelyn.

At the age of 18, Theodore entered Texas A&M College and applied for the Dwight Look School of Engineering, majoring in Petroleum Engineering. He graduated from the college in 1921 and was employed by the Halliburton Oil Company. Ted married Helen Armstrong in 1923 and three years later Helen gave birth to a boy who was named Alfred. Ted and Helen also had a daughter born to them in 1928 and they named her Elizabeth.

Al continued to smoke his Cifuentes y Cia down to a stub. It had gone out but he was so far into recounting the story that his father had told him that he didn't even notice, he was so engrossed in thought …

It was the night of the senior prom at South Park High school, June of 1943. The school band was playing their rendition of Glenn Miller's 'Moonlight Serenade' and he had Cindy Walker in his arms as they danced to the music. Al had played football for the South Park High School all four years and Cindy had been on the school cheerleading squad during that time. The world was their oyster and the war in Europe was a thousand miles away, almost meaningless to these kids at their prom.

Al turned 18 in August of 1943 and registered for the draft. All of America was geared up for the war effort; it had affected every man, woman and child in one way or another. This tremendous effort had bonded the people of America together like no other event in the history of the nation. Even the newly formed labor unions had set aside their differences with management in working together to arm the nation. President Roosevelt acknowledged this cooperative labor effort in one of his radio broadcasts to all Americans by making the statement, *"Our fundamental rights, including the rights of labor, are threatened by Hitler's violent attempt to rule the world."*

Al was drafted into the US Army in September, 1943, trained as an infantryman and served in the 4th Infantry Division in Europe which went ashore on Utah Beach on June 6, 1944. He was wounded in the Battle of Hurtgen Forest in Germany in November of 1944 and Al considered himself lucky. In that one battle 5,450 American soldiers were casualties and slightly over 800 were killed. Al was sent to the UK[1] for recuperation and by the time he was ready to return to duty it was evident the war in Europe was winding down, therefore he was sent back to the United States as a replacement to be sent to the Pacific theater. For all practical purposes, the war in the Pacific was over when the bomb was dropped on Hiroshima on August 6, 1945. Instead of being deployed to the Pacific, Al was discharged on November 10th, 1945.

After returning home, Al began to map out his future and wanting to follow in the footsteps of his father he contemplated on going to Texas A&M as his father had. However, deciding on a little relaxation prior to enrolling in school, he made a trip which changed his life forever.

Al leaned back in his chair, folded his arms across his chest and remembered the conversation he had with his Dad after about two weeks at home.

"Well, son, you've arrived a little late to get into school this semester. What are you going to do with all the time on your hands until next semester?"

"I don't know, Dad. I don't want you or Mom to take this the wrong way but …"

"You want to get away by yourself for a little while."

"Yeah … how did you know?"

His Dad chuckled, "I was young once myself, you know. There were a number of times when I was a young man that I wished that I could get away from everyone I knew and just be by myself. You've had it pretty tough for over two years and I just suspected that you would like to go somewhere where you could kick back, relax and make up for some lost time."

If you just knew, Dad. Part of it is the nightmares that I have every once in awhile about the Hurtgen forest.

"Yeah, that would be nice but I really don't know exactly where I want to go or what I want to do."

---

1. United Kingdom (England)

"This may sound ridiculous to you, son. But one of the greatest vacations your Mother and I ever had was a cruise to Alaska and if you just want to get away, relax, have great food and see some beautiful scenery then this may be just the ticket for you"

"I remember that ... you sent Liz and me to stay with Aunt Evelyn and Uncle Bill while you were gone. Do you think now the war is over, the ship lines have started cruises again?"

"There's one way to find out. We still have a 'phone you know."

Holland America had a seven day trip from Vancouver up the Inside Passage to Juneau, Skagway, Glacier Bay National Park, Ketchikan and back to Vancouver. It turned out to be a great trip in more ways than one. Not only did Al get to have a really great relaxing trip with wonderful food and beautiful scenery but he also met a young lady who, in time, became his partner for life.

Evelyn was 18 and had just graduated from high school in June, 1945. In fact this cruise was what she had asked her parents, Jim and Margaret Murphy, to give her for a graduation present. Being so young they naturally were not going to let her go on a cruise by herself so they accompanied their daughter on the trip. They were pleased when this clean cut young man of twenty met Evelyn. The two became almost inseparable and they participated in all of the shipboard activities together. The two were so compatible that the Murphy's invited Al to join them every evening at dinner.

After they returned home to Boulder Colorado, Jim and Margaret assumed the shipboard romance would dissipate and Evelyn would soon be seeking the companionship of another young man in Boulder, however that did not turn out to be the case. Evelyn matriculated to the University of Colorado in Boulder the following September and Al enrolled in the Colorado School of Mines in Golden, Colorado which was only about twenty-five miles from the University of Colorado campus. Al had purchased a 1940 Ford Sedan with some of the money he had saved from his service in the Army, and every week-end that Al could get away, he was on his way to Boulder to see Evelyn.

Al had talked to his Dad before enrolling in the School of Mines about his intended career. His Dad agreed with him that his desire to eventually own his own company just about precluded his following a career in the petroleum industry so Al did a considerable amount of research on various types of mining, concentrating on coal, and decided on pursuing a career in Mining Engineering. He went straight through college graduating in January, 1948 with a Bachelor of Science in Mining Engineering. Margaret, Jim and Evelyn came to his graduation ceremony and it was on that day that Al presented Evelyn with an engagement ring.

The visit to Alaska had intrigued Al and during school he did a considerable amount of research on coal production in Alaska. He learned that Alaska held 95 billion tons of coal reserves, almost six percent of the total United States reserves. There were coal fields in the Arctic Slope, the Bering River Field in south central Alaska, the Matanuska field near Anchorage and the Healy River field near Nenana. There were various other smaller fields in the Seward Peninsula and lower Yukon valley. Coal mining in Alaska was an untapped treasure.

A coal mining equipment firm in Fairbanks was advertising in the mining industry journals for a young engineer. Al found the ad in one of the journals he had been watching and submitted his resume'. The equipment firm sent Al a ticket on Alaska Airways and interviewed him for the opening. They were so impressed with this young graduate that they offered him the position. When Evelyn graduated from the University of Colorado in June of June, 1950, Al took a week's vacation, flew to Denver and attended Evelyn's graduation ceremony. He proposed to her that night and her mother and father agreed somewhat reluctantly because they knew their daughter would be moving to Alaska.

Al turned in his swivel chair back to his desk, took another fresh cigar from the humidor, lit it with the sterling silver cigar lighter and turned his thoughts to Evelyn who was now in a health care facility in Anchorage. Evelyn was now confined due to the early stages of Alzheimer's.

Chapter 30

Flyboys Meet

Usually, Dan never slept more than six hours but he probably was more tired than he realized as he didn't wake up until six-fifteen. He made a brew of coffee in the new pot, shaved, showered and was dressed by ten minutes after seven. He had forgotten to start the newspaper so he made a note to call the *Anchorage Daily News*. Dan poured himself a cup of coffee. He grimaced after the fist sip ... coffee never tastes good from a new pot. There wasn't time to fix a meal so instead he had a bowl of Raisin Bran and was off to Stevens Aircraft by seven twenty-five.

Dan's new card opened the automatic gate to the Stevens parking lot and he was entering the door to the Stevens FBO office at ten minutes to eight. Norman Timberlake was already there and had just poured himself a cup of coffee as Dan walked in.

"Hey, Dan. How about a cup of good coffee?"

"I'll go for that. I fixed a pot at the apartment this morning and it was lousy."

"Well, you'll have a hard time finding a better cup than what we brew here."

"Yeah, I will testify to that if this is as good as what you gave me yesterday." Dan took a sip and it tasted better than yesterday's. Probably because it was fresh.

"Norm, I need to ask a favor of you."

"Fire away."

"I need to have a talk with Harry and Tim this morning and I was wondering if you might have some space we could use for about an hour."

"Sure. My secretary has a dental appointment this morning and she won't be in 'til around eleven. You can use her office." Norm dropped himself into one of the lounge sofas.

"I really appreciate this, Norm" and Dan sat down in a stuffed chair across from him.

"No problem." Norm leaned forward in the couch. "By the way, I may have a deal for you. We have two exterior offices on the south wall of the hangar and one of them is empty. A charter outfit used it and they went belly up about six months ago. I can make you a really good rate on it."

"Just what do you call a good rate?" Dan asked.

"Well, seeing as how it is you ..." Norm was grinning now. "How about fifty bucks a month?"

"What's wrong with it. Does the roof leak and no heat during the winter?"

"No, no, it's really not a bad little office. About twenty by twenty with a desk, a couple of chairs and a naugahyde couch. I figure it's better to get something out of it rather than let it stand empty."

"Tell you what. You throw in three clothes lockers and you got a deal."

"Aw, c'mon, man. Those things cost money." Norm acted like he was in pain.

Dan smiled at him. "Norm, I saw about six of those things standing in the hangar yesterday and they looked like they had spider webs all over them."

"O.k, o.k ... I'll get one of my guys to clean up the place, put the lockers in and you can have it starting tomorrow and I won't charge you anything until the first of the month."

They both got up and shook hands on the deal. About that time a tall, lanky kid about six feet two walked in. Blonde hair was poking out from underneath a Chicago Cubs ball cap; he had a good tan on his face and even as young as he was he was beginning to get crow's feet around the corners of his eyes. This had to be a pilot.

"Hey, Tim," Norm greeted, "come over here and meet your new boss."

The kid's eyes lit up at that remark and he walked over towards Dan with an oversized grin on his face. He stuck out his hand and said,

"Gee, Mr. Nichols, it sure is good to meet'cha."

"Well, you must be Tim Morrison. It's good to meet you too, Tim." He had a real grip and he pumped Dan's arm like he was pumping water out of a well.

"Get yourself a cup of coffee, Tim," Norm offered.

"Don't mind if I do," and Tim walked over to the pot.

The door opened again and in walked Harry Abelson. He still had that dour look on his face. Dan thought, *I believe that if he smiled, his face would crack and fall apart.*

Once again Norm spoke. "Hello, Harry, have you met Dan Nichols?"

"Yeah, we've met."

Dan just nodded at him, "Morning, Harry."

All three of them stood there and looked at Harry as if someone had just crashed their party. Dan walked over to the coffee pot, refilled his styrofoam cup, turned, and spoke,

"C'mon guys, we've got a meeting to go to" and Dan walked down the hall to Norm's secretary's office with Tim and Harry trailing behind.

Dan walked over to the secretary's desk, sat the coffee cup down and sat on the corner of the desk with one leg hanging off and the other leg on the floor. Harry sat down first and Dan asked Tim to shut the door before he sat down.

"O.K., I don't intend to make a long speech but we need to get some things straight so that we all know the rules of the game. First, I've been hired to see that our aircraft are operated in as safe and efficient manner as we can make them, and to also make sure that all maintenance required by the FAA is done correctly and according to the book. All logbooks are to be filled in correctly after every trip and notations of any mechanical problems with the aircraft are to be recorded on the 'squawk sheet.'

"Also, I want you to pay particular attention to the way you operate the aircraft. Look over the manuals again and check out the proper fuel settings at altitude. Lean those engines back to peak performance but also watch your cylinder head temps. We want to get maximum gallons per hour but we don't want to damage those recips[1]. When you are on the ground don't do any more idling than you have to and if you are flying the 'three' and you are only going to make a stop of just a few minutes or so, kill one engine and let the other one idle. We need to cut every corner we can to improve our profit picture.

"Incidentally, the company has a new software program and every aircraft will be monitored for cost performance. It also allows us to cross check one pilot's performance in any given aircraft against the others who fly the plane. So be on your toes from now on. Also, we are not to make any charges to the company for any items that are not required for the operation of the aircraft. If it is necessary for you to spend any money of your own for items such as motel bills, meals, gasoline, or whatever, you will not be refunded for those expenditures unless you

---

1. Reciprocating engines

obtain a receipt. I have been told that you each have a company credit card for the purchase of fuel for the planes as well as normal expenses that I just mentioned so your need for spending your own money should be minimal. If you abuse the use of the credit card then that privilege will be taken away from you.

"We are going to have a small office on the exterior wall of the hangar beginning tomorrow and each of us will have a key to the office. When you return from a flight you are to place your logbook, the 'squawk sheet' and any receipts that you have for expenditures, in an 'IN' box which will be on the desk. I will review all of those documents after each flight. My top priority is to reduce the cost of operations and I will be required to turn in a report to Mr. Robinson each week detailing the flights made by each aircraft and the cost of each flight. Mr. Switzer and Mr. Robinson are determined to reduce costs and it is my responsibility to see that we achieve this goal. Also, three wall lockers are being installed in our new office; one for each of us. You may put a lock on your locker if you feel that it is necessary.

"Now, as for operations. I've got another hour or two in the 'three' with Norm Timberlake and also I need to get a seaplane rating. Both of you are to get checked out in the King Air and it will be my responsibility to see that you are qualified in that aircraft. The goal being that all three of us will be qualified to fly any of the three aircraft. That's about it. Any questions?"

Tim spoke up. "I can check you out in the seaplane, Mr. Nichols."

"The name is Dan, Tim. I appreciate the offer but I have to pass a checkride by a FAA inspector and I believe it would be best if I have an approved instructor so that I can keep the hours down to a minimum and get qualified as quickly as possible. Besides, you would be taking time away from your job."

"Yeah, I had forgot about that, sir." he replied.

"What about you, Harry ... any questions?"

"Only one." Harry twisted uneasily in his chair. "What did we get that damned King Air for ... we can't haul freight in it."

"Mr. Switzer explained to me that occasionally we sell a piece of equipment where it is necessary to transport engineers from the companies we purchase equipment from to go out on the job. These engineers survey the job, determine how best to use the equipment and then consult with our customers. This is when we need a comfortable and fast aircraft to pick them up at their home airports and take them to small fields near the job. The same goes for a prospective customer who may be interested in purchasing a large, expensive piece of new equipment. We can use the King Air to take the customer to the manufacturing facility to look at the equipment. By having a fast, economical aircraft like the

King Air, we can complete the trip in half the time it would take in the DC-3 or the Otter.

"Also, the King Air is being configured so that we can quickly remove a few seats and a light cargo load can be hauled if necessary. In addition, at times officers of the company have to be transported to job sites as well as trips to conduct business and the DC-3 and Otter are not as fast or as comfortable as the King Air. Does that answer your question?" Dan asked.

"Uh ... yeah, I guess so." Harry grunted.

"O.K. then. Tim, you've got a run with a load up to the Silver Creek Mine at Unalakleet. Here's your manifest and the guys should have your plane loaded by now. You know the drill, check everything out and when you get back be sure and turn in your trip sheet with all the details filled in, o.k.?"

"You got it, skipper. See you guys later." and Tim was out the door.

"Al, I'm going to get in another hour in the DC-3 with Norm and while I am gone, take these manuals on the King Air and study them. You won't absorb it all but do your best on the flight procedures and we will get in some time when I get back." Dan dug the manuals out of his chart case and gave them to Harry.

"Yeah, o.k." He took the manuals and headed for the Stevens lounge.

Dan walked down the corridor to Norm's office and found him sitting behind his desk.

"Hey, Norm. We got through a lot earlier than I expected. I know it's only nine-thirty but I thought I would check with you to see if we could push our schedule up on getting that hour in the Gooney Bird."

"Sure. I don't have anything pressing here. Why don't you get the guys to roll the bird out of the hangar and I will join up with you in fifteen or twenty minutes. How's that?"

"Fine, I'll see you out there."

Chapter 31

Angus McTavish

Angus McTavish was a giant of a man. Six foot five weighing two hundred ninety pounds and with shoulders that would make a Green Bay Packers fullback turn green with envy. Angus had just come out of the machinery building near the shaft to the No. 10 mine at Bullmose Mining in British Columbia. He slammed the door to the building so hard that the door loosened the hinges. Angus stomped on the ground with such force as he strode towards the superintendent's building that he could easily have been a stand-in for the part of the giant in Jack N' the Beanstalk. His face was a livid red which made the Scotsman's prematurely white hair stand out in stark contrast. As he marched, his white mustache twitched in unison with his steps.

Angus jerked open the door of the superintendent's office, marched past two young male clerks who cowered behind their desks and without knocking, opened the door to the superintendent's private office.

"Why don't you just come right on in, Angus." Superintendent Jim Morrison was at his desk with both elbows on the desktop, holding a document he was reading and he spoke as he peered up at the angry Scot over his spectacles. "You seem just a trifle upset."

"Aye, and that be the understatement of the day," Angus bellowed in his Scottish brogue.

"Why don't you sit down, cool off and tell me what's on your mind." Jim put down the document he was reading, picked up his pipe, leaned back in his chair and took a puff on his Kaywoodie briar. Angus remained standing.

"Ye know what's on me mind, Jim Morrison. It be that overworked, undernourished and nearrr death of that Cummins generator fer' Number Ten shaft. I've been a-tellin' ye forrr four months now that she was goin' ta cough her last and now she's a-knockin' like she's goin' ta throw all her rods at any minute! The Saints preserve us; the damn thing came over on the same cattle boat with me grandfather!"

Jim Morrison knew that Angus McTavish was undoubtedly the best deep coal foreman in all of Canada's western provinces. His grandfather, Paddy McTavish, had spent all his life In Longriggend, County Lanark, Scotland, mining coal. And, his father Sean had immigrated to Canada in 1929 and settled in Chetwynd, British Columbia and spent most of his life in the Bullmoose mine. Now Angus had taken over where his father had left off and had all those years of mining experience in his blood. One of Jim's main jobs was to keep all of that Scottish energy harnessed and channeled in the right direction.

Jim Morrison leaned forward in his chair, removed the Kaywoodie pipe from his mouth and tapped ashes from the bowl into the chrome plated ashtray on his desk that bore a Mack truck bulldog; a present from the Mack Truck dealer in Prince George.

"O.K., Angus. What do you suggest?"

"Suggest?! A plague upon ye mon!' I've been a-tellin' ye forrr four months to get a new or rebuilt generator! I'll no be responsible for me men down in that dark pit of hades any longer! Wi' no lights, no elevator and no exhaust fans to pull those gases out of that hole ye might as well condemn them to purgatory!" Jim looked at Angus' face and decided that he must be at, or near, stroke level.

"O.K., I'll tell the old man but you know what he is going to say. He can't afford it right now." Jim sighed.

"Begorrah, and you be tellin' him to make a choice. Either he buys me a new generator or I shut down the shaft and he can lose a hundred tons of production and pay me men while he sits on his arse and twiddles his thumbs! Now, put that in yer briar pipe and smoke it!" With that, Angus turned on his heel and went out of the office slamming the door behind him. The two clerks were making busy work at file cabinets and kept their backs to Angus until he slammed the outer door to the building.

Jim Morrison picked up his black book with the phone numbers in it, looked under "I" and dialed the number for Intermont Mining in Anchorage. The phone rang and a female voice answered,

"Good morning, Intermont Mining Supply."

"Yes, this is Jim Morrison with Bullmoose Mining in British Columbia. I would like to talk with someone about purchasing a new or used generator with a capacity of about eight or nine hundred kilowatt hours." While he waited Jim thought, *To hell with the old man. I can't afford to shut down that shaft and lose the best damn coal mining foreman in Canada to boot.*

Chapter 32

▼

Bullmoose Mining Order

Dan left the office and went to the hangar looking for Harry. He found him in the office that had just been rented from Stevens. It had been cleaned up and Harry was stretched out on the couch asleep. Dan jostled him and Harry looked up at him out of his left eye.

"I thought you guys had decided to fly down to Seattle or somewhere."

"Nope. Just took a little longer than I thought it would. You ready to give the King Air a whirl?"

"Why not," he replied.

Harry already had the King Air wheeled out of the hangar and it was sitting on the ramp ready to go. Just as a matter of proper procedure, Dan and Harry made the exterior walk-around inspection of the aircraft and then boarded it.

Dan had Harry take the left seat and Dan took the right. They spent about thirty minutes going over the controls, the instruments, radios and other instructions, especially the section in the manual dealing with the turboprop engines since it had been awhile since Harry had been in a turboprop aircraft. He said he had flown copilot in turboprop Embraers when he was with a commuter airline. Harry fired up the engines, received clearance for takeoff and Dan directed him out over the Chugach State park where Dan put him through a full familiarization of turboprop power management. After that they did some routine airwork but did not get into engine out procedures. That would come later. Finally they returned to the airport and Dan let Harry set up for the approach and make the landing. It was readily apparent to Dan that he was a very good pilot. It was just a matter of keeping him under control.

They put the King Air 'to bed' and Dan walked back into the Stevens FBO office to grab a cup of coffee and the girl at the desk saw him come in.

"Oh, Mr. Nichols. You have an urgent call from a Joe Johnson in your office."

"Thanks." Dan walked over to the courtesy phone by the coffee pot, poured a cup of coffee and called Joe who was in the Intermont sales office.

"Joe … Dan Nichols."

"Oh, yeah, Mr. Nichols. We have an urgent order from Bullmoose Mining for that big old rebuilt Caterpillar generator as well as a few other items. They want it delivered tomorrow for sure."

"Where are they located, Joe?"

"They're located near Tumbler Ridge, British Columbia. The order has already been sent to the warehouse and they will have it loaded and ready to go by eight tonight."

"O.K., thanks, Joe."

Dan walked back to the newly acquired office and found Harry still there rummaging around in his locker. Harry seemed startled to see Dan and quickly shut the locker door. Dan thought, *I wonder if he has already stashed a bottle of booze in there?*

"Harry, do you know where Tumbler Ridge, British Columbia is?"

"Sure … made a delivery there once."

"O.K., find the charts and meet me here at six in the morning. We've got an urgent delivery that has to be there ASAP. Joe Johnson said something about it being a rebuilt Caterpillar generator."

"Rebuilt Cat generator!? Man, ol' Al is going to get a charge out of that! He bought that generator at auction about two years ago so he is going to make a bundle on this sale, you can count on it!"

This was the most animated that Dan had seen Harry get about anything.

"O.K., I'll see you then."

Dan realized that sound from his stomach was it telling him that he had not had any lunch. The Breitling revealed that it was 1:25 p.m … no wonder his stomach was growling. No point in looking for a heavy lunch this late so he went into the Stevens Air lounge, got a Coke out of the machine and a package of wheat and peanut butter crackers out of another. This would have to hold him until he could get something more substantial. Dan went to their little office, got his laptop and briefcase and headed for the downtown office.

Once there, Dan spent the next two and a half hours in the General Offices rummaging through old records on the DC-3 and Otter which he proceeded to load into the Airspex program which would give him a baseline to compare the new operational figures with. Fred Robinson walked by and saw him sitting in the cubicle and stood in the entrance.

"How's it going, Dan? About to get everything organized?"

"Slowly but surely, Fred. I'm checked out in the DC-3, had a meeting with Tim and Harry this morning and now I'm developing background information on the aircraft so we will be able to have something to compare our present operation with."

Fred smiled, "Well, I would say you are coming along very well."

"Incidentally Harry and I will be making our first delivery in the morning. It's going to Bullmoose Mining in Tumbler Ridge. You know of them?"

"Oh, yes. They have been buying from us for several years. So you are going with Harry, eh?

"That's right. Maybe I will get to know him better."

"Well, if you do be sure and let me know how you managed it. Take care, Dan."

With that, Fred walked on down the hall and left Dan wondering just what he had to look forward to on his trip with Harry tomorrow morning.

Around five Dan put his papers and laptop in the briefcase, went down and headed the Jeep towards the apartment. Naturally there was nothing in the mailbox; not even Dan's creditors had caught up with him so far but they would soon. Dan had turned in a change of address card to the local post office when he was there last Saturday. At least the box would now be filled with 'junk' mail. At first Dan thought about cooking his first meal in the apartment but the more he thought of it the less he liked the idea. Dan looked in the Yellow Pages and saw where the ex-governor of Alaska owned the Downtown Deli on 4th Street. Since he had the late snack he wasn't all that hungry so the Deli sounded like it would be ideal. Dan left the apartment about six-thirty and headed downtown in the Jeep Cherokee.

His choice turned out to be exactly what he had in mind. The place was filled with locals and he was squeezed into a small table where he had a Fosters beer while looking over the menu. Dan decided on the house special of chicken soup with noodles, the grilled salmon and a tossed salad with the house dressing. It was a perfect meal to close out a busy day.

Back to the apartment where he took a hot shower and turned on the TV around nine-thirty to watch CNN news and catch up on what was going on in the world. He turned in early around ten p.m. and dropped off to sleep almost immediately.

Chapter 33

Tumbler Ridge

When Dan walked into the flight office the next morning at Stevens hangar, the first thing he did was to check the FAX machine. The order that had been phoned in from the superintendent of the Bullmoose Mining Company in British Columbia was on the machine. Dan checked it over: The first item was the D399 TA Caterpillar Generator—850 KWH, rebuilt to zero-hours, 600 volt, radiator cooled. Selling price: $15,800. Several other items had been ordered as well:

10—Cases Rimrock Blasting Caps
30—Cases Hercules Dynamite
4—Coils Potomont (V) Coal Cutter Cable

Harry walked into the office about five minutes after seven o'clock and Dan handed him the FAX copy. Harry looked at it and let out a little whistle. "Man ol' Harry is going to jump out of his shorts when he sees what they got for the Cat."

Dan spoke up, "Yesterday you said you had been to Bullmoose. Where's it located?"

"It's in British Columbia. You have to go into the airport at Tumbler Ridge. It's a small uncontrolled field that was built just to serve about three coal mines in the area."

"Pretty good strip?" Dan queried.

"Not too good; oiled gravel that has been packed and best I can remember it is about three thousand feet long."

Harry had not done his 'homework' like Dan had requested which was to get out the charts for the trip and have them ready. Dan didn't say a word but started fishing the Canadian charts out of his chart case, opened the one for British Columbia and laid it on the desk.

Dan looked at the British Columbia chart and said, "Let's see ... hmmm ... the field designation is CBX7 and according to the information on the chart, you are right. It is a gravel and oil runway that is 3100 feet long and 50 feet wide. No navigation aids and it appears there are no VOR's close by to help us with navigation."

Harry, peering over Dan's shoulder commented, "How about that ADF[1] right there?" and he pointed to it with his finger.

"Yeah, that's the Mackenzie ADF and it is ..." Dan took a mileage ruler from his bag and laid it on the ADF and drew a line to the field ... "it's 49 nautical miles from the NDB to the field."

"O.K., then I would say we should head for the Yakutat VOR then to the Mackenzie ADF and to the field from there." Harry suggested.

"Looks like the best route to me," Dan replied, "and there's one hell of a long distance between the Yakutat VOR and Mackenzie NDB. Let's see what that distance is." Dan took a straight edge, measured the distance and calculated it. "That's 588 miles ... we've got a lot of dead reckoning to do there."

Dan made some notes about the navigational aids and the distances on a kneepad for reference once they were airborne. He put all the information back in the chart bag and said to Harry, "Let's go check out the 'three' and see if the guys got everything loaded up last night."

They went into the hangar and found that the airstair was still at the clamshell doors. They opened them up and Dan got a shock. "Wow! That thing is *huge!*" The Caterpillar generator looked like it was about 18 to 20 feet long. Joe O'Donoghue, the warehouse manager, evidently had been involved in the loading as the manifest log, with Joe's initials on it, was on a clipboard hanging on the side of the generator. He had the weight down for the generator as 7,167 pounds. That plus the other items on the manifest totaled 8,420 pounds. Empty weight plus fuel was 21,500 so they would be pushing maximum gross weight which was 30,500 pounds. The generator was mounted on a skid pallet so it wasn't going to go anywhere but Harry and Dan checked the other items to make sure they were

---

1. Automatic Direction Finder

secured. Especially since dynamite and blasting caps were both on the load. Joe had made sure that these two items were well separated from one another.

"O.K.," Dan spoke up, "only thing for us to do is make our walk-around inspection, check the fuel and run a weight and balance on the load."

"No use," Harry said.

"No use in what?" questioned Dan.

"Running a weight and balance. If Joe was in on the loading you can bet it is within the CG^2 limits."

"Nevertheless, I'm going to run it. I'm not going to bet my life on Joe's or anyone else's say-so."

Harry just grinned that silly grin of his. Dan went to the cockpit and pulled the CG procedures from the side pocket next to the co-pilot's seat and ran the weight and balance check. After about five minutes Dan reported.

"Joe was right. It's within the limits but with no room to spare."

Harry just grinned again.

Smart ass. Dan thought.

They made their final inspection of the DC-3 and had one of the Stevens line boys pulled it out of the hangar to the flight line with a tow.

Dan spoke up.

"Harry, you take the run going down and I'll bring it back."

"Suits me." Dan thought to himself, *I hate to admit it but he has a lot more experience in the "three" than me and going into a small field with this kind of load is going to take some real skill.*

They clambered on board and Harry dropped into the left seat and Dan took the right. Harry opened the cockpit window on his side where he could see the Stevens line boy standing there with a fire extinguisher.

"Clear!" Harry yelled and hit the starter for the No. 2 engine. The Pratt & Whitney belched out a cloud of blue-white smoke, backfired one time and then caught. The engine roared into life while Dan immediately checked to see if the RPM gauge and oil gauge were working.

The process was repeated for the left engine and the line boy pulled the two-wheeled cart holding the fire extinguisher out of the way and threw a half-hearted salute.

Dan called clearance delivery and requested clearance on the flight plan he had filed before leaving the flight office. Clearance came back,

---

2. Center of Gravity

"Douglas November niner one four zero Romeo is cleared to the Tumbler Ridge airport via the Yakutat VOR and Mackenzie ADF. Climb and maintain six thousand, expect further clearance to one three thousand. Fly runway heading, squawk one four zero three." Dan copied the clearance as it was given then repeated it back to clearance control.

"Four zero Romeo, read-back correct. Contact ground control on one one eight point six"

Dan set the transponder to 1403 and switched the frequency on the comm radio to 118.6 and called …

"Ground control, Douglas November niner one four zero Romeo at the Stevens ramp ready to taxi."

Ground control replied. "Roger, four zero Romeo, taxi to runway six, hold short and contact tower on one one eight point three when ready."

"Four zero Romeo," from Dan acknowledging ground control.

Harry moved the throttles forward and turned the DC-3 to the right and trundled down the taxiway to the hold-short line where they did the "run up" on the two Pratt & Whitneys, went through their pre-takeoff check list and Harry nodded to Dan.

Dan changed the comm radio to 118.3 and called …

"Anchorage tower, Douglas November niner one four zero Romeo, Runway two six ready to go."

"Rrrrroger, four zero Romeo, *you* are cleared for immediate take-off." Dan noted the time: 7:52 on the kneepad.

Harry again moved the throttles enough to move the aircraft onto the runway, turned the aircraft to the left, lined the nose up on the centerline then moved the levers forward as Dan placed his left hand behind Harry's and pushed forward as Harry moved the throttles and prop control levers forward. As the DC-3 gained speed while Dan called out the "V" numbers. The DC-3 broke ground and a minute later Harry called, "Gear up," Dan moved the gear lever to the "UP" position. They climbed up to fifteen hundred feet and Harry called, "flaps up" and Dan moved the flap lever to the "UP" position. Dan was constantly monitoring the VSI[3], oil pressure, manifold pressure, cylinder head temperatures, and fuel flow gauges while Harry flew the aircraft. Good cockpit management whether in a reciprocal engine aircraft or a jet has always been the best insurance against having an unannounced and possibly an uncontrollable emergency.

---

3. Vertical Speed Indicator

The tower called, "Douglas four zero Romeo contact departure control on one one eight point six." then ..., "You guys fly safe now, ya' hear?" Strictly against the rules but that would be Jim O'Brien at the mike, one of the tower controllers that both Harry and Dan knew. Dan acknowledged the message with two clicks on the microphone button. Dan changed the frequency to 118.6 and reported to departure control who vectored the DC-3 to the "on course" heading and then cleared them to their assigned altitude of thirteen thousand feet. They were on their way.

Conversation in a DC-3 was not the best under any conditions and Dan was grateful for the lack of need to converse. He and Harry had little or nothing in common except the love of flying. Conversation with the control centers was sparse as the country over which they were flying was off the beaten path, so to speak, for most commercial aircraft. The weather was good with high cirrus clouds and broken clouds at around eight thousand feet so it was a trip where routine monitoring of the gauges was required and otherwise, for Dan, the opportunity to look at the beautiful scenery as they traveled southeast across the Alaska Range and the Coast Mountains of British Columbia to Yakutat. The shimmering Pacific Ocean was always in view on the right and with visibility around fifty miles it was no problem enjoying the scenery of coastal Alaska and British Columbia as the first signs of dawn were spreading across the sea.

They crossed the Yakutat VOR having traveled 323 nautical miles from Anchorage with 665 miles to go. Harry changed course seven degrees to the left to track outbound on the Yakutat NDB radial of 083 degrees. After ten minutes he noticed the needle on the VOR had drifted to the right five degrees which meant there was a wind coming from the southwest which was causing the aircraft to drift to the left of course. It was very important to find the correct heading at this time since there would not be another navigation aid for 588 miles and that would be the Mackenzie NDB which does not provide the same navigational features as a VOR. Harry corrected to 088 degrees and after ten more minutes they were holding a steady centered needle "FROM" the VOR. If the wind did not change before they got to the Mackenzie ADF they would be traveling in a straight line. About 100 miles from the Yakutat VOR they would lose the signal and then they would be 'dead reckoning' for about 400 miles or so until they picked up the Mackenzie NDB signal.

After five and a half hours out of Anchorage they began the descent down to ten thousand feet. The highest peaks in their area were at eight thousand so they would have a two thousand foot cushion. The field at Tumbler Ridge was at five thousand eight hundred feet so they would only have to descend another forty-two hundred feet to be at the runway level. At the Mackenzie NDB they made their final heading correction to 077 degrees and had seventy-five miles to the Tumbler Ridge airport.

What neither Dan nor Harry were aware of was the fact that Tumbler Ridge was a relatively 'new' town. Coal mining started in British Columbia over a hundred years ago, which meant most of the cities in the area were old. Two mines, the Quinette and Bullmoose, were about 100 miles from Chetwynd which was the closest city of any size. This meant that the miners had a very long commute to work in either of these mines. Therefore, the coal companies who owned the mines, built Tumbler Ridge in the early 1980's primarily for their employees and their families. New homes were built along with schools, police and fire departments, grocery stores, and all of the infrastructure associated with a small town. All of the miners and their families moved to Tumbler Ridge and it soon had a population of about 5,000 people. Outside of a few people who had service jobs, the main income that supported this community came from the approximately four million Canadian tonnes of coal that came from these two mines annually.

Unfortunately, not a great deal of money was spent on developing an airport. It was an oil and gravel strip which called for constant maintenance as the severe Canadian winters caused the ground to freeze. Then when the thaws came, the ground would shift causing large pock-holes in the runway surface. Dan was the first to spot the field on the right side of the aircraft. Harry flew past the field and made a turn to his left then flew outbound on a heading of 370 degrees which would be the reciprocal of the heading they would take to land on Runway 19 which was being favored by the wind coming from the southwest. After flying that heading for three minutes, Harry made a turn back to the right and set the aircraft up for the approach, props full forward, mixtures rich, ten degrees of flaps and wheels down. He turned the aircraft to a heading of 190 degrees and both pilots began to look for the field. The aircraft was slightly left of the field so Harry made the correction to line up with the runway and reduced airspeed to 100 knots.

The wind was drifting them to the left so he corrected to keep the nose lined with the runway and continued the descent at 500 feet per minute. When assured of making the runway he raised the nose slightly to decrease the speed and also to put the aircraft in a 'tail low' position which is the perfect attitude to land a DC-3. Harry had to drop the right wing to keep the proper 'crab angle' to keep the aircraft tracking on line with the runway.

Dan noticed the airspeed was now at 95 knots … a little high but Harry wanted two things; one, to make sure they didn't stall with a heavy load on board and two, to maintain directional control with a wind of approximately 20 knots quartering from their right. In this profile, the aircraft would hit on the right main wheel so when they were about ten feet off the runway, Harry lifted the right wing and applied a little right rudder which planted both wheels on the oil and gravel runway. *I'll say one thing for the son-of-a-gun, he can damn well fly an airplane!*

Harry pulled the throttle back to the detent and touched the brakes to slow the aircraft. When the tail wheel touched he applied full pressure on the brakes to stop the heavily loaded aircraft. They still had about 500 feet of runway left after coming to a complete halt. Time: 2:22 p.m. The flight had taken six hours and 30 minutes for a groundspeed of 152 knots. Dan and Harry both were beat.

As they were taxiing back to the unloading area Harry said,

"This will be the last time that we will be using Tumbler Ridge this year. The snows will start soon and we will have to make any Bullmoose deliveries into a warehouse in Prince George. We can't possibly land the DC-3 on this runway since it doesn't have any runway identification markers so when it snows, it's impossible to see the runway."

"Then I suppose Bullmoose has to send their truck to Prince George to pick up their material, right?" Dan said.

"That's right, and it is a helluva' trip by road from Tumbler Ridge to Prince George."

The sound of the aircraft was all the notice that the Bullmoose crew needed to crank up the tractor trailer which had a Hyster on the rear and head for the airport. Dan had been wondering just how they were going to unload that heavy generator. When the crew arrived, the first thing they did was chock the wheels of the aircraft. Next, they unloaded a hydraulic jack and placed the jack under a 'hard point' just forward of the tail wheel. The DC-3 had three 'hard points.' These are reinforced points in the fuselage; one in front of the tail wheel and one on each wing just inboard of the engines. These are used to jack and level the aircraft for checking weight and balance. In this case, the crew raised only the tail to get the tail cone of the aircraft in as level a plane as possible. They then backed the tractor trailer up to the clam-shell doors and with the forklift they used ropes tied to the forklift to pull the generator on its skid towards the door. Very carefully they turned it slightly and began to drag it out onto the bed of the trailer which was a little lower than the floor of the aircraft but they had also brought railroad ties and used those for blocks to ease the skid onto.

The entire unloading process took just about two hours. At 3:32 p.m. local time, 2:32 Alaska Time, Dan and Harry had their load receipt and were ready for departure. There was no doubt in either Dan's or Harry's minds about laying over. Neither was up to another six hours in the cockpit. Dan pulled a chart out of his case and looking at the chart, Prince George, BC was about 100 miles to the southwest and the closest place to refuel and spend the night. So they departed and went to Prince George.

Unknown to Dan, Harry would meet someone there who would have a profound effect on both of their lives.

Chapter 34

▼

Prince George

Prince George had a first class airport for a town of approximately 80,000 people. Upon arrival, Dan gave the FBO there an order for fuel and tie-down for the night. After they were satisfied the DC-3 was secure for the night, they took a taxi to the Best Western motel, grabbed a meal at the Ponderosa restaurant and were in their rooms by 9:30 p.m. However, unknown to Dan, Harry had a visitor a short time thereafter.

Harry received a call from the phone in the lobby of the Best Western. "Hey, Harry, it's me, Kyle."

"Yeah, come on up to Room 215, Kyle."

A few moments later there was a knock at the door. Harry opened the door and Kyle Thornburgh was standing in the hallway. Kyle was a tall, slightly built man about six feet with reddish-blonde hair, a sallow complexion and hazel eyes. He appeared to be in his middle forties and was wearing blue jeans over cowboy boots as well as a red and white checkered shirt with a sleeveless dark blue vest covering the upper part of his body.

"C'mon in and have a seat." Harry invited. "Drink?" Harry pointed to a fifth of Jim Beam sitting on the dressing table.

"Thanks, I'll have a short one … just water and ice." Harry mixed the drink and handed it to Kyle as he sat down in the only easy chair in the room. Harry picked up his drink and sat on the bed.

"It was something of a surprise when you called the house and said that you were in town. What brings you here," asked Kyle.

"Another pilot and I delivered a load to the Bullmoose Mine up at Tumbler Ridge airport and we had to come on down here to get fuel and spend the night," Harry explained. "How are things going at Vanguard Air Freight?" Harry inquired.

"O.K. I'm supervisor on the day shift right now but I will be going to nights beginning next week. The other supervisor and I alternate every other month."

"What's going to happen if the shipment happens to come in and you are on the day shift?

"No problem, Harry. The other guy and I swap off occasionally if some kind of family trip comes up or if one of us wants to go see the Rangers play, or something like that."

"You got any idea when it is going to take place?" Harry asked.

"Not really, my contact said that it should be within the next thirty days. He said for us to be ready to put the plan into action whenever he called."

Harry got up, walked over to the Jim Beam and added a couple of ounces plus some ice cubes. "Who's the guy behind this thing, Kyle?" Harry inquired.

"I don't know and I don't want to know. I met him in a bar one night after I got off from work. I still had my coveralls on that had my name and the Vanguard logo on them. He struck up a conversation with me, and after a while he asked me if I wanted to make some fast dough and one thing just led to another from there. I am sure that he had staked me out beforehand. The guy looks kind of Arabic, Harry. He didn't give me his name, just said to call him 'Abe.' I suppose he picked that name because he looks a little like Abe Lincoln with that beard of his. Skin's a lot darker than Abe Lincoln, though."

"Well, I just can't figure out who would be spending this kind of money to steal a box." Harry said.

"The 'box,' as you call it, has some kind of nuclear material in it, Harry."

"Oh, crap! You didn't tell me it was going to be something like that!" Harry fidgeted with his glass and then took a drink.

"Look," Kyle continued, "the stuff is safe. We have had shipments of those containers coming through our place for almost a year and nobody has been hurt."

"Yeah, but stealing stuff like that … you realize that both of us are going to have to leave the country, don't you?" Harry objected.

"So? I don't have anything holding me here. I've put in twenty years of working and I still don't have a damn thing to show for it. Do you?"

"No, not really. I busted my chance with the airlines, so I guess I don't have anything left to keep me here." Harry now felt dejected as he took another sip from the glass.

Kyle got up from his chair. "Mind if I use the bathroom?"

"Naw ... go ahead." Harry took two of the pillows from under the bedspread and propped them up against the headboard and leaned back on them. Kyle came back into the room.

"O.K., tell me how this thing is going to work." Harry asked.

"It's really petty simple. You know who Crossair is, don't you?"

"Yeah, they're one of the largest commercial air freight outfits in the states."

"They're also the *only* air freight outfit in the USA that has a DOD[1] contract to carry nuclear material." Kyle added. "They have flights that originate in Boston then go to Montreal, Ottawa, Winnipeg, Saskatoon, Edmonton, Prince George, and Anchorage. "Course at times if they don't have any freight to deliver to all of those cities, or pick up, they just skip them. However, they always come into Prince George because all freight they have that is going into the western part of the U.S. is off-loaded for transfer to another Crossair flight that covers the west coast. That is where Vanguard comes in. We handle all of that west coast freight for them."

Kyle got out of his chair, walked to the table and added some Jim Beam to his glass. He sat back down, lit up a Camel and continued.

"Abe did tell me this much about the deal ... I guess he had a good reason and I think you ought to know too 'cause you're going to play an important role in this heist, Harry." Kyle took a deep draw off the cigarette and inhaled the smoke before continuing.

"The stuff we will be looking for is called Tritium. It's in a steel, lead-lined cylinder and then packed in a special styrofoam case which fits into another lead lined steel case. Supposedly there are three cylinders per case. Abe told me we couldn't miss it; the case would be painted yellow with a red danger marker on it with the words, "Danger—Nuclear Material." I know that he is telling the straight about that because I remember having seen those cases come through periodically. Everybody in the warehouse was afraid to touch them until one of the guards on the Crossair flight pulled out a Geiger counter and showed us that it wasn't dangerous. He said there was no way the stuff could leak out."

"What happened to those cases?" Harry asked.

---

1. Department of Defense

"Well, the very next day a Crossair flight from Los Angeles came in with a load and they picked the case up, along with other material, and took them back to the states. I was curious enough to want to know where they were headed so one time I just casually asked the pilot about where they were going and he said they would eventually end up at a US Government facility in Nevada."

"Wonder why the place in Nevada doesn't get the stuff from one of the nuclear plants in the US?" Harry asked.

"I'm not sure but it seems I recall having read somewhere that the nuclear plants in the states stopped production on Tritium some time ago. Something to do with a non-proliferation treaty or something like that. I can't be sure about that though." Kyle reported.

"Anyway, our stuff will be coming in from the Ontario-Darlington Nuclear facility. Abe did tell me that much."

Kyle stubbed out his Camel in the ashtray on the table, immediately reached in his shirt pocket, took out the packet of Camels, and lit up another one.

"Man, this stuff must really cost a bunch of bucks. I wonder what they use it for?" Harry asked.

"Well, I had the same thoughts, plus some others so you know what I did? I went to the local library and looked up this stuff. The article I read said that it is a radioactive hydrogen isotope and that it costs somewhere around 50,000 Canadian dollars *per gram!*"

Harry let out a long whistle.

"Not only that … grab your seat … the stuff is a necessary ingredient in the production of Trident missiles. How about that?"

"*Trident missiles?*" Harry repeated. "Hey, those missiles are launched from submarines! I didn't know that anybody except us and the Russkies had subs that could fire off missiles."

"They don't as far as I know" Kyle confirmed. "Maybe somebody is figurin' on building one."

"Did you find out anything else at the library about this stuff?" Harry asked.

"I found out for one thing, that India and China both have nuclear plants that are capable of producing Tritium."

"Well if they have it, then who do you think wants to buy this stuff from Abe and his cronies?"

"How about maybe North Korea," Kyle answered.

Harry let out another low whistle. If that's so, wonder why North Korea can't get the stuff from them?" Harry questioned.

"Yeah, good question," Kyle mused. They both sat a minute and just looked at one another. Then Kyle spoke,

"How about this. Maybe India and China don't trust the 'spooks.' You've been reading about what a nutcake the son of the president of North Korea is? Kim Jong something or other. The old man's health ain't so good and supposedly the son is fast becoming the power behind the throne. Would you want to give a guy like that something that he could make a missile with and have him blow your ass off with it?"

"Yeah ... I guess you've got a good point there." Harry paused a moment. "What comes next?"

"O.K., here's the plan. Somehow or another Abe got one of the empty cases which he put in a wood crate and shipped it to my house. I took that crate, painted it a navy gray and stenciled it with these words in black, 'Intermont Mining & Supply Co.—Machinery Parts.' I will have to smuggle it into our warehouse the night before the switch is to take place. I'll fake a bill of lading that says these parts have been returned from Bullmoose Mining for shipment to Intermont on the next Intermont aircraft that comes in.

"The only thing that can queer the deal is that the crate will have to be loaded on your aircraft during the night shift since there are only two employees on duty at night. If you arrive during the day we are going to have to figure out something that will delay you until I report for work

"What about the other guy on duty, Kyle. How will you get rid of him?" Harry inquired.

"I'll send him out to get dinner for us. I do that occasionally so he won't suspect anything by me suggesting this. I'll spring for the cost and send him to a seafood place that I know of that will take him at least an hour to get there and back. That should be plenty of time. Now, you've *got* to manage to have an Intermont aircraft in here the next day to pick up the crate."

"How in hell am I going to manage that?" Harry asked.

"Well, how about this. You give me the name of a piece of equipment that Bullmoose would have to have in order to operate. On the day the case of Tritium comes in I will call Intermont and place an order for that part and tell them it is an emergency and we need it the next day. Deliver it to Vanguard and we will pick it up in the mine's truck. You make damn sure that Intermont has that piece of equipment in stock. Oh, and you find out when you get back to your office who signs the purchase orders for Bullmoose and I will use his name. How does that sound."

"Damn! You think of just about everything, don't you?" Harry grinned.

"Hey, I have to. We can't afford to screw this one up, buddy boy."

"O.K., I've got the crate and I take it back to Anchorage, now what?" Harry asked.

"You get back late so there's no one around the hangar. Leave the crate on the aircraft and make sure it is locked. Then you call me at home that night, o.k.?" Kyle stated.

"O.K. Now where do I take it ... I guess it will be early the next morning?"

"Right. Only thing is, I can't tell you where right now because I don't know. But when you leave here with the crate I call Abe and tell him you have it, then he is going to give me the instructions on where you will deliver it to."

"Just one more thing, Kyle. What about our money?"

"The money will be in a numbered account in a bank in the Cayman Islands. When I call Abe for directions on where you are to go he gives me the number. If he doesn't give me the number then you don't go and neither do I. He also knows that if he tries to double cross us that I will 'rat' on him to the CIA. I don't know his name but I can give them enough information that will make it a lot easier to track him down."

"Well, what about me ... when do I get mine?"

"Don't worry, buddy boy, I will still need you. You are going to fly us out of the country in an Intermont plane. Just make sure when you leave Anchorage that your passport is in order. I'll give you a phone number where you can reach me after you make the delivery. We will join up and find a place where we can alter the name and "N" number on the aircraft then we will be off to the Caymans. We both have to present our passports to the banker in the Caymans together or he won't release the money. How's that for a guaranty? Once we get our half a million bucks we disappear ... for good."

*   *   *   *

Dan and Jess were skiing down one of the intermediate slopes at Talkeetna with Jess in the lead. Dan noticed that she was building speed, pulling away from him slightly as she began a slalom turn to the right. Suddenly her skis hit a patch of glaze ice and both of her skis went out from under her and she slid off the trail into a stand of trees. Dan tried to brake but he saw that he was going to overshoot where Jess had landed so he laid down on his right side. As soon as he came to a stop he hurriedly unbuckled his boots, got onto his feet and tried to run to where Jess was huddled grotesquely and she was not moving. He turned her body so that he could see her face. "Jess! Jess! Answer me!" he screamed but there was no movement. He pulled off his right glove and placed three fingers on her carotid artery on the right side of her neck … no pulse! Suddenly Dan looked up into the sky and screamed out, "Oh, *NO*, God! Not again! First it was Mary and now Jess. PLEASE, God, don't *do* this to me!"

Dan bolted upright in the dark room in the Best Western motel in Prince George. He touched his forehead with his left hand and wiped beads of perspiration from it. Looking at the luminous dial of the Breitling on his nightstand he saw that it was 5:30 in the morning and he was tempted to call Jess to see if she was o.k. He realized then that it was only 4:30 in Anchorage and this was silly to even think of such a thing. No doubt Jess was all right. With that thought in mind, he got up, took his shower, shaved, dressed, and went down into the lobby and picked up a copy of the local paper. He walked over to the small breakfast area where a female employee was just beginning to put out the fare for the morning continental breakfast. He grabbed a raisin muffin and a cup of coffee and sat down and read the paper.

Around seven o'clock, Harry showed up and they both finished off a moderate breakfast, went back to their respective rooms, got their luggage and checked out. The taxi they had called dropped them off at the FBO office at the Prince George airport. Dan paid the fuel bill while Harry checked out the DC-3 which he found to be ready to go. Dan and Harry were off the ground by 8:45 local time and took a slightly different route back to Anchorage with Dan in the left seat. The only freight they had going back was the Bullmoose generator that had given up the ghost and they were hauling it back where it would be shipped off later to be rebuilt. They encountered a 30 knot headwind on the way back home which caused them to spend an additional 45 minutes on the return flight so they arrived back at the Stevens hangar at 2:05 p.m. Anchorage time on a Friday afternoon.

As soon as they got out of the aircraft Dan told Harry to take care of getting the DC-3 hangared and to call Joe O'Donoghue at the warehouse about sending a crew up to get the old generator unloaded and take it back to the warehouse.

Chapter 35

Relationships

Arriving back at Stevens Air from Prince George, Dan immediately went into the Intermont flight office, picked up the phone and dialed Jess' extension number on the intercom line.

"Jessica Lane," she answered.

"Are you O.K?" Dan asked

"Of course. Is there something that should be wrong with me?" Dan could tell she was smiling by the sound of her voice.

"Aw, no, not really. I just had a bad dream last night and you were … uh … injured."

"So, now you are dreaming about me. Well that *is* interesting."

Now she is gonna' laugh at me.

"It's not funny, Jess." Dan said somberly.

"O.K., I'm sorry. What can I do to get you to forgive me?" she said coyly.

"Wel-l-l-l … since you put it that way, how about dinner tonight?"

"Do you like chili?"

"I *love* good chili … it's one of my favorites," Dan answered.

"Well, I make the best. Why don't you drop by about seven and I will have some chili for you that will toast your buns."

Dan laughed, "O.K., sounds swell to me. See you then."

"G, bye-ee." and she hung up.

Dan put his hands behind his head, propped his feet up on the desk and leaned back in the swivel chair. *Damn! Why don't you admit it Danny boy ... you are hooked ... but good!*

To say that Dan had been burning the candle at both ends lately was an understatement. But, in spite of all of his accomplishments he had also managed to find enough time to sneak over to the local Harley Davidson dealer where he found out that it was possible to rent a Harley. So, he had the dealer check him out in riding one of the newer models. The arrangement of having the gearshift operated by the toe of a boot instead of the old fashioned handle mounted on the side of the gas tank was something that took a little effort, but he accomplished it. After about three trips, the dealer was satisfied that he could handle the bike and welcomed him to become a rental customer and hopefully a future buyer. Dan had done this with plans to give Jess a surprise with a Harley ride just as she had done to him.

Dan picked up the phone again and called the local Harley Davidson dealer.

"Chugach Harley Davidson," the male voice said

"Is Sam there?"

"Yeah, hold on."

"This is Sam, what can I do for you?"

"Sam this is Dan Nichols."

"Yeah, Dan, how ya' doin'?"

"O.K., Sam. Would you have a couple of bikes available for tomorrow?"

"Hold on a sec ..." Dan could hear the phone being laid down.

"Yeah, Dan, I can handle it. What time?"

"How's nine o'clock sound?"

"Great ... I'll have 'em for ya."

"See ya, Sam."

*   *   *   *

Dan punched the Jess's doorbell at seven twenty-five.

The door opened and Jess smiled that tremendous smile of hers and simply said, "Hi." She had her hair up, held by a clasp. This was the second time that Dan had seen her neck exposed. For some unexplainable reason it had made his heartbeat increase on both occasions. She had on two dangling silver circular earrings that appeared to be about an inch in circumference. Around her neck was a serpentine silver necklace which held a sterling silver locket. Jess was wearing a long sleeve white silk blouse cut deep enough to expose some cleavage and had on a pair of tailored black slacks with a black belt and a silver belt buckle. She also had on a pair of black leather pumps. Dan took in a deep breath and recognized the sensuous perfume. He was ready to throw in the towel right then.

"Well, are you going to come in or are you going to stand out there and stare?" She still had that voluptuous smile on her carefully made up face.

"God, Jess, ... you are just *gorgeous!*"

Jess felt the blood rush to her face. "Well, thank you, kind sir" and she raised up on her toes and brushed her red lips briefly against his. It was all Dan could do to keep from putting his arms around her and crush her to his body.

Instead he said, "Here ... these are for you." He had stopped by the florist and picked up a small bouquet of fresh flowers.

"Oh! Dan they are just *lovely!* Let me go get a vase and put them in it before they begin to wilt."

Dan stepped inside and shut the door while Jess went off in search of the vase.

From the other room she yelled, "Take you coat off and just put it anywhere."

Dan had worn a pair of grey casual slacks and his black leather flight jacket; a white dress shirt but no tie. He took off the jacket and laid it on the back of a lounge chair.

"How about a drink?" Jess called from the kitchen. "You want your vodka?"

"That'll be fine and I'll take an olive or two if you have them."

She brought a tray out of the kitchen with the vodka on it plus a Gibson. There were also some wheat crackers and Swiss cheese. She sat the tray on the coffee table in front of the couch.

"Be careful, or you'll get addicted to those things," Dan nodded towards the Gibson.

Straightening up from placing the tray on the table, Jess said, "There are worse things you can get addicted to," and she winked and smiled at Dan as she walked across the room to the stereo. Jess flicked a switch and the CD changer placed a CD in the player and the music of Glenn Miller's band playing "Moonlight Seranade" began to play softly.

"You really do like the guy, don"t you?" Dan said.

"I told you he wasn't dead, didn't I?" she grinned and walked back towards the sofa and sat down next to Dan. She reached over to the tray, handed him his vodka and she took the Gibson.

"Cheers," she clinked her raised glass to his.

"To us," Dan remarked.

"I'll drink to that," and Jess looked over the rim of her glass with those soul searching brown eyes. "So, how was your trip?"

"A real butt-buster. Over six hours down and a little over seven coming back. I'll say one thing for Abelson," Dan picked an olive out of the glass with a toothpick, "he's a really great pilot."

"He's a really great *jerk*!" Jess replied as the smile disappeared from her face.

"Hey, what's the guy ever done to you?"

"Nothing, except he has a big mouth and he's always shooting it off to everyone in the company. I don't know why Harry keeps him on. Sometimes I think he has something on Harry."

"Now why would you think a thing like that?" Dan queried.

"Oh, I don't know, Dan," and she looked straight ahead pensively, "I guess it is just my imagination but it's mostly Harry's belligerent attitude and lackadaisical approach towards his job that upsets me the most. Can I sweeten your drink?"

"Just a little ... here I will go with you."

They both got up from the sofa and walked into the kitchen where Jess had a small serving table on wheels with a cabinet underneath. She opened the doors and Dan saw a bottle of Popov vodka, a fifth of Jack Daniels, a bottle of J&B Scotch and a few liquers.

"That's a nice little stock you have there," Dan said.

Jess reached down, picked up the Popov and poured an ounce and a half in a jigger and added it to Dan's drink and then put one ounce in hers.

"Well, I do have social obligations to take care of, you know," and she raised her glass to take a sip.

"Oh, really? I suppose you have men friends coming in here all the time, huh?"

"There's usually a line of four or five waiting to get in every evening when I get home," Jess countered.

"They won't when I show up with my Colt 38."

"Well, I do 'declah, suh,' I believe you are slightly jealous," Jess replied in her best southern belle voice.

"No scalawag is goin' tuh' mess aroun' with mah' woman!" Dan replied in his plantation planter voice and they both broke out in laughter.

"Finish that drink Master Nichols and I'll feed you."

"I thought you never would ask."

Dan sat at the breakfast table and Jess filled two large bowls from a pot of chili that had been warming on the stove. She sat the bowls on the table and then went to the refrigerator and pulled out two large Italian salads with feta cheese, anchovies, onion and lettuce with a great Italian dressing. She also had a large loaf of warm, sliced Grecian bread in the oven which she placed on a tray and sat that on the table as well. Then she produced a stick of butter for the bread. They both sat and started on the meal.

"Well, you have convinced me," Dan said

"Convinced you of what?" asked Jess.

"That you are one of the best chili makers of all times."

Jess smiled approvingly of his comment and they both continued to eat and chat until the chili and salad were gone. When they were finished with the meal, Jess got up, removed the bowls from the table and placed them in the dishwasher.

"Let's go back to the living room, shall we?" Jess offered.

"That's fine with me. I just hope I don't go to sleep on that comfortable sofa; I still haven't caught up from that trip."

"You go to sleep and I'll bite you on your ear," replied Jess.

"Hey, that sounds interesting!" responded Dan.

"Always the wise guy!" and Jess took a playful swat at Dan.

When they got back into the living room the CD was playing a Tommy Dorsey tune, 'You Made Me Love You."

"Where in heck did you get all those Big Band CD's, Jess?"

"Well to be honest, I filched them from my Dad."

"But those are songs from the late thirties and forties," Dan said.

"I know. But from what I have read about that time it was like no other and all those songs seemed to be about real relationships and real honest people who when they said, 'I do' they meant it."

"And you are interested in *real* relationships?" Dan asked.

Jess looked at Dan and without smiling said, "If I am going to have another one I am."

"So am I, Jess."

They sat and looked at each other for about thirty seconds then Jess leaned towards Dan on the sofa and he brought his face to hers and they kissed. Not a long, passionate kiss but more of a gentle one which reflected the way that they felt at that moment.

Dan looked at his watch and said, "Man, time flies when you are having fun. I think I had better go before I get my ear bitten off," and he grinned at Jess.

"O.K, chicken. Go ahead and get out of here before I am tempted."

Dan got up, picked up his jacket from the chair and Jess took it and held it for him while he slipped his arms into the sleeves. Dan walked towards the door, took hold of the latch, then turned and said, "You got any plans for tomorrow?"

"Oh not anything that can't wait. What have you got in mind?"

"A surprise."

"Uh, oh. What kind of surprise?"

"Well, I went along with yours once and I wasn't disappointed. Are you willing to take a chance on mine?"

"Oh, all right. What time?"

"I'll pick you up around eight-thirty and, by the way, wear the same outfit that you wore when we went on the picnic."

"Where are we going?"

"If I tell you then it won't be a surprise."

"Oh, darn you, Dan Nichols. O.K., I'll be ready."

Chapter 36

Wasilla

The Jeep Cherokee rolled up in front of Jess' apartment at eighty-thirty five and Dan walked to the door and rang the doorbell. He heard Jess' boots on the hardwood floor in the hall then the door opened. "Right on time, aren't you?" She was wearing her leather jacket, blue jeans and boots that she had on when she had picked him up in front of the Marriott Courtyard for their motorcycle ride.

"Are you in too big a hurry for a cup of coffee?"

"Heck no ... you know me better than that," Dan moved inside the room as she closed the front door and the two of them walked into the kitchen. Jess removed two styrofoam cups from the cupboard and poured two cups ... black.

"I don't want to hold you up. I can see that you are so 'antsy' that you want to get going. I guess we can drink and drive without getting arrested, can't we?"

Dan smiled. "I can see that you are in good form this morning." Jess bumped Dan's thigh with her left hip,

"I'm *always* in good form."

Dan sighed, "You can say that again," and continued his smile.

Jess picked up her cup, "O.K. we're outa' here."

As they wended their way through the streets of Anchorage for about ten minutes, Jess said,

"Are you headed where I think you are headed?"

"Yep, I guess I am," replied Dan.

"So you want me to chauffeur you around on the bike again, is that your surprise?"

"Nope."

Jess thought for a moment and then, "Oh, *NO!* Don't tell me that you are going solo?"

"Yep," and Dan cracked a big grin.

"Uh, uh! I'm not going to be a party to your smearing yourself all over the highway!" she said with feigned concern.

Dan replied in his southern drawl again, "Now, don't you fret yoah' self none little lady, ah'm gonna show you how us boys frum the south can ride one of them motah-cycles."

Jess giggled, "Yeah, I'll *bet* you are."

They pulled into the Harley Davidson parking lot, left the Jeep and entered the showroom. Sam was talking to a biker near the customer desk. He saw Dan and Jess, excused himself and walked towards them.

"Hey, buddy. Little bit late aint'cha?"

"Sorry about that, Sam," Dan replied. "I got held up."

"Yeah, I can see that," and he looked at Jess approvingly.

"Jess, this is Sam Waterson and Sam this is Jessica Lane."

"Hi, Jess. Haven't I seen you here before?"

"Yes, I guess you have. I have been on some rides with a group that does business with you."

"Would Sue and Frank Edwards be two of them?" Sam asked.

"You got it. Sue is my best friend and Frank is her husband. Sue lets me ride her bike and she doubles with Frank when we are on a ride together."

Ah-ha! Sue is the culprit instead of Sean Connery! Dan was relieved.

"Yeah, now I got you pegged," Sam smiled. "Well come on ... I've got your bikes outside."

They went out the side door and there sat two Dyna Super Glides, just like the one that Jess had used for their first ride together. These two bikes were identical except for the color; one was red and the other was black. Jess spoke up,

"I'll take the red one."

Dan said, "That figures ... the color matches her temperament."

Jess made a face at him and stuck her tongue out slightly between her lips.

"O.K., you two. You know the rules. Insurance goes with the rental fee but I don't want my bikes banged up. You can kill yourselves but just don't scratch the bikes," and he grinned at both of them.

Jess spoke up, "Hey, we've got to have helmets," so they both marched back into the shop and had Sam get two rental helmets off the rack for them.

As they walked back to the bikes, Jess said,

"Now, Mr. Smarty Pants, where are we going?"

"Well, this is where you come in. I have to be honest and say that I don't think that on my first ride I should think about going more than about fifty miles out, what do you think?"

"I think you are finally getting some sense in that thick skull of yours," and she smiled as she fastened the chin strap of her helmet. They both then mounted the bikes.

"I'll tell you what," Jess spoke. "There's a little place north of here called Wasilla and it's just about fifty miles. It's a nice ride with some beautiful scenery along the way. As I recall there is an overlook about halfway and we can stop there and give you a rest."

"Oh, right. We will stop and give *me* a rest!"

"O.K., Hercules, let's see how it goes," and with that Jess hit the electric starter switch and the Harley rumbled to life. Dan did the same and Jess sat and looked at him questioningly. Dan raised his hand and made a motion with his index finger for her to take the lead so Jess eased the Harley out of the parking lot with Dan bringing up the rear.

Early Saturday mornings usually didn't find too many vehicles on the streets of Anchorage and Dan was certainly grateful for that. He followed Jess in line for several blocks until they got a red light. He then pulled up alongside and when the light turned green he rode off beside Jess and they rode side by side. As they went along together, Dan became more and more confident and was pleased with himself that he could match Jess' speed and anticipate her movements. Whenever they were to make a turn she let Dan know in advance with hand motions.

Before too long they had picked up Glenn Highway which turned into Alaska Highway No. 1. Dan remembered stretches of the road as this being the same route they had taken to the Chugach State Park. Jess maintained a steady speed of about 50 miles per hour, adjusting occasionally for cars ahead or those coming up behind as well. She didn't want Dan to notice but she was keeping watch through her peripheral vision as to his position. The road was now beginning to curve more and also they were gaining altitude as they rode along. True to her estimate, after they had been riding for almost a half hour they were nearing the overlook and Jess motioned to Dan they were going to make a move to the right. They pulled off, stopped, cut the engines and put down their kick-stands. The quiet was deafening. There were two cars in the parking area, one had Alaska plates and the other was from Oregon. One couple and a family of four were the only people enjoying the view.

Dan got off and walked stiff legged to where Jess was standing beside her bike. She leaned back against the bike seat and tried very hard not to, but she started laughing and put her hand up to her mouth. Dan came up and leaned on the bike right next to her and pushed against her with his left shoulder and whispered,

"Shut up!" She laughed even harder.

"O.K., o.k., so I'm not Hercules!" and he started laughing too. The couple who obviously were from Alaska turned, looked at them and started smiling at them. Jess tried to get control of herself but she kept erupting into giggles. Finally, Dan left the bike and walked over to the edge of the overlook and took in the view of the mountains in the distance with some of the clouds actually below the peaks. One thing for sure, Alaska had some of the most beautiful scenery he had ever seen in his life.

Jess came up beside him and slipped her left arm through his right one. She then reached over with her right hand and placed it on his arm as well and leaned against Dan. She said,

"This alone is worth the trip, isn't it?"

Dan took his left hand and reached across his body and put it on hers. "Yeah," he said softly, "and your being here makes it just that much better." He looked down at her as she turned her face to him and she squeezed his arm as hard as she could.

They sat close to one another on a large rock near the edge of the overlook for about 30 minutes. Near the end of the time a large hawk came swooping over, caught a thermal and effortlessly soared upwards for what looked like two or three hundred feet. Dan followed the hawk with his eyes and said,

"That's me in my afterlife."

"You really love to fly, don't you?" Jess commented as she looked at his face.

"I *do* love it, Jess. It's really hard to describe the feeling you have to anyone who has not piloted a plane. Although we have mechanical wings and not natural ones like that hawk, we still have the ability to soar and wheel in the sky just like they do. I guess it gives me a greater sense of freedom than anything else that I have ever experienced in my life. It's also spiritual too."

"What do you mean by that?" Jess questioned.

"Well, the best way I can answer that is … have you ever read the poem '*High Flight*' by John Gillespie Magee?"

"No."

"Well, it's too long and my memory is too bad but it starts off something like this, 'Oh, I have slipped the surly bonds of earth and danced the skies on laughter-silvered wings.' Then it goes on and it ends like this ... and this is what I mean by being the spiritual part ... he says, 'I've put out my hand and touched the face of God.'"

Dan paused for a second as he looked into Jess's brown eyes. "I've had that feeling on a couple of occasions. When you are way up there and there's no one else but you, you kind of get that feeling."

They were both quiet for just a couple of minutes and then Jess said,

"Who was he, Dan?"

"He was a 19 year old American kid, Jess, who just couldn't wait on World War II. He joined the RCAF[1], trained in Canada and went to England and was assigned to a Spitfire squadron."

"Did he become a famous fighter pilot?"

"No, he was killed in England when his Spitfire ran into a squadron mate of his. I think that happened in December of 1941 just a few days after the United States entered the war."

Jess squeezed Dan's arm, "So he didn't have a chance to be a hero."

"No, but practically every pilot over the age of fifty knows who John Gillespie Magee was."

*   *   *   *

Jess and Dan arrived in Wasilla around eleven o'clock and poked in and out of some of the shops on the main street of town. They still were not very hungry so they looked into going to the Transportation & Industry Museum of Alaska but decided not to since it was mostly a collection of old aircraft, cars, trucks, and railroad rolling stock. Dan said that he had seen enough antique aircraft for awhile, especially after pushing the DC-3 around the sky. So shortly after noon they rode their bikes to the Best Western Inn which was located on Lake Lucille and enjoyed a nice lunch while taking in a view of the mountain lake. After they finished, they went down to the dock and asked the elderly attendant there if they could rent one of the rowboats. He asked if they were guests of the lodge and they said 'no,' but they had lunch there. Love seems to transcend generations so the old fellow winked at them and said, "Let's just say that you are guests of the lodge, o.k.?" and he smiled at the two of them.

---

1. Royal Canadian Air Force

They got into the rowboat with Jess sitting in the stern and Dan in the middle manning the oars. They rowed slowly out into the lake. Like so many young ladies before her, Jess lowered her arm over the side and trailed a finger in the water, creating a very small wake.

"It's really lovely out here, isn't it?" Jess said.

"I think peaceful would be my description of it. The world is a far off place when you get a chance to do something like this." Dan answered.

"Just think … years ago people used to do this real often and then they would go down to the town square as evening came on and listen to the local band play in the town gazebo."

Dan replied, "Man, you are really getting melancholy now,"

"Do you ever wish sometimes that you had lived in that time, Dan? Life was so simple then. Neighborhood crime was almost unheard of and although most people weren't wealthy they seemed to have a better quality of life then than they do now. Their children used to go out into the neighborhoods and play and not come home until almost dark and their parents never had to worry about them."

"Yeah, I know," Dan mused. "I guess the world really made a bigger change than most realize when World War II came along. Everything seemed to start going to hell in a hurry after the fifties. But we still have a great opportunity, Jess."

"What do you mean by that?"

"Well, look at this place. Peace … tranquility … I'll bet the crime rate in Wasilla is practically nil. No wonder a lot of people call Alaska the 'last frontier.'"

Dan looked at his watch and was surprised to see that it was nearly three o'clock. The days were getting shorter now that it was late in September and the evenings were getting cooler earlier as well. Dan picked up the oars and rowed back to the dock.

The two of them cranked the Harley's a little after three o'clock and were back at the Harley Davidson shop in Anchorage about four. Dan settled the bill with Sam and he kidded them wanting to know how many scratches they had put on their bikes and then he told them to come back again soon.

Back in the Jeep, Jess said, "How about a pizza."

"Great. Sounds like a winner to me. Want to stop at the Pizza Hut and go in?"

"Why don't we just pick one up and go to my place?" Jess suggested.

They went through the drive-thru at the Pizza Hut, got a large supreme and headed for Jess' apartment. After entering the apartment, Jess put the pizza in the oven and turned it to 'warm.' Then she fixed two drinks and went into the living room where Dan already had his shoes off and had propped his feet up on the coffee table.

"Here you go," Jess said as she sat down beside him.

"Thanks, m'lady"

"You're welcome, m'lord."

They both looked at each other, grinned and clinked their glasses together.

Dan asked, "What's the toast this time?"

"Ohhh, let's just say … to us and peace and solitude."

"Just don't rock the boat, right?"

"Right." They sat and sipped their drinks together. Finally, Jess got up, told Dan to sit right there and went to the kitchen. She got two large plates and put them on serving trays then sliced the pizza, put it on the plates and took them back to the living room.

"Now, *that* is what I call service!" Dan remarked.

Jess walked over to the stereo, turned on the CD and then walked back to the sofa, sat down and they enjoyed the pizza and listened to Jess' collection of 'golden oldies.'

Just as they had finished the pizza, the CD changer dropped in a new disc and Frank Sinatra came on singing "Summer Wind." Jess got up and said,

"This is one of my favorites and it's a really great dance tune." She walked around the coffee table and held her hands out to Dan. He got up and put his right hand around her waist and took Jess' right hand in his left. They began to move about the carpet in their stocking feet.

Old 'blue eyes' kept singing …

The summer wind came blowing in from across the sea,
It lingered there to touch your hair and walk with me,
All summer long we sang a song and we strolled the golden sand,
Two sweethearts and the summer wind.

Jess had her head on Dan's shoulder and the top of her head was just even with his chin. He felt her lithe body moving slowly to the music and the 'Hypnotic Poison' by Dior was working its' way with him. Frank continued singing …

Like painted kites, those days and nights, they went by and by,
The world was new, beneath the blue, umbrella sky,

Then softer than a piper man one day it called to you,
I lost you to the summer wind.

Jess tightened her arm around Dan's neck. They were hardly dancing now, swaying with the music would be a better description of their movements.

The autumn wind and the winter wind, they have come and gone,
And still the days, those lonely days, go on and on
And guess who sighs his lullaby through winter nights that never end,
My fickle friend, the summer wind.

'Summer Wind' ended and Frank immediately went into the next song,

Can you find a little place in your heart for me ...

When Jess heard these words she clutched Dan's shirt with her left hand as if she was holding on for dear life and said,
"You think you can do that for me?"
"Do what for you?" Dan asked.
"Find a little place in your heart for me?" She looked up at him and he saw her brown eyes were brimming with tears."
Dan answered softly, "You're already there, Jess."
Jess put her head back on Dan's shoulder and they danced on for a few minutes then she said, "Dan?"
"Hmmm?" Dan murmured.
"I don't want to be alone tonight."

Chapter 37

Mickey Mouse

Dan awoke and it was still dark outside. The bedroom was lit by the light coming into the bedroom from the light in the hallway. He could smell coffee brewing in the coffee pot in Jess's kitchen and he lay there in his boxer shorts on top of the covers thinking back to the night before.

Then he heard Jess speak, "You planning on staying in that bed all day?" He raised his head and could see Jess standing in the doorway of the bedroom, silhouetted by the light behind her. She had her right arm raised with her hand on the doorpost on the right and was leaning against the left hand side of the doorpost with one foot crossed over the other. She was wearing a sleeveless cotton nightshirt that barely came down to her knees and the front of the shirt was practically covered with a huge caricature of Mickey Mouse. Dan broke out laughing.

"What's so funny? Jess asked.

"Who's your friend?" Dan questioned.

"So I'm a Mouseketeer ... is that so strange?" she grinned.

"Strange, no ... odd ... hmmmm, could be." and he continued to laugh.

"Odd? ... *Odd?..!!*" and she started running towards the bed and sprang with the agility of a cat on top of Dan, straddling him with one leg on one side of his body and the other leg on the other side. She caught him off guard and began to tickle his ribs.

"Oh ... damn!" Dan yelled. "Don't *do* that, I'm ticklish as hell!"

"Oh, you are, are you," and Jess was laughing too.

Dan struggled trying to unseat Jess but she hung on like riding a bucking bronco and all the time kept trying to tickle him. They were both in spasms of laughter with Jess yelling,

"Say it and I'll stop!"

Dan yelled at the top of his voice, "*UNCLE!*"

"*Wrong word!*" Jess replied and she kept trying to tickle him.

Wrong word? She wants me to say something besides 'Uncle.'…??

Although he was laughing hysterically and almost out of breath, Dan shouted "*I LOVE YOU!*"

Jess immediately stopped the tickling and still straddling Dan she panted, "Say it again!"

Dan looked her straight in the eyes and said in a softer tone, "I said, I *love* you."

Jess suddenly became serious, "Do you *really* mean that, Dan?"

"Yes, Jess, you *know* that I mean it." Dan said emotionally.

Still sitting erect, Jess crossed her arms in front of her, took hold of the hem of her nightshirt with both hands and pulled the shirt off, tossing Mickey Mouse on the floor. She then leaned forward and kissed Dan longingly as they embraced.

Chapter 38

The Hunt is On

"Conn, sonar."

"Conn, aye." Commander Julius R. Loudon, captain of the USS *Columbus* (SSN 717) took the call.

"Captain, a *Romeo* class is coming out of Wonsan, bearing two eight nine degrees.

"Very well."

Five minutes later.

"Conn, sonar."

"Conn, aye."

Sir, the *Romeo* is now bearing three four six degrees.

The captain thought, *Huh, that's a little unusual. He has turned north instead of south as they usually do.*

"Fire Control, Conn."

"Fire Control, aye."

"This is the Captain. Report the course and speed on the *Romeo* off our port bow."

"Aye, aye, sir."

"Fire Control, Captain"

"Captain, aye."

"Sir the *Romeo* is tracking zero eight zero, turning ten knots."

"Captain, aye."

Captain Loudon turned to his Executive Office, Lt. Commander Frank MacKenzie who was nearby. "Mac, I'm going below. Have the Sonar and Fire Control continue to track that *Romeo* for awhile and let's see if he continues on that northeast heading."

"Aye, aye, Captain," Lt. Commander MacKenzie replied.

The USS *Columbus* was a *Los Angeles* class attack submarine which had many capabilities including wartime functions of undersea warfare, surface warfare, strike warfare, mining operations, special forces delivery, reconnaissance, carrier battle group support and escort as well as intelligence collection. Her missiles could hit on target 75 percent of the Earth's land surface. The *Columbus* could remain on station for extended periods without having to return to port for servicing. The *Columbus* had a sophisticated ADCAP[1], carried Mark 48 anti-submarine torpedoes, Tomahawk cruise missiles and improved hull design for under ice operations. She was 362 feet long, 33 feet wide, beam of 42 feet, had a maximum depth of 800 feet and could reach a top speed in excess of 25 knots. She was powered by a S6G nuclear reactor and had a complement of 14 officers and 127 enlisted men. Her present captain, Commander Julius Loudon, Annapolis class of '76, had served on two previous submarines. The one prior to the *Columbus*, being the USS *San Francisco* where he had been the Executive Officer and was now one of the rising stars in the US Navy Submarine Fleet.

"Conn, Fire control."

"Conn, aye."

"Sir, the *Romeo* has taken up a heading of zero four five degrees, range 28 miles, speed 15 knots."

"Very well. Helmsman steer zero three five degrees, all ahead one-third."

The helmsman turned his wheel to the left.

"Aye, aye, Captain. Zero three five degrees, ahead one third."

Commander Loudon walked over to the plotting table where the Executive Officer, Lieutenant Franklin L. MacKenzie was standing looking at the charts. Captain Loudon spoke,

"Let's track the *Romeo* for awhile, Mac. A little unusual he would take up that heading coming out of Wonsan. I'm going to my quarters ... call me if you notice anything suspicious."

"Aye, aye, Captain," Frank MacKenzie responded.

---

1. Advanced Capabilities Program for Mark 48 Torpedoes

Franklin MacKenzie had been the XO on the *Alaska* for a little less than two years before transferring to the *Columbus*. He had come into the Navy through the Naval ROTC program at Vanderbilt University where he had graduated summa cum laude in the class of June '84. Lt. MacKenzie had the utmost respect for Commander Loudon and expected to learn a great deal from him while under his command.

The USS *Columbus* continued to track the North Korean submarine as it continued steadily on its northeast heading into the Sea of Japan.

Chapter 39

Cost Cutting

A lot had transpired in the past forty-five days and Dan reflected on the relationship that had developed between Jess and himself. There was no question in his mind that they loved one another but they had had no discussion about what they were going to do after they were married. *Married?* The subject had not even been brought up but he knew that his Christian principles would not allow him to become involved in a "live-in" arrangement so marriage would certainly be addressed sometime in the immediate future.

Monday morning Dan opened the flight office and noticed some orders had been faxed in. There was one for a small mine outside of Galena. They had lost a hydraulic pump and needed a replacement right away. The second order was a sizeable one that would go to an air cargo forwarding warehouse in Saskatoon, Saskatchewan. The shipment would then be forwarded on to Cameco Mining's uranium operation in Key Lake and Rabbit Lake uranium mines in northern Saskatchewan. Dan made a note to look into the profitability of this shipment. Saskatchewan was a long, long trip and the sale would have to be a very profitable one in order to make a legitimate profit.

The idea of an air cargo forwarding warehouse brought forth an interesting thought, however. When he and Harry had spent the night at Prince George, Dan remembered having seen an air freight building at the Prince George airport. Dan dialed Virginia Stewart's desk and asked her if she thought she could get the phone number for the airport manager's office in Prince George. She said she would try and in ten minutes she called back with the number.

Dan called the airport manager at Prince George, told him who he was and asked if he could give him the name of the air freight firm on the airport as well as their phone number. The manager told Dan the name of the company was Vanguard Air Freight and he also gave Dan the phone number. Dan dialed the Vanguard number and asked for the manager. When Charlie Thompson, the manager, came on the line Dan identified himself as being the chief pilot for Intermont Mining Supply in Anchorage and discussed with Thompson an idea he had. When Dan had finished, Thompson informed him that he thought they could handle the proposition if Dan could present him with a detailed plan so that Vanguard could quote a price for the service. Dan thanked Thompson and assured him he would be back in touch later.

Dan spent the next hour and a half getting some facts and figures together from accounting about purchases that had been made by three mines in British Columbia for the past twelve months. He had them FAX these documents to him at the flight office. Dan grouped the invoices by account, did some analysis including totals of purchases for all three of the mines. Dan then dialed Fred Robinson's extension and asked if Fred could give him about thirty minutes to discuss a plan he had for saving money for their airfreight operation. Fred said to come on over to his office. Dan was there in twenty minutes and began to lay the program out for Fred. Fred stopped him after the first ten minutes and said, "We need to get Al in on this," so he called Al and was told he was in a meeting but to come on up to his office in half an hour.

Dan and Fred were there thirty minutes later and Virginia Stewart said to "go right in, Mr. Switzer is ready for you." Fred went in first and Dan followed.

"Dan, how are you my'boy." Al rose from his chair, placed his cigar in the silver ashtray and shook Dan's hand vigorously.

"Fred says you have a plan that will save us some money. That is always music to my ears ... let's hear about it."

"Well, here it is in a nutshell. I looked over our list of clients in British Columbia and I found three mines we have been servicing that are all within a hundred miles of the Prince George airport in British Columbia. Now, Prince George is a first class facility; it's an all weather airport with an ILS[1] which will permit us to land there under all but the most severe weather conditions. I asked the accounting office to FAX me copies of all the invoices from these three mines

---

1. Instrument Landing System

for the past year, namely Bullmoose, Quintette, and Clear River. As you can see from this spread sheet," Dan pulled two copies out of his brief and gave one each to Dan and Fred, "it's a sizeable piece of change.

"What is interesting about these purchases is that about seventy-five percent of the items are repeat products, such as casings, cables, pumps, wiring, underground lamps, dynamite, etc., and only occasionally do we have a very large piece of equipment to be delivered such as the big generator which Bullmoose just ordered. Now I have talked with the manager of the Vanguard Air Freight Service at the Prince George airport and discussed with him the possibility of being a freight forwarder for us. He said that it was entirely feasible and if we would present our plan that he would give us a cost figure for the service.

"However, the key to this is to present this to the management of the three mines and tell them that if they will make up an order every month for the items they need and we can consolidate these orders and deliver them all at one time that we possibly could reduce their freight costs by as much as twenty-five percent. Of course they would have to truck their respective shipments from the airport to their mines but that shouldn't be a deterrent to the program; they have to do some trucking as it is. Even so, over a year's period of time it would be a sizeable cost reduction for them and a very nice improvement in profits for us."

All three of them were seated around Al's desk looking at the papers that Dan had presented. Then Al looked at Fred and they both had looks on their faces like "why didn't we think of this ourselves?" After pouring over the details and agreeing that the plan had merit, Al placed calls to the plant managers of the three mines and briefly described what he had in mind. He received a good reception of all three and all three managers agreed to meet with Al, Fred and Dan on Tuesday of the following week at the airport manager's office in Prince George at eleven o'clock in the morning. When they left Al's office, Fred said that he would run some cost figures and then contact Vanguard to see what they would charge for the warehousing fee.

After the meeting broke up, Dan hustled back to the flight office and by that time Tim and Harry had arrived and were in the hangar doing some cleaning on the aircraft and checking the oil, tire pressures, etc. Dan asked if they had seen the FAX'es in the office for the run to Galena and Saskatoon. They both verified they had seen them. Right away Harry spoke up,

"Hey boss, if you don't mind I would like to make that Saskatoon run with Tim. He needs all the twin engine time he can get and I think he could use some more multi-engine instruction from a first class pro." Harry was actually smiling, Dan noticed.

Boss? That's the first time he ever called me that. He must be after something.

"That's fine with me, Harry. I need the time in the Otter and would like to see what's going on in the Galena area for myself."

What I really want to do is get away for a day. Get up in the air where I can think about some things and sort through all that has been going on the past few months and figure out where I am headed ... if I can.

Chapter 40

Time for Thought

Days were definitely much shorter now as the third week in October had arrived. Tuesday morning Dan was on his way to the airport in the dark and arrived at the Stevens hangar at 7:20 a.m. Parking the car he proceeded to the flight office and found it empty. Taking a quick look into the hangar revealed that the DC-3 had departed. Tim and Harry apparently wanted to get a head start on their long flight to Saskatoon.

Dan sat at the small desk in the flight office, opened up his flight chart and removed the Alaska Lo Altitude chart to plan his flight to Galena. Laying a straight edge on the chart from Anchorage to Galena he found that the distance was 286 nautical miles. Providing for no wind and using a cruise speed for the DHC 3-T Otter of 150 knots, the flight should take approximately two hours. Dan picked up the phone, called the number for Flight Service and got a weather briefing then filed his VFR flight plan. It looked as if there would be some low broken clouds with bases approximately 1,800 feet above ground level then after getting up to three thousand feet it should be clear with visibility of 20 to 30 miles.

At first glance, the DHC 3-T Otter is an ungainly looking bird. The large body sitting on a pair of floats with wheels, which are retractable, gives the appearance of a cumbersome flying machine. However, it was designed to be a workhorse and that is exactly what it was. With a Pratt & Whitney PT6A-135 turbine engine it could develop 750 SHP.[1] The aircraft had an 8,000 pound gross weight rating which afforded it the ability to carry a sizeable load. Another feature which came in handy in areas with a great deal of snow in the wintertime, was the fact that the floats could be removed and a combination ski/wheel landing gear could be installed.

Not seeing any Stevens personnel around, Dan cranked up the tow and pulled the Otter out of the hangar to the flight line. First order of business was to check the cargo against the manifest to make sure the customer's order was as it should be. He then conducted his walk-around inspection, fired up the Pratt & Whitney PT6A turbine engine and ran his engine checks. He checked the transponder to make sure he had it set on 1200 which was the normal setting for a VFR flight plan. If Anchorage center wanted him on another frequency, they would let him know. Dan called Anchorage clearance and confirmed his VFR flight plan, then Anchorage ground control took him to the end of runway six left. Dan called the tower and got clearance for takeoff, climbed through the low broken clouds and departure control turned him to a heading of 300 degrees as he climbed to his assigned altitude of ten thousand five hundred feet.

After reaching five thousand feet, Dan clicked on the autopilot and let "George" take the aircraft to its assigned altitude and onto the 300 degree radial from the Anchorage VOR. He was already drifting into his own thoughts after scanning all the instruments to make sure the Otter was performing as required.

Dan's mind drifted around to the subject of marriage. Jess was not the type to go to Knoxville and be a housewife; they both would be bored to tears in a short time without some plan of action. Traveling together would be great but after every place they had in mind had been visited they would be right back at square one. Dan thought that Jess would have a great relationship with Tom and Mary Ann but they could, by no means, be her whole life. They weren't even *his* whole life although he loved them dearly. So, what would be the answer?

Anchorage center called and said there was a Cessna Caravan at his ten o'clock position, VFR five miles, and report contact. The Caravan had its strobe lights on so Dan picked him up in a matter of seconds and reported he had the traffic in sight.

The flight should be a piece of cake this morning. He had a load of various pieces of equipment on board, plus the much needed hydraulic pump for the Illinois River mine which was a medium size gold mine. He also had a number of miscellaneous pieces of merchandise as well including a set of dog harnesses.

---

1. Shaft Horsepower

What the heck they were going to do with that he had no idea unless they had their own dog sleds for winter travel in the mine vicinity.

Al had told him that since getting in the equipment business that many of the smaller mines had looked at Intermont as something of a general store. Many would place an order and then say, "as long as you are coming how about bringing up six dozen 100 watt light bulbs" or something else as strange as that. It was a matter of convenience for the mine owner; he would be willing to pay a premium just for the convenience of not having to scramble around for two or three different companies to take care of their miscellaneous needs. Al was willing to take care of their requests as he more than made up for any inconvenience in getting and keeping their equipment business.

Dan also learned that as Intermont grew they had diversified. For example Intermont now had a contract with AVEC (Alaska Village Electric Cooperative) which was an association of 51 villages which operated 144 diesel generators to produce their electricity. Some of the items that Intermont normally carried, such as generators and electrical cable, could be used by these co-ops. Also, AVEC requested Intermont carry a few transformers in inventory for them. Intermont's ability to transport these items quickly to one of the remote villages could mean the difference between their being out of power for a matter of a couple of days versus perhaps a week or more. It had proved to be a good arrangement for both parties.

Dan's mind switched gears again. Of course both Jess and he could probably stay with Intermont and build a life together in Anchorage which more than likely would not be boring since they both would be pursuing their interests. Dan wondered however if that kind of life would be appealing to the two of them after the "new" of their relationship had worn off. Something to think about.

As he got within 40 miles of the Galena VOR, Dan noticed that the clouds close to the surface seemed to be thickening. There was no weather reporting at Galena, even the AWOS[2] was unavailable. The airport was 'uncontrolled,' that is there was no tower there and other than a possible radio maintained by the FBO, if there was one, it would be the only source of weather and traffic. Dan trimmed the aircraft for descent and was dropping altitude at the rate of 500 feet per minute. By the time he reached the GAL intersection which was the IAP[3] he was at the specified altitude of 2,000 feet for the ILS approach to Runway 25. The altitude of the field was 152 feet

---

2. Aircraft Weather Observer System
3. Initial Approach Point

AGL and the MDA[4] was 402 feet so if he did not have the runway in sight at 552 feet he would have to execute a missed approach.

Just to be on the safe side, Dan tuned the communication radio to 122.8 which is the Unicom frequency used at all airports without a control tower. Approaching pilots broadcast "in the clear" giving their approximate location and their intentions just in case there was another aircraft in the vicinity with plans to land on the same runway. Failure of pilots to do this systematically had occasionally resulted in aircraft flying into each other, usually on final approach, with devastating results. Therefore, Dan announced, giving his "N" number, a description of his aircraft and his intention to land on Runway 25.

He set his No. 1 NAV radio on a frequency of 109.5 for the ILS approach and the needle was two dots to the left of center in the crosshairs of the HSI and the "fly up—fly down" needle was above the centerline. Dan adjusted his heading from 247 degrees to 242 and the vertical needle began to move towards the left. When it centered, he made another correction to 244 degrees and began to track the ILS centerline. Passing over the AMIRA intersection, the "fly up—fly down" bar centered and Dan reduced the power, dropped five degrees of flaps and kept that needle centered horizontally. He was now in the clouds at 1300 feet and continued to keep both the needles centered. At 800 feet the runway appeared dead ahead and Dan slowly reduced speed to 85 knots, planted the wheels on the runway and taxied to the only small building on the airport.

The airport appeared to be deserted of any form of human life. Once he had shut down the engine and left the aircraft, he walked to the building and saw a pay phone. He dug in his billfold and found the number for the Illinois River mine office. Dan dropped in a quarter and dialed the number. A male voice answered. Dan identified himself and the person on the other end of the line said their truck would be there in twenty minutes. The office was locked so Dan returned to the aircraft to await the arrival of the truck.

After some twenty-five minutes the truck arrived and there were three men aboard. The driver got out of the truck with a thermos in his hand. He asked Dan if he had a thermos, which Dan acknowledged affirmatively, and the driver said he had some coffee they had brewed at his office just an hour ago and wanted to know if Dan would like some. Of course he did, so the driver graciously filled Dan's thermos above the halfway mark. The men all pitched in and with Dan's help they had the aircraft unloaded in a little over an hour and Dan was soon airborne on his way back to Anchorage.

---

4. Minimum Descent Altitude

The trip back was as uneventful as the trip up and lost in his thoughts again, the time passed quickly and Dan made a routine landing at Anchorage International, hangared the Otter and went to the flight office. There was a message on the answering machine for him to call Virginia Stewart at the main office. As soon as she answered she told him to hold on for Miss Lane. Very astute of Jess, Dan thought.

The phone clicked as the call was transferred.

"Hi, I see you are back in one piece."

"Well, actually I am in two pieces. You are talking to my head but my body is still strapped in that damn airplane." Dan replied.

"Smart ass. You doing anything tonight?"

"Well, I was hoping that some gorgeous black haired woman would call and ask me for a date." Dan chuckled.

"Will I do?" Dan could just see her smiling.

"Wel-l-l-l, I suppose so."

"Actually I have a couple coming over for dinner and I would like for you to meet them."

Uh, oh. Looks as if I am going to be put under the microscope at last.

"What time?" Dan asked.

"Seven-ish?"

"Sounds like a winner, I'll see you then pretty lady."

"Thanks for the compliment," she said approvingly. "Bye."

"Bye." Dan responded.

Dan looked at his Breitling ... fifteen 'til one. He walked over to the main terminal, grabbed a Reuben sandwich and a Diet Coke. He picked up a copy of the USA today while he ate and checked the stock market. Actually the market was in an upturn and he hoped all his investments were still putting money in his account. *Maybe I should call my broker and see* how *things are*, he thought.

Back at the flight office Dan took his laptop out of his flight bag and went to work on his cost efficiency program. Promptly at five o'clock he packed up the bag, put it in the Cherokee in the parking lot and headed for the apartment. It was already dark. The days were growing shorter but it was unseasonably warm weather in Anchorage for this time of the year. He was totally unprepared for what was about to happen.

Chapter 41

Friends

Dan pulled up to Jess' apartment at ten minutes after seven and noticed a light blue BMW 450i four door sedan parked at the curb. He pulled the Cherokee in behind the 'Beamer,' walked to the front door and pushed the doorbell. Dan heard sounds of laughter and then Jess' high heels on the hardwood foyer floor. The door opened and Jess said, "Hi!," and touched her lips to his briefly and said, "Come on in … I want you to meet two of my friends." The young woman had gotten up from the couch and the man was already standing.

"Dan, this is my best friend Sue Edwards and her husband Frank." Sue was a blonde, just a little on the plump side and looked to be a couple of years older than Jess. She was just about two inches shorter than Jess and had what could be called a 'pixie' face. Frank looked to be about six feet with black hair that had just a hint of grey at the temples. He had finely chiseled features, with a small cleft in his chin and the complexion of Cary Grant. He was well built and gave the total appearance of someone who should be in the movies.

Sue came forward first and said, "Hi, Dan, it's great to finally get to meet you. Jess has told me *so* much about you." She held out her hand and Dan shook it. Her handshake was firm for a woman which he was glad to see.

Then Frank approached Dan. "Hello, Dan, glad to meet you," and his handshake was that of an athlete, firm and hard.

Dan said "Hello, how are you. It's good to meet the two of you."

"Well," Jess said, "we've been waiting for you to have our drinks so why don't you and Frank sit on the couch while Sue and I bring them out." Frank and Dan sat down and Frank said,

"How do you like Anchorage so far?"

"So far, so good, Frank. I have been just a little surprised at how warm it has been though."

"Yeah, it's been unseasonably warm but the forecasts indicate that we are going to start having typical October weather in just a few days."

"What about snow," Dan questioned. "I suppose just about everyone from the states expects to see snow in Alaska by this time of the year."

"Normally we begin to get some light snows in November but the heavy snows don't usually hit us until the middle of December and later." Frank replied.

"Well, I'm the sentimental type that would like to see a white Christmas so maybe I won't be disappointed."

"If past history is any indication, in all probability you won't be," Frank said.

Sue entered the living room with a tray that had four drinks on it. "Here, Dan, this is your vodka with the olive and Frank, this is your ginger ale. The two 'stiff drinks' here are for Jess and myself" and she gave Dan a little wink. Dan wondered about the ginger ale for Frank but he didn't say anything.

Jess had the gas logs in the fireplace on and she sat close to Dan on the couch with Frank in the recliner and Sue in the overstuffed lounge chair. It was very cozy and they seemed to be a great couple and the conversation was flowing back and forth with the usual questions about what Dan had done for a living and about his children. Evidently Sue was correct, Jess *had* told her a great deal about Dan. Eventually it was time for dinner and Jess had decided to serve buffet style. They all went to the kitchen where Jess had the food lined up on the counter top. They all took a dinner plate and began to fill them with the baked chicken, mashed potatoes, peas, carrots and there was a tossed salad in a large bowl. Also hot rolls and butter plus a gravy boat were at the end of the line. Dan was impressed with Jess' ability as a cook and said so.

Sue spoke up, "Oh, she is a great cook among other things." and Dan noticed that Jess' cheeks flushed slightly. Dan seemed to catch a little innuendo here from Sue about something other than just food.

Conversation at dinner followed very much along the line of the small talk made while they all sat in the living room. However, Sue brought up the subject of motorcycle riding.

"Dan, I understand that you renewed your interest in riding bikes after you came to Alaska."

"That's right, after taking a ride with your 'friend'" and Dan looked over at Jess and smiled, "I thought that I needed to ride by myself or take the risk of getting killed."

Jess looked at Dan and made a face, "Yeah, right."

Sue then said, "I understand that the two of you took a trip up to Wasilla one Saturday."

"We sure did and I managed to stay on the thing all the way up there and back," Dan replied.

"Well, I was just thinking," Sue went on, "if the good weather holds until Frank gets a week-end off, all of us could ride down to Seward for Saturday and Sunday. We could stay over and Jess and I could bunk together in one room and Frank and you could stay in the other." Sue looked at Dan with a knowing smile on her face and then transferred her eyes to Jess. Jess looked at Sue like she could kill her.

Trying to make the best of a rather testy situation, Dan replied, "Well, I guess we will just have to wait until Frank gets a chance to take off and see what the weather is like at that time."

Eventually, everyone had finished and Jess said, "Why don't you guys retire to the living room while Sue and I clean up the table. Frank and Dan got up and walked to the living area while the two women began to clear the table.

When the two men sat down Dan noticed that Frank looked at his watch. Frank looked at Dan and saw that he had noticed his action. Dan thought he would relieve any embarrassment this may have caused by saying,

"That's a habit that I have too … always checking the time."

"Yeah, same way with me. I have an early flight out in the morning so I was just checking to see how long it would be before I have to leave."

"Business trip?" Dan inquired.

Frank laughed, "Well you might say that. I'm a pilot."

"No kidding? Who do you fly for?"

"Alaska Airlines." Frank replied.

"You're kidding! Jess didn't tell me that you were an airline pilot."

"Well, I guess she has gotten so used to it that she just forgot to tell you."

"What are you flying, Frank?"

"Right now I'm copilot on a 737-200."

"Man it would really be a blast for me to get to fly one of those things … if I could handle it."

"What's the largest plane you have flown, Dan?" Frank asked.

"The King Air."

"Oh, you wouldn't have a problem. You know, I thought that once I got into the bigger jets that it would really be tough learning to fly them. The flying isn't the hardest part; learning the systems and how to react to emergencies is what's so demanding."

"Yeah, I guess you're right but I'm not going to ever have to worry about that. What time do you leave in the morning?"

"We get out at 6:15 for Seattle, lay over there for a little over and hour and then go on to Denver. We RON[1] there, take the same route back the next morning and then get back in here that evening."

"I suppose that is part of a pilot's life, isn't it … hanging around in airports."

"You got it."

About that time the girls came back into the kitchen and they all sat around and talked until about 8:30 when Frank said, "I hate to break up a great party but I do have to get going. Got an early flight out, as usual." They donned their jackets and they all said their good-byes and then Sue and Frank departed.

"Well," Jess smiled at Dan, "what do you think?"

"Oh, they are a great couple, Jess. Why didn't you tell me that Frank was a pilot with Alaska Airlines?"

"I don't know. I just forgot it I suppose."

"Well, evidently you didn't forget to tell Sue about our 'roll in the hay.'"

"What did you say!?" Jess said with great emphasis.

"Aw, c'mon, Jess. You surely caught the implications that Sue was tossing around all night. Didn't you tell her what a 'great stud' I was?"

"I certainly *did not!* And as for your being a 'great stud,' you said it, I didn't." and her eyes were literally blazing.

That really got to Dan. "Well, you sure as hell seemed to enjoy it!" Dan's voice was getting louder.

"Dan Nichols, you are a *chauvinist!* Not only that but you are certainly not the gentleman that I thought you were!"

Things were getting out of hand, Jess had turned her back to Dan and he tried to put his hands on her arms to get her to look him in the eyes. She whirled around and said, "Don't you touch me! I think you had better leave!"

"Aw now, Jess. I'm sorry. We've both had a couple of drinks. Let's just forget the whole thing."

---

1. Remain Overnight

"No! I will *not* forget the 'whole thing.' If there is one thing I will *not* discuss with anyone, including Sue, is my sex life!" She had folded her arms and she was staring straight at Dan. "I want you to leave … now!"

That really ticked Dan off so he grabbed his jacket and said, "O.K., if that's the way you want it!"

And he slammed the door as he went out. Dan got in the Jeep, started the engine and spun the rear wheels as he left the curb. By the time he arrived at his apartment there was a knot in the pit of his stomach about the size of a softball and he felt sick. *What a stupid, blithering idiot you are, Dan Nichols!* he thought to himself.

Chapter 42

Vanguard

Dan immersed himself in his work the next few days. The days were now much shorter and although all three of the Intermont pilots were qualified to fly at night, they would all admit, if pressured, that flying at night in Alaska was something that they did not look forward to. Most of the trips were planned to leave early in the morning so that their arrivals would be in daylight and then returning to Anchorage after dark was not so bad because of the outstanding airport navigation facilities and radar coverage at Stevens Anchorage International.

One thing that took up an entire day and half a night, was preparing the three aircraft for an emergency landing during the winter months. Alaska had a law that all commercial aircraft, including aircraft that carried any passengers for a fee, were required to carry emergency gear during the winter months. This entailed having enough food on board that would sustain each person for two weeks. Also, an axe, a first aid kit, a hunting knife, matches, mosquito headnets, gill net, fishing tackle, a pistol or rifle with ammunition, sleeping bags for every person, snowshoes, and wool blankets, were required. In addition, an ELT (Emgergency Locator Radio Transmitter) was also required. Most aircraft carried an ELT anyway, but this became a mandatory requirement for all aircraft during the winter. If an aircraft crashed, the impact would set off the ELT automatically and it would send out a radio signal which could be picked up by search aircraft and pin-point the downed plane. The device could also be set off manually if the plane crash impact was not great enough to activate the device. In addition to all this equipment, Dan had also ordered a hand-held battery operated transceiver which was a standby combination transmitter, receiver and also had ILS receiving capabilities. In the event the aircraft had an electrical failure, this portable transceiver could actually become a lifesaver. The range was limited, of course, but dead-reckoning navigation could usually get the aircraft in receiving range of an FAA transmitter. Getting all this gear together for all three aircraft took time but it was time well spent.

Complying with the emergency order plus three flights took up the rest of the week. When the week-end rolled around, Dan forced himself to keep busy so that he would not think about Jess. Well, not think about her all the time, anyway. Consequently, he continued to work on his cost analysis program and also gather information for the forthcoming meeting in Prince George on the following Tuesday. Meals were the loneliest time of all and on Saturday and Sunday night he brought in a pizza one night and on Sunday night he threw together some canned vegetables and a baked chicken that he picked up in the deli of the local supermarket.

The following Monday, Al, Fred and Dan boarded the King Air for the flight to Prince George. They wanted to make sure they would be there on time Tuesday morning for the meeting with the three mine superintendents at the Vanguard manager's office. Fortunately the weather going down was quite good. Dan was afraid they might encounter turbulence that just might have an adverse effect on either Al or Fred, and at worst both of them. They arrived just before nightfall and checked into the Best Western Inn. After they got settled in, they all went to the local Outback Steakhouse where they had a couple of drinks and an outstanding steak dinner. Afterwards they all went back to the motel and went to their individual rooms.

Dan hadn't been in his room five minutes until the phone rang. His instinct told him it was Jess calling to say that she was sorry and hoped they could put the recent episode behind them. He answered the phone.

"Hello."

"Dan, this is Al. Have you gone to bed yet?"

"Oh, no, Al. I was just getting ready to go get a bucket of ice."

"Would you mind coming down to my room for a chat. I'm in 241."

"Why no, I'll be right down."

Dan went into the hallway, oriented himself and walked off five rooms to number 241 where he knocked on the door. It was opened by Al.

"Come right in, Dan," Al invited. "Have a seat."

Dan walked over to one of the two upholstered chairs and sat down.

"Dan, I've had something on my mind for several weeks now and I thought this just might be the time to discuss my thoughts with you."

"Sure, Al. What is it?"

Al picked up a cigar from the ashtray on the side table but did not light it. He just put it in his mouth and chewed on it for a few seconds.

"Dan, did you know that Evelyn and I don't have any children?"

"Why, no. Frankly, I just assumed that you did."

"No. We tried for a long time ... even eventually thought about adoption. But it just became one of those things we thought about and never got around to doing then one day we woke up and realized we were too old to adopt a child."

"I'm sorry, Al. Children are a responsibility but the joys far outweigh the problems."

"Yes, I'm sure that is true." Al replaced the cigar in the ashtray, got up and poured a glass of ice water. "Would you like a glass, Dan?"

"Yes, that would be nice, thank you."

Al sat back down and took a swallow of water. He put the glass back on the plastic tray and then looked Dan in the eye.

"I've ... uh, ... come to sort of look at you almost as a son, Dan. I know I'm hardly old enough to be your father but I have been really impressed with what you have done since you have been with us and several times I've thought that if I had had a son, I would have wanted him to be like you."

"I really appreciate that, Al ... more than you probably realize."

"Thank you. Now, there is something else that I think I need to tell you. Did you know that Evelyn is in an assisted living facility because she has early Alzheimer's?"

"No! I certainly was not aware of that."

"Well she is."

Dan noticed that Al's eyes were beginning to tear up slightly and there was just a slight quiver in his voice when he spoke.

Al continued, "I am beginning to feel terribly guilty, Dan, because I promised Evelyn that when I got the business well founded that she and I would travel and enjoy life together and I was always so involved in the business that I kept putting it off and putting it off. Now there is no hope of that happening."

Al paused for a minute while he picked up the glass and took a big swallow of water. It was as if he was stalling for time in order to compose himself. Then he spoke again.

"I'm telling you all this, Dan, because I need to spend more time with Evelyn while she can still recognize me and know who I am." Al was now on the verge of tears.

"I can certainly appreciate that, Al. Is there *anything* that I can do?" Dan said sincerely.

"Yes there is. After another couple of months, once we get this deal working with Vanguard smoothly and can tie up another few loose ends in the business that you are not aware of, I would like for you to come into management."

"Well, that certainly is a compliment. Just what would you have in mind for me to do?"

"Eventually, I would like for you to be president of the company and part owner with an option to buy the company at some point in time. That is, if you would want it."

Dan was dumbfounded. A full minute passed before he finally spoke. "Man, that's something that I never *dreamed* about doing. What about Fred or even Jess?"

"No … Fred is definitely not interested. I have discussed it with him on two occasions and he has turned it down flat. Fred is a wonderful man with money, Dan, but he is not a salesman and doesn't have the knack for managing people and he admits it. As for Jess, she is a very capable young lady but can you see her dealing with the roughnecks and tough managers that we run up against in the mines? She just wouldn't be able to handle it."

"Yeah." Dan paused while he thought on that. "I can see where you are coming from, Al."

"Well, I wanted to tell you about my ideas now. You have been with us for almost four months and I didn't want to drive up to our six months agreement and then drop this on you. I have done more checking up on you than you probably are aware, Dan, and you are as clean as a bedsheet and you don't particularly need the money. The only thing is, since you have had a taste of retirement, will you want the hassle?"

"I honestly don't know at this point. I will have to give it a great deal of serious thought. But I do appreciate the confidence that you have in me."

Al got up out of his chair and Dan did likewise. Al put out his hand and Dan took it. Al then put his left hand on top of Dan's and they shook hands.

"You think it over. Get a good night's sleep, Dan."

"Thanks, Al. You too."

Dan was lying in the bed with the lights out thinking. *Do I really want to climb back into the management 'saddle' again or do I want to continue doing what I love best ... flying. Maybe something will happen that will influence me one way or the other.*

Chapter 43

Sealed Deal

Al, Fred and Dan were all at the Vanguard office by nine o'clock the next morning and were ushered into Charlie Thompson's office, the manager of the operation. The three of them wanted to get there a little early to have a brief discussion with Charlie prior to meeting with the three mine managers.

Charlie Thompson already had a proposal prepared for them to look over which would cover the unloading of incoming Intermont flights and the transfer of the material into their warehouse, the storage fees based on the length of time the articles were in the Vanguard facility and then the loading of the three mine companies' trucks when they arrived to pick up their respective loads. The contract looked in order as far as Al and Fred were concerned but they informed Thompson they would have to defer an agreement of acceptance until the conference with the mine managers would take place. Thompson said he certainly understood their position and then showed the three of them to a conference room where they could have the meeting with the incoming managers. Thompson then had one of the Vanguard employees bring in a large urn of coffee, some coffee cakes, sugar, cream and cups. Al thanked Charlie profusely and they awaited the arrival of the others.

The three gentlemen all arrived within ten minutes of each other. Sam Edwards from the Bullmoose mine, Robere Chalmont from the Quintette mine and Claude Monroe from the Clear River mine. Introductions were made all around including Charlie Thompson. All of the managers wanted to take a tour of the facility so all but Dan and Fred left the meeting room for the tour. Dan and Fred remained and had a cup of coffee and conversation together.

When all of them returned, Charlie Thompson excused himself and the three managers with Al, Fred and Dan sat down around the conference table. Fred led the discussion, divulging the information on the freight costs involved in a full load of materials being delivered from Anchorage to Prince George. The warehouse fee was also presented and all charges would be pro-rated based on the weight of material going to each of the three mines. Also, the three managers were advised they would have forty-eight hours to remove their material from the Vanguard warehouse before a demurrage charge of one hundred dollars per day would be incurred. They all seemed impressed with the arrangement and all agreed to have their individual acceptance of the plan back to Fred by Friday of the next week.

After they departed, Al, Fred and Dan met briefly with Charlie and informed him the proposal was generally acceptable and if all three responded in the affirmative by Friday of the following week, then Fred would send Intermont's signed agreement with Vanguard to Charlie Thompson by the early part of the following week. Al, Fred and Dan shook hands with Charlie and took a taxi to the Prince George airport. Dan inspected the King Air and they were airborne by two o'clock for the four hour plus run back to Anchorage. They would be arriving in the dark.

Enroute at twenty thousand feet, Dan stole a look into the passenger compartment and Al and Fred were sitting in the 'conference arrangement' of the seats. One seat faced aft and one forward with a drop-down table between them. They had some papers spread out on the table between them, probably going over some of the details of the meeting. When they were about ninety miles from Anchorage, Vancouver Center cleared the King Air to descend to 8,000 feet. Dan tuned in the Anchorage ATIS[1] on the comm radio on frequency 118.2 for the current weather. The recorded male voice intoned:

"Anchorage International information Echo, zero two two zero Zulu. Wind two niner zero at one two, visibility one mile in snow. Braking conditions fair. Sky conditions; ceiling one thousand one hundred broken, temperature minus five, dewpoint minus one five. Altimeter two niner five six. ILS runway two four left in use. Advise controller on initial contact you have information Echo."

---

1. ATIS–Automated Terminal Information Service

Well, winter has finally arrived with a vengeance, Dan thought. *My first night landing in the snow in Alaska and I have the company president and vice-president on board. That's just dandy!*

Dan turned on the "Fasten Seat Belt" sign just as Al appeared in the cockpit and sat down in the right seat.

"What's it look like out there, Dan?" Al asked.

"Aw, we just got a little snow and the visibility isn't all that great but we're o.k." Dan did his best to try and put Al at ease. Al sat there and stared at the dimly lit instruments on the panel and wondered how the heck someone could keep tabs on all that information and still fly the airplane.

"I don't guess there is anything I can do to help, is there?" Al asked rather anxiously.

"You might try praying." Dan looked at Al and grinned. That loosened Al up a bit and he put a smile on his face.

Dan thought to himself, *We may need it.* They were now forty-two miles from the airport and Vancouver Center turned them over to Anchorage approach control. Dan tuned the comm radio to 118.4, the frequency that Vancouver had given him. Dan clicked his transmitter button,

"Anchorage approach, King Air November zero four five Kilo with you at eight thousand, heading two seven zero, squawking one seven four two. We have information Echo."

The Anchorage approach controller came back on the radio.

"King Air November zero four five Kilo, radar contact. You are now three five miles from the Anchorage airport. Descend and maintain two thousand one hundred. Turn right to heading two eight five until intercepting the localizer. Runway two four left in use. You are cleared for the approach. Contact tower on one one eight point three."

Dan repeated the clearance word for word, acknowledging he had received the transmission. He set up the approach heading on the HSI for 245 degrees and set the autopilot for the auto approach. He flipped the switch to change to a backcourse approach and then monitored all the instruments to make sure the instruments were configured to make the instrument approach. Ten miles from Stevens, he slowed the aircraft to 120 knots and dropped one notch of flaps. The speed then dropped to 110 knots and Dan noticed the vertical needle of the localizer indicator beginning to move to the left. The autopilot captured the localizer and began to turn the aircraft to a heading of 245 degrees. When the horizontal needle of the glide slope reached the center of the dial, the autopilot started the descent as Dan dropped the landing gear and made an adjustment of the throttles to keep the speed on the 'blue line' at 110 knots. He then called the tower on one one eight point three and reported inbound on the localizer. The tower cleared him for the landing.

Dan spoke to Al in the right seat.

"Al, now you can do something for me. Keep looking ahead and shortly you should see sequential strobe lights that will look like they are running towards the end of the runway. We call those lights the 'rabbit.' As soon as you see them, let me know, o.k.?"

"O.K., Dan," Al replied just a little nervously.

The aircraft was continuing its descent and Dan flipped on the windscreen wipers to keep any of the blowing snow from sticking to the Plexiglas. Dan kept his eyes glued to the instruments and ran his final check as he looked at the three green lights above the landing gear switch to confirm that the gear was down and locked. He continued to keep the airspeed on the 'blue line,'[2]. They were now at 850 feet and if they did not have the runway in sight at 340 feet he would have to declare a 'missed approach.' Dan stole a quick glance at the windscreen and it was black as pitch outside. Just at that moment Al cried out,

"I see it Dan ... I see it!"

Dan looked up and verified they had the lights of the 'rabbit' in sight and he immediately went back to the instruments for a second just to make sure everything was as it should be. Then he looked up in time to see a series of horizontal green lights which were the REIL lights.[3]

Dan pulled back on the yoke slightly to put the aircraft just a bit tail low. He remembered the ATIS message warning of 'braking conditions fair.' Retarding the power levers, he let the speed bleed off and when the main wheels made contact with the runway he began to brake just slightly. He had a ten thousand five hundred foot runway so there was no need of risking a skid off the runway into what would surely be soft ground that just might cause a ground loop. When the nose wheel touched the runway Dan began to brake evenly and not encountering a skid he brought in the reversers. Once the aircraft came to a stop, the tower handed them off to ground control who directed them to taxi to the Stevens ramp.

---

2. 'Blue line speed.' Speed at which a multi engine aircraft can maintain directional control if an engine fails.
3. REIL–Runway End Identification Lights

When Dan had cut the engines and flipped all the switches to the "Off" positions, he heard Al give an audible sigh of relief. He turned and looked at Dan and said,

"I'm glad I am paying you enough money." They both had a laugh together and Al slapped Dan on the back. They both got up from their seats, gathered Fred and all three exited the aircraft.

Al said, "Let's all stop by the pub and I'll buy."

Chapter 44

▼

La Perouse Strait

While Captain Johng Ho Kim was asleep in his quarters in the *Romeo* class UB235 submarine of the Democratic People's Republic of Korea, his Executive Officer *Taewi* Huang Sun Lee poured over the charts lying on the plot table. The UB235 was holding on course of zero four five degrees as it moved at a speed of 6 knots further into the Sea of Japan.

Lieutenant Huang was concentrating on a point in the course much further from their present position. He was perusing the chart where the international waterway ran between the Russian island of Sakhalin and the Japanese island of Hokkaido. La Perouse Strait was named for the French explorer, Count Rouse, and it separated the dé La Pe Sea of Okhotsk from the Sea of Japan. It is 27 miles wide at its narrowest part and varies in depth from 167 to 387 feet. It is noted for its extremely strong current and is normally closed by ice in the winter. Lieutentant Huang was considering just how tricky a December passage through this strait might be.

Chapter 45

Weather: 'Go No Go'

It had been nearly a week now since Dan and Jess had their little 'spat.' He realized that they had something else in common—they were both stubborn. As he drove from the Stevens hangar to the main office he swore to himself that he would not be the first one to break the silence.

Dan had to take his laptop to the main office to upload more statistics that he had gathered pertaining to the operation of the aircraft department. Secretly, he had hoped that he might accidentally encounter Jess and they would be forced to 'break the ice.' However, when he entered the reception room and greeted Virginia Stewart, he nonchalantly inquired if Miss Lane was in and Virginia informed him that she was attending an environmental conference in Fairbanks and would not be back until tomorrow. Dan then walked down the hall to the administrative office where he proceeded to upload his information into the mainframe computer.

While performing this operation, one of the clerks approached him and said that Mrs. Stewart was on the 'phone. Dan picked up a nearby handset and spoke. "This is Dan." Virginia Stewart informed him that Mr. Switzer wanted to speak to him and made the connection.

"Hello, this is Al Switzer."

"You wanted to speak to me, sir?"

"Oh ... yes, Dan. Say, I have some good news and some bad news."

Dan chuckled. "Well, I think the usual procedure is to ask for the good news first."

"That's the usual response, Dan." Al laughed in reply. "You know that I have been trying for some time to do business with the Alyeska people up in Prudhoe Bay. Well, they are in a bind for a couple of large pumps for the pipeline and their usual supplier said it was impossible for them to get the pumps to them tomorrow. Alyeska reminded me that I had been bugging them for a long time for some business and if I could deliver they would be inclined to share some of their regular business with us."

"Hey, that sounds great, Al. I know how hard you have worked on this and how much it means. So what is the bad news?"

"In talking with them up there they said that the weather was a little bit dicey but that is usually the case at this time of the year anyway. However, I don't want you, Tim, or Harry to take any unnecessary chances. You be the judge, now. If you feel that it is too risky then let me know and I will tell them 'thanks but no thanks.'"

"I have no idea what the weather forecast is for Prudhoe or Deadhorse, Al. Let me check it out and I'll get back to you."

Dan hung up the phone and then dialed the number for Flight Service and asked what the twenty-four hour forecast was for Prudhoe Bay. The specialist came back and said that the temperatures for the next day would range from minus fifteen degrees Fahrenheit to plus two degrees. There possibly would be some blowing snow which would reduce visibility at times but it should not restrict visibility to the point to where an instrument landing would be impossible. The specialist went on to say there was a low pressure trough sitting about 100 miles off the coast northwest of Point Barrow. Presently it was moving very slowly, however once it reached the mainland it could pick up speed and create icing conditions aloft. Dan thanked him for the information and hung up. Dan immediately called Al and told him that he didn't see a problem in making the delivery. Al said that he would call Joe O'Donoghue at the warehouse and take care of having the material loaded on the DC-3. Dan could tell from the tone of Al's voice that he was quite pleased.

Dan hustled back to the flight office in the Stevens hangar and out of habit, when he entered the office, he looked at the FAX machine. There was an order there for Unalakleet for tomorrow which could easily be handled by the Otter. He stood there and thought for a few moments. Should he send Harry and Tim to Deadhorse since there was a possibility of bad weather coming in tomorrow or the next day? Finally he reasoned to himself that he had to get experience in flying in Alaska under adverse weather conditions so he and Tim would take the Deadhorse trip and Harry could handle Unalakleet.

Time to get my feet wet, bad weather or no.

Chapter 46

Deadhorse or Die Trying

Dan was up early on this December morning and went to the kitchen in his apartment where he put on a pot of coffee. While that was brewing he went to the bathroom, showered, shaved and completed his morning routine. Back to the kitchen, he took a mug of coffee with him into the bedroom while he dressed. This morning he put on a pair of long underwear, blue jeans, a red and black checkered flannel shirt, wool mid-calf socks and a pair of leather waterproof boots that were also mid-calf.

Going into to the kitchen he made a cheese omelet, link sausages and wheat toast. While eating his breakfast and having a couple of cups of coffee, he got out his Alaska chart and the tentative route he had made from Anchorage to Deadhorse. The plan going up was to fly the VOR's from Anchorage to Big Lake, Talkeetna, Nenana, Chandalar Lake and on to Deadhorse. He calculated the mileage as being 549 nautical miles and if the DC-3 could average 150 knots on this trip then it should take around three hours and forty five minutes to get there.

The plan was to leave Anchorage around nine o'clock in the morning. It would still be dark as the sun was scheduled to rise today at 10:14 a.m. and would set at 3:42 p.m. He and Tim should arrive in Deadhorse around 12:45 p.m. when there would be some 'visible light.' At this time of the year the sun actually never rises above the horizon but they do have two to three hours of what they call 'visible light.' This way the cargo could be unloaded in the best of visible conditions if they could not get access to a heated hangar. If they were fortunate enough to get away in two hours they should be back in Anchorage around 7:00 p.m. Finishing his breakfast, Dan rinsed out the dishes in the sink, put them in his dishwasher and filled up his thermos with the remainder of the coffee. He slipped on a wool sweater and donned his fleece lined parka which had a hood. He checked the parka pockets to make sure the lined waterproof gloves were there. The last article of clothing was a University of Tennessee ball cap which he had brought with him from Knoxville.

He was glad he had an apartment with a garage as the Cherokee was like ice inside. The temperature in Anchorage was around twelve degrees and there was about two inches of snow on the ground. The Cherokee turned over after three cranks and he backed out of the garage, closed the door with the remote and headed for the airport.

When he walked into the lighted hangar, which was also heated, he found that Tim had already beat him there and he was walking around the plane checking it out. Dan went into the flight office to see if there were any more faxes on the machine but it was clear. Harry had not showed up yet but he didn't blame him. He didn't have a long run and there was no point in leaving all that early. About that time Tim came into the office.

"'Mornin' skipper. You all set to go?"

"I guess I am as set as I am going to be, Tim. Have you checked the aircraft?"

"Yep. She has a full load of gas and the oil in both engines is right to the mark."

"How about the tires; did you look at them?"

"Sure did," Tim replied. "They both are 'aired' and I didn't see any cracks or bad wear marks."

"Good. Is the rifle on board?" Dan asked.

"You planning on knocking off a polar bear or two?" Tim grinned.

"I'm not planning on it but you never can tell. What about the water containers; have you checked them out?"

"Nope. I hadn't gotten around to that," Tim replied.

"Well, let's be sure and check that and let's make sure that the sleeping bags and the food box are in good order before we go."

"Roger," Tim replied. "I'll go check them out right now." And he went out the office door into the hangar. Dan made one final check of his 'brain bag.' His mag light was in there, all necessary Jeppesen charts, the .38 Colt revolver, two Snickers bars and his coffee thermos. All set. He walked out into the hangar and noticed that Tim had a pail of water which he was taking into the DC-3, apparently to 'top off' the water reservoir. Dan clambered up the ladder into the aircraft and checked all the emergency gear to make sure they had everything that was needed. The rifle was in the locked rack so he checked to make sure they had the key so they could get it out if needed. The next item he checked was the Emergency Locator Transmitter; he pushed the "Test" button to make sure the batteries were still charged. He also checked out the small locker on the back of the wall separating the pilots' compartment from the cargo hold which held the Very[1] pistol which would be needed if they had a forced landing. Dan and Tim then inspected the cargo lashings to make sure that the load was secure. Once the two of them were satisfied, they returned to the flight office to check with the Flight Service Station on the weather.

The FSS weather advisor informed Dan that Anchorage had broken clouds at 1500 feet, Temperature 12, Dewpoint 18, winds out of the north at 3 knots, barometric pressure was 29.42 steady and visibility was 10 miles. There would be an overcast at 10,000 feet with occasional breaks. The weather at Deadhorse was not as promising. They were reporting the current temperature as 'zero,' dewpoint as 'zero,' winds from the west at 18 knots, barometric pressure 29.44 and falling. Visibility was 3 miles in snow and fog. There was also an AIRMET out for the Brooks Range Area. Mountains were obscured. Occasional overcast at 1500 feet, visibility 3 miles in blowing snow. Passes: Anaktuvuk and Atigun, IFR, visibility 3 miles in blowing snow. Ice and freezing level: isolated moderate rime ice in clouds; 1500 to 10,000 feet. Freezing level; surface. Dan inquired about forecast conditions for the following day and the specialist advised that the forecast for the next day would be 'more of the same.' With some misgivings Dan proceeded to file the IFR flight plan he had worked up for the flight to Deadhorse with the FSS specialist who was still on the line.

Dan swore under his breath. He gathered from this that the low level trough that had been off the coast was now moving inland. This undoubtedly would bring with it warm air which would override the colder air. With the relative humidity at Deadhorse being 83, this could mean that the moisture in the upper levels of the warm front would produce rain which would fall down through the very cold air and probably form freezing rain. He sat and thought about the situation for a few minutes and if it had not been for the fact that Al was counting on getting this load to Alyeska so badly, he would have either cancelled or, at best, delayed the flight.

---

1. Very pistol. A gun which fires a signal flare.

Tim questioned Dan, "Well, whaddya' think, Skipper?"
"Oh, I think we can handle it o.k. Let's get the bird out of the hangar."

Chapter 47

Alyeska

The Intermont DC-3 was 'wheels up' off runway six at Anchorage International at 0855 Alaska time. Anchorage departure control vectored the aircraft to intercept the 350 degree radial to the Big Lake VOR and cleared N9140R to 'climb and maintain eleven thousand feet.' Tim Morrison was sitting in the left seat and he turned the DC-3 to the left until it was on the 350 degree radial from the Anchorage VOR. Dan had decided to let Tim fly the leg to Deadhorse as Tim needed all the multi-engine time that he could acquire. Dan, sitting in the right seat, would handle the radio transmissions and assist in monitoring the gauges as well as doing the navigation work.

At eleven thousand feet the outside air temperature gauge read minus eight degrees Fahrenheit. Since there was no apparent moisture in the air the pilots were not too concerned at this point of having ice form in the engine carburetors. They were still below the overcast and visibility appeared to be somewhere between five and ten miles in the pre-dawn darkness. They still had about an hour to go before the sun would rise although it was doubtful they would be able to see it. Being only 26 miles from the Big Lake VOR they were on it in short order and then set up to follow a heading of 330 degrees to the Talkeetna VOR. They passed the Talkeetna VOR within three minutes of their estimated time so there apparently was no wind directly on their nose. At Talkeetna they had tuned the comm radio to 135.2 and picked up the Deadhorse terminal forecast. It was practically the same as they had gotten from the FSS in Anchorage: temperature minus one degree, dewpoint zero, winds from 290 degrees at 18 knots and barometric pressure 29.42. Visibility was still 3 miles in snow and fog. As they progressed northward they noticed no difference in the 'visual daylight' and were flying in a semi-dark environment.

Sixty miles out from Deadhorse they began their descent and since there was no FAA facility there, they would provide their own navigation to intercept the ILS approach to runway two two. The windscreen and pitot[1] heaters had been turned on at takeoff and when the aircraft started its' descent, Dan flipped the switch on the right electrical panel to turn on the pump that would inject de-icing fluid into the carburetor of each engine. This prevented ice from forming in the carburetors as the engines were operating below their normal temperature ranges. When this procedure is initiated, there is normally a drop in the RPM gauge for each engine. Dan noticed the right engine RPM drop was slightly less than the left.

Visibility dropped markedly as they turned to the heading to intercept the ILS and at two thousand feet they both estimated the visibility to be less than two miles. They had tuned the comm radio to the ATIS frequency of 118.4 and the recorded voice intoned the same information they had received over Talkeetna. The landing lights had been switched on and they both could see the blowing snow reflected in the beams of the lights. Fortunately, the blowing snow had not covered the runway lights entirely and they still offered some guidance in lining up the aircraft with the runway. Tim concentrated on following the needles of the ILS which offered guidance down to 260 feet while Dan attended to handling the gear, flaps, mixture and throttle controls. Tim made a very good approach and touched down solidly with a wheel landing. The 6,500 foot runway allowed them to brake gradually without skidding. Dan checked his Breitling; three hours and fifty minutes … just seven minutes more than their planned flight time. As they taxied up to one of the hangars they noticed an Air Alaska Boeing 737-200 loading at the terminal for a run down to Anchorage. Their time would be a little better … one hour and twenty minutes. Ah, well, such is the price one pays for being the tortoise rather than the hare.

Lady Luck was smiling on them and they were able to pull into a heated hangar. This would not only keep the engines warm but also facilitate the unloading of the cargo, Tim and Dan went into the FBO office with their lunch bags in hand. They found a spot at an empty table and had their coffee and a sandwich

---

1. Pitot: venturi device mounted on exterior of aircraft that determines the airspeed.

they had brought along. In about fifteen minutes the Alyeska truck arrived and they began the process of unloading the cargo from the DC-3. At 1450 (2:30 p.m.) the aircraft was unloaded and ready to head back to Anchorage. Before leaving, Dan called the FSS number posted on the wall near the telephone in the FBO office and got the latest weather report. His worst fears were confirmed.

The warm front had moved inland and now was just south of Prudhoe Bay traveling from northwest to southeast at 15 knots. As the warm, moist air moved upward over the colder air beneath, it was producing rain which, when falling into the colder air, was turning into sleet and freezing rain. The specialist stated that the leading edge of the trough was at 18,000 feet at the present time and would drop to 12,000 feet in approximately two hours. The specialist also informed Dan that the front was not expected to reach Nenana until 1650 hours. Dan went ahead and filed a flight plan back to Anchorage and told the specialist that if they decided to "go" that he would activate the plan after taking off. Dan thanked him for his assistance and put the phone back on the hook.

Dan and Tim talked it over. It was 340 miles to Nenana which was about two hours away. If they could manage the flight for that period of time then they should be able to make it on to Anchorage without a problem. They both decided it was worth a try. If it looked too bad, they would turn around and come back to Deadhorse. They prepared the DC-3 for takeoff.

Chapter 48

Nenana or Else

At 1510 the DC-3 was rolling down the runway on takeoff from Deadhorse with Dan at the controls and Tim as the co-pilot. As they climbed through the murk of blowing snow, Tim tuned in the Flight Service Station at Barrow on 132.15 and activated their flight plan which called for them to climb to 9,000 feet on a heading of 170 degrees for the Bettles VOR. Dan and Tim had decided to return via Bettles, Nenana, Talkeetna, Big Lake and then to Anchorage. Although they would be flying a more westerly route, it afforded more safety. The Bettles VOR was located on the airport which offered a VOR/DME approach. Also, the Nenana airport had a VOR and an ADF approach. Although the field was not manned, it did have a lighted runway. This route they were taking back to Anchorage afforded more options for a forced landing than the one they had taken on the northbound flight to Deadhorse.

At eight thousand feet Dan was able to contact the Anchorage Air Route Traffic Control Center by means of one of the RCO's[1] on frequency 135.35. ARTCC directed him to squawk 1422 and Tim set the transponder on that frequency and pushed the 'squawk' button. Immediately Anchorage acknowledged with "radar contact." That message afforded some relief and feeling of security to both Dan and Tim. As they were climbing, Tim had turned the pitot heat and

---

1. Remote Communications Outlet

carburetor heat "On." When Tim flipped on the carburetor heat Dan noticed the right engine RPM needle dropped more than the left engine again.

They had leveled off at 9,000 feet and 70 miles from the Deadhorse VOR they noticed a slight amount of frozen precipitation began to form at the lower corners of the windscreen. They both looked at one another with that 'here it comes' expression on their faces. The southeasterly wind was giving them a slight tailwind and when they had tuned in the Bettles VOR and were able to get a 'fix' they determined they were making 160 knots over the ground. If this continued they should have a total flight time to Anchorage of three hours and thirty-five minutes even though this route was 25 miles further than the one going up.

Ninety miles from Bettles the precipitation began to increase. Dan reached down on the left side to a small panel which had an "on—off" in-line valve. He turned that valve to the "on" position them flipped a toggle switch to "on" and this started a pump in the forward baggage compartment where a six gallon container of ethylene glycol was located. The fluid was pumped up to de-ice the windscreen. Tim and Dan both could see the freezing rain swirling at them through the darkness and Dan said, "Tim, call Anchorage and ask them to clear us down to 8,000 feet." Tim did so and Anchorage came back and immediately approved the change in altitude. Forty-five minutes into the flight, Dan said to Tim, "Take the mag light out of my case and see if you can see any ice formation on the wing."

Tim did so and answered, "I can't tell for sure, Dan. It may be clear ice instead of rime and that's why I can't see it."

"O.K.," Dan replied. "Let's pressurize those boots just the same and then see if you can tell if anything breaks loose."

Tim turned on the valve which used compressed air to inflate the rubberized "boots" along the leading edge of each wing. In just a minute or so they heard what appeared to be pieces of ice hitting the tail assembly which evidently had been broken off the wing. Tim took the flashlight once more and focused it on the wing surface.

"Dan, I can see now where the ice has broken loose." Tim said.

"O.K., we will have to wait now for more ice to build up before we can pressurize again." Dan turned in his seat to where he could see the pump behind his seat which pumps de-icing fluid from a four gallon tank located by the pump to the slinger rings mounted on each propeller just behind the propeller hub. Dan turned the petcock on the tank to the "On" position then flipped the "On" switch on the electrical panel which started the pump. He then turned a rheostat next to the supply tank to adjust the flow. Hopefully this would eliminate ice building on the propellers.

Thirty miles from Bettles, Dan checked the instruments and noticed that the RPM needle for the left engine had dropped 50 RPM's. Dan thought: *Either something appears to be wrong with the engine mechanically or perhaps the venturi in the anti-icing system that injects the alcohol into the carburetor is partially clogged allowing some ice to build in the carburetor.*

They crossed the Bettles VOR at 1628 hours which Tim calculated to be a groundspeed of 160 knots. Another 30 minutes passed and Dan noticed he was having to keep back pressure on the yoke to maintain altitude. Normally he would have flown the plane using the autopilot but he had purposely flown it by hand using the trim tabs to keep the aircraft in level flight. By doing this he maintained a 'feel' for what effect the ice may be having on the aircraft.

"Take another look at that ice, Tim." Dan instructed.

Tim picked up the mag light and pointed it towards the right wing. "I can't see a damn thing, Dan. It's got to be clear ice for sure." There was a note of anxiety in his voice.

"O.K., well, let's pressurize again."

Once more Tim began the pressurization process hoping that the boots would break the ice loose from the wings. Tim then took the flashlight and moved it back and forth across the surface of the wing.

"Dan, I think the wing surface is being covered with that ice. It seems to have a glazed appearance to me."

"Yeah ... I think you are right. It's getting harder for me to hold altitude without increasing the angle of attack and that is decreasing our airspeed."

Just about that time the left engine backfired one time and the RPM gauge dropped to 1200 RPM's. Dan moved the left throttle, manifold pressure and mixture control handles full forward but it didn't have any effect on increasing the RPM's. He also had to start holding more right rudder to attempt to counteract the tendency of the aircraft to turn into the engine that was generating less power. Dan began to move the rudder trim tab to compensate for the torque but he could see that wasn't going to have the desired effect. Dan told Tim to contact Anchorage and tell them they were icing and also were having mechanical troubles. Tim got on the radio.

"Anchorage Center, Douglas November niner one four zero Romeo is nine five miles south of Bettles VOR, heading one two eight degrees, eight thousand. Encountering icing conditions, have mechanical problem with left engine and losing altitude, over."

"November four zero Romeo, Anchorage. Understand icing, mechanical problem and losing altitude. Are you declaring an emergency?"

Tim looked at Dan who shook his head. "Not at this time ... four zero Romeo."

"Roger, four zero Romeo. We still have you radar contact squawking one four two two. Keep us advised." Anchorage replied.

"Roger, November four zero Romeo, out."

Ten minutes later the DC-3 was at seven thousand five hundred feet and Dan had dropped the right wing and was holding right rudder trying to keep the aircraft on the assigned heading. His right leg was beginning to ache from the pressure so he told Tim to get on the rudder with him. The aircraft was still losing altitude and Dan could see that in just a few minutes they were going to be passing through seven thousand feet. This was the critical altitude for maintaining radio contact because of the mountainous terrain. There was no way they could keep the plane in the air for long. Dan told Tim to contact Anchorage and tell them they were going to make an emergency landing at Nenana.

"Anchorage Center, Douglas November niner one four zero Romeo is making an emergency landing at Nenana. I repeat, emergency landing at Nenana."

(Silence)

"Try them again, Tim," Dan requested.

Tim repeated the message ... there was no answer.

"O.K., Tim. Squawk 7700[2] and get out the ADF approach chart for Nenana."

---

2. Transponder Code for Emergency

Chapter 49

'Gooney Bird' Down

The radar controller in the Air Route Traffic Control Center in Anchorage was peering at his radar screen keeping a close check on that DC-3 which had reported having icing and mechanical problems. He had them tagged at seven thousand feet squawking 1422. He had just glanced at them and was turning his attention to an Air Alaska flight when there was a glow on the DC-3 blip and the numbers 7700 appeared. He turned to his supervisor.

"Hey, George, my DC-3 out of Deadhorse just went seventy-seven hundred!"

George Mynatt, the senior controller and supervisor of the shift came over to Bob Andrews' scope.

"Have you tried to raise them?"

"Nope, it just happened when I called you."

"Well, see if you can get them on the horn."

"Douglas November niner one four zero Romeo, Anchorage Center."

A moment or two passed ... "Call them again," George insisted.

"Douglas November niner one four zero Romeo, Anchorage Center."

"What altitude were they at the last time you talked with them," asked George.

"They had been losing altitude down from nine thousand and the last time I got them they were just at seven thousand." Bob replied.

While the two of them were looking at the scope, the DC-3 with the 7700 "blip" disappeared from the screen.

"O.K., that's it!" George declared. Let's get the word out. I'll have the front desk call the Air National Guard Rescue Unit and Civil Air Patrol to initiate search and rescue. Where did you have the last fix on them?"

"Sixty miles north of Nenana," Bob replied.

"All right, I'll pass along that info. I doubt that anything can be done tonight in the lousy weather they have up there but let's do our part. Bob, do you have any other aircraft in the area that might relay a transmission for us?"

"Not right now." Bob answered.

"Well, make sure you tag it as an item to brief your relief about. In the meantime, put out a general request for any aircraft to monitor for an ELT."

Chapter 50

Premonition

Frank was laying over in Denver so Sue called Jess and invited her over.

"Come on over and we can have a bite of dinner and just 'hang out.' You might bring your nightie and just spend the night."

"Well, I don't know about spending the night but I will bring it and we will see," Jess replied. She was in her car and over at Sue's condo in twenty-five minutes.

Sue opened the door and Jess said,

"Hi," and walked into the foyer with a small overnight bag.

"*Well,* aren't you the jolly one," Sue remarked. "Why the long face?"

"Dan and I had a little tiff about a week ago." Jess offered.

"A little *what?*" questioned Sue.

"A 'tiff.' You know … an argument. It was my fault as much as his but we haven't spoken to each other since and I am just sick about it." Jess furrowed her brow.

"Well, well, the love birds have had their first run-in," Sue grinned.

"Ain't funny, dammit," Jess replied, taking her coat off revealing a high necked grey wool sweater. She had on a gold chain belt and a long black skirt with her black patent boots.

"At least you still look good," Sue remarked.

"Thanks. But I sure as hell don't feel good."

"Ahhh, the damsel in dismay." and Sue continued to grin. "Come on ... let's go into the kitchen and have a little glass of wine. That will warm you up and lift your spirits."

"I need *something* to lift my spirits," Jess said. "Dammit, Sue. I miss him."

"I would say that would be natural seeing as how you are in love with him," Ann smiled as she filled two wine glasses about half full with White Zinfindel.

"Love? Who said I loved him?" Jess answered with a tone of indignation.

"Aw, *c'mon*, Jess. It's written all over your face ... and your butt too, probably."

Jess plopped down in one of the kitchen chairs and suddenly a grin spread across her face.

"You've been peeking!"

"Atta girl ... now, you feel better don't you? Honest confessions are good for the soul."

Jess lifted her glass and sipped the wine.

"I'm hooked, Sue ... I may as well admit it. And I'm worried too."

"About what?"

"Dan and Tim flew up to Deadhorse today on a 'turn-around.' They should be back by now. Also the weather up there today was terrible ... snow and freezing rain. I called Stevens Aviation just before coming over here and they haven't heard from them."

Jess was sitting in the chair rubbing her left arm with her right in an effort to ease the tension in her body. Sue walked over to her and put her arm around her shoulders, patting her.

"Now, don't worry. Dan's a great pilot ... if the weather got too bad they probably put the plane down somewhere to wait it out. C'mon, let's have some dinner and you will feel better."

"I hope so, Sue. I just have this awful feeling in the pit of my stomach.

Chapter 51

▼

Emergency Landing

"How far to the Nenana VOR, Tim?" Dan could feel perspiration forming on his forehead and under his armpits.

"Forty-two miles. I've got the chart right here and I'm plotting our outbound heading from the VOR for an approach to Runway two one right." Tim replied. "How are we doing? Are you still able to control the heading?"

"Yeah ... I've reduced the RPM's on the right engine to about 1500 since we've got to lose altitude anyway but the controls are getting a mushy feeling. If that right engine keeps turning up I think we may be able to make it in. We've got to get this thing on the ground before too long though or it may just fall out of the sky." Dan had an anxious tone to his voice.

"O.K., here's what I've got, Tim replied. "Nenana has an ADF on the field, frequency 525." Tim reached for the ADF tuning knob and dialed in 5-2-5. The needle immediately sprung to life and pointed about twenty degrees to the right of center.

Tim continued, "Let's see ... we are on a heading of one two eight ... which is good. We need to depart the VOR at 3,000 which is the MSA[1] for this area. Heading of one two zero. On that heading, when the ADF needle reads ninety degrees we can turn right to a heading of two one zero which should line us up with the runway. We can then descend to the approach altitude of 2000 feet."

---

1. Minimum Safe Altitude

"What's the field elevation and length of the runway?" Dan asked.

"The elevation is 360 feet and the runway is 4,967 feet long and it's an asphalt runway."

"That's good." Dan replied. "I can't wait for that needle to read ninety degrees though. We can't risk too tight a turn with this ice load. We need to 'lead' the turn by at least ten degrees I would think."

"O.K., Dan. You're the boss."

Yeah ... some boss. I'm the one who got us into this damn mess. Dan thought to himself. *At least the precipitation stopped about twenty minutes ago so we aren't picking up any additional ice.*

Ten minutes later Dan noticed the left engine had dropped down to 1000 RPM's. *Oh, God, don't let us lose it now!* The DC-3 was now at thirty-two hundred feet and twelve miles from the Nenana VOR. Dan reduced power on the right engine to twelve hundred RPM's and continued to hold the right wing a little low and kept pressure on the right rudder, trying to maintain their heading.

They crossed the VOR at two thousand seven hundred feet and Dan turned the aircraft slightly left until they were on the one two zero heading outbound from the VOR. Dan had to run the right engine back up to 2200 RPM's to maintain altitude and he was having real difficulty in keeping the aircraft from yawing to the left. He dropped the right wing a little more and increased the pressure on the right rudder. He noticed they were losing altitude at the rate of about 300 feet per minute but there wasn't anything he could do about it. He just prayed there was a safety factor built into that MSA.

Tim had tuned in the 150 degree radial 'FROM' the Nenana VOR and watched the needle. When it centered that would be the point at which they could begin the descent from 3000 feet into the airport. Tim then shifted his attention to the ADF needle so that when it read 80 degrees to the right he could inform Dan to start his turn towards the runway.

"O.K., Dan, time to start the turn," Tim informed him.

Dan started turning the aircraft gently to the right and when the ADF needle centered on zero they were headed towards the ADF beacon located on the field. Tim then shifted his eyes to the VOR needle. When it centered he told Dan,

"O.K., Dan, we can begin the descent. Dan said nothing to Tim about the fact they were already down to 2,500 feet.

Tim asked, "You want me to drop the gear?"

"*No!*" Dan replied. "I don't want to do anything to disturb the airflow right now. I'll let you know when." Dan could now reduce the power on the right engine and relieve some of the pressure on his right leg. The aircraft was still in a descent of 300 feet per minute as prescribed on the ADF approach chart. They had estimated that the time to the field would be seven minutes.

After six minutes had elapsed Dan was just about to shove both of the throttles to the firewall and tell Tim they were aborting the approach when Tim shouted,

"Look! To your left Dan ... I see runway lights!"

Fortunately Nenana, although unattended at night, had an automatic lighting system which turned on the lights at a certain ambient light reading. Dan looked to his eleven o'clock position and saw the lights. He called out,

"Gear down!" and he turned the aircraft slightly to the left. Tim moved the gear lever to the down position.

A few seconds later Tim called, "We have two green." The two green lights near the gear lever indicated the two main wheels were down and locked. Dan reduced the speed to ninety-five knots which was a little excess speed but he was reluctant to cut it back any further, afraid the aircraft might stall with the extra weight caused by the ice.

"It's got to be right the first time, Tim. I don't believe the ol' gal will be able to generate enough power for a go-around. Make sure your seat belt is tight. I'm going to put it on the ground regardless!"

Tim checked his belt and said a prayer. It had been so long since he had prayed that he felt guilty but he hoped the Lord would still be listening. Dan was so tense the muscles in his neck were beginning to spasm but there was no time for anything else at the moment but to get the wheels of the DC-3 on that runway.

When Dan was sure they were going to make the runway he began to come back on the power and as the airspeed indicator read eighty-five knots the aircraft stalled and the stall warning horn began to blare. Ten seconds later the wheels hit the asphalt runway with a jolting bounce. Dan had to fight the rudder pedals to maintain directional control as the aircraft wanted to slide to the left. Finally the tail began to come down and the snow on the runway helped slow the aircraft. Fortunately the snowfall had not been so deep that it obliterated the light coming from the runway lights. They were still glowing through the snow. Dan let the aircraft roll until only about a third of the runway was left then he began to apply brakes. The DC-3 started to slide to the left as there apparently was ice under the snow. Dan flipped off the Master Switch then released the brakes and let the aircraft roll a few feet further then stepped on the left brake to try and straighten the plane. He let it roll further and just touched the brakes occasionally. Soon he managed to bring it to a halt without running off the side of the runway.

"Whooooo-Ahhh!," Tim shouted and slapped Dan on the back. Dan sat motionless for a moment. He noticed that his hands, still locked around the control wheel, were shaking. He and Tim then went through the shut down procedures.

There was no sign of life on the field. They could make out the small office in the dark but there was no sign of a light. After a few minutes they decided to disembark and see if they could possibly find a telephone in the office. Before leaving the aircraft, Dan turned on the ELT just in case search aircraft managed to get out this evening. He also took the Very pistol and put it in the pocket of his parka. If they managed to get inside the office they might want to stay in there all night. If they did hear any search planes he could run outside and fire off a flare. They put on their parkas and gloves, got the mag light, put the ladder down from the cargo door and got out of the aircraft, closing the door behind them.

They walked through the snow to the office and found it was locked. They shined their flashlight through one window and saw a desk with a phone on it. Then they went to the small hangar and found a door open on the side of the building. Inside were two aircraft, a Mooney and a Maule STOL with a ski/wheel combination gear. The door from the hangar into the office was locked but it didn't appear to be a dead bolt lock so they both put their shoulders to the door and after a few shoves they were able to force the door open, splitting the door jamb.

Inside the office they found a light switch and turned on the lights then Dan picked up the phone receiver and didn't get a dial tone. Evidently there was a switch located somewhere that turned the phone off when the office was locked for the night. That, or else the line may have broken due to the ice load. They searched for the switch but eventually gave up. Fortunately there was a pot bellied stove in one corner of the room and there was some wood in the firebox. Dan started a fire while Tim went back to the airplane to get their sleeping bags.

In the plane, Tim opened up the food locker and got two cans of vegetable soup, some packaged dried beef, canned tomatoes, cheese, crackers and a can of sardines. He also got a small pan so they could heat the soup. Tim put all of those items in one of the sleeping bags and zipped it up so they wouldn't fall out. He then rolled up the bag and dropped both bags out of the plane into the snow, recovered them and headed back to the office.

Dan had the fire going by the time Tim got back and they went to work preparing their meal. They heated the soup in the pan and ate the canned tomatoes, dried beef and some crackers with sardines. At least it was enough to satisfy their hunger.

"I wish there was some way to let the FAA know that we're o.k.," Dan remarked. "But it would be stupid for us to set off on foot in this weather. We wouldn't have the foggiest idea of which way the town would be."

"Yeah, I know," Tim replied. "I guess we have done about all that we can do. No doubt the airport manager is going to be really ticked off about us breaking in his door though."

"It couldn't be helped," Dan said. "Hell, we couldn't stay out there and freeze in that airplane when there is a better place to be."

After eating their meager rations, they unrolled their sleeping bags. Dan threw a couple of more logs in the stove and hoped they would have enough wood left to keep it going until morning. Dan looked at his Breitling and it read twenty minutes after nine. They were due in Anchorage at ten minutes after seven. He wondered how many at Intermont knew that they were missing and he also wondered if Jess knew and if she was worried about him. Dan heard Tim breathing heavily which indicated he must be asleep. Ten minutes later Dan joined him.

Chapter 52

USS Columbus

Commander Julius Loudon entered the control room of the *USS Columbus* with a cup of coffee in his hand. Lieutenant Gary S. Monroe, navigator of the *Columbus* was standing at the plot with a compass in his right hand tapping it lightly on the chart he was studying. Commander Loudon approached.

"Good morning, Lieutenant."

Lieutenant Monroe looked up from his charts and straightened up. "Good morning, Captain. How are you this morning, sir?"

"Very well, thank you. What's our present position?"

Lieutenant Monroe took one pointed end of the compass and placed it on the chart he had been studying.

"Right here, sir. Forty-five degrees north and one hundred forty degrees east."

Just at that moment, the Executive Officer, Lieutenant Commander MacKenzie came out of Fire Control and joined them.

"What does sonar have to say about our 'friend,' Mac?" asked Captain Loudon.

"He's held to his course all night, Captain. He stopped dead in the water twice and remained silent for about ten minutes each time."

"And I assume that we did the same?" questioned Loudon.

"Oh, yes sir. No chance he heard us, Captain. We have remained beyond his sonar range," replied Lt. Commander MacKenzie.

"Very well. It appears that he may be headed for the La Perouse Strait." Testing his Executive Officer's acuity, the Captain asked,

"That being the case, Commander MacKenzie, what would you say would be his options once he has traversed the strait?"

"Well, sir." Lieutenant Commander MacKenzie picked up a pencil and pointed to the Island of Sakhalin to the north, "He could be heading to the east side of Sakhalin or to the west coast of the Kamchatka Peninsula," and he moved his pencil to the right to Kamchatka. "Of course," continued MacKenzie, "he could continue on eastward across the Kuril Ridge."

Captain Loudon said, "Assuming that he does cross the Kuril Ridge, Commander, where do you think he could possibly be heading then?"

MacKenzie moved his pencil eastward on the chart. It stopped and the Lieutenant Commander turned his head to look at the Captain who was already staring at him.

"The Aleutians?" asked MacKenzie.

Captain Loudon tore off a sheet of scratch paper from a pad lying on the plot table and began to write. When finished he handed the note to MacKenzie.

"Get this off to Pearl, Mac."

Lt. Commander MacKenzie looked at the note. It read:

TO: COMSUBPAC—PEARL HARBOR

FROM: SSN COLUMBUS

CONTINUING TO TRACK DPRK ROMEO CLASS SUBMARINE. POSSIBLY HEADING FOR KURIL RIDGE. POSSIBLE DESTINATION MAY BE ALEUTIANS. WILL CONTINUE TO TRACK AS PER OPERATIONAL ORDER DTD 15 DEC 88.

J. LOUDON COMMANDER USN

"Yes sir, right away sir," MacKenzie replied.

Chapter 53

▼

Eleven O'Clock News

Sue and Jess, having nothing much else to do, had watched a re-run of Clint Eastwood in the movie *High Plains Drifter* on Anchorage Channel 3. Jess was sitting on the couch in a silk two piece pajama set with her legs crossed underneath her. She had a 'throw' covering her lap and legs. Sue was in a long cotton gown with a pair of cotton pajama socks leaning back in a large recliner. The movie ended and immediately went into commercial announcements.

Sue said, "Well, we've been up this long so we may as well catch the eleven o'clock news."

Jess replied, "O.K., but I guarantee it won't be anything but bad news," and she took the final sip from her cup of decaf coffee.

The announcer for Channel 3 News came on the screen: "Good evening Ladies and Gentlemen, this is Brian O'Connor with your late breaking Channel Three News. Topping the headlines this evening is a report of a missing DC-3 cargo aircraft owned by Intermont Mining & Supply Company of Anchorage. The aircraft was returning from Deadhorse where it had made a delivery of oil drilling equipment to Alyeska. According to a report from the Federal Aeronautics Authority the aircraft disappeared from the radar screen of the Anchorage Air Route Traffic Control Center around six p.m. local time after the pilot had radioed the DC-3 had encountered heavy icing and mechanical problems. It is suspected the plane is down in the vicinity of Nenana. The only persons on board were the company chief pilot and co-pilot. We will keep you posted on any late breaking news pertaining to this accident. Now to other local news we had a ...

Jess's face turned ashen white, she dropped her empty cup and saucer into her lap, put her hands to her face and let out a scream, *"Oh, God ... No, No, No!"* and she began to sob uncontrollably. Sue jumped from her chair, sat down on the couch beside Jess and put her arm around her shoulders. Jess buried her face in Sue's bosom and continued to cry. With both arms around Jess, much like a mother would comfort a hurting child, Sue said,

"Oh, Jess. Don't give up, honey. They just said the plane is missing and you know that Dan is a good pilot. You've got to have faith that he and Tim are both going to be O.K."

They both sat on the couch in that position for nearly a half hour as Sue continued to attempt to console Jess whose body was still jerking with each sob. Finally Sue convinced her that they both should go to bed and try to get some sleep so Sue helped Jess to the guest bedroom. Sue helped tuck Jess into bed, stepped into her bathroom and got an Advil. Sue returned to Jess with a glass of water and the Advil.

"Here, honey, take this. It will relax you and help you to get to sleep."

Jess sobbed, "Oh, Sue, it won't help. I know I'm just going to lie here all night and cry.

Why did this have to happen to Dan and me? We were so happy together."

Sue convinced her to take the Advil and stayed in the room with Jess for awhile, sitting in a barrel back chair that was in the room. Finally Jess showed signs of beginning to drift off to sleep. Sue turned out the light on the nightstand beside the bed and eased out of the room.

Chapter 54

Search & Rescue

A rattling sound awoke Dan and he realized it was sleet lashing against the window of the small Nenana airport office building. Apparently the storm had moved further south and was now over Nenana. Dan was thankful that they had been running on the front edge of the bad weather and had time to get into a safe haven. He looked at the luminous dial of his chronograph and saw that it was 11:20 p.m. The room was still warm even though Dan could see from the vents in the opening of the door on the pot-bellied stove that the fire was slowly dying. He crawled out of his sleeping bag, went to the wood box, picked up two medium sized logs and opened the door to the stove. As he was placing the logs in the opening, Tim roused and sleepily asked,

"What time is it?"

Dan told him, "It's nearly eleven-thirty."

"You think air rescue will be looking for us?"

"You hear that sleet hitting the building? I don't think those guys are idiots, Tim."

Tim grunted and rolled over. Dan went back to his sleeping bag and crawled back in, hoping that he could sleep until morning.

* * * *

The call from the Anchorage Air Traffic Route Control Center had come in to the charge of quarters of the 71st Air Rescue Squadron at Elmendorf Air Force Base at approximately seven forty-five p.m. Senior Airman Robert Adams, who had taken the call wrote down all the details pertaining to the downed DC-3 and immediately contacted Captain Josh Williams who was Officer of the Day. Captain Williams was just finishing up his dinner in the Officers' Club and he immediately drove over to the 71st Headquarters building where Airman Adams was located.

Captain Williams went over the details with Airman Adams and then the captain called the Anchorage ARTCC office to see if they had any later information. They informed him they did not. Captain Williams then called the base weather office and talked with the specialist on duty informing him of the details that were available pertaining to the downed DC-3. The specialist told Captain Williams that the ice storm that was moving in a southeasterly direction would be over Nenana in approximately an hour to an hour and a half and would, in his opinion, prohibit any rescue aircraft from operating in that area. Captain Williams thanked him for the information and asked the specialist to continue monitoring the weather in that area and to notify the 71st Headquarters when it appeared that the weather would be suitable to mount a rescue mission. The specialist confirmed that he would follow Captain Williams' orders. Just to "cover his six," the captain contacted Colonel Frank Walker, the commanding officer of the 71st at his quarters. Captain Williams explained the situation in detail and related the information he had gathered from the weather specialist.

"Sir, it is just about two hundred miles from Anchorge to Nenana and by the time one of our helicopters could get to the Nenana area they would no doubt be in the thick of icing conditions." Captain Williams reported.

"I concur, Captain. It appears that you have the situation well in hand. There is nothing we can do until that weather system moves out of there. Thanks for informing me of the situation. Keep me posted."

"Yes sir, thank you sir." Captain Williams hung up the receiver.

Chapter 55

The Survivors

Tim woke up at 5:30 the morning after the forced landing and the first thing he noticed was the silence. He crawled out of the sleeping bag and as he did so he heard Dan stirring. Tim made his way over to the window and looked out into the darkness. Apparently the storm had departed the Nenana area.

Tim's stirring awoke Dan. "You see anything out there? "Dan asked.

"Heck no. You couldn't see your hand before your face out there."

Dan crawled out of the bag and walked to the door where the light switch was located and turned on the light in the office.

"Well, at least the storm didn't knock out the power," Dan reported.

"I don't see how unless they have buried electrical lines up here." Tim replied.

"If they do, then the 'phone line would be buried as well." Dan said.

Dan walked over to the wood box and picked up two more logs and put them in the stove.

"I hope somebody shows up soon. We've only got about four logs left in the wood box."

"What now?" Tim asked.

"Well, for one thing, I'm hungry. Did you notice if there was any coffee in the food locker when you got the food last night?"

"Yeah, I believe there was a couple of pound tins of some kind of coffee there. Am I going to have to go out there just so you can have your coffee?" Tim asked.

"Nope. I'm going to go get it myself and also anything else out there that is edible."

"Awww, surely you aren't going to do that, are you?"

"Man, I can't navigate without my coffee. You stay here ... I can manage."

"You sure you don't need me?"

"I said for you to stay *here*, didn't I?" Dan said a little testily. "Tell you what. You look around, I'll bet there is a coffee pot here somewhere and maybe a pan we can use to cook with if we need it."

With that, Dan put on his parka, his Tennessee ball cap, put on his mittens and wrapped a muffler over his nose and mouth. He got the mag light and pulled the hood of the parka over his head before opening the door to the hangar. He walked through the hangar and opened the door to the outside. The arctic air hit the exposed part of his face like a thousand needles but he trudged out into the darkness in what he hoped was the right direction to the DC-3.

In about five minutes, following the beam of his mag light, he saw the hulking shape of the aircraft in the darkness ahead. The ladder was still at the cargo door so Dan carefully climbed the ladder but there was no way he could open the door. The ice had frozen it shut. Dan backed down and shined the light on the wing and the tail empennage. Icicles were hanging off every surface. It was as if the airplane was in an ice cocoon. Dan retraced his steps back to the office.

Opening the door into the hangar and then the one into the office, he saw that Tim had, indeed, found an old porcelain coffee pot with a strainer inside. Apparently it was used quite regularly.

"Where did you find that?" Dan asked.

Tim grinned. "In the lunchroom."

"In the *what?*"

"The lunchroom. C'mere."

Tim opened the door to the hangar and took a 90 degree turn to the left and walked towards the back wall. There was a door opening into a small room. Tim reached to his right and flipped on a light switch. This room apparently was used as something of a pilot's lounge and a place for them to eat their lunch and snacks. There was a two burner hotplate on the counter next to a sink. On the back wall were several shelves with some foodstuffs. There was a part of a can of coffee, two cans of Spam, one can of stewed tomatoes, and two cans of Campbell's tomato soup. In the small refrigerator was a package of American cheese and also two Irish potatoes were in the crisper bin. Not exactly the fare you would find at the Crow's Nest but it would have to do.

Chapter 56

▼

Air Force Alert

"Seventy-first Air Rescue Squadron, Senior Airman Adams."

"This is Tech Sergeant O'Brien in Base Weather Ops. The latest weather for the Nenana area reports no icing conditions from the surface to fifteen thousand feet. This is from a PIREP[1] by a C-130 transiting the area at 0530 flying at 11,000 feet. Our forecast estimates visibility to be five miles with probability of increasing to ten miles by 0830. Sorry the information is so sketchy but, as you may know, we have no actual reporting facilities within seventy-five miles of Nenana."

"Thanks, Sarge, I'll pass this on to the O.D." Adams noted the time; it was 0556.

Airman Adams called Captain Williams number at his quarters. The captain had gone to bed but was wide awake after hearing it was Airman Adams calling. The captain was given the information and he told Airman Adams to alert the search and rescue crew and he would be at Headquarters in thirty minutes.

Airman Adams found the duty roster for the day and dialed the number for Lieutenant Donald Fontana.

"Lieutenant Fontana," the voice said sleepily.

---

1. Pilot reports from aircraft.

"This is Senior Airman Adams, Lieutenant. Captain Williams is mounting a SAR for a downed DC-3 in the vicinity of Nenana and asks that you alert your crew and report to headquarters ASAP."

"Thank you, sergeant. I'm on it."

Captain Williams was in the headquarters office by 0641 and within ten minutes 1st Lt. Jake Fontana arrived. Five minutes later 2nd Lieutenant David Groves arrived with Paramedics Technical Sergeant Mike Harper and Staff Sergeant Greg Smith following minutes later. The entire crew assembled around a plotting table with Captain Williams and they hashed out a search pattern for their Sikorsky HH-60 Helicopter which had been configured for emergency medical evacuation.

The 'copter was equipped with Bendix color weather radar, Doppler navigation, GPS, INS, moving map display, new HF, VHF and satellite comms, IR jammer, FLIR, refueling probe, IR strobes, ESSS, HUD, and digital data BUS. Cruise speed of 110 knots. The crew boarded the helicopter at 0720 with Lt. Fontana at the controls and Lt. Groves as co-pilot. They were off the ground at 0732 headed for the Nenana area.

Chapter 57

Jess' Revelation

The next morning Jess arose, took her shower, fixed her hair and attempted to cover up the redness around her eyes with make-up. She could conceal the cosmetic change in her appearance but she could do little about the sad expression on her face. Jess went into the kitchen where Sue, still in her robe and house shoes, was fixing some cereal and toast.

"Why don't you call in sick this morning, Jess? You know that you won't be able to concentrate on your work once you get there."

"No, Sue. If I sit around here I will just be glued to that television set all day and that will be worse than if I go on to the office and try to get my mind on other things although I'm afraid that I won't be able to."

"O.K., honey. You know what you have to do but you know that I would be glad to have you stay here and I would be here with you."

Jess walked over to the stove where Sue had the bread in the toaster. She put her arms around Sue and gave her a hug.

"Sue, I don't know what I would do without you. You and Frank have both been *so* good to me since I have been here. I couldn't possibly have any friends better than you two."

Sue gave Jess a big squeeze, patted her on the back then they both sat down at the table and had their cereal, toast and coffee.

* * * *

Jess walked into the lobby of the Intermont office about nine-fifteen and it was all she could do to look Virginia Stewart in the eye. Virginia looked at her and said,

"Good morning Miss Jess. Have you heard about Mr. Dan and Tim?"

Jess said solemnly, "Yes, I have, Virginia."

"Oh … Miss Jess. Mr. Switzer said when you came in he would like to see you."

"Thank you, Virginia."

Jess went into her office, picked up the phone and dialed Al Switzer's extension.

"You wish to see me, Al?"

"Yes, just come on in, Jess."

Jess walked to the door which connected the two offices, opened it and went into Al's office. He was standing by the coffee table where the four easy chairs were located.

"I suppose you have heard about Dan and Tim?" Al asked.

"Yes, sir." Jess stood still with her two arms hanging loosely in front of her with her hands clasped, her head slightly bowed.

"I suppose the thing we should do is issue a statement to all of the employees about this unfortunate circumstance telling them how badly we feel about the accident and that we all have faith and hope that Dan and Tim will be found safe and sound," Al said looking at Jess.

Jess looked up at Al and tried to compose herself. She started to speak.

"Al … I … I just can't …" and she broke out in tears and put her hands to her face.

Al looked at her, perplexed at first, and then it suddenly dawned on him what the situation was. He walked over to Jess and put his two hands on her shoulders. Jess looked up at him with tears streaming down her face and Al knew for sure then that his suspicions had just been confirmed. He reached in his suit pocket and took out a handkerchief and gave it to Jess and ushered her over to one of the chairs and guided her into the seat.

She sat in the chair wiping her eyes with the handkerchief while Al sat in the chair directly across from her with his arms resting on his legs, hands clasped in front of him and leaning forward towards Jess.

"My Lord, Jess! What a fool I've been … I'm so sorry … I had *no* idea!

"I know ... I know ... no one knows, Al. We've tried to keep it quiet since we both work for the same company. We didn't want to embarrass you or anyone else in management."

"*Embarrass* me? Why, I think it's *wonderful!* Dan is a superb young man and I don't think that he could have found any young lady any more beautiful and with such talent as you!"

Jess put her hands in her lap still clutching the handkerchief, looked at Al and managed a weak smile.

"Thank you, Al. But now ... it ... it's too late!" and she started crying again.

Al reached over and patted Jess on the shoulder.

"Now, now ... don't you talk like that. I have all the confidence in the world that those two young men are safe and sound. Now don't you worry, everything is going to be all right."

Jess had her face practically covered by the handkerchief and with her face buried in the handkerchief and her hands, she nodded her head up and down accepting Al's statement.

"Don't you worry yourself about that announcement to the employees. I'll have Fred take care of it. Now, I want you to take your time and get your face all prettied up and go home and rest," Al said to Jess.

"Oh, no sir." Jess removed the handkerchief. She looked at Al still sniffing and dabbing at her eyes again. "I want to be here because I know this is where the news will come when they have been found."

Jess's face grimaced when she said, "found." Once again she fought another rush of tears. "I'm going to be o.k."

Al got out of the chair and went to the bookcase on the nearby wall. He opened two doors to reveal the bar, took a bottle of brandy and poured a small amount into a glass. He walked back to where Jess was seated.

"Here you go, sip on this. It will help you more than you realize." Al offered the glass to Jess

"Thank you." Jess took the brandy and took a sip of it.

Al walked over to his desk, lifted the phone and dialed Virginia Stewart's number. She answered the phone.

"Yes, sir?"

"Virginia. I want you to hold all of Miss Lane's calls. She isn't feeling well."

"Yes, Mr. Switzer.

Chapter 58

Air Force Rescue

Breakfast for Dan and Tim consisted of Spam covered with melted cheese, warm stewed tomatoes and french fries which Dan had made by slicing the potatoes and frying them in the grease from the Spam. They washed the food down with two cups of coffee which had been perked in the porcelain coffee pot. At least the meal satisfied their hunger and they were sitting around drinking their third cup when they heard an engine noise. Dan looked out the office window and saw a Jeep Wrangler pulling up to the building.

In a few minutes Dan heard a key being inserted in the front door to the office, the door opened and a huge burly figure all wrapped up in a fur trapper's cap, parka, blue jeans and hunter's laced boots walked in through the door.

'Waal, you must be the fellers what came in here last night in that frozen igloo parked out there on the runway." The man pulled off one glove and stuck out a size twelve hand. "I'm Stoney Ferguson, the owner of this shebang," he grinned.

"Dan Nichols, Mr. Ferguson, and this is my partner, Tim Morrison," Dan said as he shook the big hand. Tim got up and walked over and shook hands also.

"Glad to meet'cha. Sorry I couldn't be here to welcome you last night but the weather wasn't fit for man nor beast. I'm surprised you got that old C-47 down in one piece," Stoney said.

"You weren't half as surprised as we were," Dan replied. "I apologize for having to break in your door to the office but our company will reimburse you for the damages as well as the food we just had for breakfast."

"Hey, don't worry about it. This whole damn building ain't worth very much anyway and a busted door jamb ain't goin' to make that much difference."

"Nevertheless, it was a Godsend to Tim and me and we will certainly see that you are well paid," Dan replied.

"Have you called anybody to let them know you are o.k.?" Stoney inquired.

"Well, no we haven't. The phone is dead." Tim spoke up.

Stoney let out a big laugh that would have made a moose jealous. "Oh, it ain't dead ... I just cut it off. Guess you fellers couldn't find the switch, huh?"

Stoney walked over to the desk, got down on his knees and stuck his hand up under the kneehole space.

"There ... try it now," Stoney grinned.

Dan picked up the receiver and got a dial tone.

"Well, I'll be damned. We looked all over the place and couldn't find a switch."

"Yep, I had to hide it good. Dang kids around here would come in at night and call all their friends in Alaska, Canada and the U.S. One month my phone bill was over three hunner'd dollars so I had to find a way to stop 'em."

"I'm going to call my boss in a few minutes, Stoney, but before I do I need to find out if there is some way I can get that DC-3 de-iced. We need it back in Anchorage as soon as possible as we have a trip scheduled for that DC-3 to Prince George in British Columbia."

"Well, I'll tell you what, Captain. There's a farmer about a mile down the road who has a lot of acres in oats, barley and field peas. He has to do a lot of spraying during the growing season and he ain't doin' nuthin' right now. He just might be willin' to bring one of his spraying rigs up here and de-ice that thing for you if you can get the de-icer fluid up here. Also, he has a blade on the front of his tractor and he jus' might clear the runway of snow at the same time," Stoney offered.

"If he will get the plane de-iced and the runway cleared in twenty-four hours from the time the ethylene glycol gets here, I'll see that he gets three hundred dollars for his efforts," Dan said.

"Hey, for that kind of money he'll probably jump through a hoop for ya," Stoney laughed. "These here farmers are hard up for money this time of the year." Dan looked at his watch and saw that it was 9:50 a.m. He dialed the "800" number for Intermont and Virginia Stewart answered the phone.

"Good morning, Virginia, this is Dan Nichols. Is Al there?"

"Oh ... Oh, *thank GOD*, Mr. Nichols! He sure is, hold on."

Dan heard Al's phone ringing, then, "Dan ... thank the Lord, where are you?"

"We're at the airport in Nenana, Al, and Tim and I both are o.k … we don't have a scratch on us and the plane is in good shape but it's covered with ice."

"Well, don't worry about the airplane. I'm just happy you two are safe. The Air Force rescue unit is on the way up there. They left here around seven o'clock this morning and should be there any minute now." Al said.

"Great! Listen, Al, I have someone here who can de-ice the plane and clear the runway for three hundred bucks. We need to get the "three" out of here so we can make that Prince George run so here is what I suggest. Have Joe O'Donoghue load two fifty-five gallon drums of ethylene glycol on the King Air and have Harry hot-foot it up here. Once the "three" is de-iced, Tim and I will fly it back and Harry can bring the King Air back, o.k.?" Dan suggested.

"No, Dan, that's *not* o.k. I want *you* back here as soon as possible. Tim can bring the King Air back and Al can bring the DC-3 back by himself. He has flown it solo before and he can do it again." Al answered.

"But, Al …" Dan began.

"*No but's,* Dan! I want *you* back here on that Air Force helicopter … understood?" Al demanded.

"Well … since you put it that way, Al … o.k., I'll come back with the rescue unit," Dan agreed.

I wonder what put a burr under his saddle? Al has never talked to me that way before.

Just about the time he hung up the phone, Dan heard the "whap-whap-whap" of rotor blades. He quickly picked up the Very pistol from the top of the desk, ran out into the darkness and fired a signal flare to let the helicopter know there was someone below. An instant later he heard the pitch change on the blades and in just a minute or so he picked up the sight of the flashing strobe and running lights of the Sikorsky H-60.

A searchlight from the 'copter had been turned on and the pilot was looking for a suitable spot to land. The helicopter settled on its skis and the whine of the turbine engine began to wind down. Immediately four figures popped out of the helicopter and started running towards the lighted office building.

Chapter 59

The Reunion

Once the men were inside they introduced themselves all around and Dan apologized to them for not having been able to notify anyone by phone earlier. He explained to the helicopter crew about the disabled phone and they all took it as well as could be expected. After all, flying a little over two hours on what turned out to be a fruitless rescue was not exactly their idea of a 'Sunday drive.'

Dan apologized to Tim about his being ordered to return and Tim being left behind and assured Tim that this was not the way he wanted it. Tim apparently didn't mind. He told Dan that he understood someone had to stay and he had no reason why he had to be back in Anchorage at a given time. Dan thanked Stoney Ferguson profusely and assured him he would be getting a check from Intermont in the next few days and it would include the three hundred dollars for his farmer friend.

So, the crew all had a cup of coffee, used the 'head' and after about thirty minutes the four crewmen plus Dan piled in the H-60 and headed back to Anchorage. As soon as the helicopter reached cruising altitude, 2nd Lieutenant David Groves called in to Elmendorf Air Force Base and informed the controller they were on the return flight with the captain of the downed DC-3.

* * * *

The H-60 was hovering over the helicopter pad at Elmendorf AFB at 12:52 p.m. Anchorage time and Lieutenant Jake Fontana put the helicopter down lightly on the skis. All five of the men exited the helicopter and started walking to the Base Operations office. About 50 feet from the building, the door of the office flew open and a female figure started running towards the men. Dan suddenly realized it was Jess and she never broke stride. She spread her arms and hit Dan so hard with her body that he had to take a step backward to keep from falling. Jess' arms were wrapped around Dan's neck and she was crying.

"Dan ... oh, Dan! I thought I was going to *die* when I heard you were missing. Please, please, forgive me! she cried.

Dan took her face in his gloved hands and asked, "Forgive you for what, honey?"

"For the way I acted about Sue and Frank. Can you *ever* forgive me?" she sobbed.

Dan, still holding her in his arms, looked into her dark brown eyes and said, "Jess that's all history and it's forgotten. All that matters is that we are together again and I love you very, very much." Dan smiled at her.

They kissed briefly and stood there holding one another as the four crewmen looked at each other and smiled. The trip had not been for nothing after all.

Walking to the office with Jess hanging onto his arm, Dan understood then why Al had demanded that he come back right away. When they walked into the Base Ops office, Al was standing there. He walked up to Dan and instead of extending his hand he gave Dan a hug, "We're all so thankful that you are back, my boy," Al said.

Chapter 60

COMSUBPAC

Captain James L. Madison, USN, walked to the door bearing the nameplate 'Admiral Horatio B. Crownover' and knocked. A booming voice from the other side said, "Enter!" Captain Madison opened the door and entered the Admiral's office,

"Good morning, Admiral."

"Good morning, Jim. What wonderful tidings do you have for me this morning."

Captain Madison merely laid the message received from the *SSN Columbus* on the desk in front of the Admiral.

"Well, well, it looks as if 'Jules' may have sniffed out a rabbit for himself. The Admiral pushed back in his desk chair, leaned back and looked at Captain Madison over his reading glasses. It was often said about Admiral Crownover in Naval circles, that when Admirals Arleigh "31 Knot" Burke and William "Bull" Halsey had graduated from Annapolis, the bolt of cloth they were both cut from was saved so that enough would be left over for Admiral Horatio B. Crownover.

Admiral Crownover's grandfather had been an Admiral in the U.S. Navy, his father had been a fleet commander in World War II and now Horatio Crownover was the Commander-in-Chief of the Pacific Fleet and was reputed to be every bit as hard nosed as his two 'namesakes,' Admirals Burke and Halsey.

"Jim, to your knowledge, have we ever had a North Korean sub this far north?"

"Not that I can remember, Admiral."

"Hmmmmm," the Admiral, leaning back in the large leather chair, stroked his chin with his left hand, still holding the message in his right.

"And 'Jules' and his boys think they are heading through La Perouse bound for the Aleutian Bay? What do you think, Jim?"

"I would say that due to the Korean sub not having deviated from his course nor significantly reduced his speed at any time, that this may be a distinct possibility, Sir."

Admiral Crownover stood up, turned his back to the Captain and looked at the huge wall map of the Pacific ocean that was on the wall to the rear of his desk. He stood with his hands clasped behind his back for a good two minutes looking at the map then turned around to face Captain Madison.

With a great deal of sarcasm in his voice, Admiral Crownover said, "Well, their timing just couldn't be any better. Secretary of State Baker is presently engaged in negotiations with the North Koreans for better relations and they are sneaking a submarine right into our back door. Keep your eye on this one, Jim, and if that 'gook' crosses into the Aleutian Bay let me know immediately. This will certainly stir up things in the Pentagon to say nothing of the White House."

"Yes, sir, Admiral. I'll stay on top of it." The Captain stood erect, turned smartly and exited the office.

Chapter 61

Welcome Home

The Jaguar Vanden Plas left the Elmendorf visitors parking lot with Al, Jess and Dan all in the front seat. Al was driving and Jess was sitting in the middle snuggled up to Dan. She was still holding on to Dan's left arm with her right. She also had her left hand holding on to Dan's arm as well.

Al spoke, "How about some lunch? We all have been so excited about your return, Dan, that we forgot to eat anything. Are you starved?"

"Yes, sir, I sure am. That fried Spam and warm stewed tomatoes are wearing a little bit thin," and they all had a laugh as Dan described his and Tim's meal in Nenana.

Al pulled into the parking lot of Applebee's.

Inside they were seated immediately and the waitress brought three glasses of water and menus. When they all had made their selections, Al spoke up,

"Dan, I can't tell you how happy I was when I got the call from the sergeant at Elmendorf and he told me that you and Tim had been found safe and sound."

"Thanks, Al," Dan replied. "I appreciate your concern and both Tim and I are really pleased that we were able to get the plane down without any damage."

"Don't you think for a minute I was concerned about that airplane," Al continued. "I still have a guilty conscience about sending you up to Deadhorse in that kind of weather."

"Hey, it was my decision to make. You know the final decision is always up to the pilot and I should have laid over but I was concerned about getting back here so we could make that delivery to Prince George on time," Dan replied.

"Well, you don't have to worry about that. I have already called all three of the mines and explained the situation. Not a one of them is in dire need of anything on the order. By the way, one of Stevens' mechanics went up to Nenana with Harry in the King Air to check that left engine and make sure it will be in good mechanical condition for the flight back. They should be in here this evening with the aircraft if everything is o.k. Joe O'Donoghue is having a crew stay over and load it so Harry and Tim can get out of here in the morning," said Al.

"I really should to be going on that trip, Al."

"No, I want you to go by the office in the morning and have a meeting with Fred. We are working on the budget for next year and all he needs is your approval of the figures for the aircraft division to finish it up." To himself Al was thinking, *"And there is someone else who needs you here too."*

The waiter arrived with their orders and they began to eat their lunch.

All three were eating their food and finally Al spoke again,

"Jess, I went by the health care center yesterday evening and visited with Evelyn."

Jess asked, "How is she getting along?"

"Not well at all."

Dan looked at Al as he took his napkin and wiped his mouth. Dan thought he saw tears forming in Al's eyes. Al could hardly speak of his wife now without becoming emotional.

"When I greeted her, she looked at me, smiled and said, 'Can I do something for you?' She didn't know who I was. This has been going on a lot lately." Al definitely had tears in his eyes.

"Oh, Al, I'm *so* sorry!" Jess took her hand and patted Al's forearm.

"Well, I knew that it was just a matter of time. I should have been prepared for this but I suppose no one wants to face a situation like this. The doctor told me this time that the day would probably come in a few months when she wouldn't recognize anyone she has known." Al put down his fork and took several swallows of water. He set the glass down and continued. "When we finish lunch I want you kids to take the rest of the afternoon off and rest. The two of you have had a couple of real rough days."

Dan and Jess both objected but Al insisted. When they left the restaurant they drove to the Intermont parking lot.

Dan suddenly remembered that he had left the Jeep Cherokee in the Stevens parking lot. Jess told him not to worry about it, she would take him out there in the morning and pick it up. Al went towards the office building while Jess and Dan got in her Corvette and departed.

"Do you feel like stopping by the grocery store for a few minutes?" Jess asked.

'Why sure," Dan smiled. "You think I am a basket case or something?" Dan replied.

"Well … I'm not sure but I intend to find out," she said with a mischievous look on her face.

Jess whipped the Corvette into the Chugach Supermarket and they both went in. Jess got a cart and began to pick up several items including two strip sirloin steaks that looked really nice. They went through the checkout line and Dan tried to pay for the groceries but Jess would have no part of it. Back in the Corvette, they were at her apartment in fifteen minutes.

When they got inside and put the groceries in the kitchen, Dan asked,

"You mind if I take a shower?"

"You go right ahead. You want me to lay out something for you to put on?"

"Like what?"

"Well, I could let you borrow my Mickey Mouse nightshirt," she laughed.

"You *do* that!" Dan exclaimed. "If I get my hands on that damn thing I'm going to burn it"

"Over my dead body," Jess replied. Again the mischievous smile appeared.

"That's my favorite 'nightie.'"

Dan took his shower and put his same clothes back on and went into the kitchen. Jess was putting the steaks into the refrigerator when Dan moved up behind her and put his arms around her waist. She closed the refrigerator door turned around and put her arms around his neck and they engaged in a long, long, kiss.

"Oh, Dan," Jess breathed. "I really, really felt like I was going to die when I heard that you and Tim were missing."

"I know, I know," Dan said. "The last thing I thought of when we were heading in for the landing was, 'Oh, Lord, let me get this thing down in one piece so I can be with Jess again.'"

"Did you *really?*"

"Yes, I did … *really*."

She relaxed her arms, gave Dan a little kiss and said, "Now get out of here before I lose control. I've got to fix our dinner."

Later that evening the two of them sat at the dinner table where Jess had placed two candles and they enjoyed a wonderful dinner she had prepared and they ended it with a glass of red wine.

Dan said, "You keep cooking like this and I may have to marry you."

"Is that a promise?" Jess replied with a smile.

Dan leaned back in his chair, raised his glass of wine and finished it off.

"Well, I may have to domesticate you first," he said, placing the empty glass on the table.

Jess looked at him very coyly and said, "I'm ready … just anytime."

They both removed the plates from the table and Dan helped Jess clean up the pots, pans, and placed the dishes and silverware in the dishwasher. They then retired to the living room to watch the news on TV.

There was an old John Wayne movie coming on at seven o'clock which they both decided to see for the second, or third, time. They settled down on the couch close together and Jess reached over and held Dan's hand in hers. The movie had been on for about thirty minutes when Jess heard Dan breathing heavily. She looked over at him and he was sound asleep. Jess got up and lifted his legs onto the couch. She unbuckled his belt, unzipped his trousers and pulled them off as well as his shoes. She went into the bedroom, got a pillow and a blanket and returned. She lifted Dan's head, placed the pillow under it and threw a blanket over him. She leaned over and kissed him on the forehead and whispered, "Welcome home from the sea, sailor." She turned off the TV and the lamp and stole out of the room.

Jess undressed, pulled back the covers and sat down on the edge of the bed. She set the alarm for six o'clock, got under the covers and turned out the light. "Dammit!" she murmured and turned over on her side.

Chapter 62

Christmas Plans

The steady buzz of the alarm clock awoke Jess at five minutes until six o'clock. She jumped out of bed, slipped on her robe and bedroom slippers and went into the kitchen where she started a pot of coffee. She then went into the living room, turned on the floor lamp and shook Dan.

"Huh … huh? What's going on?" he said.

"It's time to get up and go fly somewhere," Jess replied.

Rubbing his eyes with his fists, Dan replied, "Go fly? Fly where?"

Jess let out a laugh. "Oh, I don't know, but I'm sure you will think of somewhere."

"Oh … damn! I'm sorry, Jess. I guess I was more tired than I thought I was." Dan sat up on the couch. Jess sat down in his lap and put her arms around his neck and gave him a kiss. Dan slipped his arms under her robe around her body feeling the warmth and softness.

"I really screwed up, didn't I?" he said.

Jess smiled at him and said softly, "No, you didn't … that's the problem."

"Well, come here," Dan grabbed her as he fell back onto the couch.

"Oh, no you don't!" Jess laughed and pulled away, standing up. "You had your chance and blew it. Come on in the kitchen and I *may* let you have a cup of coffee," and she got up and walked into the kitchen with Dan tagging along behind.

They stood in the kitchen, Jess in her robe, nightgown and scuffies and Dan in his sock feet, T-shirt and boxer shorts, drinking their coffee.

Dan said, "You know, it just dawned on me that I haven't changed clothes in three days. I also need a good shave. What do you say I borrow your car, drive over to the apartment and shave and change and come back by. I'll take you to the International House of Pancakes and try to make amends for last night."

"All right, but don't think you are going to buy me off for a couple of old pancakes," Jess said.

Dan was back in an hour and ten minutes, picked Jess up and they were at the IHOP by eight o'clock. They both ordered the 'special.' Two eggs, two pancakes, sausage links, bacon and coffee. While waiting on their meal Dan took a sip of his coffee and asked,

"What have you got planned for Christmas? It's only ten days away you know."

"Yes, I know, but I really haven't made any plans."

"How would you like to spend three nights at the Denali Overlook Inn?" Dan inquired.

"Are you nuts! That place has probably been booked up for at least two months." Jess replied.

"I know. I booked three rooms there the 15th of October."

"*Three* rooms? How many are going?"

"You, me, Sue and Frank."

"You're *kidding*? Have you asked them?"

"Yep. I called Sue two weeks ago and asked her not to tell you. I wanted it to be a surprise."

"*Dan Nichols!* You dog! Oh, I *love* you!" Jess got up and moved over beside Dan, hugged him and gave him a kiss.

Several of the customers looked over at them and smiled. Jess actually looked a little embarrassed and then asked quietly,

"Why *three* rooms?"

"Well," Dan grinned at her, "that was before I got to *know* you so well ... if you know what I mean."

Jess nudged him in the ribs with her elbow. "You can cancel one of the rooms, you know."

"Yeah, I know ... but I don't think I will." Dan replied.

"Why not?" Jess said with a frown on her face.

"You might get mad at me again and I would have to bunk in with Sue and Frank."

Jess burst out laughing. "Dan Nichols, you're incorrigible!"
"Just like I told you the last time you said that ... I sure hope so."

Chapter 63

Connection Plans

Harry and Tim were late getting away from Anchorage on their flight down to Prince George in the DC-3. They pulled up to the unloading area of the Vanguard warehouse a few minutes after eight p.m. The floodlights from the overhang above the loading dock were illuminated and it lit up the area almost as if it was daylight. One of the Vanguard employees appeared on the dock and said, "We'll be with you in just a minute."

Five minutes later, Kyle Thornburgh appeared riding on the forklift which would be used for unloading the cargo. Kyle drove the forklift down a ramp to ground level and approached the aircraft. The other Vanguard employee walked down the ramp and joined Kyle, Tim, and Harry. Kyle introduced the Vanguard employee as John Hanson and Tim and Harry proceeded to remove the "dogs" from the skids which held the skids locked down to the floor of the aircraft.

The unloading began and as the skids nearest to the door were unloaded, Tim and Harry, by means of a block and tackle, moved skids located fore and aft in the aircraft to the doorway to facilitate the unloading. Once the cargo was unloaded, Kyle spoke up.

"You guys want to come in and have a cup of coffee?"

"Sure," Harry replied and the four of them walked into the building. Harry noticed that about eighty percent of the warehouse floor space was available for general warehousing but there was about twenty percent which was behind heavy duty woven steel wire that ran from the floor to the ceiling of the warehouse.

There were two large doors, mounted on wheels, which rolled back alongside the framed in area. The doors when closed were locked by a remote locking mechanism, no doubt controlled electrically from inside a nearby office.

Kyle spoke to Harry, "You want to come into the office and finish up the paperwork?"

"Sure," Harry replied and the two of them walked towards an enclosed office at the end of the warehouse leaving Tim and John near the outside door where the unloading had taken place.

Once inside the office, Kyle said,

"We've got to be quick about this ... I don't want to arouse any suspicion on the part of John."

"All I want to know is *when?*" Harry said.

"It's getting close. I would say within two weeks."

"What's taking so damn long?" Harry wanted to know.

"I've told you all along that Abe says it is about timing; something to do with the vehicle that is going to pick the stuff up after you deliver it. Incidentally, they only need three of the containers. The stuff degrades over a period of time and they apparently only need that much to do their testing with. This may mean that we will have only one case to deal with instead of two."

"That suits me fine." Harry replied. "By the way, it isn't going to be as hard for us to make the connection here now since we are bringing in about a load every other week."

"Yeah, but you still have to be here within twenty-four hours of when Crossair delivers the stuff."

"I don't think that's going to be too big a deal," Harry replied.

Kyle signed Harry's bill of lading for the equipment that had been delivered and they both walked back down the warehouse to where Tim and John were waiting.

"You ready to head for the motel?" Harry said to Tim.

"I sure as heck am. I'm still short of sleep from that Deadhorse trip," Tim replied.

Harry laughed. "Yeah, that'll teach you to fly with some guy who hasn't got enough sense to stay out of icing conditions."

Tim thought to himself, *"I'd like to kick your big fat ass."*

Chapter 64

Maturity—Male Vs. Female

Jess had been sitting on the couch reading *The Body in the Library* by Agatha Christie, one of her favorite mystery writers. She removed her reading glasses and looked at her watch. It was a few minutes after ten and she decided she would take her shower and get to bed early.

In the shower, she began to think about Dan. *Hell, he's about all that I think about when I'm not working.* She still felt a little rebuffed about his dropping off to sleep on the couch and hesitated to attribute that to his age. *Forty-six really isn't that old and there's only nine years difference in our ages. Does nine years really affect your libido all that much?*, she wondered. *My gosh, he has the physique of someone seven or eight years younger and he certainly doesn't have the personality of someone that old. The way he kids around and acts you would think he wasn't a day over forty-one at the most.*

She stepped out of the shower and couldn't help but look at herself in the full length mirror on the back of the bathroom door. *Not bad for a thirty-seven year old*, she thought. *Everything is still firm and stacked in the right places. Wonder what it will look like when I am sixty and Dan is sixty-nine? Who will give a damn at that age anyway?* She toweled off, put her hair up and slipped into a two piece silk pajama suit. *No doubt Dan would like this better than the Mickey Mouse nightshirt.*

She slipped between the cool sheets, turned off the lamp on the nightstand and lay there in the dark thinking. *I know he loves me ... you can just tell when someone has deep, sincere feelings for you.* She recalled when she was in high school as a freshman that she was attracted to senior boys and they to her. She had always seemed to be more mature for her age than her peers.

She began to think about Ben, her first husband. *Ben was only one year older than me and come to think of it, that is probably the main reason that our marriage didn't work. He always acted as if he was about five years younger than me. It seems that marriages are more stable if the male is a few years older than the female,* she reasoned. *Probably females mature faster than males, especially when they are younger. This is why the relationship with Dan just has to be better for me ... I need a more mature man.*

Jess slipped off to sleep thinking about the forthcoming trip to the Denali Inn. She had a feeling that this could well be a real turning point in her relationship with Dan.

Chapter 65

Five Days Out

The Submarine UB-235 of the Democratic Peoples Republic of Korea had just traversed the Kuril Ridge and now had taken up a more northeasterly track paralleling the Kuril Trench. The submarine was running on the surface for three reasons; to bring fresh air into the submarine to replace the stale air that permeated the entire vessel, to recharge the batteries that were running quite low, and they could make fifteen knots on the surface as opposed to the eleven or twelve while submerged. Captain Johng Ho Kim and two lookouts were braving the elements on the bridge of the conning tower. Although Captain Johng had a real adversity to cold weather, he thought it necessary to set an example for his men for him to spend time on the bridge in bad weather just as they had to. He had on his full uniform plus his long greatcoat, scarf, leather gloves, and foul weather hat which was fur lined and had covers for his ears. The sea was white-capping and the spray would occasionally blow back over the conning tower. Ice was beginning to form on the steel structure of the submarine.

Captain Johng heard someone coming up the ladder from below, turned and saw that it was his Executive Officer, Huang Sun Lee.

"The navigator has given me our latest position, Captain," Lieutenant Huang reported.

"And it is?" asked Johng.

"Estimated to be three thousand three hundred and sixty kilometers from our destination in the Aleutian Basin, Captain," Huang reported.

"And the estimated time is …? Johng inquired.

"One hundred and forty hours, sir."

Johng did a quick calculation in his mind. A little under six days.

"Very well. Thank you, Lieutenant. Sound the klaxon."

Lieutenant Huang pressed a button on the control panel of the conning tower and the klaxon began to blast.

"Lookouts below!" shouted Huang, "Dive, dive, dive."

Captain Johng was the last man down the ladder. He pulled the hatch down behind him and turned the wheel to seal the hatch as the submarine had already started its' descent.

Captain Johng took this thought with him as he descended the ladder into the control room. *My destiny will either be fulfilled or destroyed within six days.*

Chapter 66

All Aboard!

Snow was already on the ground in Anchorage and now it was snowing again the evening of December 23rd, 1988. There was little doubt that Anchorage and environs would be having a white Christmas. Normally, during November and December, snow that had fell would be around throughout the winter. Temperatures in the Anchorage area this time of the year were normally in the low twenties to low thirties with days rarely reaching fifty degrees for a short period of time. Due to the days being short, approximately five and a half hours during the winter, the snow usually does not melt. Most people in the lower 48 states are of the opinion that temperatures are sub-freezing in Alaska during the winter but the weather in the southern part is normally not as severe as cities such as Chicago, Cleveland, Buffalo and Boston. Anchorage is spared some of the worst winter weather due to the high mountain ranges north of the city which often diverts the bad weather to the northeast, a lot of it engulfing Fairbanks.

Dan, Jess, Sue and Frank were excited about spending three nights together at the Denali Overlook Inn and especially looking forward to being there on Christmas eve as well as Christmas night. All of them had packed their winter clothing, as well as one semi-formal outfit to wear for dinner on Christmas night. It had been decided that since Dan's Cherokee had the most room, they would all ride down to the Alaska Railway station in Anchorage together and leave the wagon there and take the train to Talkeetna. It would be a trip of 112 miles and would, according to the Alaska Railway timetable, take three hours and five minutes. Of course, the time could vary according to any problems due to weather.

On the morning of December 23rd, Dan loaded his one suitcase and accessory bag into the Cherokee, cranked up the vehicle and went by Jess' apartment. He rang the doorbell at 7:05 a.m. and she answered the door promptly.

"Hi," she said. "Would you believe I am ready?"

"No." Dan grinned at her.

"Well, I am, so get your rear in here and help me with the bags."

"Bags? You mean you have more than one?" Dan said, needling her.

Jess shot him a glance with those brown eyes and remarked, "I guess you have an old barracks bag that you have your stuff in?"

"Aww, I'm just giving you a hard time to see if you are alert this morning."

And with that he picked up two suitcases while Jess put on a stunning light brown suede coat with a white fur collar. She had a peaked hat made of the same suede, ringed at the bottom with matching fur. When she put on the coat and hat with her mid-calf black leather boots and her long black hair, she looked like a young czarist princess right off the set of Dr. Zhivago. She locked the door to her apartment and followed Dan down the walkway to the Cherokee.

The two of them chatted amicably as they drove the four or five miles to Frank and Sue's condominium. They too, were ready and by 8:05 a.m. they were at the railway station where they checked their bags. Dan and Frank went to the ticket window where they picked up tickets which they had reserved for the trip up to Talkeetna. The agent informed them that the train was on time and it should be pulling into the station around 8:15 for boarding; departure time was scheduled for 8:30. Dan and Frank walked from the ticket window to the small refreshment area where Jess and Sue were waiting for them with coffee in four styrofoam cups. They sat drinking their coffee and chatting until the diesel powered locomotive pulled four passenger cars into the terminal boarding area. The four of them boarded the train which departed promptly at 8:30 a.m.

The train was not completely full and they walked through two cars until they found where there were two seats facing two others so that all four could sit opposite each other. Coats were removed and placed in the overhead racks and then they all sat down for the three hour run up to Talkeetna. Time always passes more quickly when conversation is lively and entertaining and these four had a great deal to talk about. Frank and Dan were engaged most of the time discussing aircraft and some of their varied flying experiences whereas Jess and Sue were interested in relating their latest adventures in shopping for bargains in clothes, cosmetics and household items.

Occasionally the four of them would notice an outstanding view they were passing and would comment on the natural beauty which had been enhanced by the overnight snowfall. The shortest day of the year, December 22nd, had just passed which offered five hours and twenty-eight minutes of daylight. It was now nine-thirty and it was not yet full daylight which should be more noticeable in about another hour. The forecast had called for a clear day, so during the time that the sun would reach its' zenith in the southern sky, it should make the landscape quite brilliant with glistening snow.

Just seven minutes past the scheduled time for arrival, the Alaska Railway train pulled into the Talkeetna station. Passengers scheduled to disembark at Talkeetna left the train and those who had checked their bags headed for the baggage claim area. While Dan and Frank were retrieving the luggage, Jess and Sue were looking for the van from the Denali Overlook Inn. They found it parked in the lot outside the terminal building and hailed the driver who left the engine idling and came to help Dan and Frank load the baggage. They soon had all the luggage loaded and began the five mile drive to the Inn.

Chapter 67

Denali Overlook Inn

The Inn was a frame three story building with the lowest floor partially underground. The building sat on the tip of a spectacular bluff which provided an unobstructed view of three mountains; Mt. McKinley (20,320'), Mt. Foraker (17,400') and Mt. Hunter (14,573'). All were, naturally, covered with snow and when the four entered the main floor great room they were all amazed at the spectacular panorama. Those who had visited the Inn in the past had commented that the location offered the most definitive view of Mt. McKinley of anywhere in the area. The Great Room was stunning to say the least. Fifty-two feet across and accentuated by ten foot ceilings, open archways and magnificent masonry, post and beam construction. There was also a Bose music system, and a surround sound theater. A huge stone fireplace was situated in the center of a wall opposite the large windows that overlooked the mountains.

If one faced the fireplace in the great room, the dining room was to the right with windows that looked out on a magnificent view. To the left was a very large sitting area. A superbly equipped kitchen was adjacent to the dining room and also on the first floor was a very large room on the opposite end of the building from the kitchen. In this room was a huge hot tub with several pieces of exercise equipment which afforded an opportunity to keep fit when the weather outside precluded any sport activity.

In one corner of the great room stood a huge fir tree that just touched the ten foot ceiling. It had been beautifully decorated with Christmas lights and ornaments of every description. Around the base of the tree, which had been covered with red felt, were a number of brightly wrapped packages. Holly, mistletoe, and other Christmas ornaments were hung around the spacious great room, lending an appropriate holiday atmosphere to the inn.

Upstairs was the huge master suite with an outdoor deck and five other guestrooms. Dan had reserved the master suite and two other bedrooms. The cost of these rooms for the three nights would cost him well over two thousand dollars but he had a very good reason for wanting to pay for this outing. Dan took the master suite which was connected to one adjoining guest room and the four other bedrooms were across the upstairs hallway. One of the bedrooms across the hallway was reserved for Sue and Frank. After they had all settled in, they met downstairs in the dining room to have a late lunch.

After they had been seated in the dining room for lunch, the owners of the Overlook Inn, Jayne and Kirk Hammond, came to the table and introduced themselves.

"Hello folks, I am Kirk Hammond and this is my wife Jayne. We're the owners and we welcome you to our establishment and hope that you have a wonderful Christmas with us."

Dan spoke up, "We're glad to meet you two. This is Sue and Frank Edwards, two very close friends, and this young lady is Jess Lane and I am Dan Nichols. We feel very fortunate to have gotten reservations with you so late in the year."

"Well, as I told you on the phone when you called, Dan, you called just at the right time. We have six people who have been coming every year at Christmas for about the last six or seven years. This year, one of the men died suddenly and the two remaining couples didn't feel like it would be appropriate not to be with the surviving widow at Christmas this year," explained Kirk.

"Now," Kirk continued, "as you can surmise from having only six guest rooms in the inn, we normally don't have more than about twelve to fourteen people with us over Christmas. So, we have had a tradition of inviting about five couples who are very close friends of ours and who live in the community, to come and have dinner with us on Christmas Eve. This makes for a nice group for the social hour and for dinner. We also have a local musical group who comes and they play carols for us and those who dance may do so after the dinner is over. Cocktails are served at six o'clock and we hope you will join in."

The group of four looked at each other and smiled with pleasure at Kirk's announcement.

"Hey, that sounds like a really nice arrangement," Frank replied. "Now, can you tell us what we might do for entertainment this afternoon?"

Jayne Hammond answered Frank. "Well, we have ski boots and ski's in our equipment room down on the lower level and we have a few snowboards there as well. Also, there is a pond behind the inn that has frozen over, naturally, and we have several pairs of ice skates which you may use if you like ice skating. Then, if you would like to take a sleigh ride before dinner, we have a local resident who has a team of fine horses and a sleigh and we can contact him to come over and take you for a sleigh ride. His charge is quite nominal we think; he charges forty dollars for an hour's ride."

This really delighted Jess and Sue who looked at each other smiling.

Jess said, "Why don't you give him a call and ask him if he can be here around four o'clock if that's o.k. with you guys," and Sue looked at Frank and Dan questioningly.

"That's fine with me. What do you say, Frank?" Dan asked.

"Whatever makes the ladies happy just tickles me to death," Frank said with a laugh.

Jayne said, "I'll call him right now and see if he can be here at four."

The waiter appeared with their meal and Jayne and Kirk left the two couples to eat their lunch.

After lunch the group asked the waiter how to get to the equipment room in the basement. The waiter disappeared and returned in about ten minutes with a young athletic type who appeared to be in his early twenties.

"Hi folks, my name is John, and if you will follow me I'll take you down to the equipment room and see what we can find for you."

They followed John down a flight of stairs and he opened a door into a well lighted room where there were several pairs of skis in racks plus boots, ice skates, a couple of snowboards and off in one corner was a toboggan that would carry four people.

Dan looked at his Breitling and saw that it was two o'clock.

"It's only two hours until the sleigh is going to be here so we haven't got a lot of time. What say we throw on some warm jackets and go tobogganing for an hour or so and we can try out some of this other gear tomorrow?"

"That sounds like a winner to me," Frank replied.

They all departed for their rooms and in about twenty minutes they were back in warm coats, hats and boots. Frank and Dan pulled the toboggan out of the room and headed for a slope down the road about a quarter of a mile away that John had told them about.

When they had found a likely looking 'jumping off' place, Frank got in front, Sue and Jess behind with Dan bringing up the rear. Dan gave a shove and then jumped on the toboggan as it started its' slide down the hill. Just one thing they had forgotten. The toboggan didn't have any brakes and it picked up speed rapidly which didn't seem to concern the foursome who were all laughing and giggling like a bunch of kids. Frank was yelling at Dan to "put on the brakes!" and Dan was laughing, "There ain't any."

Finally Dan said, "I'm bailing out" and he went over the side followed by Jess. The two of them were lying in the snow laughing at Sue and Frank who were still barreling down the hill. Eventually they, too, rolled off into the snow and let the toboggan continue where it eventually ran into a bank of snow at the bottom of the run. Frank retrieved the toboggan and started pulling it back up the hill, gathering Sue on the way.

They loaded up the toboggan and made one more run down the hill but this time they all four stayed on until the last minute before 'bailing out.' They all lay there in the now for a few minutes, laughing and trying to get their breath. They had forgotten how strenuous exercise at such a high altitude can exact such a toll on the human body. Finally they all four picked themselves up and Frank retrieved the toboggan.

Trudging back up the hill, Dan and Jess were in the lead with Sue and Frank about fifteen yards behind. Sue stopped, packed a snowball and threw it at Jess which hit her in the back.

"Now you've done it!" yelled Jess and she packed a snowball and threw it at Sue. Then followed a chain reaction as all four were making snowballs and in a few minutes there was a mad snowball fight going on with all laughing and yelling at one another. After about 20 minutes they were all exhausted and started back to the inn with the toboggan in tow. They stowed the toboggan away and went up the stairs to the great room where they warmed themselves in front of the fire in the huge stone fireplace.

One of the waitresses appeared with four mugs of hot chocolate with a marshmallow topping each one. They all eagerly took a cup and began to warm their insides. They no more had finished their refreshment when John appeared and told them that their sleigh had just pulled up at the front entrance.

Chapter 68

▼

Winter Sleigh Ride

A few minutes after four the sleigh arrived, pulled by two fine looking horses. The driver looked to be in his early sixties, a tall lean gentleman with a white mustache and, of all things, a top hat to go with his long coat and muffler tied around his neck. Standing in the great room looking out one of the large windows, Dan whispered to Jess, "He reminds me of caricatures I have seen of Charles Dickens' Mr. Scrooge." The driver was standing by the sleigh when the foursome exited the inn and approached him.

"Ladies and gentlemen, my name is Edward and this is 'Dolly' as he patted the forehead of one of the horses and this one is 'Horatio," and he rubbed the forehead of the second one. "We will be your hosts for your ride this evening."

Sue and Frank sat on one bench behind the driver's seat and Dan and Jess sat on the other facing them. Edward made sure they were all tucked in well by the blankets and then he mounted the sleigh, took his whip and cracked it above the two horses, saying "Giddy-yap" and they were off with the bells attached to the trappings jingling merrily. Edward took them down some paths that were well packed with snow and all four began to sing 'Jingle Bells' and some other Christmas songs they were familiar with. The cold air was exhilarating and their breaths created a fog as they sang their songs.

The hour went by in a hurry and they returned to the inn. Frank and Dan had agreed to give the driver fifty dollars and they had split the amount prior to leaving. Frank gave Edward the money and expressed the groups' thanks for a very nice drive. Sue and Jess stood by the horses as Frank settled up with Edward. They gave each of the horses a pat on their foreheads and then all four dashed into the inn and went immediately to their favorite place in the great room; the very large hearth where they warmed themselves by the fire for the second time that day. They all soon agreed to retire to their rooms, clean up and dress in casual attire for the evening since the next evening would be Christmas Eve and they would want to 'dress' for that occasion. Dan was back down in thirty minutes and arranged with one of the waitresses to have their cocktails by the fire. Frank and Sue came down next and a few minutes later Jess arrived. They were all dressed in basic slacks and sweaters and sat around the fire where there was a large sofa and several lounge chairs. They sipped on their drinks as they laughed about their toboggan fiasco, relaxed and enjoyed the fire and the evening.

Around seven o'clock one of the waitresses approached the group and informed them that dinner was being served in the dining room. Dan got up from the sofa and extended a hand to Jess and Frank did the same for Sue, then all four walked over to the dining area where they were seated by one of the waiters at a table for four. They noticed that there were two other couples in the dining room. One couple appeared to be in their sixties and the other looked as if they were more their own age; perhaps in their early forties. They all smiled at each other as they were being seated.

The dinner was served family style. The entrée that evening was prime rib au jus with several vegetables and a choice of either Waldorf salad or hearts of lettuce with bleu cheese dressing. The bread was the chef's specialty, freshly baked yeast rolls. For dessert, what else … baked Alaska.

Conversation during dinner was animated, ranging from how delicious and filling the food was to what a unique place the Denali Overlook Inn was. All four were enjoying talking about the trip up to Talkeetna, their snowball fight and now this wonderful dinner.

Frank was the first to say, "Man, I've had it. I just can't eat another bite." But he said that just as he had eaten the last bite of his baked Alaska.

Dan mentioned, "I see that you managed to get that dessert down before you said you were finished, Frank." and Sue and Jess laughed at Dan's comment.

"You bet … I certainly wasn't going to let a bite of that be wasted," Frank replied.

Jess spoke up, "I think that we all would have to agree that this is one of the finest meals that we have had in months," and they all chimed in with agreement to her statement.

At that time the elderly couple had gotten up from their table and walked over to the group. The gentleman spoke as he approached Dan's chair.

"We couldn't help but see what a wonderful time you young people are apparently having and my wife and I wanted to come over and just say 'hello.' I'm John Williams and this is my wife, Nancy. We are up here on vacation from Idaho."

Dan got up, shook hands with John and introduced himself, Sue, Jess and Frank. Frank also stood and shook John's hand. Dan explained that all four of their group lived in Anchorage and were up for the Christmas holiday.

"Well, we don't want to interrupt your party. I'm sure that we will be seeing one another again in the next couple of days," and the two of them walked off towards the sitting area.

The waiter came by and wanted to know if there was anything else that anyone wanted and they all agreed they were completely satisfied. He then informed the four that a movie would be shown in the sitting area beginning at eight-thirty. The name of the movie was *The Accidental Tourist* with Geena Davis, William Hurt and Kathleen Turner. He also mentioned that it had been nominated for best picture of the year by the Academy Awards committee but had lost to *The Rain Man* with Dustin Hoffman and Tom Cruise.

"Oh, I saw *The Accidental Tourist*," Sue said. "One evening when Frank was on the Denver turnaround I went with Sally Edwards. You remember, Jess, we called you and you said that you had to work late that evening."

"That's right," Jess replied. "And I remember your telling me a couple of days after that how good it was."

"It's good enough that I would like to see it again if all of you would," Sue said.

"Fine with me." Dan answered.

"Hey, far be it from me to be the lone dissenter," Frank agreed as he walked over and put his arm around Sue.

So they all moved away from the table and went to the sitting room where John and Nancy Williams were already seated.

In a few minutes the younger couple came in and Dan and Frank were still standing so they went towards the couple and introduced themselves. They learned that their names were Francis and Eleanor Andrews and were from Sacramento, California. They had taken one of the cruise ships from Seattle which offered a five day layover in Alaska and they would return on the same cruise line after their five days were up. Frank invited Francis and Eleanor over to meet Sue and Jess, which they did. A few minutes the waiter announced they had the movie ready for showing so the lights in the sitting area were turned off and the movie began.

Around ten o'clock the movie ended and the lights came on in the sitting area. All four of them arose and Dan suggested they go back to the fireplace in the great room. Once they were there, Dan sought the waiter that had shown the film and asked him if they happened to have any Grand Marnier in the bar. The ?waiter said that he thought they did so Dan asked him to bring four apértifs if they had the liquer. In a few moments he returned with the four small apértifs. It added warmth to their insides as the fire warmed their outsides.

They sat for awhile talking about the movie they had just seen and finally Frank let out a yawn which he apologized for and said that he was accustomed to getting to bed about this time every night so he and Sue said 'goodnight' to Dan and Jess and departed. Dan and Jess were sitting on the sofa and he had his arm around her as she snuggled up to him.

"Dan, this is just marvelous. I know that Frank and Sue are having as wonderful a time as I am. How about you?" and she looked up into his blue eyes.

"Jess, I couldn't be any happier than I am right at this moment." He set his glass down on the table at the side of the sofa, took his right hand and turned her face up to his and gave her a gentle kiss. Jess felt a chill run down her spine.

"I wish we could stay right here forever," she said.

"Don't you think we would eventually get hungry?" Dan said as he grinned at her. Jess took her right elbow and shoved it into his ribs.

"You're about as romantic as a bull moose." Jess complained.

Instead of answering her, Dan moved her face to his again and gave her another kiss … this one lasting quite a bit longer than the first.

"I think we had better go to bed," Jess said.

So they both got up from the sofa and walked upstairs to Jess' door to her room. Dan took out the key, opened the door for her and said, "It's getting quite late, Jess. Good night." and he gave her a little kiss on her cheek, handed her the key and walked towards his door.

Jess walked into her room, slammed the door and began to take off her clothes and literally throw them at a chair. When she had completely undressed she walked over to the closet and opened the door. Inside was a Victoria's Secret black silk and lace naughty nightie hanging there which she had purchased especially for this trip. She said out loud, "I don't know if I am going to get my damn money's worth out of you or not!" She then walked to the dresser, opened one of the drawers and took out her Mickey Mouse nightgown, put it on and went to bed. She took her fist and started pounding on the pillow to make a place to put her head. Once her exasperation had subsided, she turned out the lamp on the bedside table and lay in the dark for a few minutes thinking, *I believe I will go over there and knock ... no, KICK that damn door down,* referring to the connecting door between her room and Dan's. She turned over and after her heart rate had returned to normal, she finally dropped off to sleep.

Chapter 69

Christmas Day

The next morning, Dan left his room, walked a few steps down the hall and knocked on Jess' door. Dan heard her call out, "Just a minute" and he heard footsteps approaching the door. It opened and Jess' face appeared. Dan could see that she was in her robe.

"I thought I would check and see if you were ready to go down for breakfast."

"No, not quite. You go on down and I'll be there in a few minutes." She did not give Dan her usual smile.

"O.K., I'll see you shortly," and Dan walked on down to the dining area where he saw Frank and Sue were already seated at their table.

"Hi. Where's old 'sleepy-head?'" Sue asked.

"She's not quite ready … said she would be here in a few minutes. How you doin' this morning, Frank?" Dan asked.

"I'm sore as hell from falling off that sled and thrashing around in the snow," Frank replied.

Sue laughed at him and playfully hit him on the shoulder, "To say nothing of all those hits you took from the snowballs!"

"Aw, c'mon. You're a lousy pitcher and you know it," Frank rejoined.

The waiter appeared and asked if they were ready to order. Dan informed him they would wait for the other member of their party but said all three would take some coffee. In just a few minutes he returned with a carafe of hot coffee and sat it on the table. In a few more minutes Jess appeared wearing skin tight black stretch knit pants, the legs of which disappeared into her black snow boots. She was wearing a matching black sweater with little white snowmen wearing red scarves. Instead of her black hair hanging down to her shoulders she had it pulled it back into a sleek pony tail clasped at the base of her neck with a gold clasp. As usual, she looked stunning.

"Hi, gang, what's up?" she asked.

"Well, 'old folks' here is feeling his age this morning," Sue said as she grinned and bumped her shoulder against Frank.

"You're a great one to talk," Frank answered. "I had to drag you out of bed this morning."

"Well, I didn't have that problem," Sue said wryly as she lifted her coffee cup to her mouth.

Sue looked at Frank and then both of them looked at Dan. Dan just took a drink of his coffee and said,

"Man, that coffee tastes good this morning."

Frank quickly said, "I could eat a horse. Where *is* that waiter?"

The waiter appeared and gave each of them a breakfast menu. All four placed their orders and in no time they were all busily engaged in eating a delicious breakfast.

After breakfast they all went into the sitting room and turned on the TV to pick up the weather forecast from Anchorage. Partly sunny with patchy morning fog, high near 22 with evening lows of 13 to 18, light winds out of the southwest, was what the weatherman was predicting. The report also offered the sun would rise today at 10:25 a.m. and set at 3:38 p.m. All four decided they would lounge around until the sun made its appearance and Dan and Frank said they would get skis and head for a ski slope which was about a half mile from the inn. Sue and Jess opted to find a pair of skates and try their hand at ice skating even though both professed they were certainly not experts at skating. They agreed to meet back in the dining room somewhere between one and one-thirty in the afternoon for lunch.

Dan and Frank went to dress leaving Sue and Jess at the table to drink their last cup of coffee. At ten o'clock, Dan and Frank reappeared, gave the girls a kiss on the cheek and went to the equipment room to get their skis. They wanted to be at the slope just as it got good and light to begin their ski session.

After they had left Sue said, "It didn't go according to plan last night, huh?"

"I don't want to talk about it," Jess said dourly as she sipped on her coffee.

"What's wrong with him, Jess?" Sue demanded.

"Hell, I don't know ... maybe it's *me!*"

"Oh, come *on!* You *know* that isn't true."

Jess took another sip of her coffee then replied thoughtfully, "I think he has a guilt complex."

Sue turned that over in her mind for a few seconds, put her elbows on the table and cupped her face in her hands.

"You know ... you may be right? In his mind he may be thinking that he is cheating on his wife, right?"

Jess put her cup down, looked directly at Sue,

"That's the only thing I can come up with, Sue. It sure isn't because he isn't virile."

"*Well!* That's sure a twist. What's next?" Sue asked.

"Oh, hell, I don't know. Let's go skating."

* * * *

Frank and Dan returned about one-fifteen and immediately went to the roaring fire in the great room to thaw out. Sue and Jess were in the sitting room, saw them and headed for the fireplace.

"Well, how did it go," Sue asked.

"Old Jean-Claude Kiley here, walked off with the gold cup today," Dan grinned.

"Yeah," Frank replied. "I ran one poor old guy off the course into a snowbank and then I lost my balance and crashed into the same bank. If it hadn't been for Dan coming and pulling both of us out we probably would have still been there."

"What did the 'old guy' have to say when you pulled him out?" Jess asked.

"Soon as I had both of them sitting up, the older guy reached inside his jacket, pulled out a flask and said, 'I think we all need a drink.' It was straight vodka. We all three had a swig and after that we didn't care much whether we did any more skiing or not," Dan said. They all laughed uproariously.

"How did your ice skating go?" said Dan.

Sue looked at Jess and Jess looked back at Sue then they both broke out laughing. "Oh, it was hilarious!" Jess said still laughing. "We were both hanging on to each other trying to stay upright and we hadn't even made one circle around the rink when we both fell at the same time landing right on our butts."

"We ... we ..." Sue was laughing so much she could hardly speak. "We ... finally got to our knees still hanging on to each other then Jess got upright and tried to get me up. Of course I was pulling on her and just as I was about to stand up Jess slipped and we both went crashing back down again."

For the next five minutes they continued to tell of their exhibition on the ice and by the time they got through Dan and Frank were laughing so hard they had tears in their eyes while Sue and Jess were holding their sides from laughing so much.

"O.K., enough ... I can't stand anymore," Frank said. "So what do we do now?"

"Well, you won't guess what we found in a cabinet in the sitting room." Sue said.

"What ... a bottle of Scotch?" Frank asked.

"No, silly ... a Monopoly game!" Sue answered.

"A *Monopoly* game?" Frank replied.

"Yes. And Jess and I want to play you and Dan."

"Ha!" Frank exclaimed. "Well, that's not going to be any contest."

Sue replied, "Well, we will just see about that!"

Sue went to the dining room, found a waitress and asked if she could serve some sandwiches and drinks in the sitting room, explaining they wanted to play Monopoly while they ate. The waitress told Sue that would be no problem and she headed to the kitchen. All four of them retired to the sitting room, got out the Monopoly game and squared off ... Sue and Jess against Frank and Dan. The waitress brought in a serving table, set it up and said she would be back with some sandwiches and drinks in a few minutes.

After three games, Jess and Sue had Frank and Dan down two to one. Frank was demanding they play another game when Sue looked at her watch. It was ten minutes until five.

"No way! Do you realize what time it is ... it's nearly five o'clock and the cocktail hour for the dinner party starts at six so we've got to break this up."

"Well, o.k., but you two wouldn't have won that last game if you hadn't cheated," Frank said.

"What do you mean, *cheated?*" Sue demanded.

"You dang well know ... you rolled one of the dice off the table and it came up with a "one" and you said that didn't count because it rolled on the floor. You rolled again and it gave you enough to get on Boardwalk and you bought it. That gave you Park Place and Boardwalk and that's what beat us." Frank complained.

"Oh, come on, you sore loser ... let's go get dressed," Sue said disgustedly.

They all four walked up the stairs together, Sue and Frank turning left off the hallway into their room while Dan and Jess turned right towards Jess' room. Jess took her key out of the pocket of her slacks and handed it to Dan who unlocked the door.

"When you get dressed, knock on the connecting door, Jess, and we will go down together if you like," Dan said.

Jess replied, "I like," and she gave him a brief smile.

Chapter 70

Christmas Dinner

Dan entered the master suite, took a hot shower and shaved. After toweling dry he walked back into the main room and took a tuxedo out of the closet. Dan and Frank had met at the Squire's Shop in Anchorage one afternoon Frank was free and both had bought tuxedo's. They agreed they would say nothing to the girls about having purchased them. Dan had wondered how Frank would keep it from Sue. Frank told him later that he had gotten it into the condo undetected by hiding it in a hanging bag that he occasionally took on his overnight trips.

Dan was standing in front of the full length mirror on the back of the bathroom door and checked out his attire. It had been years since he had tied a bow tie but it looked presentable so he walked into the sitting area of the suite, turned on a floor lamp by the easy chair and sat down to read a copy of *Flying* magazine which he had brought along. In about ten minutes there was a tap on the connecting door. He got up and opened it.

Jess was wearing a fitted ankle length black velvet dress with a high collar which accentuated her lovely neck. Her only jewelry was a pair of sparkling drop diamond earrings. She held her sequined black evening bag and black velvet jacket. Jess had let her hair down and it was softly curled at the bottom; the black sheen of her hair glistened as it caught the room light. Dan immediately picked up the scent of the perfume. Dior had certainly named the perfume correctly … he was hypnotized.

Jess turned her back to Dan, "Would you zip me up, please?"

The zipper was right at the waist line and Dan zipped it up slowly, admiring her beautiful bare back as he pulled it up to the neck. Just before he reached the stop, he leaned over and kissed the nape of her neck. Jess felt a chill run all the way down her spine. She turned, dropping the bag and the jacket on the carpeted floor and put her arms around Dan's neck.

"You'll mess up your lipstick," Dan said.

"To hell with it ... there's more where that came from," she whispered as she closed her eyes. Dan kissed her very passionately and longingly. They separated and Dan said,

"Now you've done it," he grinned. "You better go to my bathroom and repair the damage." Dan stooped, picked up her bag and handed it to Jess and placed her suede jacket on the bed. Jess went into the bathroom with her handbag.

She called him from the bathroom.

"My gosh ... look at this *bathtub!* It looks like a small swimming pool and it's a Jacuzzi, too!" she exclaimed. She then proceeded to put more lipstick on.

"Yeah, I know." Dan replied. "All I have had time for is a shower so far but I plan on using that thing before I leave here."

I may have to take a plunge in that thing myself, Jess thought.

As soon as Jess came out of the bathroom, Dan went in and removed the lipstick from his lips. They both exited Dan's room and walked towards the stairs.

The musical group had arrived and had taken up positions next to the grand piano in the great room. Most of the visitors had arrived as well, and Sue and Frank were mingling with them, being introduced around by Jayne and Kirk Hammond. The band was now playing "White Christmas" just as Dan and Jess started down the stairs. One couple noticed them coming down and turned to another couple. It was almost as if the domino effect had taken over and one after another of the entire complement of some thirty people turned to look at the attractive couple as they descended the stairs. Frank and Sue left the group and went to meet Dan and Jess.

"Talk about the belle of the ball!" Sue smiled.

"What ... this old thing," Jess replied.

"Yeah, right. Where the heck did you get *that!*" Sue asked.

"If you must know my Mom got it for me. I told her what I wanted and she found it for me at a ladies shop in the Watergate Hotel. I did have to take it to a seamstress and have the sleeves of the jacket taken up slightly. She did such a good job that you can't even tell it," Jess replied.

"I think it is just *gorgeous,* Jess." Sue exclaimed.

"Well, you don't look so bad yourself, Sue. My gosh, I haven't seen that dress before. You look stunning in it." Jess said.

Sue was wearing a medium blue sleeveless dress with sequins. The dress had a slightly plunging neckline which exposed Sue's ample cleavage. Her neckline was accentuated by a string of cultured pearls and she was also wearing pearl earrings. Sue looked as if she had been melted and poured into the dress which accentuated her hourglass figure.

"Well, after you two get through admiring yourselves, you might have something to say about your two escorts," Frank said.

"Oh, you two are always handsome but I will say that you pulled one off on us with those tuxedos. You two look absolutely marvelous!" Sue replied.

Jess had her arm through Dan's and she pulled closer to him, looked up to his face and said, "We've got the best good looking guys in the room, Sue," and she meant it.

"You're right, Jess. Without a doubt," replied Sue.

Jayne and Kirk Hammond came over and greeted Dan and Jess then began to introduce them around to their friends and the other guests. The band continued to play Christmas carols as the 'happy-hour' began and people went to the bar that had been set up in the great room. After about forty-five minutes, Kirk Hammond went to the bandstand, asked the leader to stop for a minute and announced that dinner was being served.

Extra tables had been set up in the dining room which forced a few to be placed in part of the great room. Place cards had been put by the plates and Sue, Frank, Dan and Jess had all been assigned their regular table for four. This time a buffet table had been set up so after being seated and having a glass of wine, they joined with the people who were going through the serving line. There was a wide selection of salads, fresh vegetables and the main entrée was a very large sirloin of roast beef which the chef was carving to order.

The band continued to play all of the old Christmas songs as well as the favorite, "White Christmas." Couples were not only enjoying food but also the music and, as some finished their dinners, they left their tables and were beginning to dance.

Chapter 71

The Ring

One couple finished their dance and had ventured out on the deck. They returned to the dining room telling others that the Aurora Borealis was just beautiful tonight and other guests then began to go out on the deck to see the display. As most of the group outside began to return to the great room, Dan asked Jess if she would like to go out and look at the view. She agreed, so as she stood, Dan took her jacket and held it for her.

They then proceeded to the deck and looked at the magnificent display of the 'Northern Lights.' The Aurora Borealis was offering a brilliant display this evening with colors of a medium shade of green fading into a mixture of light green, light yellow and pale pink. The display looked as if it was coming up from behind Mt. McKinley in the far distance and then swirling upwards in what the locals called the 'water hose effect' as it climbed towards the heavens.

Dan and Jess were standing side by side looking at the outstanding display of one of nature's marvels. Jess remarked,

"Isn't that the most beautiful thing you have ever seen?"

"Almost." Dan answered as he looked toward her standing beside him. Jess turned her face to look at him and realized that he had been speaking of her. She pressed her body against his and he put his left arm around her shoulders. They stood there silent for a moment and then Dan said,

"Jess."

She waited for him to go on but he said nothing so she turned to face him. Dan also turned to face her.

"Jess, I do love you with all my heart."

Dan reached his hand into his right pocket and removed an object. He then took her left hand with his left, raised it slightly, and slipped a ring on her left ring finger. She stared at it for a moment and then she said,

"Oh, Dan, it *is absolutely gorgeous*!" It was a two carat diamond solitaire mounted on a white gold band which also had two smaller diamonds of half a carat each mounted on each side of the solitaire.

Jess was almost breathless as Dan said to her, "Jess, will you marry me?"

"Oh, YES, Dan, *Yes, Yes*!!" and tears begin to run down her cheeks.

Dan leaned over slightly and gave her a soft kiss as they clung to one another. Tears were still making their way down her cheeks as they separated. Dan pulled a handkerchief from his left pocket and absorbed the tears.

"Oh, Dan … I'm the happiest girl in the <u>world</u>!" she said.

He put his hands on her hips and she had hers resting on his broad shoulders. He kissed her gently again and said,

"And I am the happiest guy in the world, Jess."

After Jess had composed herself, she and Dan walked back into the great room where Sue and Frank were still sitting at the table. Sue saw Jess coming towards them and it appeared that perhaps Jess had been crying. Sue thought,

"If that son-of-a gun has upset her again I'll kill him!" But then Jess broke into a huge smile which confounded Sue. Jess walked up to her, put out her left arm and said,

"Look!"

Sue looked at the diamond … her mouth dropped open then she stood up, screamed, *"Oh my God!"* and threw her arms around Jess.

They both stood hugging one another as those in the immediate vicinity of their table looked on wondering what was happening. Jess and Sue began to cry as they still hung on to each other. Frank, finally realizing what was taking place, stood and started pumping Dan's hand up and down.

"Congratulations, old man! You have gotten one of the best gals in the world. I suppose you know that though."

"Yeah, I sure do, Frank. And thanks." Dan replied.

Finally Sue and Jess sat down and Sue continued to hold onto Jess' hand and look at the ring. Sue said,

"I believe that is the biggest diamond I have *ever seen*!"

Jess let Sue hold on to her hand but she turned to Dan sitting next to her and said,

"Yes, and the greatest guy in the world gave it to me." The tears were still glistening in her brown eyes.

The two couples sat and talked awhile then Dan and Jess got up and went onto the dance floor and danced to the Christmas music. After several dances, Frank came over and cut in and Dan went to Sue and asked her for a dance. As Dan and Sue made their way around the floor, Sue said to him,

"Dan, you know you have just made that girl the happiest she has been since she started in college."

"Yeah, I kind of realize that, Sue," Dan replied.

"And you know that if you make her miserable that I'm going to break your neck," Sue looked at Dan right in the eyes, but she smiled.

"Yeah, I realize that too, Sue. But that's one thing you aren't going to have to worry about," Dan continued' "You've been a tremendous help to her, Sue, and I appreciate it very much." Dan leaned forward and gave Sue a little kiss on her cheek.

Sue smiled at Dan and said, "You're a great guy, Dan. I think we may just keep you in the family."

Chapter 72

End of a Perfect Day

Finally, around eleven-thirty, the musical group struck up 'Auld Lang Syne' which was a signal that they were winding up their presentation for the evening. When they finished, the couples who were visiting began to put on their coats. Good-byes were said to new acquaintances and they began to depart. Frank and Sue said they were ready for bed and they made their way up the steps. Dan looked at Jess and said,

"Do you want to sit by the fire for a little while?"

"I'd love it," Jess replied. So the two of them walked over to the dying fire and sat on the large sofa facing the fireplace. They sat for almost thirty minutes looking at the flickering fire while holding hands. Occasionally Sue would look at her engagement ring and smile at Dan.

Jess broke the silence. "Dan?"

"Hmmm?"

"There's something I would like to know. Promise me that you won't get mad at me for asking."

"O.K., I promise." Dan said.

"You know that I wanted to sleep with you last night, didn't you?"

"Yes."

"Was it because of Mary … it being Christmas and all?" Jess asked.

"Partially, but that really wasn't the main reason."

"Well, what was it then?" Jess asked seriously.

"I suppose it is because I am somewhat old fashioned, Jess. Of course I knew something that you didn't and that was, I knew I was going to give you that ring tonight and I would just feel better about our being intimate after I had made a commitment to marrying you."

"Thank you for sharing that with me," and Jess squeezed his hand. She turned her head so that she could look up at the ruggedly handsome features of his face. "That just makes me love you all the more … if that is possible." and she let out a little sigh.

"As long as we are baring our souls, I have one for you," Dan said.

"O.K., fire away," Jess replied.

"That night in my room at the Marriott after you had taken your shower, if I recall correctly you seemed to have made a sexual overture, right or wrong?"

"You're right." Jess answered.

"Well, were you disappointed that I didn't accept your offer?" Dan asked.

"I would have been highly disappointed if you had. I wouldn't have gone through with it and you would have answered a question I had in my mind at that time."

"Which was?" Dan asked.

"Whether you were interested in *me* or just interested in my body. I wouldn't be sitting here tonight if you had tried."

So I did have it figured right. Dan thought.

They sat in silence, close to each other, and continued to watch the flickering fire until the time came when they were the only ones left in the room.

Finally, Jess said, "You ready to go up?"

"Sure," Dan replied so they got up and arm in arm and they made their way up the staircase to the second floor.

When the two of them approached Jess' door, Dan already had her by the arm so he just steered her past her door and on down the hall to the entrance to his room. He unlocked the door and they went in together. Once inside, Jess said, "Ill be back in a few minutes." She then went through the connecting door into her room. Dan removed his shoes then took off his tuxedo and hung it in the closet. He removed his undershirt and got into bed with his boxer shorts still on. The only light on in the room was the lamp on the nightstand by the bed.

In just a few minutes Jess appeared in the doorway, silhouetted against the light still on in her bedroom. She had on one of the filmiest black 'nighties' that Dan had ever seen. As she drew nearer to the bed, Dan could see the outline of a very brief bikini underneath the 'nightie.' Jess walked around the bed to the right side where Dan was lying and sat on the edge of the bed.

"How do you like my Victoria Secret 'special?'" She asked, smiling at him.

"Well, it sure has Mickey Mouse beat hands down," he replied. "It's so delicate aren't you afraid that it might get damaged?" he grinned.

"That thought has crossed my mind," she replied. Having said that, Jess stood up, pulled the 'nightie' over her head and dropped it on a chair close to the bed. Dan pulled back the sheet and Jess sat on the side of the bed. She then turned out the bedside lamp and Dan pulled her into the bed alongside him.

* * * *

Dan awoke in the morning darkness and felt the warmth of Jess' silky skin next to him. She was lying on her stomach so he took his hand and moved his fingers down her spine to the hollow of her back. She moaned slightly and said,

"Oh, that feels *so* good!"

Dan asked, "Would you like to have a rub-down?"

"Oh, would I!" Jess replied.

Dan then straddled her body and began to massage the muscles where her neck joined her shoulders. After a minute or two of that he then began to massage the muscles running alongside her spine all the way down to the small of her back.

Jess rolled over and said,

"Oh, that was wonderful. I feel much more relaxed now."

She then reached up with her hands and pulled Dan down so that she could kiss him.

Suddenly she said,

"You know what I am going to do?"

"What?" Dan asked.

"I'm going to try out that hot tub!" And she wiggled out from under him and ran into the bathroom. Dan just dropped back into the bed and listened to the water running in the tub. In a few minutes the water stopped and there was silence for a period of time then he heard the jets of the whirlpool engage. Jess called out.

"Dan?"

"What?"

"Come here a minute I want to show you something."

He walked into the bathroom wearing his boxer shorts. Jess had put her hair up on top of her head and she was up to her chin in frothing bubbles. Evidently Jess had found some bubble bath salts.

"Where did you find the bubble bath?" Dan asked.

"It was in the cabinet under the sink. You ought to get in here and see how this feels ... it is absolutely wonderful!" and Jess was grinning from ear to ear.

"I think I will." Dan removed his shorts and got into the tub.

"What did I tell you? Doesn't this feel great?"

Dan remarked, "It sure does."

"Not *me*, you dirty old man!" Jess squealed! "I meant the bubble bath!"

"Oh ... sorry about that."

CHAPTER 73

UB-235 ON SCHEDULE

It was an unusually mild day for December in the Aleutian Basin. The temperature was 35*F with a wind chill factor of 25 degrees. Visibility was unlimited, barometric pressure 30.05 and rising and, the wind was from the west at 12 knots which favorably affected the North Korean submarine UB-235 which was running on the surface making 12 knots on a course of 085 degrees.

Captain Johng Ho Kim had been on the bridge for almost an hour and he was enjoying what he considered to be a 'mild' day. Occasionally he would lift the binoculars hanging around his neck and intuitively scan the horizon for any ships. The UB-235 had crossed the International Date Line just two hours ago and was on an easterly heading which would skirt the northern edge of the Rat Island Ridge. The navigator had just given Captain Johng a position report a few minutes previously which placed the submarine approximately seven hundred and seventy five nautical miles from their assigned destination point.

If they continued to make 12 knots, which they should, their arrival time would be around 1700 hours on Sunday. Captain Johng left the bridge and approached the plotting table. He took a message form and wrote a message to be sent to the Korean Naval Headquarters in Wonsan advising them of their ETA[1] at their appointed destination.

---

1. Expected Time of Arrival

DPRK Naval Headquarters in Wonsan acknowledged receipt of the message from the UB-235. The seaman who had received the coded message, decoded it and took it to the duty officer in charge. The officer, in turn, took it to Admiral Kwan Il Soong's aide, *Chungwa*[2] Kim Mi-young. *Chungwa* Kim knocked on the Admiral's door, entered and gave the message to Admiral Soong. The Admiral read the message without comment, wrote a short memorandum on the bottom and instructed his aide, "Take this to the radio room and instruct them to code this message and send it immediately to the agent we have in Canada." The aide bowed from his waist and left the room.

---

2. *Chungwa*-Commander

Chapter 74

Altercation

The foursome returned to Anchorage on Monday, December 26th and the next day, everyone was back into their routine. Frank was off on a regularly scheduled run to Denver, Jess was back at her desk and Sue was the luckiest one of the foursome ... she didn't have to work. The mines were all shut down from Christmas until the following Monday so there was very little demand for any flying trips. Dan busied himself putting the final touches on the budget for 1989 plus conferring with Fred about the cost analysis program. Fred was well pleased with Dan's efforts and told him so. "For the first time ever, Dan, we are very soon going to be able to determine just how profitable our flying operation is after we have factored in realistic delivery figures."

Dan left the office about four in the afternoon and decided to drop by the hangar to see what Tim and Al had accomplished for the day. He entered their flight office from the exterior door and finding no one in the office, he went into the hangar. Tim was putting a wax coat on the Otter.

"You doing all that by yourself?" Dan asked Tim.

"Naw ... Harry was here but he knocked off about an hour ago."

"Well, it's nearly five ... you want to go somewhere and have a beer?" Dan asked.

"Sounds great to me."

"O.K. Where do you want to meet?" Dan said.

"What do you say we go to the Blue Parrot. We might run across some of the guys there."

The Blue Parrot was a respectable pub where a number of the Stevens Aviation guys went and also some of the tower and radar room controllers showed up there after getting off from work. Both Tim and Dan cranked up their automobiles and headed for the pub.

As soon as they got in the door, Tim looked towards the back of the pub and saw Harry sitting in a captain's chair with the chair rocked back on the rear two legs, his back against the wall.

"Hey, Dan. There's Harry back there. Why don't we go back and join him?"

"I don't know, Tim ... from the looks of those empty bottles it appears as if he has taken on a lot more than he should." Dan recalled Al's statement about Harry's problem holding his liquor.

"Awww, come on ... he really isn't a bad sort of guy."

Dan grudgingly agreed and they started walking back towards Harry. Before they reached him, Harry turned his head and saw them coming. He immediately displayed his sardonic grin.

"Well, look who's here ... the 'big man' himself. I thought maybe you would be out with your whore."

"Who do you think you're talking about?" Dan demanded, his face becoming vividly red.

"You know who the hell I'm talking about," he slurred. "Ol' Al has finished with her and now he's tossed her off to you." Harry said, loudly enough for those in the immediate area to hear him.

As quick as a cat, Dan took his foot and kicked one of the front legs forward causing the chair to crash on its' back, dropping Harry and the chair to floor. Dan grabbed Harry by the belt with his right hand and Harry's shirt and jacket at his neck with his left. Dan lifted the trunk of his body about two feet off the floor and with Harry's feet dragging the floor, Dan ran him across the room and slammed him into the wall on the opposite side. Harry's head hit the wall with a sickening thud and Dan dropped him to the floor. Harry was lying there in a half conscious drunken stupor with a glazed look in his eyes. Dan dropped to one knee, put his face up close to Harry's and said,

"You sick bastard! If I *ever* hear you mention her name again I'll beat your damn brains out!" Dan stood up and turned around to Tim who was standing there wide-eyed with his mouth open.

"Let's get out of here, Tim. I can't stand the sight of him." The two of them walked out of the Blue Parrot as a few of the men in the back moved over to see about Harry.

* * * *

The following morning, Wednesday, Dan drove directly to the Intermont Mining Supply downtown office, parked his car in the lot and took the elevator to the fifth floor. He looked at his chronograph as he exited the elevator and noticed the time, 8:46 a.m. Entering the office he walked over to Virginia Stewart's desk and spoke to her.

"Virginia, if Al is in I would like to talk with him for a few minutes. It's a matter of some importance."

Virginia dialed Al's extension and related Dan's message to Al.

"You can go right in, Mr. Dan," Virginia said.

Dan opened the door to Al's office and Al had already gotten up from his chair and was walking towards him with his hand outstretched. Al noticed that Dan was not smiling as he usually was.

"Good morning, Dan. You look rather serious this morning."

Dan took Al's outstretched hand and shook it. "I'm afraid I have some bad news, Al."

"Well, have a seat and let's see what it is."

Dan spent the next five minutes relating to Al the altercation that took place between Harry and himself in the Blue Parrot last evening. While Dan was relating the details, Al sat silently with his right elbow resting on the arm of his chair, holding his chin in his right hand while slowly stroking it with his right thumb. When Dan had finished, Al pushed back from the desk, dropped both hands into his lap and heaved a big sigh.

"Dan, you realize there is not a word of truth in the charge that I had any kind of intimate relationship with Jess. My Lord! ... I look upon her as I would a daughter!" Al stated.

"I know that, Al. Harry just infuriated me so much that I lost my temper but I'll have to be honest and admit that I am not sorry that I took the action I did."

Al locked his fingers and twiddled his thumbs for a few moments. "This is the end of it. I've done my best to stand by Harry during his numerous indiscretions but he is going to have to go, Dan," Al said.

"You want me to do it? I know that you and he have had a long relationship and perhaps you would rather that I do it."

"No, no ... actually I think it would be best if I talked with him. I would have let him go before now if it had not been for his mother. I have known her for many, many years and have procrastinated in not taking action before now. I just hate it for her sake but it must be done.

It couldn't come at a more inopportune time. I have a dinner meeting scheduled with one of the Alyeska management people in Fairbanks tomorrow evening. I want you to run me up there in the King Air and also have dinner with us. I think it would be a great opportunity for you to meet this gentleman just in case that you decide you want to accept my offer that we discussed. Pack your overnight bag and we'll come back on Friday morning."

"You know that I will be very pleased to make the trip with you, Al, and I certainly would like to meet the gentleman as well." Dan replied.

"Good!" Al stood up and walked around the desk. As the two of them walked towards the door, Al put his arm around Dan's shoulders, "Look ... I think it would be advisable for you to avoid any contact with Harry today. Why don't you take the rest of the day off; surely you have some personal matters that you would like to take care of. We won't be leaving until around noon tomorrow so I will call Harry and have him come to my office in the morning and have a talk with him. What do you think about that?"

"Whatever you say, Al. You're the boss and it's obvious that you know how to handle Harry better than I do."

They got to the door, Al opened it and patted Dan on the back as he went through the door.

"Dan?" Al said as Dan passed through the door.

Dan turned and looked at Al. "Yes?"

Al spoke in a low voice, "I would appreciate it if you would keep this to yourself for a few days."

"Don't worry, Al. I won't say a word to anyone."

Dan stopped at Virginia's desk. "Is Miss Lane in, Virginia? If she is and has a minute, I'd like to see her."

Virginia smiled at him rather slyly and said, "I'll see, Mr. Dan." She buzzed Jess on the phone and then told Dan, "She said to come right in," and she literally beamed at Dan.

Somehow she knows about Jess and me ... she must have seen the ring, Dan thought. Dan hit the door with his knuckle twice and then opened the door.

Jess was wearing the red outfit that she had on the first day that he, Al and she had met in Al's office. It had gotten to the point where every time he was away from her for awhile and then saw her again, he got that old familiar ache in the pit of his stomach. Jess had gotten up and was walking around her desk to meet Dan when he spoke.

"Good morning. Is it permissible for the Chief Pilot to kiss the Vice-President?" he grinned.

"You better if you don't want to get a pink slip with your paycheck," and she put her arms around Dan's neck and they kissed.

"Hey, I just dropped in to see if you had anything planned for this evening," Dan asked.

"Yes, as a matter of fact I have," Jess replied.

Dan's countenance dropped and he merely said, "Oh."

"You jerk," she said, "you know darn well I wouldn't plan anything without including you."

"Well, I thought we might go out to dinner if that was o.k. with you."

Jess replied, "Wouldn't you rather drop by and have some of my great chili?"

Dan pulled her close to him again and said, "See you about seven?"

"Seven will be fine, don't be late!"

After Dan had stepped into the lobby, Virginia spoke to Dan.

"Oh ... Mr. Dan?"

"Yes, Virginia," Dan turned and looked at her.

"You may want to use these," and she pulled two Kleenex from one of her desk drawers.

Dan blushed and took the Kleenex from her, wiped his lips and dropped the Kleenex into her wastebasket. "Thanks, Virginia,"

"You're quite welcome, Mr. Dan," and she beamed another smile at him.

Chapter 75

Harry Defined

The snow crunched under his feet as he made his way from the Jeep Cherokee to Jess' front porch. It was colder than blazes; the six o'clock weather report was minus one degree centigrade with a wind out of the northwest at five miles per hour which gave a wind chill factor of minus ten degrees. He rang the doorbell and Jess opened the door. She was wearing a black pant suit and her black patent boots. She had on a black turtle neck sweater under a white blouse with a gold necklace and earrings. Dan couldn't believe how lucky he was.

"Hello, stranger. Is there something I can do for you?" she flashed her perfect white teeth.

Without saying a word, Dan encircled her waist with his arms and pulled her to him tightly and kissed her.

"Whew!" Jess remarked as they broke the embrace. "It just gets better all the time!"

"Hey, you ain't seen nothin' yet," Dan said as he removed his parka and hung it on the back of a rocking chair. "You got something to warm my 'innards.?'

"You bet … just follow me."

They both walked into the kitchen and Jess had set the breakfast room table with two floating candles in the middle. Jess picked up two wine glasses from the table and poured them about half full with a nice white Zinfandel. They both clinked their glasses.

"Ahhhh, that's what I needed," Dan remarked. "Some antifreeze."

They went back into the living room and Dan removed his boots and propped his feet up on the coffee table, feeling the warmth of the gas firelogs. Jess was sitting close to him and they both sipped their wine.

Dan looked at her, then took her right hand with his left.

"Honey, I've just got to tell you something but before I do you have to promise me that you won't say a word about this to anyone ... including Sue. I promised Al that I wouldn't tell anyone but I think you need to know."

Dan proceeded to tell Jess about the altercation between Harry and himself. When he got to the part about Harry calling her a 'whore,' Jess' face turned as red as the fire in the fireplace. She burst out, "Just wait 'til I see that ass! I'll kill him!"

"No ... we all know him for what he is ... a liar and a drunk. Afterwards I was almost sorry for what I had done. He's a pitiful case and he needs professional help but he's too stubborn to admit it. I don't know what's going to become of him once Al lets him go."

Jess sat still for a few moments and gradually regained her composure.

"I guess you're right ... but do you remember one time when I told you he had a 'big mouth?'"

"Yeah, I do."

"Well, he had made a remark to one of the girls in the office a few months before you got here about my being a 'kept woman' by Al. The person knew him well enough that she told only me about it. I started to tell Al what he said but I thought better of it."

After finishing their wine they went into the breakfast room where Jess served up some of her delicious chili along with a Grecian roll and a tossed salad. After they had finished, Dan helped her clean up the table and they returned to the living room. Jess had turned on the stereo and they listened to some of the 'golden oldies' tapes for awhile. About ten o'clock, Jess asked Dan if he wanted to 'stay over.'

"You know I'd love to but I really should get on back. Al and I have to take the King Air up to Fairbanks about noon for a meeting tomorrow night with a VP from Alyeska."

"Well, you know best," Jess replied.

"You're ticked off at me, aren't you?"

"No ... really I'm not. I should get a good night's sleep myself."

Dan got up, put on his parka and pulled the hood over his head. He and Jess embraced again then he went out into the cold night air.

Chapter 76

▼

Harry The 'No Show'

Since the sunrise was scheduled for 10:15 a.m., Dan was in no hurry to get out to Stevens International for Al's and his trip to Fairbanks. This was the morning that Al was going to lower the boom on Harry so there was no possibility that he would encounter Harry at the airport.

Dan arrived at their small airport office at 11:30 a.m. and he immediately went to the FAX machine. An order had come in from AVEC for two transformers to be delivered to the village of Minto. He looked it up on the chart and found that it was about thirty-five miles west of Fairbanks. The chart also did not show an airfield at Minto. Dan looked in his phone book and dialed the number for the AVEC office in Fairbanks. When they answered he told them they had a plane that would be in Fairbanks around two-thirty or three o'clock this afternoon and he could deliver the two generators to the Fairbanks airport if AVEC had some means of getting them over to Minto. AVEC said there was a road from Fairbanks to Minto and they could transport them by truck with no problem and they appreciated the prompt service. Dan called Joe O'Donoghue to bring the two generators over to the hangar, remove most of the passenger seats in the King Air and load the transformers.

The mailman had delivered some updated charts from Jeppesen so Dan whiled away some time placing them in his chart books and after that he went over to the terminal and found Norm Timberlake in the coffee shop having lunch. Since Norm was by himself, Dan went over and the two of them had

- 301 -

lunch together and, as usual, got around to discussing late news pertaining to the aircraft industry. Around one thirty they both walked back to the Stevens facility. Dan went into their hangar and saw the guys from the warehouse were in the process of getting the generators loaded.

Going back to his office, Dan checked the local weather which he found to be fairly decent. Temperature 26 degrees F., winds calm, barometer 29.12 steady, sky overcast at 6,000 feet with scattered clouds at 1,500 feet, visibility 10 miles. He also checked the Fairbanks weather and found it to be about the same so he and Al should have some nice weather going up. Sunset was at 3:48 p.m. and twilight should be around 4:50 p.m. so they shouldn't have any problem getting in before dark.

Al arrived at five minutes after two o'clock and after greeting one another, Dan asked him how the meeting with Harry had gone.

"It didn't." Al said.

"What do you mean?" asked Dan

"I mean he didn't show up at *all!*"

"Well, you did talk with him the evening before about getting together, didn't you?"

"Yes. I caught him at home yesterday evening and told him I wanted him to be in my office this morning at 10:00 a.m."

Dan frowned and then said, "Do you think he got wise?"

"There's no way, Dan. No one knew about this besides you and me."

"Well." Dan paused. "What now?"

"Nothing to do but go to Fairbanks and have our dinner meeting this evening. I'll run him down for sure first thing Monday morning and I will have it out with him then," Al replied.

They both boarded the King Air, departed Anchorage and had a smooth ride all the way into Fairbanks. Upon arriving there Dan made arrangements with the FBO to unload the two AVEC transformers and hold them in their hangar until the AVEC truck showed up. Al and Dan then took a taxi to the Princess Riverside Lodge where they would entertain the Vice President from Alyeska that evening.

Unknown to Al or Dan, Sam Edwards with Bullmoose Mining had called in not more than 30 minutes after their departure from Stevens International and had talked with the order department of Intermont. Edwards wanted to know if it would be possible for their scheduled delivery to be pushed up so it would arrive by noon on Monday as they were in a real bind for a couple of items on their order. The clerk who took the call checked quickly with Fred Robinson.

Fred told the clerk he saw no reason why this couldn't be done and to tell Edwards the plane would be there no later than noon. Fred then called Joe O'Donoghue, the warehouse manager to make him aware of the request. Joe assured Fred there was no problem since the order had already been placed and the warehouse crew was in the process of loading the DC-3 as they spoke.

Next, Fred called the Intermont flight office and Tim, who had just returned from a delivery in the Otter, answered the phone. When Fred told Tim of the Bullmoose request, Tim said that he would track Harry down and make sure they got off to an early start.

Chapter 77

Harry—The 'Artful Dodger'

Harry walked into his apartment at 10:10 p.m. and the phone was ringing. He picked it up.

"Hello?"
"Harry, this is Tim."
"Yeah ... whaddya want?"
"The order department got a call from some guy at Bullmoose saying they were in a hurry for some of the items on their load and want it in Vanguard's warehouse no later than noon Monday. I've got an idea." Tim paused.
"Yeah ... what's that?"
"What do you say we leave around noon on Sunday. That way we can have a night out in Prince George at the company's expense."
Harry thought for a minute. *He had gone to the Blue Parrott after Al had called him Thursday evening and gotten bombed out of his skull. Some broad had picked him up and they spent the night in her apartment. He was so soused the next morning that he had missed the appointment with Al who was probably really pissed by now. Al must have wanted to chew him out about the fracas he had gotten into with Dan so maybe the longer he stalled on having to face Al the less likely he would be to really lower the boom on him. Whenever he had gotten into serious trouble before, he always*

delayed in facing Al so that Al would have time to cool off. Maybe it would work one more time.

"You still there?" Tim asked.

"Yeah ... yeah ... I was just thinkin'. I think you just might have a good idea there, Tim. 'Spose we meet Sunday morning at the IHOP about ten o'clock for breakfast and we can leave from there."

"Great! I'm going skiing with some friends up in the mountains all day tomorrow so I'll just meet you there, O.K.?

"Yeah ... yeah, O.K., Tim."

Harry took two aspirins and had hardly laid his head on the pillow when the phone rang again. He picked up the receiver and belligerently yelled,

"Hello!"

"Where the hell you been? I've been trying to find you all evening!"

"Who is this?" Harry queried.

"It's Kyle, you numbskull. Who do you think it is?" Kyle said disgustedly.

"Oh ... yeah ... whaddya want, Kyle?"

"The package is going to be here Monday around noon."

Harry sat up in the bed and hung his legs over the side.

"Man ... that's a coincidence. We have a trip scheduled for delivery and Tim and me are going down Sunday evening so we can be there by around noon Monday."

"You think that was a *coincidence?* You remember the last time we got together and I told you to give me the name of someone at Bullmoose who was in authority pertaining to orders? Well, that was *me* that called your office."

"How in hell did you know that we had an order?"

"Man ... where is your brain? I called, said I was Sam Edwards with Bullmoose and asked them if they had gotten my order yet. The guy had me hold on a minute, came back and said that they had it."

"I'll be damned! What would have happened if they said they didn't have it?" Harry asked.

"You've got a short memory. I also asked you to tell me the name of an item that they couldn't operate without and you told me that it was an electrical control panel, remember? If they had told me that they didn't have an order I was prepared to use our emergency plan to get you down here no later than noon Monday. I guess they would have sent you down here in the Otter."

"Bullmoose probably could have found one of those electrical control panels in Prince George, you know." Harry said.

Kyle grinned as he said, "Yeah, I know that but by the time the kid in your office thought of that you would already be on the way down here. Remember ... you've got to find a way to hold that aircraft on the ground until I show up for work Monday evening. See you Monday, buddy."

"Sure thing, Kyle. G'night."

Just before he dropped off to sleep, Harry smiled and thought, *Well! I'm not going to have to face ol' Al ever again.*

Chapter 78

Meeting In Fairbanks

Around 6:00 p.m. Al picked up his room phone in the Princess Riverside Lodge and asked the operator to dial Mr. Mark VanWaters room. The phone on the other end of the line rang three times.

"Hello."

"Mr. Van Waters?"

"Yes it is." There was a trace of a British accent to the voice.

"This is Al Switzer with Intermont."

"Ah, yes, Mr. Switzer. Did you have a nice trip up?"

"Very good indeed, thank you. Would you like to meet in the bar say around seven for a drink before dinner?"

"That would be delightful. Since we have never met, I will be wearing a blue double breasted jacket with grey slacks and a red and blue striped tie."

"Fine. We will see you there." *The tie undoubtedly would be the 'old school' tie,* Al thought.

Al knocked on Dan's door at ten 'til seven and they both went down to the bar and selected a table. Promptly at seven o'clock a gentleman wearing the clothing that Mark VanWaters had described walked into the bar room. He was a good six feet two inches, very trim in every way and had a salt and pepper moustache and the same color hair except it had turned completely white at the temples. He easily could have passed for Stewart Granger, the movie star.

Al got up from the table and went over to meet him. They shook hands and then walked back to the table where Dan was waiting. Dan arose and shook VanWaters hand as Al introduced him.

"Mr. Van Waters, this is Dan Nichols, manager of our aircraft division and soon to be one the officers in our company."

"I'm very pleased to meet you, Mr. Van Waters," Dan replied.

"Mark, please." VanWaters replied with a smile.

The waiter appeared and they gave him their drink order.

"So, you are a pilot, Dan?" Mark VanWaters asked.

"Yes, sir. I started flying in high school and have been at it off and on ever since."

"That's interesting. I've had a few hours myself."

"Really? What have you been flying?" Dan asked.

"Have you ever heard of the Gypsy Moth?" Mark asked in his British accent.

"Have I! That aircraft is a legend in private aircraft circles."

"Yes, indeed. I had about nine hours in it before I soloed. After I had accumulated about twenty five hours, a friend of mine who had purchased one of your Stearman PT-17's gave me about ten hours in that aircraft. I eventually soloed that as well."

The conversation dwelled on flying and aircraft as they had their drink. Al was delighted to just sit and listen to the dialogue, pleased to see that the two had something in common. In about forty-five minutes they adjourned to the dining room, ordered their dinner and continued to discuss flying adventures and eventually the conversation turned to mining and the Alyeska operation.

Mark VanWaters remarked.

"We at Alyeska were very pleased with the manner in which you responded to our request in getting the material delivered to us recently in very adverse weather conditions. Whether you are aware of it or not, your ability to perform in that instance reached the highest level of our management. That is why I wanted to meet with you tonight and discuss some arrangements that possibly will be advantageous to both parties."

VanWaters then turned to look directly at Dan.

"I also have learned, Dan, that you nearly had what could have been a fatal accident on your return flight."

"Well ... my copilot and I did have a very interesting flight that evening, Mark." Dan replied with a grin.

All three of them had a chuckle at Dan's comment. As the evening went on, the conversation took on a serious tone and the groundwork was laid for Alyeska to present a proposal to Intermont for pricing on a wide variety of products. If Intermont's response was favorable then a contract for twelve months would be signed by both parties.

Mark VanWaters looked at his watch.

"My goodness ... it's nearly ten o'clock already. As the saying goes, time flies when you are in good company. I must get to bed, I need to catch a commuter flight over to Galena at nine o'clock in the morning to look at one of our operations there."

Dan looked at Al.

"Al is there any reason that you need to be back in Anchorage early in the morning?"

Al, catching Dan's drift said, "Why no. Tomorrow's Friday and I don't have a thing planned."

"Well, why don't we run Mark over to Galena. It's only about an hour from here in the King Air."

"Oh, no. I couldn't impose on you like that!" Mark replied.

Dan looked at Mark. "I'll let you ride co-pilot over there."

Mark's eyebrows lifted in surprise. "Deal!" he said and extended his hand.

As Al and Dan walked up the stairs to the second floor, Al said,

"You are a natural born salesman, you know that don't you," and he had a big smile on his face.

"That's the way I made my living for nearly twenty years, Al."

"And that's why I want you to take over my business, son. I think you and Jess can take the company to the next level in five years."

They reached the door to Dan's room first. They both paused at the door. Al turned, looked at Dan and said,

"Think about it, Dan."

"I have been thinking about it a lot, Al. I'll let you know one way or the other by the end of the month."

"Fair enough. Get a good's night sleep. We will be carrying important cargo in the morning." Al slapped Dan on the shoulder as he turned and walked to his room.

The weather cooperated nicely on the flight over to Galena and even though it was still dark, Dan turned the controls over to Mark VanWaters after they had reached altitude and leveled off. Mark kept turning and looking at Dan, grinning from ear to ear. He was like a kid with a new Christmas toy.

When they had landed at Galena, Dan cut the left engine and kept the right one turning over while Mark shook hands with Dan and Al, picked up his suitcase and departed. They now had a friend in a high place in Alyeska. After taking off again, they resumed their flight on down to Anchorage and landed a little after ten Friday morning. Dan pulled the King Air up to the Stevens hangar, shut everything down and as they came down the airstair door one of the Stevens line boys approached Dan.

"Mr. Nichols, Nancy on the front desk said that she had an important message for you."

"Thanks, son. Will you put the King Air in the hangar for me?"

"Sure will, sir."

Al and Dan got their bags and walked towards the Stevens Air office. As they entered the office Dan said,

"Nancy, do you have a message for me?"

"Yes, sir, I sure do." She handed Dan a slip of paper. "Call Jess at office ASAP."

Dan used the phone on the desk and dialed Jess' direct office number.

"Jess Lane."

"Hi, you looking for me?"

"Sailor home from the sea," she laughed. "I sure am ... are you free for the rest of the week-end?"

"Well, I suppose so. What's up?"

"Frank is off this week-end and we thought that we would make that trip down to Seward that we talked about not too long ago."

"Sounds good to me ... are we biking down or are we driving?"

"It's a little chilly for biking so we thought we would go down in the 'Beamer' if that's o.k. with you."

"Suits me. I'll have to run home and pack a bag."

"No problem. Suppose we pick you up there about two?"

"Great. See you then."

Dan hung up the phone, turned around and saw Al standing nearby with a big smile on his face.

"You need me to drop you somewhere, Al?" Dan asked.

"No, no ... I've got my car out in the lot. You run along and have a great time and I'll see you Monday."

Al picked up his bag and left by the front door. After Al left, Dan had a fleeting thought about going to their airport office but decided, *to heck with it*. Therefore, he didn't get to see the FAX from the downtown office lying on his desk concerning the trip lined up for the DC-3 for a delivery to the Vanguard warehouse on Monday.

Chapter 79

A Friendly Wager

Captain James Madison was in Admiral Horatio Crownover's office delivering another message from the *SSN Columbia*.. The Admiral looked at Captain Madison over the top of his reading glasses after having read the message.

"So the 'gook' has crossed the International Date Line, has he? You get a message off to the CNO[1] in the Pentagon, Jim, and bring him up to date on what has happened since our last message. Also, get one off to Commander Loudon and tell him to stick to that sub like glue on wallpaper. If that *Romeo* enters our territorial waters and engages in any hostile action, I want the *Columbus* to be in position to blow that 'gook' sub to hell and gone if he so much as bats an eyelash. You put that in the form of an Operational Order, Jim."

"Yes, Sir, Admiral ... I will get on it right away." Captain Madison got out of his chair and left the Admiral's office.

* * * *

Commander Julius "Jules" Loudon, captain of the *SSN717 Columbus* was sitting alone in the officers' wardroom at 2100 hours having a cup of decaf coffee when his Executive Officer, Lieutenant Commander Franklin MacKenzie walked

---

1. Chief of Naval Operations

in, picked up a cup and filled it from the urn sitting on the sideboy. He sat down, pushed his cap to the back of his head and exhaled heavily.

"How is it on top, Mac?" the captain asked.

"Not a bad night really. Temperature is around twenty degrees and you can actually see the stars for a change. The sea is rather smooth for this time of the year as well." Commander MacKenzie paused for a moment then continued.

"It has turned out to be a dull trip so far hasn't it, sir?"

"Yeah, it has been rather boring but that may change. Is our *friend* still holding the same course?"

"Yes sir, ... right on zero eight five at twelve knots."

The captain took a sip of his coffee, slumped in his chair and extended his legs.

"I expect him to change his course before long."

"How do you figure that, Captain?"

"Well, if he is headed for the Pribilof Islands, he will make a correction of about ten degrees to the northeast. If he is heading for one of the Aleutian Islands he will make a considerable correction further to the southeast."

"Which one do you think it will be?" asked MacKenzie.

"I'll bet you five bucks it's one of the Aleutians," "Jules" Loudon said.

"You're on, Captain!" said MacKenzie.

They shook hands as they both grinned at each other.

Chapter 80

Course Change

Commander 'Jules' Loudon of the *USS Columbus* was standing at the plot with the navigator, Lieutenant Gary Monroe, when Lt. Commander Frank MacKenzie came through the passageway to the bridge. He continued his walk over to the plotting table. Captain Loudon looked at his Executive Officer, grinned and said, "You owe me five bucks." Lt. Commander MacKenzie looked at the blue line on the chart depicting the course of the *Romeo*. The course line had changed to the southeast revealing that the North Korean sub was on a heading of one three zero degrees.

"Well, I'll be damned. Where do you think he is headed, Cap'n?"

"That's the sixty-four thousand dollar question, Mac. There's little or no shipping in these waters except mostly for coastal vessels and an occasional tanker. If he had any intentions of sinking anything he surely wouldn't be in here for that purpose. If I had to make a guess right now I would say that he may be intending to offload some agents in a raft."

"What now, Captain?" MacKenzie asked.

"You saw the message we got from ComSubPac. We don't have a choice but to lie close by and wait him out. He has to make the first move.

"If he maintains his heading and speed, you know that he will be in our territorial waters before too long, sir." MacKenzie said.

"Yes, I know, Mr. MacKenzie. I hope he does, then if he commits any act that we deem dangerous to the security of the United States, we will be absolutely justified in any action we take to deter him, or even eliminate him, as long as we are in compliance with the operational directive we have received from COMSUBPAC."

Chapter 81

Kenai River Drifters Lodge

Friday evening, Sue, Jess, Frank and Dan were in Frank's BMW just about fifty miles from Anchorage. Frank was driving with Sue beside him and Jess and Dan were huddled up in the back seat together. Instead of going all the way to Seward on the way down, they decided to check out the Kenai River Drifters Lodge that Frank had heard about.

What they found was a resort that had two story lodges with two bedrooms and bath upstairs, a downstairs with a living area with a fireplace and a small kitchen with fridge, microwave and coffee pot. Meals were served in the adjacent lodge so they decided to spend two nights there. On Saturday the guys tried their hand at fly fishing in the river and Frank caught two salmon and Dan caught one. The girls sat on the bank and kibitzed until Jess said she wanted to try. After hooking her fly in the trees on three consecutive casts, she decided to join Sue again in the 'peanut gallery.'

The salmon were charcoal grilled that evening on the outdoor grill where Frank and Dan nearly froze in the process but they had a wonderful salmon dinner. There probably was not a more compatible group than these four and they enjoyed one another's company immensely.

They all slept in on Sunday and spent most of the day lounging around before the fire, resting and watching a little satellite TV. They did muster up enough energy to take a short hike along the river's edge but gave it up after a little over an hour due to the cold. Just before departing that evening the two pilots insisted on checking the weather on the Weather Channel. Seward was having temperatures of 14 degrees with a northerly wind of 28 miles per hour which produced a wind chill factor of minus six degrees. Sunset was at 3:59 p.m. so they departed in the dark with Frank having to do some fancy driving due to the gusts which at time reached 39 miles per hour according to the forecast. However, the highway was free of snow so that was one plus and they arrived safely in Anchorage around 9:00 p.m.

Dan was blissfully unaware that Tim and Harry were at the Prince George Best Western Motel at that time and Harry was hatching a plot that would endanger his life as well as Tim's.

Chapter 82

Prince George—Final Visit

Tim and Harry met at the International House of Pancakes for breakfast on Sunday just as they had planned. After finishing up, they both drove their cars out to the Stevens parking lot, entered the hangar and proceeded to preflight the DC-3 as well as check the Vanguard load to make sure that everything was tied down. Finding everything to their satisfaction, they filed their IFR flight plan over the phone in the flight office, towed the DC-3 out of the hangar, boarded the aircraft, fired it up and departed Stevens International at 12:06 p.m. Alaska time.

The weather was overcast with a ceiling at twelve thousand feet, broken clouds at six thousand, temperature 31 degrees Fahrenheit on the surface, and winds from the northwest at eight knots. Tim was piloting the aircraft on the trip down and Harry was sitting in the right seat reading the Sunday edition of the *Anchorage Daily News*. They were tooling along at their assigned altitude of nine thousand feet. Tim had just run a calculation and estimated their ground speed at one hundred fifty-five knots. They should be in Prince George by around seven-thirty British Columbia time.

The Intermont Mining and Supply DC-3 touched down at the Prince George International Airport at seven thirty-nine British Columbia time. Tim taxied the aircraft to the Vanguard Freight Company ramp where they would lock the aircraft down for the night. Tim and Harry retrieved their overnight bags, went to the terminal and got a taxi to take them to the Best Western motel.

After they had settled in they went to the Outback Steak House and ordered a Fosters beer apiece. Harry finished his off while Tim was still drinking and Harry ordered a second. Tim was concerned that Harry might get on another of his 'binges' but after the second, Harry said he was ready to order. When they finished dinner it was close to ten o'clock so when they got back to the motel they went to their separate rooms and turned in.

Chapter 83

Al's Past

Al stopped by at his favorite breakfast place, Wanda's Diner, at six forty-five on Monday morning to read the morning paper and have his breakfast. One of the waitresses approached him.

"Good morning, Al. You want your usual?"

"Yes, Dolores, that will be fine." Al turned the newspaper to the local news section.

In just a few minutes Dolores returned with two eggs over medium, link sausage, hash browns, biscuits, orange marmalade and coffee.

"Anything else, Al?"

Al looked at the plate. "No thanks, Dolores, I think that will do it.

Al smiled at Dolores and laid the paper down as he started eating his food.

He wasn't looking forward to what he had to do today. George Abelson had been Al's very best friend. They had gone through basic training together, went overseas together, went in on D-Day together and more or less took care of one another until they got to the Hurtgen Forest.

During that terrible battle, George and Al were in a bunker one night trying to keep from freezing to death when George told Al, "Al, I've got a funny feeling. I just don't think I'm going to make it." He handed Al a small envelope and made Al promise him that if anything happened to him that he would personally visit Virginia Stewart, his fiancé, when he got back home and give her the envelope.

The next day two of their squads had been pinned down by a German machine gun nest. After exchanging fire and grenades with the Germans for three hours it appeared their squad, which was on point, was eventually going to be decimated by the enemy fire. Suddenly George jumped out of his foxhole and started running from tree to tree evading the machine gun fire until the last moment. George had just lobbed a grenade into the machine gun nest when he caught three bullets in his chest. He fell immediately just as the grenade exploded in the nest and killed the four Germans. George was awarded the Silver Star posthumously for his bravery.

When Al was discharged, he went to Tyler, Texas and found Virginia. She and George had planned to be married but George would have no part of it until he got back home safely. What George never knew, of course, was that Virginia had given birth to his son while he was overseas and she had never written George that she was pregnant. Virginia had recorded her son's name on the birth certificate as Harry George Abelson. However, she retained her maiden name and was working as a secretary while her mother took care of little Harry.

Al kept in touch with Virginia down through the years and when he could, he would send Virginia money to help with her expenses. She always insisted that Al not continue doing this but Al never stopped. After Harry was old enough to go to college, Al insisted that Virginia allow him to pay for Harry's tuition which he did for one year. However, Harry dropped out of college and became an airport bum, working at odd jobs and spending what he could on flying lessons. Harry became an alcoholic in due time and also became a source of worry and trouble for his mother.

After Al had acquired Intermont Mining and Supply, he sent for Virginia and hired her as his secretary and hired Harry as one of the company pilots after he had washed out with Air Alaska. Al insisted that Virginia not tell Harry of the relationship between himself and George, his father. Also, no one in Intermont knew the true identity of Virginia Stewart. Only Al, Evelyn and Virginia knew the entire story.

Al finished his breakfast, left a tip for Dolores, paid his check and those in the restaurant that morning who knew Al by his being a regular customer at Wanda's, could have no idea of how heavy his heart was as he got into the Vanden Plas to head for the Intermont office.

Chapter 84

Harry Skips Town

Dan arrived at Stevens Intenational at 7:30 a.m. Monday and went to Intermont's flight office. The first thing he saw was the FAX for the Vanguard order lying on his desk. He opened the door to the hangar and saw that the DC-3 was gone. He picked up the phone and called the Stevens International control tower. When a male voice answered, he asked if Jim O'Brien was on duty. Dan was asked to wait and then another voice came on the phone.

"Jim O'Brien speaking."

"Jim, this is Dan Nichols with Intermont."

"Oh ... hi, Dan. What can I do for you?"

"Do you have anything on a departure time for our DC-3?"

"Just a minute, Dan."

Dan could tell by the sound that Jim had laid the phone down. He was gone a good three minutes.

"Yeah ... it left yesterday afternoon at 12:06 p.m ... filed IFR for Prince George International."

"*Yesterday!?*" Dan exclaimed.

"Yep ... that's what the log sheet says, Dan."

"Oh ... O.K., Jim. Thanks." He put the receiver back in the cradle then immediately picked it up again and dialed Al's extension number.

"Al Switzer."

"Al, this is Dan."

"Good morning, Dan. How was the week-end?"

"Oh, it was great, Al. Would you believe that Harry and Tim left for Prince George yesterday afternoon?"

"Is that right? What on earth for?"

"Apparently there was an order that came in for Vanguard just after you and I left for Fairbanks on Thursday."

"It looks as if Harry keeps dodging my bullet, doesn't it?"

"It sure does. Well, I guess there isn't anything we can do about it until they get back."

"You can rest assured, Dan, that I have *not* changed my mind about Harry. I will see him first thing in the morning and he *will* be terminated. He has caused us a problem for the last time."

"Oh, I'm not concerned about that at all. I just wanted to be sure that you were aware of where he is."

"Thanks, Dan. As I said, I will see Harry in the morning."

Chapter 85

▼

Lying in Wait

Lying at periscope depth about five and a half miles off the coast of Dutch Harbor in the Aleutians, the North Korean Submarine UB-235 was quietly waiting. Just minutes ago the radioman had received a message from Headquarters Eastern Fleet in Wonsan. He delivered the message to the Executive Officer who took it to Captain Johng Ho Kim who was in the officers' mess having breakfast. The captain read the message which had been decoded:

To: Commanding Officer UB-235

FROM: Commanding Admiral

Eastern Fleet

Condition yellow. Package due to be delivered approximately 1300 hours 05 Jan 1989.

Captain Johng looked at his Executive Officer and smiled. "Only one more day of waiting, Huang."

"Yes, my Captain," and Huan Sun Lee returned the smile.

* * * *

Just one nautical mile away, to the west, the *SSN Columbia* was also waiting at periscope depth. The *Columbia's* Executive Officer, Lieutenant Commander Franklin MacKenzie, went to the intercom, "Captain to the Conn."

Captain 'Jules' Loudon had been in the torpedo room making an inspection when he heard the call. He made his way back to the Conn.

"What's going on, Mac?" he asked.

"Sir, Pearl just intercepted a message from North Korean Fleet Headquarters which they think may have been directed to the sub we are stalking. Captain Loudon read the message.

"Well, if this *is* for our 'friend,' then it looks like he may be picking someone, or something, up instead of dropping an agent off as I suspected. O.K., we will just have to wait a while longer."

Chapter 86

The Game Is On

A thousand or so miles away, Harry Abelson and Tim Morrison had finished their breakfast and checked out of the Best Western Motel in Prince George, British Columbia. As they were riding in the taxi from the motel to the airport, Tim remarked,

"Well, you sure took your time getting up and getting ready this morning."

"What's the big deal? You got a heavy date waiting for you back in Anchorage?"

"No, but Vanguard said in their FAX that they needed this load by noon today."

"Don't sweat it. It's only 10:45 ... there's still plenty of time."

They pulled into the parking area for Vanguard, paid the cab driver and walked towards the Vanguard warehouse. As they approached the warehouse door they noticed a security guard carrying what appeared to be a Colt 45 on his belt.

"Can I see some identification from you gentlemen?" the guard asked.

"What's going on," Harry grinned, "is the Queen Mother arriving this morning?"

"Just a little added precaution today, sir. May I see that I.D., please?"

Harry and Tim both produced their drivers' license plus their FAA license and an Intermont credit card.

"Thank you, gentlemen. Just be sure that you are accompanied by a Vanguard employee while you are inside the warehouse, please."

"Sure, captain." Harry remarked, and he and Tim went up the steps to the loading dock. Harry stopped short and said,

"Look. You go on in and get things lined up for the unloading and I will go out to the "three" and get it ready for taxiing to the unloading area."

"O.K., Harry."

Harry went back down the steps and walked across the ramp towards the DC-3. At the plane he looked back towards the warehouse and noticed that the guard had been watching him. No doubt about it, the "stuff" was coming in today. Harry put the ladder up against the DC-3, unlocked the door and went up to the cockpit. He pulled a small tool chest out from behind the co-pilot's seat and removed a Phillips screwdriver. He quickly pulled the plate cover from the number one comm radio and slid it out. He then took a pair of needle nose pliers he very carefully broke a connection to one of the diodes. Then he slid the unit back in, replaced the cover and tightened the screws. That should do it he thought.

Harry knew that the FBO had a radio repairman on duty during the day and just before takeoff Tim would learn that the number one communication radio was inoperative. The radio repairman would be able to finally find out what the problem was but Harry was counting on it taking him two or three hours to find it. The repairman would have to pull the unit and take it to the test bench in the hangar in order to diagnose the problem and that would take some time. Harry looked at his watch ... 11:15. He still might have to find a way to stall at least another hour.

Harry looked out the windscreen and Tim was standing on the dock waving his arms. No doubt they were ready to unload so Harry cranked up the No. 2 engine then took as much time as he could to get No. 1 started and began to taxi slowly to the unloading area.

*   *   *   *

Across town in Prince George, Kyle Thornburgh was at home having a late breakfast when the phone rang.

"Hello," Kyle answered.

"This is Abe."

"Yeah. How's it going, Abe."

"It's going ... it should be there about any time now."

"Good. You got some 'news' for me?" Kyle asked.

"Yep. Here it is. Delivery point is the airport at Dutch Harbor. You know where that is?"

"Sure do. What else?"

"Have your contact call this number when he gets there ... 886-5102. Tell your man to tell the contact, 'Abe sent me.' You got that?"

"Yeah, 886-5102. Abe sent me." Kyle repeated.

"Correct. The guy has a pickup truck so they can transport the case."

"Where does our man take it?"

"He doesn't need to know ... the contact knows, O.K.?"

"O.K., anything else?"

"Two things. One, he has to arrive during daylight hours ... as close to noon as he can. Two, he *must* accompany the contact to the final delivery point. Tell him he has to get the vehicle number from the final carrier. The clue is that it will be two letters 'UB' plus three numbers. You have to phone me back that information before I will release your money, O.K.? Now repeat this information back to me so there won't be any slip-ups."

Kyle repeated the information back to Abe just as he had copied it down.

"Correct. Now tell your man not to screw this up. If he does then I will come looking for him. You tell him that."

"Sure, Abe, he will take care of it."

"He'd better." The line went dead and Kyle heard the dial tone. Kyle realized that his heart rate had increased considerably. Kyle folded up the piece of paper that he had made the notes on and stuck it in his billfold. He had another cup of coffee and looked at his watch. It was ten minutes after one. Good ... if I can stall just a little bit longer.

Chapter 87

The Switch

The Vanguard workers had about half of the material on the Intermont DC-3 unloaded when a Crossair Boeing 727 taxied up to the ramp. The hyster driver took the pallet he just unloaded from the DC-3 over to the dock, set it down and then got off the hyster and told Tim, who was standing on the dock, "Hey. We will have to knock off on you guys and take care of that Crossair flight first." Tim jumped off the dock and walked out to the DC-3 where Harry was standing in the door and repeated what the hyster driver had told him. Harry almost smiled. This was the delay he had been hoping for.

When they opened up the door to the Crossair 727, the first person to get off was a security guard carrying a shotgun. He also had a pistol on his belt. Tim and Harry stood on the ground next to their DC-3 as the unloading began. After about thirty minutes, Harry saw them offload a yellow case with a red triangle warning sign on the side. *There it was ... there was the 'stuff.'* Harry's heart beat a little faster.

The armed guard followed right along with the hyster and when they put that case on the dock, the guard followed it on into the warehouse. Tim remarked,

"What have they got on that plane ... gold?"

"I dunno," Harry replied, "but it sure must be worth something." *A quarter of a million bucks to put in my pocket,* he thought.

Another thirty-five minutes went by and then the Vanguard personnel began to load several crates back onto the Crossair 727. The pilots got back aboard, the jet engines began to spool up and the aircraft taxied out for take-off. Harry looked at his watch. It was 3:05. Perfect.

Finally the DC-3 had been unloaded and Harry was in the pilot's seat and Tim was in the right seat. Harry looked at his watch and saw that it was 3:55 p.m.

"Call Clearance Delivery and get our clearance, Tim."

Tim clicked the 'mic' button on the yoke and spoke into the microphone on his headset.

"Clearance Delivery this is Douglas November niner one four zero Romeo at the Vanguard ramp ready to copy clearance, IFR to Anchorage." Tim paused waiting for the reply. Nothing.

Tim repeated the message and got no reply. Next he switched over to Comm No. 2 and sent the message for the third time. Clearance Delivery answered immediately.

"Douglas November niner one four zero Romeo, Clearance. You are cleared to the Stevens International Airport as filed. Climb and maintain six thousand, expect further clearance to one two thousand ten minutes after departure."

Harry said, "Tell 'em we have a problem with our number one transceiver."

"Number two is working o.k., Harry," Tim pleaded.

"You want to get halfway to Anchorage, run into instrument weather and have the number two radio to go out on us, you numbskull? Tell 'em we got a delay ... our number one transceiver is inoperable!"

Tim's face turned red and he got back on the radio, called Clearance Delivery back and reported a delay due to the primary radio being inoperable.

Harry and Tim both climbed down from the DC-3 and headed for the FBO to find the radio technician. Harry could have pulled the set himself and taken it with him but this would take up more time by having the repairman go out to the aircraft.

The repair technician went out to pull the radio so Harry told Tim, "Let's go over to Vanguard and hang out in their canteen while we wait." It was now a little after four o'clock. They told the guard on duty what had happened and asked if they could go into the canteen. He told them to wait a minute while he checked on something. He came back in about five minutes and said they could go in.

They were in the canteen having a couple of Cokes and some peanut butter crackers when five o'clock rolled around and the shift changed. Harry noticed that the armed guard left with the first shift. Kyle Thornburgh came out of the main office and walked down the aisle to the canteen. He said 'hello' to the two of them and asked why they were hanging around. Tim spoke up and told him about the radio trouble and Kyle said that was too bad ... he was sure they were anxious to get back home.

The three of them heard the hyster start up and then Kyle's fellow employee on the night shift came rolling down the aisle with a pallet loaded with several crates which he took to a certain section of the warehouse and placed it. Kyle said,

"That's some of the stuff you guys brought in. We have to place it so that the three mines it is consigned to will be able to pick it up in the morning without any delay."

Tim spoke up, "I thought Bullmoose said they had to have their order by noon today?"

"Well, apparently they didn't, did they?" Kyle replied.

The repair technician from the FBO walked in the door and said,

"Hey, I've got your unit ready to go back in."

Harry looked at Tim, "Tim, why don't you go out to the plane with him and make sure it works."

"O.K., Harry." Tim and the repair technician left.

The forklift came back down the aisle and Kyle stopped him.

"Bill, why don't you go get our dinner while these guys are around. If I need any help I know I can get them to pitch in."

"Sure, Kyle. What do you want to eat?"

"How about some seafood from Freddie's?"

"That sounds good to me," Bill replied.

"O.K., here's twelve bucks and the keys to my car. Just get me the 'usual.'"

Bill took the money and the keys and left.

Kyle looked at Harry, grinned and said, "How's that for luck! C'mon, you can help me."

Kyle went into the office and Harry heard a metallic 'clang.' The lock on the caged area was disengaged. Kyle came out, climbed on the hyster and went down the aisle and came back with a crate painted Navy grey with letters on the side, "Machine parts. Return to Intermont Mining Supply Co." Kyle jumped off, opened the doors to the restricted area and the two of them carried the crate inside. Kyle had the top of the crate already loosened so it was easily opened. Inside was another case painted exactly like the one that was to be 'hijacked.' Harry and Kyle removed it and put the one just brought in by Crossair into the Navy grey crate, put the lid back on and moved it out of the caged area. He went back into the office and Harry heard the lock being reset.

Kyle came out of the office, went to a tool box near the canteen area, took out a hammer and some nails and nailed the lid on the grey crate. He then brought up the hyster with an empty pallet on it. The two of them put the crate on the hyster and Kyle told Harry to get on the crate and sit on it. Kyle drove the hyster slowly down the ramp and out to the DC-3. They lifted the crate on board as Tim stuck his head around the bulkhead to the pilot's compartment and wanted to know what was going on.

Harry said to Tim, "Kyle just noticed a crate of parts that had been returned by Bullmoose for us to carry back."

Tim replied, "Oh."

Harry went back to the warehouse with Kyle and they were sitting in the canteen talking. Kyle handed the piece of paper to Harry with the notes on it. They didn't notice that Tim had come into the building. Tim was in earshot in time to hear Kyle say,

"Have you ever been to Dutch Harbor before?"

Harry answered, "Yeah ... twice."

Just then they both heard Tim's footsteps and turned to see that it was him. Kyle immediately said,

"Well, I hope to get down there someday. I understand there are some charter fishing boats there and they have some good deep sea fishing at certain times of the year."

"Yeah, that's what I have heard too," Harry said. He looked around at Tim again.

"Is the radio working o.k.?"

"Yeah. I checked it out, Harry, and it's working fine. The radio man said they would send the company a bill for the service."

"Good. You ready to get under way?"

"I sure am. We aren't going to get home 'til early in the morning."

Harry and Kyle stood up and Kyle shook hands with Harry.

"Good luck on your trip."

"Thanks, Kyle." Harry and Tim walked out to the DC-3 and after checking everything out for the final time, they taxied out to the end of the runway and took off for Anchorage.

Chapter 88

The Chase

Driving to the airport on Tuesday morning, Dan was reflecting on the events that had taken place during, and shortly after, Christmas. He was thinking about how fortunate he had been to meet a wonderful girl like Jess and then to find two friends like Frank and Sue. What a great couple they were and he could see the four of them having some great times together as time went by. The Intermont air operation was shaping up with the only problem being Harry and that should be taken care of after today. The only other thing he was having a problem with and that was the short days in the winter. Just like today, the TV weatherman said the sun would rise at 9:52 a.m. and set at 4:02 p.m. Oh, well, it will just take some getting used to.

Dan parked the Cherokee and went into the Intermont office. He checked the FAX machine and there was an order for a large hydraulic pump to be delivered to the Cripple Creek mine at Koyukuk but they said any day this week. That's a twist ... they usually want it right now!

"Hey, Dan, how ya' doin' this morning?" Dan turned around to see Tim entering the office.

"I'm just fine. What time did you two get in last night?"

"It was actually this morning ... around one-thirty"

"What happened? Why so late?"

"Our number one transceiver went out and it took over two hours to get it repaired. By the way, Bullmoose sent a crate of machinery parts back for some reason. I guess I had better go out and check on it and then call O'Donoghue to come and pick it up."

Tim went through the door to the hangar and five minutes later he returned.

"Dan, the crate isn't in the "three" and the Otter is gone."

"What?" Dan got up and walked out into the hangar trailed by Tim.

"What did you say was in the crate?" Dan asked.

"It was a grey crate and stenciled on the side 'Machinery Parts—Bullmoose Mining' and the guy at Vanguard said Bullmoose sent the crate to them and said put it on the next plane going back to Intermont."

"Wait a minute." Dan walked back into the office, picked up the 'phone and dialed Al's extension.

"Al Switzer."

"Al, this is Dan. Did Harry show up for your meeting this morning?"

"No, he didn't Dan. I was just getting ready to call you and see if he was there."

"He isn't here, Al, and not only that, the Otter is missing as well as a crate that Tim and Harry brought back from Vanguard last night."

"What was in the crate?"

"Tim said it supposedly was machinery parts sent back by Bullmoose but I'm beginning to doubt that. I'm going to call the tower and see if they have a record of the Otter leaving."

"Fine. Keep me posted, Dan."

"I sure will."

Dan dialed the Anchorage control tower number.

"Anchorage Tower, Jim O'Brien speaking."

"Jim ... Dan Nichols."

"Oh, Hi, Dan, what can I do for you?"

"Jim, our Otter is missing. Apparently it has been stolen and I need to know if you have a record of departure on it. The registration number is November seven four three two Oscar."

"O.K., hold on a sec, Dan." Dan heard the 'phone being laid down and papers riffling.

"Yeah, here it is. The aircraft departed at 6:48 this morning on an IFR flight plan to Yakutat."

"Yakutat?" Dan asked.

"That's what it says, Dan."

"Jim, would the radar controller at that time still be on duty?"

"Probably. You want to hold on while I find out?"

"Yeah, I'll hold." Dan heard a 'click' while Jim put him on hold. About three minutes later someone came on the line.

"This is Ralph Manning in departure control, Mr. Nichols. Can I help you?"

"Yes, Ralph. Were you controlling the Otter flight, November seven four three two Oscar when it departed this morning."

"Yes sir, I was."

"How far were you able to follow the flight? I understand the destination was Yakutat."

"That's what he filed for, Mr. Nichols, but a funny thing happened. When he got to Cordova he apparently turned off his transponder and turned southwest almost like he was heading for Kodiak. I followed him for awhile but then I got busy with other traffic and lost him after that."

"Thanks, Ralph ... you've been very helpful. Oh, one other thing, Ralph. Would you please notify your supervisor that the Otter apparently has been stolen and would he please notify the proper FAA authorities and get out a 'watch' on it?"

"I certainly will, Mr. Nichols."

Kodiak is out. Dan thought. *It would be too easy for Harry to be found, and trapped, in Kodiak. No ... he has to be heading somewhere else.*

While Dan had been talking, Tim had brewed a pot of coffee. Tim was sitting on the naugahyde couch drinking his cup. Dan poured himself one and returned to the swivel desk chair.

"Tim, during the return flight did Harry mention *anything* to you about going on a trip or any clue that might give you some idea what he might be up to?"

"No sir, not a thing."

"Come on, now, Tim. Put your mind to it. Any conversation with *anyone*. What about the people at Vanguard ... did the two of you have any conversation with anyone there that might that would give us a lead?"

Tim sat for a few minutes, sipping his coffee and suddenly his eyes brightened. "One thing I do remember, Dan, was that Harry was sitting talking to this guy Thornburgh in the canteen at Vanguard when I walked up on them and I don't think they heard me coming because they acted surprised when they saw me. But all I heard was this guy Thornburgh asking Harry if he had ever been to Dutch Harbor. I believe they had been talking about fishing. Harry said he had never been there but he wanted to go sometime."

Dan got up and walked over to the wall where he had previously put up a piece of wallboard and glued a large aviation map of Alaska to it. He had put a small nail on the spot where Anchorage was and then tied a long string to the nail. By stretching out the cord from Anchorage to any city in Alaska and then referencing the length to the mileage index, it would be easy to quickly estimate the distance to any point in Alaska from Anchorage.

Dutch Harbor ... Dan was thinking to himself. *Dutch Harbor is on the island of Unalaska in the Aleutian Island chain.* Dan ran his finger down the Aleutian chain until he found Unalaska. *What the heck could be so important about that island? It's really not close to anything except it has one of the best airports in the chain on it. If I was looking for the best airport to land a plane in the Aleutians it would be Dutch Harbor.* Dan took the string and ran it from Dutch Harbor to the nearest city on the coast of Russia. *One thousand miles roughly ... it would be possible, but risky, to try and make a flight from Dutch Harbor to the Russian mainland in a small aircraft which would be easier to fly underneath the Air Force Early Warning Radar System. Or ... a boat! A boat would be less likely to draw attention and a trawler wouldn't be suspected at all in those waters with American registry painted on it! That must be it. Whatever they have would be easier to transport out of there by boat than by a plane.*

Dan stretched the string to Cordova, held it there with a finger of his right hand then extended it further with his left hand westward to Dutch Harbor. Referencing the total length to the index gave a mileage of approximately 750 miles. Dan went back to his desk and got out his small calculator.

"O.K., Tim, we've got a total distance of 750 miles. Divide that by the cruising speed of the Otter, 140 miles per hour and we come up with five point four hours or five hours and twenty-four minutes. He left at 6:48 so add 5:24 to that ... his arrival time at Cold Bay should be twelve minutes after noon."

Tim said, "*If* that is where he's going."

"We don't have many other choices, do we?" Dan asked.

"No, sir, I guess we don't."

"O.K., then. I say we roll the dice on Dutch Harbor and just hope and pray we are right."

Back at the board once more, Dan stretched the string from Anchorage to Dutch Harbor and calculated the distance ... seven hundred and twenty miles. Dividing that by the cruise speed of the King Air gave him two hours and eighteen minutes. He looked at the clock on the wall ... it read 9:15. If they could leave in 30 minutes it would be almost a 'dead heat.'

"Tim, how long would it take you to get to your apartment and back?"

"Oh, about a half hour I guess."

"O.K., you run home and get that hunting rifle of yours ... the one with the scope on it. Make sure you bring some extra ammunition. You got a pair of binoculars?"

"Yes, sir."

"O.K., I'm going to have the King Air rolled out, check the fuel and be ready to go in 30 minutes. You be on the flight line at that time, o.k.?"

"Yes, Sir!" Tim jumped up and ran out the door.

Dan made sure the Colt 38 Detective Special was in his flight case along with the charts. He then called Al and told him where Tim and he were going. Al objected at first but Dan was adamant so he finally agreed and wished them well. Dan went out and checked the gas on the King Air ... it was 'topped off,' did a quick walk-a-round, rolled the King Air out of the hangar and went aboard to check everything out in the cockpit. At 9:50, Dan fired up the number one turbine and two minutes later Tim came running around the corner of the hangar with his binocular case and the Winchester .203 with the Leupold scope. He pulled up the airstair door after he got aboard and made his way to the cockpit.

"I'm all set, Dan, let's go!"

Chapter 89

Dutch Harbor

The Otter had made better time than Harry had estimated. He had confidence that his 'feint' towards Cordova would lead anyone astray who might check on his flight plan and attempt to follow him. Once he had gotten close to Cordova, he changed his route and headed towards Dutch Harbor, turning off his transponder to prevent flight following by Anchorage radar. Although he would still be painting a 'blip' in secondary radar coverage, he probably would be lost in the ground 'clutter.'

It was just ten minutes until noon and he could see Unalaska Island dead ahead. Ten minutes later he overflew the Unalaska airport at Dutch Harbor and began a left turn to parallel the runway. Harry noticed the windsock was favoring landing on runway two. Two miles from the airport he turned to heading two zero and saw the runway ahead slightly to his right. On final approach he corrected his heading and put the Otter down "on the numbers" for Runway two As he taxied in towards the FBO office he saw a line boy come out of the office to direct him to the ramp. He braked to a stop and motioned the boy to the side window which he opened.

"I want a tie-down for the night and will gas it up in the morning," he yelled at the boy.

"O.K., mister, just follow my signals."

The young man directed Harry to the tie-down area where Harry parked, disembarked and the two of them tied down the Otter.

Harry walked into the office and asked if there was a 'phone he could use. The attendant behind the desk pointed to a handset sitting on a table in the lounge area. Harry walked over to the 'phone, dialed 886-5102 and a male voice answered.

"Hello."

"Yeah, I'm here. Abe sent me."

"You at the airport?"

"Yeah."

"O.K., I can be there in fifteen minutes. I'll be driving a red Ford pickup so just come on out when you see me drive up."

"O.K., I'll see you then." Harry hung up the phone and walked outside. Harry looked at his watch ... it was ten minutes after twelve.

Chapter 90

Unalaska Marine Center

At twelve-twenty, Dan and Tim were at four thousand five hundred feet and could see the Unalaska airport dead ahead.

"Tim, I'm going to drop down to about two thousand feet and overfly the airport. Take a look and see if you can spot the Otter." Dan said.

"O.K." Tim responded.

Dan pulled back on the power levers and dropped down to two thousand feet and flew just south of the airport, keeping Runway three zero in sight. Tim was in the cabin of the King Air with his binoculars. He scanned the field and then stuck his head back in the cockpit.

"Dan, there's a red Otter sitting on the field!"

"O.K., get in your seat and strap in. I'm going to do a two hundred degree turn and fly down runway two."

Dan turned the King Air to the right and came to heading two zero and descended to one thousand feet and flew down the runway at 120 knots. They both got a clear look at the Otter and saw the identification number on top of the wing of the Otter. It read N7422 O.

"That's it!" shouted Tim.

Dan extended the downwind leg, did a one hundred eighty degree turn and dropped the gear and flaps and hit runway two dead on the numbers. He braked to a stop at the first turnoff, did a hurried taxi to the tie-down area and stopped right next to the Otter. Tim was out the airstair door while the props were still turning and ran over to the Otter and looked inside. Dan was right behind him.

"Damn! He's gone, Dan, and so is the crate."

They both started running towards the office when the line boy who had assisted Harry came towards them.

"Can I help you fellas?" he asked Tim and Dan.

"Yeah," Dan said, "did you see the guy that brought this Otter in?"

"Sure did."

"How long ago?" Dan asked.

"Oh, about thirty minutes ago."

"Do you know where he went?"

"Nope ... a man in a red Ford pickup truck drove up and they took a box out of the Otter and left."

"So you don't know where they went?"

"No," the young man said. "I do know the guy that picked him up though. His name is Bill Nolan and he is a charter boat captain."

Tim and Dan exchanged looks at one another. "Where does this man Nolan have his boat docked?" Tim asked.

"Usually he runs out of the Unalaska Marine Center."

"Can you take us down there?" Dan asked. "It's really important. The man who flew in here stole that Otter."

"Yeah, I got a truck and if the boss will let me go, I'll run you down there."

"Tim, you go get the rifle and binoculars while I go talk to this young man's boss." Dan said.

Tim took off running for the rifle and binoculars while Dan and the young man headed for the FBO office. By the time Tim had retrieved the rifle and binoculars, locked the King Air, and got back to the FBO office, Dan and the young man were coming out the door. All three of them took off for the parking lot where they got into a white Chevy pickup and headed for the Marina.

On the way the young man told Dan and Tim his name was Don Strong and the reason he knew Bill Nolan was because he had worked on the boat with Bill Nolan one summer baiting hooks and cleaning fish. Don said that Bill had not paid him what he had promised and Don quit working for him.

* * * *

Harry and Bill drove into the parking lot of the Unalaska Marine Center where Bill parked the truck and told Harry to stay there until he came back. In ten minutes Bill came back with a two wheel dolly. The two of them unloaded the case from the Ford truck and placed it on the dolly. Harry had wrapped the case in a piece of heavy duty polyethylene and taped it so that the wording on the case would be hidden. They proceeded to push the dolly across the gravel parking lot and came to an asphalt walkway which led down a slight incline to the wooden dock.

There was a tow-headed young man hosing down the deck and cockpit of a fiberglass cruiser tied up to one of the slips and he gave them a cursory glance as they proceeded along the wooden walkway towards the slip where Bill's fishing boat was tied up. Harry noticed the registration number on the hull, A K 5 6 5 8. *Well, this isn't it ... I need the letters UB and three numbers.* Bill and Harry loaded the case in the open cockpit of the boat then they stepped aboard and went up the steps to the flying bridge. Bill inserted a key into a lock, turned the key and then hit the starter button. The Ford diesel engine came to life.. He put the engine in reverse and they backed out of the slip and then headed slowly out of the inlet towards the Aleutian Bay.

"I guess you know where you are going," Harry said.

"Yep. I head out of here on a heading of three hundred fifty degrees and hold that until we get out about five miles. Then I will fire off that Very pistol you see over there (Bill pointed to the shelf on the right of the cabin) and then the boat will approach us."

"How do you know it is there and what kind of boat is it?" Harry asked.

"The answer to both of those question is, 'I don't know.' I get paid for this job whether or not the boat shows up."

Harry thought, *I wish I could say that.*

Chapter 91

The Noose Tightens

The Chevy pick-up screeched to a halt on a gravel road at the Unalaska Marine Center office in a cloud of dust. Dan already had a twenty in his hand and he handed it to Don and said, "Thanks … you did good." Tim and Dan were out of the truck with Tim still holding the rifle and binoculars. Dan had put the Colt 38 in his jacket when they had gotten off the King Air. They didn't even go in the marina office, they just headed down the path to where they saw a young man cleaning on a boat.

"Did you happen to see a couple of guys around here that were carrying a case of some kind?" Dan asked?

The young man answered, "Yeah. They were by here about ten or fifteen minutes ago."

"Where did they go?"

"They took the case and put it on Captain Nolan's boat, the *Betty Sue*."

"What does the boat look like?" Dan asked?

"Oh, it's a regular charter fishing boat … about thirty-two feet long with an in-line diesel engine, white with blue stripe down the side and the name on the stern."

"Do you know where we can get a fast boat with a radar on it?" Dan asked.

"Well … I don't know," he said hesitantly.

"Do you have a boat?" Dan asked.

"No, not really."

"What do you mean, 'not really?'"

"Well, Mr. Anderson let's me use his boat sometimes. I do a lot of extra work for him and don't charge him anything much so he let's me use his boat for fishing just about whenever I want it."

"Look ... I need a boat *bad* and I'm willing to pay for it"

"Wel-l-l-l.." the young man was looking at Tim's rifle.

"Oh, you think we are going to shoot someone. That gun is strictly for self defense. The heavy-set guy with Nolan stole an airplane from my company which he landed over at the Unalaska airport. And, we are sure that case holds some kind of contraband that has also been stolen. Now, if you want to take us out on Mr. Anderson's boat and help us find the boat that just left, I will give you a hundred dollars."

The young man's expression changed instantly and he said, "Let's go!"

*   *   *   *

The *Betty Sue* was running through a sea of light chop under an overcast sky with visibility of about five miles. Harry turned to Bill standing behind the wheel and said,

"Can't you get any more speed out of this tub?"

Bill turned to look at Harry with a sneer on his face. "Look, this is a fishing boat, not a damn speedboat. Fifteen knots is a good cruising speed for it and I don't see the need to go busting through this chop. If it's too slow for you then you can jump overboard and swim!"

Harry sulked over to the opposite side of the flying bridge.

Chapter 92

Prepare to Fire!

The UB-235 had been at periscope depth for over twelve hours. Captain Johng Ho Kim had risked surfacing for two hours shortly after midnight and had allowed three or four of the crew at a time to come up to the sail. This had not only given the crew an opportunity to stretch their legs and get some fresh air, but also to refresh the air inside of the boat. Now the UB-235 was once again in a waiting mode.

"Control, Sonar"

"Control, aye"

"Captain, I have propeller sounds, bearing zero nine zero. Appears to be a slow moving fishing boat."

"Up periscope." Captain Johng commanded as he took the handles of the periscope as it went upward. Peering through the periscope, Johng could barely make out the bow of a boat which apparently was coming out of Dutch Harbor.

"Down scope. Helmsman come right to heading one seven zero, all ahead slow." The North Korean submarine started a slow turn to the right and now had definitely left International waters proceeding into United States territorial waters.

* * * *

On board the *SSN Columbus* the sonarman noticed the blip on his screen beginning to move and simultaneously recognized the distinct sound of the North Korean Romeo.

"Conn, Sonar"

"Conn, aye."

"Captain, the *Romeo* is moving, bearing zero four six. He appears to be heading towards land."

"Sonar, conn, aye."

"Fire Control, give me an intercept heading to the *Romeo*

"Captain, the intercept heading is one five zero, range nine thousand four hundred yards."

"Aye, aye. Helmsman come to heading one five zero, all ahead one-third."

"Aye, aye, sir. Coming right to heading one five zero, all ahead one-third."

Captain Loudon turned to his Executive Officer.

"Mac, when the *Romeo* stops, which I am sure he will, I want to close slowly to approximately one thousand yards and set up for a bow shot at his midships. Although our sonar is now active, I am counting on the distraction of the *Romeo* meeting the two approaching boats to allow us to close without being noticed."

"Aye, Aye, Captain." Lt. Commander MacKenzie acknowledged the plan.

Chapter 93

Ship Ahoy!

Dan had learned the young man who was piloting their boat was named Tom Blackwell and he had the express cruiser on the step doing approximately thirty-five knots. Dan was standing beside Tom peering at the radar screen which showed a blip ahead of them and slightly to their left. Tim was also in the pilot house peering through his binoculars.

"I see 'em!" shouted Tim above the roar of the engine. "There ... just off to our left!" Dan peered ahead to where Tim was pointing and he could barely see what appeared to be the stern of a boat. Tom spoke to Dan and told him that they should overtake the boat in no more than six or seven minutes. Just at that time all three of them saw a flare which had been shot into the air from the boat they were pursuing.

"That's got to be a signal from them for the boat that is going to meet them, "Dan said.

"I wonder what kind of boat they're meeting," Tom asked. "I've got this radar on the ten mile range and I don't see another boat."

In another three minutes Tom said, "Look! There it is ... what the heck is going on ... there wasn't anything there a minute ago and now we've got two boats on the screen. They traveled on for another few minutes and then Tim shouted.

"*Holy shit*! It's a submarine!"

Dan and Tom couldn't see it with the naked eye but Tim had picked it up through his binoculars. They were rapidly gaining ground on the boat they were pursuing and they now could definitely make out the details of the craft they were following.

Dan turned to Tom. "You got a radio on this thing?"

"Yeah, why? Who do you want to call?"

"I want to call the Coast Guard."

"Oh, man," Tom groaned, "you're going to get us in trouble."

"We're already *in* trouble if you didn't know it! Now get on the horn and call them … *right now!*"

Tom turned on the radio, set the frequency for the Coast Guard and spoke into the microphone,

"Cruiser *Handy Andy* calling the Coast Guard. Cruiser *Handy Andy* calling the Coast Guard."

"Coast Guard to *Handy Andy*, go ahead."

"Coast Guard, stand by one … I have a passenger who wants to talk to you." He handed the microphone to Dan.

"Coast Guard, can you hear me?"

"Yes sir, loud and clear."

"My name is Dan Nichols and I am the chief pilot for Intermont Mining and Supply in Anchorage. One of our employee pilots stole our DH-3T Otter amphibian, registration number November seven four three two Oscar. I reported the theft to the FAA this morning. We are in pursuit of the thief who is in a boat called the … standby …

Tom said, 'it's the Betty Sue out of Dutch Harbor.'

… it's the *Betty Sue* out of Dutch Harbor. Have you got all of that?" Dan asked.

"Yes sir. Stand by one."

In just over a minute the Coast Guard radioman came back,

"Mr. Nichols, the FAA put the information out over the net this morning just as you said and we were notified of the theft. Over."

"O.K., now here is something you probably are not going to believe. Our 'ex employee' pilot on the *Betty Sue* has stolen some type of contraband. We know that for a fact, and he apparently is attempting to deliver the contraband to a submarine which has surfaced just about two to three miles ahead of us. Over."

There was a pause by the Coast Guard and the *Handy Andy* was now only about two hundred yards behind the *Betty Sue*. Tom had wisely dropped astern to cut down on the chance of being seen by those on the *Betty Sue*.

"Coast Guard calling the *Handy Andy*."

"Go ahead, Coast Guard, this is the *Handy Andy*." Dan answered.

"We have the cutter *Courageous* about thirty-five miles from your position. They will make all haste to attempt to assist you but it will take approximately forty-five to fifty minutes for them to reach you. Over."

"Thanks, Coast Guard. We don't know what we will be able to do but we will try and think of something. *Handy Andy* out."

"Coast Guard out."

* * * *

Harry was elated! The North Korean submarine had surfaced and he saw the number 'UB-235' which had been painted on the sail. Those three numbers, 2-3-5 were like winning the lottery … his quarter of a million was now guaranteed! The hatch on the conning tower was open and crewmen were coming through the tower and down a ladder onto the deck. Apparently they were in the process of inflating a rubber raft. Just at that moment Harry caught something out of the corner of his right eye. Dan had decided to pull ahead of the *Betty Sue* and attempt to position their boat between the *Betty Sue* and the submarine.

The North Korean UB-235 was sitting with its bow and stern at a ninety degree angle to the two approaching boats. Still unknown to Captain Johng, the *SSN Columbus* had silently maneuvered itself one half mile on the side of the UB235 opposite the two approaching boats with its bow looking directly at the middle of the North Korean submarine.

Chapter 94

Battle Stations!

"*Man your Battle Stations! Man your Battle Stations!*" BONG! BONG! BONG! BONG! The call and klaxon rang out throughout all sections of the *USN Columbus*. Off duty sailors emptied their berths, cooks left their stoves, off duty officers left their compartments and all hands began to dash as fast as possible to their assigned battle stations.

Captain Loudon was looking through his periscope while his Fire Control was feeding the coordinates into the firing solution.

Executive Officer MacKenzie reported to Captain Loudon,

"Sir we have the firing solution. Range nine hundred yards, heading one eight zero two."

"Very well. Set depth for thirty feet, open outer doors one and two."

"Fire Control, aye, aye, sir. Depth set for thirty feet, opening outer doors one and two."

Captain Loudon turned to his Executive Officer, "I think we have waited long enough, Mac. Send him two pings."

"Sir?" Lt. Commander MacKenzie questioned.

"I repeat, Commander, *send him two pings!*"

"Aye, Aye, sir."

"Conn, Sonar."

"Sonar, Conn."

"Send two pings to the target."

Sonar, aye, aye, sir, two pings."
PINGgggggg ... PINGgggggg
"Sonar, Conn. Good strong echo from the target, sir."
"Very well," Lt. Commander MacKenzie responded.

* * * *

Aboard the UB-235 the sonarman, who had been distracted by the activity going on outside the boat, was shocked beyond belief to hear the two pings. He rapidly ran a scan on his scope and picked up the submarine that had sneaked up on them. *It had to be a US Navy submarine*! He immediately called the captain who was on the bridge.

"Sonar to Captain Johng! Sonar to Captain Johng!"

Captain Johng on the bridge spoke into the microphone mounted there.

"Sonar, Captain."

"Sir, we have taken two pings from an American submarine, bearing zero nine zero to port, range eight two two meters. They have opened their outer doors!" The sonarman was practically screaming!

Captain Johng was frozen in his tracks momentarily. He looked through his binoculars to his left and saw the tip of a periscope in the distance. He then came to reality quickly. *The American pigs are looking right down our throats and are prepared to shoot! How did this happen?!!* The captain immediately pressed the button on the bridge control station and the klaxon began its' sound as Captain Johng began to yell,

"Clear the bridge, clear the bridge! All hands below immediately!"

The crew members dropped what they were doing. The half inflated raft slipped over the side and floated away as the men scurried up the conning tower and down the hatch. Captain Johng was the last one down shouting, "Emergency Dive! Emergency Dive!

* * * *

On board the *SSN Columbus*. Captain Loudon picked up the microphone.

"Conn, Fire Control."

"Fire Control, Conn."

"This is the captain. Continue to track the *Romeo* maintaining a firing positon as she goes. If she gives any indication she is taking an attack position, we will blow her out of the water."

"Aye, aye, Captain."

* * * *

As soon as Captain Johng's feet hit the deck of the control center, he gave the command, "Level off at one hundred meters, all ahead slow. Helmsman come to heading one five zero."

The helmsman responded, "Aye, aye, captain. Leveling off at one hundred meters, all ahead slow, coming to new heading of one five zero."

* * * *

Aboard the SSN *Columbus,* the Fire Control Center and the Sonar controller monitored the movements of the North Korean submarine UB-235 as it slowly continued its movement forward for approximately one half a mile then turned very slowly, keeping its' stern towards the *Columbus,* as it turned its' bow to the heading of two three zero. The *Columbus* maintained a firing position on the UB-235 until Captain Loudon was satisfied that the North Korean submarine was only concerned with beating a hasty retreat back into international waters and on its way out of the Aleutian Bay. Thus the *Columbus* had prevented the international incident that the White House, Pentagon and COMSUBPAC were concerned about taking place.

Chapter 95

Harry's Revenge

Harry Abelson was stupefied. The Korean submarine had disappeared before his very eyes and the dream of a quarter million dollars disappeared below the waves with the UB-235.

Both the *Betty Sue* and the *Handy Andy* had drifted to a complete stop and they were practically alongside each other, separated by a distance of perhaps ten yards. Both Harry and Bill had left the flying bridge for the open deck of the *Betty Sue* as did Tim, Dan and Tom on the *Handy Andy*.

Harry looked across at the other boat and yelled,

"I might have known that you two would be on that boat! I don't know how you sons-a-bitches did it, but this is one time you are going to pay for screwing up my life!"

He reached inside his jacket and pulled out a Glock nine millimeter semi-automatic handgun and pumped off five rapid shots. The first one grazed Tim's neck, the next went into Dan's lower right abdomen and the other shots went wild.

Tim dropped to his knees and grabbed the Winchester .203 which had been leaning against the bulkhead next to the door going into the cabin. He very carefully and coolly braced the barrel of the rifle on the railing of the side of the boat and fired one shot. Looking through the Leupold scope, Tim had aimed for Harry's heart and that was exactly where the bullet went.

Harry staggered backwards from the impact of the bullet. Off balance, he fell against the railing of the boat which was just about the height of where his buttocks met his thighs and his momentum carried him backward over the side of the boat into the icy water. Bill rushed to the side of the boat and looked overboard. Apparently Harry's body had already begun to sink as Bill made no effort to try and retrieve him.

Tim handed the rifle to Tom and said, "Here, keep this rifle trained on that guy," meaning Bill. Tim immediately unbuttoned Dan's jacket, ripped open his shirt, unbuckled his belt and found the bullet wound in Dan's abdomen which had already begun to bleed profusely. Tim turned to Tom and asked him if he had anything on the boat that would do for a bandage. Tom told him there were some sheets on the two bunks in the cuddy cabin.

Tim went below and came back with a sheet which he was ripping apart. Dan was lying on the deck on his back, groaning. Tim pulled Dan's trousers down far enough for him to see where the blood was coming from. He wiped the blood away until he could see where the bullet had penetrated his abdomen. Tim made a small pad out of a piece of the torn sheet and placed it each over the hole where the bullet had entered and then began to take strips of the sheet, winding it very tightly around and around Dan's torso trying to get enough pressure on the wound to stop the flow of blood.

Tim then took time to look at Dan's face and saw that Dan was looking at him through glazed eyes. A medically trained person would have recognized that Dan was on the verge of going into shock. After stanching the flow of blood as best he could, Tim tried to comfort Dan by telling him, "Hang in there, buddy. We are going to get you to a doctor as soon as we can."

Tom was still standing, guarding Bill with the rifle. Tim took the rifle from him and then told Tom to get something to pull the two boats close together. In a few minutes he came back with a rope with a grappling hook on the end which he used to pull the craft together.

"O.K., Nolan, get down on your knees." Tim ordered.

"For Christ's sake ... you aren't going to kill me are you?" Bill cried.

"Oh, hell no! We're just going to rope and hog-tie you." Tim had Tom tear the remainder of the sheets into long strips and tie Tom's hands behind his back. Then he had him tie his ankles together. Once that was done they rolled Bill on his stomach and tied his hands to his ankles.

"There, that ought to hold you awhile." Both Tim and Tom hopped back on the *Handy Andy* and tried, as gently as they could to get Dan down in the cuddy cabin and cover him with blankets. In minutes they heard a very loud ship's horn. Tom ran up on the deck and saw the Coast Guard Cutter *Courageous* close by.

Chapter 96

Coast Guard to the Rescue

The *Courageous* came within hailing distance and Tom shouted, "We have a seriously wounded man on board. Please send a doctor if you have one!"

One of the officers on board the *Courageous* picked up a megaphone and yelled back, "We don't have a doctor but we will put a pharmacist's mate aboard immediately."

No sooner had the officer finished his message than a small boat was soon being lowered by the davits with four of the *Courageous'* crew aboard. As soon as the boat pulled alongside the *Handy Andy* the first person to come aboard was a pharmacist's mate with a black satchel. Tom ushered the pharmacist's mate down into the cuddy cabin of the boat where both Tim and Dan were. The mate immediately noticed that Dan was in a state of shock so he removed a syringe from his bag, filled it with morphine and injected it into Dan's arm. He then took cotton pads, applied a generous amount of Betadine to the pads and began to cleanse the blood from the area around the wound. When he had removed all the blood, he applied more Betadine to the area and then applied a compress to stop the bleeding.

Turning to Tom the pharmacist's mate asked, "Are you from the island?"

Tom answered, "Yes, I am."

"Do you have a hospital there?"

Tom said, "No, but we have a medical clinic with a doctor."

The pharmacist's mate turned to one of his crewmen standing close by and said, "Andrews, tell the captain that we need to move this man to the island as quick as we can and I recommend we do it by means of this boat. He is in too critical a condition to take him aboard our ship."

"Right away, chief," the crewman answered and turned to go to the deck of the *Handy Andy*.

The crewman returned in just a couple of minutes and said, "Captain Thigpen said to take the wounded man ashore ASAP, chief."

The chief spoke to the three crewmen who had come aboard with him. "Andrews, you Standefer and Simpson check out the guy in the other boat and also see if you find anything suspicious that they may have aboard. Report what you find to Captain Thigpen."

"Aye, aye, chief," and the three crewmen boarded their boat.

The pharmacist's mate turned to Tom. "You know how to run this boat?"

"Sure. It's my boat."

"O.K., then let's haul ass for the island and call ahead on the radio to someone ashore if you know anyone who can arrange for transportation of this man to the clinic"

"No problem, chief. I'll call our marina and have a vehicle ready."

The pharmacists' mate then looked at Tim whose shirt was soaked with blood, by this time, from the wound in his neck. "O.K., now let's see what I can do for you."

CHAPTER 97

▼

ADAK

Sweeping across the mainland of Mongolia, the jet stream dipped further to the south than normal and crossed the Sea of Japan where it sucked warm, moist air into the atmosphere and then hurried it northeastward toward the Aleutian Islands. Approaching the small island of Adak, the temperature of the air near the surface reached 29 degrees at the same time the dewpoint achieved that same magical number. Mother Nature dictates that when this anomaly occurs, fog forms. On this January morning Jack Frost took his magic wand and coated all inanimate, and animate, forms in the small community of Adak with miniscule glistening droplets of frozen fog.

This caused little inconvenience to most of the inhabitants of the island because at this hour of six o'clock on a Saturday morning most were still asleep and could care less about what was taking place outside their dwellings.

However, one particular young female had just taken her shower and was in the process of putting on her freshly starched nurse's uniform, white hose and white athletic type shoes. She then slipped on a parka and went out the front door where her ice encrusted 1982 Ford F-100 pickup truck was parked. She slipped the key in the ignition, started the engine and stayed in the cab just long enough to make sure the engine would idle without further encouragement, then she returned to the house, removed the parka and went back into the bathroom.

Looking into the mirror, she picked up a reddish-brown eyebrow pencil and darkened her light eyebrows ever so slightly to blend more perfectly with her beautiful auburn hair. She then applied a soft layer of a similar color of lipstick remembering what her Irish mother had always told her. "Tis' a God-given gift from yer Irish grandmother that ye' have that be-yootiful head of hair, Patricia, and ye' ne'er want to do nuthin' to detract frum it."

Satisfied with the results, the nurse donned the parka again, slung her purse over her shoulder and looked at the white nurse's cap with the two black bands resting on the chest of drawers. She seldom ever wore it to the small clinic on the island but today was a very unusual one so she decided she would wear it once she was inside the clinic. She picked up the cap and carried it since she had the hood of the parka pulled over her head.

The cab of the Ford was getting warm and the defroster had removed most of the ice from the windshield. Her Scotch-Irish dad had taught her to always warm up a cold engine and make sure the oil was circulating around the cylinders before putting a load on the engine. She engaged the clutch of the six year old pickup and moved slowly into the fog bound road which she knew so well and began the one and a half mile drive to the clinic. She had purchased the truck second-hand from a local fisherman shortly after her arrival on the island and it had served her faithfully the two years that she had owned it.

Driving slowly to the clinic in the heavy fog, she had plenty of time to recount the arrival yesterday afternoon of the two men that had been brought into the medical facility with gunshot wounds.

Chapter 98

Attack at Sea

The afternoon of the day before, had begun with an almost frantic call from Tom Edmunds, the Unalaska Marine Center owner. He had received a marine radio message from the Coast Guard Cutter *Courageous* lying offshore about three miles, who reported they had intercepted two fishing boats whose occupants had been involved in a gun fight. Two men had been wounded and were enroute to Edmund's marina in one of the cutter's small boats with a Coast Guard Pharmacist's Mate and two other seamen aboard.

As soon as the boat arrived at the marina, the two wounded men, one walking and another on a stretcher, were loaded into Edmund's Chevrolet Suburban and were rushed to the clinic. On arrival at the clinic, the victim on the stretcher was immediately removed and the pharmacist's mate, holding a bottle of saline solution which was being fed into the wounded man's arm, walked alongside him as he was being carried inside.

Patricia recalled that after rushing the patient to the operating room, Dr. Erickson found a gunshot wound to his lower right quadrant of the abdomen. The two of them had prepared the patient for the operation with Patricia administering the anesthesia as she was also a nurse anesthetist. After the abdomen had been opened they found a perforating wound of the intestines which the doctor repaired. Patricia remembered Dr. Erickson saying that there was so much blood in the abdomen it was a miracle that the patient had survived. Removing the bullet would have to wait until the patient could be transferred to a hospital on the mainland where an ample supply of blood would be available in the event a transfusion was necessary.

* * * *

As the Ford F-100 neared the clinic, Patricia began to see the yellowish glow of the fluorescent lights from inside the building spilling out through the windows to form multi-colored prisms on the still dark ice covered landscape. Under other circumstances she might have spent more time enjoying this winter wonderland of nature but her mind was focused on getting inside the clinic as soon as possible.

Parking the Ford, she gathered her purse and nurse's cap and quickened her step as she hurried towards the main entrance of the clinic. She was anxious to see if the patient who had been rushed in yesterday afternoon with the gunshot wound to the abdomen was still alive.

Chapter 99

The Patient

Registered Nurse Patricia Cavanaugh stepped onto the portico of the Iliuliuk Family & Health Center, pulled open the glass door and walked into the empty combination waiting—registration room. As she removed her purse and parka she immediately smelled the aroma of what had to be a freshly brewed pot of coffee. She hung her parka in the closet, put on her cap, and moved down the hallway past Dr. Erickson's office on the left. Glancing in the darkened room, she saw the doctor, fully clothed, asleep on the couch in his office. The next door to the right was the examining room and she looked through the doorway to see a nurse sitting there reading a book. Patricia Cavanaugh entered the room.

"Hi, Jean, how's he doing?"

"Mornin,' Trish. He's still alive," the Licensed Practical Nurse said as she looked up from her book.

Trish Cavanaugh walked over to the bed that had the guardrails in the up position and looked at the ashen face of a ruggedly handsome male who appeared to be in his mid-forties. She took his wrist and compared the faint heartbeat she felt with the second hand on her watch. Pulse fifty-six. Trish looked at the chart held by a clipboard that was lying on the bedside table. She noticed that all the 'vitals' had been checked every hour on the hour either by the LPN or the doctor. The readings had remained fairly constant for the past five hours.

"What time did the doctor go to bed, Jean?"

"Oh, he laid down on the couch about midnight but made me promise to get him up at two o'clock. He came in and checked him over then walked out telling me to call him again at four. I guess he has had maybe three or four hours of sleep since you left at eleven last night."

"Let's let him sleep as long as he can. You want a cup of coffee?"

"That would be nice, Trish. Just a tad of sugar … no cream."

"Yeah," Trish smiled. "I don't know why you bother with the sugar."

"Just a habit, I guess."

Trish left the room and went to the small canteen area where they had a small sink with some cabinets, a coffee pot, a table with four chairs and a small refrigerator. She poured Jean's cup, added a half teaspoon of sugar, fixed a black cup for herself and returned to the patient's room.

"I don't suppose he has regained consciousness?"

"You guessed right … not a word. He does groan ever so often and frowns. I know he must still be experiencing quite a bit of pain."

"What about his friend … Tim, isn't it … with the wound to his neck? Is he o.k.?"

"Yeah, he's doin' all right. He was really lucky. The bullet that got him was right at the juncture of his neck and shoulder. A few more inches to the right and it probably would have ruptured his carotid artery and that would have been all she wrote for him. I gave him a sedative and told him to take one of the beds in the ward room. He turned in right after you left. By the way, his name is Tim Morrison and our patient here is named Dan Nichols."

"Well, it's good to know who we have been working on, isn't it?" Trish remarked.

"What does Dr. Erickson think? Has he wagered a guess as to his chances?" Trish asked.

"He told me the last time he checked on him that if he can make it until noon today that he believes he will be o.k."

Trish finished her coffee and set the cup on the table by the bed and checked the bottle of liquid antibiotic that was being dripped intravenously into the patient's arm. The flow rate looked good. She then turned and looked at Jean who was showing the signs of a rough night. Dr. Erickson was lucky to find an LPN on this island. Jean was the wife of Tom Edmunds, the marina owner, and she was always willing to help out whenever they had an emergency that required a twenty-four hour vigil which, fortunately, was not very often. The last time was when Tom Matthews, a commercial fisherman, had stepped on a gaff that penetrated his shoe and cut his foot severely. Like so many stubborn working men,

Tom thought his fishing business was more important than his health so he resorted to self-treatment. Consequently, the foot became infected and by the time he decided to see Dr. Erickson it was too late ... gangrene had set in. Dr. Erickson had no choice but to amputate the foot right above the left ankle. Now, Trish thought, it looks as if the doctor may have a chance to save a second life. This little community was just not aware of how fortunate they were to have an experienced physician/surgeon as they had in Dr. Glenn Erickson.

"Jean, has Tom learned anymore about what happened out there on the bay?" Trish asked.

"Oh, rumors are flying left and right according to Tom. Do you know Tom Blackwell?"

"No, I don't believe I do," Trish replied.

"Well, he's the young fellow who does a lot of miscellaneous work on the boats at the marina, ... works on some of the engines and cleans them up. He does a lot of work for Jim Anderson who owns that express cruiser the *Handy Andy*. Mr. Anderson lets Tom Blackwell use his boat just about any time he wants to so when Tim and our friend here showed up at the dock asking about any boats that had just left the dock recently, Tom told them about some guy who had loaded a box on Bill Nolan's boat the *Betty Sue* and they had left about ten minutes ago. So, the two of them, Tim and Dan, hired Tom to take off after the *Betty Sue*. When they caught up with it a gunfight took place between the two boats. That's about all he would say."

Jean took a sip of her coffee and then continued.

"My Tom says that Tom Blackwell is scared to death. The Coast Guard arrested Bill Nolan and has taken him into custody and the captain of the Coast Guard cutter told Tom Blackwell not to discuss any of the details of what happened as the FBI has entered the case since something happened out there that is a matter of national security."

"Wonder what happened to the guy that was on Bill Nolan's boat?" Trish asked.

"No one knows unless the Coast Guard has him too." Jean answered.

"Look, Jean," Trish remarked, "you've been here too long already. Why don't you head on home and get some sleep. I'll wake the doctor up soon now and I'm sure the two of us will be able to handle everything."

"Thanks, Trish, I think I will." Jean walked over to the bed and lightly patted the still unconscious patient's head. "You hang in there, now. You're going to be o.k." She turned, smiled at Trish, and said, "I think he will be all right if he ever comes to."

Trish thought, *That has a definite ring of finality to it ... if he ever comes to.*

As Jean left the room, Trish turned around and looked at the patient again. Suddenly a frown came across his face and a low moan issued from his mouth. Trish stroked his forehead lightly and the frown receded.

She thought, *What's going on in that mind of yours ... if anything? Are you trying to remember what brought you to this place? Is there someone somewhere who wonders where you are and what has happened to you?*

Chapter 100

Close Call

Registered Nurse Patricia Cavanaugh could hardly believe it had just been slightly more than twenty-four hours since the patient she was now looking at had been brought into the clinic on a stretcher with the Coast Guard pharmacist's mate carrying a bottle of saline solution which was being intravenously fed into the patient's arm. She recalled how feverishly she and Dr. Erickson had worked during the operation to repair the damage to the patient's intestines in his lower right abdomen, stopping the flow of blood into the cavity and then maintaining a vigil since then to see if the patient would have the strength to survive.

His temperature was now just two points above normal, his pulse rate was at a steady 58 beats per minute as a result of the shock, and his blood pressure was 120 over 80, all good signs that he was well on the road to recovery. Now if he would just regain consciousness. Nurse Cavanaugh was aware of footsteps coming down the hall.

"Good morning, nurse. How's he doing? Tim Morrison, the patient's friend had just entered the room.

"He's doing fine, Mr. Morrison. If he would just regain consciousness I think we would all breathe a sigh of relief however."

"Do you think it would do any good if I talked to him?"

"It certainly wouldn't do any harm. Why don't you try it?" Nurse Cavanaugh replied.

Tim moved close to the side of the bed, put his hand on Dan's right shoulder and leaned over the bed.

"Hey, old buddy, it's me ... Tim. How about waking up and talking to me a bit?"

There was no response. Tim looked around at Nurse Cavanaugh and she motioned with her head as if to encourage him to keep talking.

"Come on now, the sooner you get better the sooner we can get back in the King Air and go back home to see Jess."

At the sound of the word 'Jess' Dan's eyelids moved slightly.

"Yeah, I called Jess last night and told her you were o.k. and we would probably be coming back in a day or so. You wouldn't want to disappoint her, would you?"

Dan's eyes flickered open and he stared up into Tim's face.

"Did you say you talked to Jess?" Dan asked. "How is she?" he asked weakly.

Tim glanced at Nurse Cavanaugh quickly and she was smiling and had clasped her hands and was holding them over her head like a fighter who had just had a victory.

Tim smiled broadly at Dan and replied, "She's doing great, Dan, and she told me to tell you to hurry up and get well and get back home."

"How did I get here, Tim? Am I going to be o.k.? I mean, I'm not going to be crippled or anything am I?"

"Heck no, man ... you are going to be just fine. That Coast Guard cutter we called arrived and the pharmacist's mate patched you up. Then the mate, Tom, and I brought you in on the *Handy Andy.*"

Dan noticed the patch on Tim's neck. "What happened to you? Did you get shot?

"Awww, it was just a nick, Dan. Ol' Harry was a lousy shot and I'm surprised that he was able to hit you."

"What happened to him, Tim?"

Tim's countenance dropped and he said, "I hated to do it, Dan, but I had to put him away."

"You did what you had to do, Tim. Don't blame yourself."

Nurse Cavanaugh had slipped out of the room and now she had returned with Dr. Erickson who moved in alongside Tim.

"Well, how are you feeling, Mr. Nichols? I'm Doctor Erickson. You gave us quite a scare there for awhile but you are making progress now."

Dan slowly raised his right arm and extended his hand. "I sure am glad to meet *you,* doctor, and I want to thank you for saving my life."

"You are a very fortunate man, Mr. Nichols. I don't want to give you any concern but if that bullet had hit you in your *left* abdomen ... well, it more than likely would have been a very different situation. Thanks to the pharmacists mate and those who rushed you here, you are now well on your way to recovery."

"How soon before I will be able to go home, doctor?"

Doctor Erickson laughed, "Well, that is a sure sign you are doing well. Anytime a patient asks if he can go home I know he is doing well. Let's not be too hasty though. You are still in a very weakened condition and I want you to be strong enough to endure that flight back to Anchorage. Maybe in a couple of days. We will see."

'Thank you sir," Dan replied. He smiled weakly and said, "I'll be ready when you are."

"Fine," replied Dr. Erickson. "Now I suggest we get out of here and let you get some more rest."

Dr. Erickson and Tim left the room and the nurse checked on Dan's vital signs one more time. Tim decided he would go to the canteen and see if he could find a cup of coffee. He pulled a handkerchief from his pocket and wiped away a tear in his right eye.

Chapter 101

Nurse Patricia Ann Cavanaugh

Tim was sitting at a table in the canteen drinking his cup of coffee when Nurse Cavanaugh walked in.

"I decided that I could use a cup of that myself," and she selected one of the china cups and filled it from the pot sitting on the warmer.

"Say, since it looks like we may be here another night or two can you tell me if there is a motel here in town?" Tim asked.

The nurse smiled and said, "No motel. This is a very small community and we don't get a lot of visitors here except in the fishing season. There is a fishing lodge here which stays open all year, mostly to serve meals during the off season as there aren't many good restaurants in town. I know the owner and if you like I can call down there and see if he can put you up for the night … or for whatever time you are here."

"I'd sure appreciate it … is it Patricia? Tim asked.

"Yes, but everybody calls me 'Trish' … and you are Tim, right?"

"Yep, that's right. Say, is there a 'phone I can make a credit card call on. If you don't mind, while you are making your call I'll make mine. There are some people in Anchorage I need to call and let them know what's going on."

"There's a phone in the reception area you can use. You will have to dial 'zero' for the operator. We don't have a direct dial system here yet. When you get through look me up and I'll Let you know what I found out about your room."

Tim made his call to the Intermont office and caught Al there. He gave Al a complete report on everything that had happened and to say that Al was shocked would be putting it mildly. Al told Tim to stay with Dan regardless of how long it might take before he would be able to make the trip and he also told Tim that he would let Jess know how Dan was doing. Al also told Tim to be sure and call back first thing in the morning and let him know how Dan was progressing. Tim said he would do that and finished the call. He then walked back to the nurse's station and found Trish seated at the desk filling out some charts. As Tim approached, she looked up.

"They've got a room for you down at the lodge, Tim. Mr. Sanders said that he would be glad to put you up for the nights you will be here and they will be serving dinner tonight at seven o'clock. They serve family style so I need to call him back and let him know if you are going to be there as they set only enough places for those who are going to be there for the meal."

"Hey, that sounds great, Trish. When you call back, why don't you tell him to fix *two* places."

Trish looked at Tim a little surprised and said, "Well, thank you. I can use some good home cooked food for a change so I will accept your invitation. By the way, I get off at five o'clock so if you want to hang around until then I'll be glad to drop you off at the lodge. I'll have to go home and change and then come back for dinner if that's o.k."

"You've got a deal, Trish," and Tim smiled expansively at her.

On the way to the lodge in Trish's '82 Ford pickup, Tim realized that he was in need of some toiletries as well as something to sleep in. Trish said she had just the ticket for that and pulled up at a general store type facility in the village where Tim was able to buy the necessary items and a small zippered overnight type canvas bag to put everything in. Trish went into Sanders Lodge with Tim and introduced him to Bill Sanders, the owner, and then she left for the two rooms she rented in a private home.

Bill took Tim up to the second floor and unlocked the door to a single large room which had a large feather bed, a rocking chair, a small desk with a lamp, a straight chair and a small fireplace where kindling and a few logs had been laid. There was an ample supply of logs for the fireplace. The room was rudimentary but clean.

"I think it would be a good idea to start that fire," Bill said as he struck a match and lit the paper under the kindling. "It's gonna get pretty cold in here before morning so you'll want to keep that fire going, Mr. Morrison."

"Thanks, Mr. Sanders, I'll sure take care of it."

"Fine, if you need anything, just let us know. Remember, dinner will begin at seven sharp. Oh, I nearly forgot ... the bath is at the end of the hall." With that, Bill Sanders left and closed the door.

Tim took his canvas bag and exited the room, turning left down the hall towards the bathroom. He counted off nine other doorways as he walked the hall so the lodge had accommodations for at least twenty people if there were two to a room. He entered the large bathroom, filled the tub with hot water and took a much needed luxurious bath followed by a shave. Tim only realized then what a stressful day it had been.

* * * *

Tim was in the large combination lobby and 'great room' at six thirty. There was a huge fireplace in the room and a blazing fire was going. One large sofa and several easy chairs were arranged in front of the fireplace. The entire structure was built of oak flooring and oak paneling. Large twelve inch oak beams spanned the 'great room' as well as the adjoining dining room. Supporting pillars of the same size as the overhead beams were strategically placed to support the second floor of the structure. The building looked as if it must be seventy-five years old at least.

At six forty-five, Trish Cavanaugh entered the lodge. She had on a knitted wool cap over her auburn hair and was wearing a heavy overcoat and boots. Tim walked over to meet her and helped her remove the overcoat. Trish removed the cap and put it in the pocket of the coat which Tim hung on a hall tree. As Tim turned around he, for the first time, appreciated what a stunning young lady Trish was. She had on a white knit wool sweater with a crew neck and a long wool skirt. Tim noticed that the leather boots were knee high. Two gold circular earrings dangled from her ears and when she smiled at Tim, she revealed perfect white teeth which were accentuated by the makeup that was more noticeable than it had been at the hospital. Tim also realized for the first time that she had two beautiful green eyes.

"Hi," Trish said.

"Hi, yourself," Tim replied. "Hey, you look great in 'civvies.'"

"Well, thanks ... you're just full of compliments, aren't you?"

Tim blushed. "Aw, heck, I'm sorry ... I meant you look *great!*"

"Oh, come on," Trish laughed as she took him by the hand and led him into the dining room.

There were a total of six other people besides Bill and Elizabeth Sanders. Apparently the three other men and three women were 'locals' who had come for dinner. They all stood around the table while Bill Sanders said 'grace' then they sat and Bill started passing the plates full of food. The meal was a typical family style dinner and there was more than enough to go around. No one left the table hungry that evening.

After dinner, Trish and Tim went to the fireplace and sat on the large sofa. Tim brought up the subject of Dr. Glenn Erickson looking so young and Trish explained that he had graduated from the University of Washington School of Medicine and had done his internship and residency at one of the major hospitals in Seattle. He had been offered a grant in aid if he would accept an appointment to a rural community hospital for a minimum of two years after he finished his residency. Trish also explained that they had met during Dr. Erickson's residency and she had been a nurse anesthetist in the same hospital. When Dr. Erickson learned he was being assigned to the community hospital at Dutch Harbor, he talked Trish into coming along to be the chief nurse at the facility.

"Oh, I didn't know," said Tim.

"You didn't know what?" asked Trish.

"Well ... you know ... I guess you and he ..."

"Oh, no! It's nothing like that. Glenn is married and he and his wife have an eight month old baby. He just talked me into coming since he said that I would get experience here that I couldn't possibly get in any other hospital with the limited experience that I had. I assist Glenn in surgery and he is training me to become a surgical nurse. When he leaves there will be a replacement doctor coming in to take his place and I will be leaving to go to a larger hospital somewhere."

"Like Anchorage, maybe?" Tim looked at her inquisitively.

"Wel-l-l-l ... it could be Anchorage," Trish smiled at him.

The two talked on until it was almost nine o'clock when Trish said that she needed to be going.

"I have to be at the hospital by seven o'clock. Would you like for me to stop by and pick you up?"

"Yeah, I sure would ... I want to be there as early as I can."

Tim walked Trish to the door and helped her on with her coat. She put on her wool cap and turned to face Tim.

"Thanks for the dinner tonight, Tim."

"It was my pleasure, Trish. I really enjoyed your company and I appreciate your coming."

Trish reached in her coat pocket, took out two leather gloves and said, "I'll see you in the morning." and she was gone.

Chapter 102

Adak—Day Three

Trish picked Tim up at twenty 'til seven and they were in the hospital ten minutes later. The two of them went immediately to Dan's room and found that Dan was sitting up just finishing off a breakfast of oatmeal, dry wheat toast, a fruit cup and coffee. The I.V. was still in his arm but the color was back in his cheeks and he looked much, much better.

"Hey, man," Dan said as they came into the room, "am I glad to see you."

"You feeling better this morning?" Tim asked.

"Oh, heck yes. I think I am going to live," Dan grinned at him.

Tim walked over to the bed and gave Dan a playful punch on his right shoulder.

"You sure *look* a lot better than you did when I left here last night." Tim turned and took Trish by the arm and ushered her close to Dan's bed. "Dan, this is Nurse Trish Cavanaugh. She was in surgery with you when the doctor patched up your 'innards'."

Dan extended his right hand, "Thanks, Miss Cavanaugh. I surely appreciate all that you and Doctor Erickson have done for me."

"You're quite welcome, Mr. Nichols. We thought that we might have to admit this fellow here too ... he was so worried about you." Trish replied.

"Yeah, I know ... he really came through for me when the chips were down," Dan said.

"Well, look, you two have some things to talk about I am sure and I have other patients to attend to as well so I will check back with you later," and Trish left the room.

Dan looked up at Tim, "Hey, buddy, I have something that I need to ask of you."

"Sure, Dan, anything you want."

"Look in my pilot case in the King Air, get my check book and bring it to me. I want to write a check to that kid ... what's his name ... Tom Blackwell? ... for two hundred dollars. If you would, take it to him and tell him to buy his friend who owns the boat a set of new sheets and keep the rest for himself. Will you do that, Tim?"

"Sure will, Dan. I'll get on it right away."

"Oh, have you called Al?"

"Yeah, I have."

"Did you tell him about Harry?"

"Yeah, I did, Dan. And, I also told him about you and asked him to tell Jess."

"Damn. I'll bet she will cry her eyes out ... and spoil her make-up." Dan smiled.

Tim laughed out loud. "Dang, Dan. You will probably be cracking jokes when you draw your last breath."

"I will if I can think of one."

The two of them chatted for a few more minutes then Tim said he was going to see if he could borrow Trish's pickup and go to the King Air to get Dan's checkbook.

* * * *

Tim returned with the checkbook about an hour and a half later and when he entered Dan's room there was an officer there that Dan introduced as the local sheriff. He was investigating the shooting and when Tim entered, the sheriff asked him some questions, probably just to corroborate what Dan had told him. The Coast Guard had contacted the sheriff concerning Bill Nolan and the fact that the Coast Guard was keeping him in custody until the FBI could interview him.

Tim asked the sheriff if anything suspicious had been found on the boat. The sheriff told Tim and Dan that a case of material had been recovered that had been classified as hazardous material and that was all he knew. The sheriff also said in talking with the Coast Guard he had been requested to contact both Dan and

Tim to let them know the FBI would want to talk to both of them after they returned to Anchorage. In the meantime, they were not to discuss any of the details of the encounter with anyone.

Dr. Erickson made his rounds with Trish Cavanaugh around 10:30 that morning. He checked Dan over very carefully and informed him that he was very pleased with the progress he appeared to be making and in all probability he would be able to travel back to Anchorage after one more day in the clinic

Chapter 103

Return to Anchorage

The morning of the fifth day in Adak for Dan and Tim was cold, dark and overcast. Trish had picked up Tim again at Sanders' lodge and they arrived at the clinic a few minutes before seven o'clock. They went direct to Dan's room and found Dr. Erickson there listening to Dan's chest through his stethoscope. He then took his pulse and his blood pressure and then picked up his chart and reviewed it while Tim and Trish stood by in silence. After he had finished, Dr. Erickson turned and addressed all three of them.

"All right. Now, I believe that Mr. Nichols is ready to be transported to Anchorage but here are the ground rules. First of all, Mr. Morrison, you contact the FAA weather facility and find out what the enroute weather looks like between here and Anchorage. If there is any unusual turbulence forecast between Adak and Anchorage the flight is off. Understood?" The doctor looked directly at Tim.

"Yes, sir." Tim responded.

"Second." Dr. Erickson continued. "Nurse Cavanaugh, I would like for you to accompany Mr. Nichols on the flight to Anchorage and be sure you have all necessary emergency medications and equipment to deal with any situation enroute. You can return to Adak on the first available flight by Reeve Aleutian Airways and the clinic will pay for your expenses, of course. Is that agreeable with you?"

"Yes sir, that will be fine with me." Nurse Cavanaugh replied.

"Finally, Mr. Morrison," the doctor continued, "you are to remain on your stretcher in a prone position for the entire flight and do exactly what Nurse Cavanaugh tells you. Do you agree?"

Dan replied, "Absolutely, doctor."

"Good. Now we all know what is required of each of you. Mr. Morrison, as soon as you have your weather report you and I will get our heads together and see if the flight is on."

With that the doctor and Tim left the room. Trish Cavanaugh looked at Dan and gave him a smile and a wink. Dan smiled and gave her a responding wink.

Tim made a long distance call and got in touch with the FAA Flight Service Station which covered the Adak area. The forecast for the day was for an overcast sky with no turbulence and no freezing precipitation. It should make for a smooth ride back to Anchorage. Tim reported this to Dr. Erickson and the preparations began for the evacuation flight.

Trish Cavanaugh dropped Tim off at the Sanders' lodge to pick up his gear while she went on to her apartment to pack an overnight bag. She picked up Tim on the return trip and they were both back in the clinic by around ten o'clock.

Dr. Erickson had called the Adak Marine Center and asked Tom Edmunds if he would volunteer his Chevrolet Suburban for the trip from the clinic to the airport. He said he would and he would drive the truck. He also said he thought he could get Tom Blackwell and one other employee to volunteer to come along and assist in loading and unloading the stretcher.

Trish and Tim left the clinic at ten-thirty in her Ford pickup for the airport. Tim would pre-flight the King Air and Trish would arrange for fresh water to be placed aboard plus loading her medical gear. She would leave her pickup at the airport so it would be available when she returned from Anchorage on Reeve Aleutian Airways.

Just a few minutes before noon, the Chevrolet Suburban arrived at the airport and Tom Edmunds, Tom Blackwell, Tim and one of Edmunds' employees loaded the stretcher aboard with Dan strapped to the stretcher. After getting Dan aboard and placed, Tom Blackwell knelt beside the stretcher, shook hands with Dan and said,

"Good luck, Mr. Nichols. If you ever want to go fishing come to Adak and look me up. I'll be glad to take you out as long as you don't have a rifle with you," and he grinned at Dan.

Dan grasped Tom's hand. "Thanks, Tom. You're a great guy and I will always remember what you did for Tim and me."

"No problem, Mr. Nichols. And thanks a lot for that two hundred bucks. I'm going to make good use of it."

"I know you will, Tom. You're a fine young man."

Dan waved good-bye to all of them as Tim pulled up the air-stair door and walked back up the aisle to the cockpit. Trish Cavanaugh settled in one of the seats adjoining where she could see Dan's head as he was lying on the stretcher in the aisle. She buckled up as Tim started up the turboprop engines and then taxied out to the end of the runway. Five minutes later they were off the ground on their way to Anchorage International Airport.

There was an overcast sky and winds were light so the ride back to Anchorage was very smooth. Trish made Dan take a sleeping pill which would cause him to sleep most of the way home and occasionally she would check his pulse, blood pressure and check the bandages to make sure there was no bleeding.

In approximately two hours and a half, Tim received clearance from the Anchorage tower to land. Tim put a lot of effort into making the landing a "greaser," which it was, and Tim taxied the King Air up to the main ramp at Stevens Air. Just as Tim expected, Al and Jess came running out to the plane as the props stopped turning.

Chapter 104

Welcome Home!

One of the Stevens line boys opened the airstair door and Jess was the first to come aboard. Nurse Cavanaugh had gotten out of her seat and walked forward to the cockpit. Jess went up the aisle, got down on her knees next to Dan and began to cry. He opened his eyes.

"Hey, hey, I'm not dying you know," and he smiled at her.

Jess laid her head on Dan's chest and sobbed as he took his right hand and stroked her jet black hair.

"Oh, I don't know what I am going to do with you," she cried. "I guess I am just going to have to get a ball and chain and keep you tied down so you will keep from getting into all these terrible messes."

Al came up the steps and stopped close enough to where he could speak to Dan.

"Are you doing all right, Dan?"

"Sure, Al. I'll be good as new in a few days."

"Well, you just take all the time you need. I'm sorry that I had to put you through all of this."

"What the heck do you mean, Al? None of this was your fault."

"Oh, yes it was. I should have gotten rid of Harry long ago but I was just too soft."

Two Emergency Medical Service attendants went aboard the King Air, checked out Dan's vital signs then picked up the stretcher and handed him down through the door of the aircraft to Norm Timberlake and two of the line boys who were on the ground. The EMS personnel, plus two of the Stevens line boys, transferred Dan from his stretcher to a gurney that came from the EMS ambulance. Norm had an opportunity to say a few words to Dan as the EMS personnel wheeled the gurney to the waiting ambulance. Jess boarded the ambulance with Dan who would now be taken to a local hospital where he would be checked in and be prepared for the operation to remove the bullet that was still lodged in his abdomen.

As soon as they had left, Tim approached Trish Cavanaugh.

"Trish, I'm going to escort you over to the terminal and see about getting you on a flight back home. You know that Intermont is going to pay for your ticket, don't you?"

"There's no need for that, Tim, Dr. Erickson gave me enough money for the return ticket."

"Our boss, Mr. Switzer, just told me that we are going to pay for your expenses while you are here as well as your ticket back home. Here, I'll get your bag out of the baggage compartment and we'll head for the terminal.'"

Trish smiled at Tim as they began their walk to the terminal and thanked him for his attention. It turned out that the last flight on Reeve Aleutian was sold out so Tim booked her on the first flight out the following morning.

"Well, gee. Now I guess I'm just going to have to put you up at the Marriott Courtyard and take you out to dinner tonight. That will give us some time to talk about which hospital here in Anchorage that you might want to work for."

Trish laughed and said, "Has anyone ever told you that you are a 'fast worker?"

"Who, me?" Tim laughed, and they walked off together to get in Tim's car.

Chapter 105

The Operation

The day after Dan arrived at the Alaska Regional Hospital in Anchorage, he was prepped for the operation to remove the Glock 9 mm. bullet from his abdomen. The operation went smoothly, the bullet was excised, and Dan was out of the recovery room and into a private room by two o'clock that afternoon.

Jess took two days of her vacation so that she could 'mother' Dan during his recovery. The third day his doctor said there was no evidence of any infection or complication and he should be able to be dismissed the next day. He would, however, be confined for four or five days thereafter to make sure that the incision had healed and would have to be checked at that time.

Jess was visiting with Dan at noon on the second day after his surgery when one of the nurses walked into the room.

"Mr. Nichols, there is a gentleman outside who wishes to see you. He said he is with the FBI."

Dan looked at Jess and she had a startled look on her face which mirrored that of the look on Dan's face.

"Show him in, please." Dan responded.

The nurse left the room and Jess and Dan heard her say, "You may go in, sir."

In walked a man in a dark pin striped suit who would have easily passed for the movie star, James Garner, physique and all. He reached out with his right hand to shake that of Dan.

"Mr. Nichols, my name is Dwayne Roberts, special agent with the Federal Bureau of Investigation," and he reached inside his jacket, removed a leather wallet to which was affixed the badge of the FBI which he held close enough for verification by Dan.

Agent Roberts continued, "I appreciate your seeing me, sir, and I trust that you are making a nice recovery from your wound."

"Oh, yes, I am mending nicely, thank you." Dan replied. "Agent Roberts I would like for you to meet my fiancé, Jessica Lane, and Dan nodded towards Jessica who was sitting in a chair at Dan's left side.

"How do you do, Miss Lane." Agent Roberts said. "And, congratulations … I understand you two are to be married in a church close to Fairfax in the next few weeks."

Dan and Jess once more exchanged surprised looks.

"Well, you certainly seem to know about our arrangements, Mr. Roberts," Jess replied.

"Oh, yes. As a matter of fact we know a great deal about the two of you. After all, that is our business." Agent Roberts smiled in response.

Agent Roberts continued, "I know the two of you are wondering why I am here so I will get right down to business. Mr. Nichols, just how much do you know about the material that was in the crate that was recovered by you, Mr. Morrison and the Coast Guard?"

"Very little, actually," Dan replied. "I assumed that it was some type of contraband but I have no idea just exactly what it was."

"Good. That is all to your credit. So far the Canadian Security Intelligence Service and the FBI have been able to downplay this episode with the media. As far as they know at the present time, you and Mr. Morrison were involved in apprehending Mr. Abelson because he had stolen an aircraft from Intermont Mining Supply Company. They know nothing about your encounter with the submarine in the Aleutian Bay. We have put a lid on that. If you should happen to be interviewed by the press, radio or TV people, we would appreciate it very, very much if you would indicate that your interest was solely in retrieving your stolen aircraft."

"I certainly have no problem with that," Dan replied. "I must admit that I am curious about that submarine and why it disappeared so quickly though. The Coast Guard cutter wasn't even in sight at that time according to Tim Morrison. Under the circumstances, don't you think that I deserve to know just a little more about that situation?"

Agent Roberts stood silently for just a moment then said, "I think you can be trusted with this much. That was a Korean submarine and it would have presented a very serious threat to the security of our country if that crate had fallen into their hands. As for their leaving in a hurry, you can credit the United States Navy with their beating a hasty retreat." and Agent Roberts smiled at Dan.

At first, Dan was perplexed with the explanation of the Navy having been responsible for the Korean sub retreating then it finally sank in that a *second* submarine must have been on the scene.

Agent Roberts continued, "You may not have been aware that Secretary of State James Baker was in Korea having a meeting with the Korean President at the time of this altercation. It would have been most embarrassing, and detrimental to the safety of our nation, if the transfer of the crate had been made. President Reagan has asked me to convey to you his sincere appreciation, as well as to Mr. Morrison, for the part you two played in interfering and preventing this transfer from taking place."

Jess got up from her chair, sat on the edge of Dan's bed and stared at Agent Roberts in amazement.

"The *President!* You mean that *President Reagan* was aware of this?" Dan's jaw went slack.

"Oh, yes. The President had been receiving daily briefings on the possibility of an international crisis resulting because of this incident. Of course I can't reveal all the details but this action started about a month ago."

Dan turned and looked at Jess in total amazement.

"Well ... this is certainly news to me. I can't imagine that Harry Abelson would be able to cause this kind of trouble," Dan said.

"Oh, he wasn't working by himself, Mr. Nichols. There were at least two others involved. One was a Canadian national working for the Vanguard warehouse in Prince George. He has been apprehended by the Royal Canadian Mounted Police and is in custody in Alberta. The Canadian Security Intelligence Service has had him under suspicion for some time because of telephone conversations he was having with the third party whom we believe to be connected to a terrorist cell in Pakistan. So far, this foreign agent has eluded the RCMP but they are hot on his trail."

"Well, I'll be damned!" Dan said in amazement.

"Here's my card, Mr. Nichols. Agent Roberts removed his wallet again and gave Dan a calling card. "Since you and Miss Lane will be traveling to Fairfax soon, the President has requested that I give you this card which has the Washington Bureau's telephone number as well as my office. After you and Miss Lane become Mr. and Mrs. Dan Nichols, please call the Washington office and let them know at least two days in advance when it would be convenient for you and Mrs. Nichols to visit the White House. President Reagan said he wanted to shake your hand personally and tell you how much he appreciates what you have done for our country."

"Well, I'll be damned." Dan said for the second time. "Please pass along to the President how much I appreciate this honor and Mrs. Nichols and I will certainly be pleased to visit with him."

"I'll see that he gets the message, sir. Thank you for your time and I hope you have a speedy recovery and a wonderful wedding." Agent Roberts shook Dan's hand again and left the room.

Jess stood up, jumped up and down a couple of times as she clapped her hands together.

"*I can't believe it!* We're going to get to meet *President Reagan!* Oh, I can't wait to tell Sue ... she will just *die* with envy."

"Hey, if it's going to make you all that happy I'll see what I can do about getting shot in the other side of my body," Dan laughed.

"Oh, you!" Jess walked around to the right side of the bed, sat on the edge, leaned her face close to Dan's and said, "Do you know what you just called me?"

"Yeah ... Mrs. Nichols."

"Has a nice ring to it, doesn't it?"

"Sure does. C'mere."

Jess leaned close to Dan and gave him a gentle kiss.

Chapter 106

Final Cruise

The UB-235 had cleared the LaPerouse Strait two days ago and was now well into the Sea of Japan on a course for the Naval harbor at Wonsan. The North Korean submarine was submerged and the second watch had just taken their stations. Captain Johng Ho Kim was sitting in his compartment thinking about the disgrace that he had brought upon himself and his family by having failed to complete his mission. As he thought about that fateful day when the United States Navy submarine had forced him into making an ignominious retreat, he arose and went to the wall safe in his compartment, opened it and took out a standard issue US Army .45 Colt Revolver. Admiral Kim Mi-young had given him the weapon the day that he had been commissioned as the captain of the UB-235. Admiral Kim had taken this pistol from a dead US Marine Captain at the battle of Chosin Reservoir and had presented it to his favorite understudy upon his appointment to the UB-235. Admiral Kim had told Captain Johng to keep this pistol as a reminder of his deep affection for the new captain and to serve his country with honor and dignity.

Captain Johng removed the clip and verified that it was fully loaded. He went to his locker and removed the sword which he carried at all military dress functions. He then sat down at his desk, laid the sword on the desk in front of him, opened his mouth and fired a single shot from the Colt .45. Executive Officer Huang Sun Lee had just come down from the control center to get a cup of coffee in the officers' wardroom. He heard the shot and dashed into the captain's compartment to find Captain Johng slumped forward in his chair with the Colt .45 lying on the floor. After getting over the immediate shock of seeing his captain sitting there dead, he stepped into the corridor to see if anyone else had heard the shot. No one was in sight.

Sojwa[1] Huang lifted the microphone from its' holder in Captain Johng's compartment and called for the officer of the deck to come to the captain's quarters immediately. When he arrived, the two officers cleaned the floor of blood, dressed Captain Johng in his first class uniform and wrapped his body in a blanket tying it with cord which they obtained from the quartermaster. They then placed the captain's body back in his bunk. Lieutenant Commander Huang opened the UB-235's logbook and made an entry. "At 2210 hours on 22 January 1989, Captain Johng Ho Kim died of a grievous wound which had been inflicted by a submarine of the United States Navy."

The next morning, the Democratic Peoples Republic of Korea's Submarine UB-235's complement of officers and enlisted men stood respectfully at attention below decks while Lieutenant Commander Huang, the temporary Captain, and four seamen moved Captain Johng's body to the deck of the *Romeo*. The two officers rendered a hand salute as the four seamen slipped Captain Johng's weighted body into the deep in the Sea of Japan.

---

1. Lieutenant Commander

Chapter 107

Wedding Bells

Dan was discharged from the hospital on the morning of the fourth day and Jess took him to her apartment and insisted that he go to bed for the rest of the day. Dan balked but Jess persevered so Dan gave in just to keep from getting into an argument. By the morning of the third day he had spent in Jess' apartment, Dan said he had had enough of 'recovery' and wanted to go down to the office.

That morning they drove down in Jess' Corvette and went up the elevator to the office. When they went into the lobby, Virginia Stewart got up from her desk and approached Dan and Jess. Virginia placed her right hand very gently on Dan's arm. Dan noticed that she had tears in her eyes. "Mr. Dan, I just want you to know that I don't hold any ill will whatsoever about the incident involving Harry." And she turned around and went back to her chair, sat down, took out a handkerchief from her purse and began wiping her eyes.

Dan looked at Jess questioningly and Jess just raised her eyebrows signifying that she didn't know what Virginia meant either. They both then walked to Al's door and knocked. He said, "Come in." and they both entered his office.

Once inside and seated, Jess told Al what Virginia had said. Al, pushed back in his chair, put his hand over his eyes and said,

"Oh, my! I had hoped to talk to you two before you saw Virginia. I'm *sorry*."

And he told both of them about his relationship with Harry's father and how he had died. As the entire story unfolded, Jess and Dan sat and both felt the agony that Al, and no doubt, Virginia, had been through.

After Al had finished, Dan said, "Al, Jess and I have something that we need to discuss with you."

"Well, you just go right ahead. I'll clear my desk for the rest of the morning if you want me to."

"Oh, I don't think it will take that long." Jess was sitting on Dan's right and he reached over and took her hand.

"First, we want to get married right away."

Al stood up and without a word he walked around the desk, took Jess' free hand and said,

"Jess, would you give an old man a hug? I feel like my own daughter is getting married." She stood and gave Al a big hug. He then turned to Dan and laughed,

"I can't hug you but but I can sure shake your hand," which he did. He returned and sat down in his chair.

"Well, that's not all, Al ... we want to take you up on your offer to buy Intermont."

Al thrust both of his arms straight towards the ceiling. "Hallelujah! The Lord has sure answered my prayers today! That is the most wonderful news I have had in a long, long time. To know that the two best people I have are going to continue my company just makes me feel ... well, I just don't have the words to describe it."

When Al had settled down, Dan said, "Well, I suppose we should talk about the terms of the purchase."

"No, no ... don't bother yourselves about that right now. I want you to have your marriage and a wonderful honeymoon then we can get down to the nitty-gritty stuff later. I assure you though, that I am going to bend over backwards to see that you two kids get the deal of a lifetime. What can I do with money? I don't need it. Evelyn, bless her heart, can't use it and I have no heirs. You two are the only heirs I have," and tears welled up in his eyes.

Dan looked at Jess and she looked at him.

"Well ... what can I say, Al. You are one in a million and without a doubt the most considerate and kind man I have ever met in my life."

Jess spoke up. "Al, I've always considered you as my second father, you know that, and that presents a problem. Because of my parents, and Dan's children, we need to get married back in Virginia. There is a small country church several miles out of Fairfax and I want to get married there. Just a simple ceremony with family and a few very close friends."

"Well, what's wrong with that, Jess?" Al asked.

"What's wrong with that is that you won't be there, Al!"

"Who said so?" he said with mock indignity. "You plan on having your wedding on a Saturday or a Sunday and I'll be there. Northwest Airlines fly planes on the week-ends, don't they?" and he spread a big smile across his face.

Jess got up, walked around the desk, leaned over and gave Al a big kiss on his cheek. "Al, as Dan said, you *are* one in a million."

Chapter 108

Homeward Bound

On the morning of January 23, 1989, Jess was sitting in a window seat of a Northwest Airlines 747 with Dan sitting next to her. He was holding her left hand, rubbing the diamond ring with his right thumb and forefinger. "Best investment I ever made in my life," he said.

"The ring?" she asked.

"No, you."

She smiled that alluring smile of hers and Dan got a whiff of the perfume that had such an effect on him that first night he arrived in Alaska. He thought, *that stuff has finally taken control of my life and I couldn't feel better about it.* He leaned to the right, she met him halfway and they kissed each other softly.

They were at forty-two thousand feet over Iowa as a cattle farmer came out of his house to go check on his feed lot. He heard the sound of a large jet up in that clear, blue, January sky. He looked up to see the four white contrails behind the silver plane and said to himself, *just think ... there's probably a couple of hundred people or more in that thing. All of them either returning home or heading off somewhere to a new adventure. I'll bet some of them really have some more kind of story to tell.*

FINIS

978-0-595-43674-3
0-595-43674-9

Printed in the United States
201983BV00003B/178-189/A